I THINK HE KNOWS

A ROMANTIC COMEDY

DONOVAN FAMILY BOOK 2

KATIE BAILEY

Cover Vectors by
JOANNEWHYTE AND MSANCA

ELEVENTH AVENUE
PUBLISHING

1

LANA MAE

NEARLY TEN YEARS AGO...

Call me Idiot.

And believe me, I don't say this lightly.

In fact, I'd like to offer my sincere apologies to Mr. Melville for paraphrasing his most famous opening line, perhaps the most famous opening line in literary history (except for *The Holy Bible*'s "In the beginning" and maybe *Anna Karenina*'s "All happy families are alike"—which is plain wrong, by the way, but I'll get to that later). But I need to make this known to all: Idiot is my new name, and I'm off to court first thing tomorrow to make it official.

Do, da do, do-oo dah do do, do dah-do do do...

The opening bars of Billy Joel's "Piano Man" blast through the room, cutting through my thoughts and propelling me back to the present, where for some inexplicable reason everyone in my vicinity is climbing up on the furniture. Judging by the rickety state of most of it, this particular activity looks like it poses serious risk of injury for a room full of very, very drunk people. Not that I'm an expert on drunken injuries. Unless you count the time my

Uncle Sam drank too much bourbon on Christmas Eve and accidentally set his hair on fire.

Which I don't, obviously. Because that would just be... sad. And something I would never do.

A boy with overgrown biceps that mismatch his cherubic baby face pounds the ceiling with a staff made out of taped-together empty beer cans, and yells "DRINK, DRINK, DRINK!"

Everybody drinks.

I take another sip of my water and look around with something between fascination and horror. It's like being in a Discovery Channel nature documentary. I can almost hear David Attenborough's smooth, British lilt: "And here, we have the Neanderthal male, inflating his chest while performing a show, of sorts—an alcohol-fueled mating call, in hopes of attracting a willing female. More often than not, these valiant attempts at copulation are resoundingly unsuccessful, and the male must retreat back to his stinky-sheeted nest, alone."

Unfortunately for me, the show is about to become interactive. The guy on the table to my left swings his arm a little too vigorously in his attempt to raise his red cup to his mouth, which makes me the lucky recipient of a shower of lukewarm keg beer.

"Eeee!" I squeal as I spring out of the way. But it's too little, too late, and my honey-colored hair, once carefully waved to vintage perfection, is now plastered to my skull in wet, snakey strands.

Drunkypants doesn't even notice his blunder. Instead, he burps, tosses the rest of his beer back, and flings his cup with abandon.

Of course it hits me in the face.

Fabulous.

Let's crash a college party, Lana, they said. *It'll be fun,* they said. *We promise you won't get left on your own, we'll be right by your side.*

They were liars.

"They" being my friends, Nora and Bethany. Who I have now decided are my ex-friends, given that they ditched me the second I got here. So now I am not only an idiot, but a friendless one, too.

I glance at my phone for the thousandth time, checking the time (9 p.m.) and my messages (none).

Where is he? And why is he not messaging me back?

A sudden wave of nausea crashes over me and I splay a hand across my belly, inhaling sharply to breathe through it. Probably sick from the nasty stink of beer I'm now wearing.

It may be nine o'clock on a Saturday, but I wish I was in bed with a hot water bottle in my lap and my nose in a book. Even if that book was *Moby Dick*.

But sadly, I am not tucked up in bed. Instead, I am standing in the sticky, dank residence of the Gamma Kappa Rah Rah Frappuccino fraternity house, watching Bethany search for her dignity in the mouth of a profusely sweaty hockey player who's wearing a necktie around his head like a bandana. Meanwhile, Nora has been unceremoniously tossed over the shoulder of a particularly rowdy frat member, and is currently being helicoptered in clumsy circles at the center of the dance floor while she clutches at the hem of her skirt, making a valiant (yet unsuccessful) attempt not to flash the entire room.

My friends and I have just started our senior year of high school, and we've often discussed how cool it would be to go to one of the famed Frat Row parties at Central Georgia State. However, now that I'm finally at one, I don't see what all the fuss is about. It smells like BO in here, there are no snacks (which are surely a Party 101 essential), and there's a distinct lack of Taylor Swift on the playlist.

I can't picture myself living in a place like this. Or even going to places like this on a regular basis. In fact, I imagine my own future college experience will be very different from what Steven's current one apparently is—more time spent participating in roundtable literary discussions and sipping black coffee at slam poetry events than attending drunken frat house parties.

Steven and I will have to do... lunch together. Or something.

And speaking of Steven, seriously, where the actual hell is he?

I can hardly surprise my boyfriend at college if he isn't here to surprise.

My eyes rake across the room again, searching. Nada. If he's not here, then I'm seriously considering going home to cuddle with my cats, because this party stinks. Literally. I open my phone and check my Uber app—this cool new ridesharing thing everyone's using.

Ouch. A cab home will cost me pretty much all of the tip money I saved this summer bussing tables.

With a sigh, I begin moving through the throng of bodies, each step more squelchy than the last. Maybe before I resort to booking an Uber, I can look upstairs. As far as frat party etiquette goes, I'm not sure where this falls on the scale of acceptable, but if anyone questions me, I'll tell them my boyfriend lives here. Which is true. The only weird part will be when I can't locate said boyfriend's room, because true as the "boyfriend" status is, he's been at college for over a month now, but has never actually invited me here. Which may be one of the reasons I agreed to this little surprise tonight.

As I make my way across the crowded room, my eyes land on the only other person at the party who doesn't look like they're having the time of their life. He's standing at the bottom of the stairs, leaning against the railing in the most grumpy stance I've ever seen. He's maybe a year or two older than me, and his scowl does nothing to detract from his startling good looks. And I do mean *startling*. He's tall and broad-shouldered and square-jawed. His brown hair is at that perfect stage of just-a-touch-too-long and pokes out from under the sides of his baseball cap.

There's an intensity about him that's almost visible, radiating off of his tense body in waves as he glares at the ground. I wonder what on earth his deal is...

Girlfriend dumped him? He flunked a test? His Greek letter hoodie suggests he's a frat boy, and that this could be his house. Maybe he's scheduled for clean-up duty tomorrow morning?

That would suck.

But I have no time to feel sorry for intense, prickly, handsome strangers. I need to go upstairs and look for Steven, and then, if I can't find him, my carriage (AKA a blue Honda Accord driven by Viv, who's rated four point eight stars) awaits. The boy glances in my direction as I continue to move towards him, and I'm immediately amazed by his eyes. I've never seen eyes so blue. Or eyes that look so... decidedly pissed off.

I shoot him a tentative, sympathetic smile. A knowing sort of smile that says *"Hey, buddy, I feel your pain right now. We're in this party-hating camp together. So please, please do me a solid and step aside to let me upstairs without incident."*

Because every little kindness helps, right?

Wrong.

Hot, pissed-off frat boy looks at me blankly for a moment, before making me the new recipient of his light-blue frosty stare. It steals my breath and I stumble slightly. This makes him smirk.

Jerk!

In response, I smile back sweetly, then flip him off. I don't know where this moment of reckless bravery comes from—probably the fact that I'm damp and sticky and sour-scented from the beer shower, or that I rode in the back of Bethany's deathwagon to get here tonight, or that Steven still isn't replying to my texts. There's a pit beginning to form in my stomach, signaling something isn't right.

Frat boy's eyebrows raise for a fraction of a second before his lips twitch at the corners, widening that irritating little smirk of his into a full-blown smile.

I *really* don't have time for this. My mascara is running, my red lipstick is smudged, and my heart-print hunter-green romper with its ridiculously cute little half-cap sleeves is soaked through and sticking to my curves like wet cement. I just want tonight to be over already.

And so, with a deep breath, I straighten my spine, try to forget my romper wedgie, and take a few steps towards him. When I get close, I toss my ropey hair over one shoulder. It hits my back with a weird, slurpy *slap* that sounds like raw hamburger being shaped into patties. Yuck. The mere thought of raw meat brings another wave of nausea, stronger this time. I clap a hand to my mouth and swallow.

The boy's smile widens further. He steps up onto the bottom stair, effectively blocking my path.

Instinctively, I take a half step backwards. His light-blue eyes are frosty, yet they smolder like they're ablaze.

Dry ice. Smoking and frozen and ready and willing to cause serious damage.

I breathe out shakily. "Hey."

He raises one dark brow. "Hi."

Now is the time to say something witty and dazzling. Something that will make him think I'm sharp-tongued and clever and not to be messed with...

"You're in my way," I say.

Nice one, Lana. Real original.

"Or are you in my way?" he counters. Flirtily. I think.

It's difficult to figure this guy out.

"I have a boyfriend," I blurt, in case he's one of those IRL Christian Grey types who thinks being all alpha and demanding is flirting (Oh, and if my mom asks, I have *not* read those books).

"Oh?" He smiles, clearly amused, and I blush like a tomato when I realize I misread his tone. But he still doesn't budge.

Frustration builds in my chest. "You are literally blocking my way upstairs."

"And you are literally blocking my view of the party."

"Well excuse me for inhibiting your front-row viewing platform to the eighth wonder of the world."

He laughs. It's a short, surprised laugh, but a laugh nonetheless. "Are you usually this sarcastic?"

"Are you usually this insufferable?"

This draws another laugh from him, and the ice in his eyes melts to reveal irises the vivid hue of alpine lakes in the sunshine.

"No. At least, I hope not. I'm just having a bad night. Or, I *was* having a bad night, I should say." He grins suddenly. A dazzling grin that could make millions on the big screen. But somehow, I get the feeling he uses this smile exclusively for getting girls, and for getting what he wants. "What's your name?"

I swallow. And then, for some reason, I give it to him. "Lana, um, Lana Mae Donovan."

"Lana Mae Donovan," he repeats my name thoughtfully, like it tastes sweet on his tongue. Then, he fixes those light-blue eyes on me. I feel a bit wobbly all of a sudden, like I've sprouted baby deer legs. "I'm Carter

James Callahan, if we're being so formal as to include middle names."

I shake my head. "My first name is Lana Mae. No middle name."

"No middle name." He's still staring, his lips quirked in a vaguely amused smirk. "I like that."

I can't help but register that he doesn't show any recognition of my name whatsoever. If this guy knows Steven, he surely would have heard my name before, right? Double-barreled first names are a given here in the south—every girl group has at least one—but Lana Mae isn't the most common.

I swallow, but before I can open my mouth and ask him if he's acquainted with my boyfriend (and if so, where I can find him), he blinks at me, erasing all traces of his smirk.

"Do you want to get out of here, Lana Mae No-Middle-Name Donovan?"

2

CARTER

"Oh my! Do you say that to all the girls?" The very damp, very pretty, panda-eyed girl in front of me tilts her face to the side and mockingly thrusts a hand to her forehead in a fake swoon.

I like this girl. In fact, I was having an altogether awful night until she showed up with her dark, flashing eyes and gangly awkwardness. I feel bad for being so cold to her. At first, I thought she was another sorority girl coming over to hit on me, which normally wouldn't be a problem but was literally the last thing I was in the mood for tonight. That sounds arrogant, I guess. But it's true. I'm beyond tired, and want to go to bed. Alone.

However, Lana Mae has unexpectedly made me laugh to the point where I can almost forget why I was annoyed in the first place.

She kind of reminds me of a baby deer, in a good way.

"Only the cute ones," I reply.

She rolls her eyes and shivers. "Gee. Glad I made the cut."

"So do you? Want to get out of here?" I pause. Smile.

"I'm assuming that's a yes with the way you were making for the stairs like an Olympic sprinter."

She scowls. "Do I look like the sort of person who'll go home with a stranger for a night of unbridled passion? After I just told them I have a BOYFRIEND?"

"Night of unbridled passion, huh?" I cock a brow and fix her with my gaze, unable to resist teasing her. "Tell me more."

My stupid comment confirms something I've been wondering about since locking eyes with her across the room: despite having golden, tanned skin, her cheeks go red as fire trucks when she blushes.

"There's no more to say." She crosses her arms over her wet outfit and glares up at me. "Because unlike some people, I have standards."

"I'm very glad to hear that. You absolutely should have standards." I match her glare with a sly grin. "And now that we've established that, would you like to get out of here *to find a towel and a dry sweatshirt*? Unless it's a night of unbridled passion that you are actually after?"

The look on her face is priceless.

"Wait, you're offering to get me a towel?" Her voice is laced with disbelief.

"You appear to be in need of one, so yes."

"And you're not pulling a move to attempt to seduce me or something?"

Her choice of words makes me chuckle. "Absolutely not."

She narrows her eyes at me. "You said that a bit fast."

"Maybe I'm not into going home with strangers either." I shrug. "No matter how cute."

This tugs a smile out of her. "I don't believe you."

"You shouldn't."

At this, she laughs. It's a weird, snorty, high-pitched

laugh unlike anything I've heard before. At the sound of her own snort, she claps a hand over her mouth, her blush deepening.

I'm beginning to feel a bit envious of this so-called boyfriend of hers.

"Come on, Miss Lana Mae. Your no-strings-attached access to the last clean towel in our linen closet awaits."

She snorts again, and I indicate she should go up the stairs in front of me. Not so that I can check out her butt. Honest. I avert my eyes, like the gentleman I actually am under my teasing. The girl may be beautiful in that irresistibly sweet, whimsical way, but she said she has a boyfriend, and I don't mess with that.

Unlike my roommate from hell, who's up in our room with a sorority girl when I know for a fact that he has a girlfriend back home. One he never mentions. And one who apparently has no idea he's working his way through the entire female population of our freshman class while still dating her.

I clench and unclench my fists at the memory of his smug face as he ushered the petite brunette into our room about an hour ago. He simply shrugged at me while I stood in the hall wearing nothing but my shower towel. "Sorry, bruh," he said, wiggling his eyebrows. "But you know how it is."

I retorted that no, *bruh*, I did not know how it was, because while I was perfectly capable of picking up a girl, I didn't do so while in a relationship. He had the gall to laugh. "Whose fault is that?" he asked before he slammed the door of my own bedroom in my face.

Which is how I ended up at this stupid party in the first place. I had to borrow clothes from one of my buddies down the hall (resulting in me looking like this century's most enthusiastic frat boy), and then resorted to hanging out by the stairs, chugging water and waiting for the aforementioned petite brunette to reappear, which would signal that I could finally get some sleep before my 5 a.m. alarm tomorrow.

I have to be up early in the morning for an audition. Like, a movie audition. Which sounds weird, even to me.

Truth is, it's a Hail Mary. I'm currently working a landscaping job most mornings, and on top of that, I've started picking up night shifts at a warehouse. Fitting both jobs around my college courseload is exhausting, and after falling asleep in class twice last week, I realized I needed to figure out a more sustainable way to pay for my education. I might have no idea what I want to do with my life, but I know I want to make something of myself. Succeed. And getting a college degree is the first step.

When I heard that extra parts in movies here in Atlanta pay pretty well, I was kinda skeptical.

But honestly, I'll give *anything* a fair shot if there's a chance I can at least quit the night shifts.

Meanwhile, my *bruh* drives a Range Rover and has daddy's credit card on hand for his tuition and expenses. Which I know I shouldn't be butt-hurt about, but it's hard not to be when he's such a jerk. I feel terrible for his girlfriend, and I've never even met the girl.

"So, you live in Frat Boy Paradise then?" Lana Mae asks, looking over her shoulder as she steps onto the landing. Half the guys' bedrooms are up here, and more often than not, everyone's overflow crap ends up in the hallway.

I quickly kick away a couple of rogue jerseys and beer cans. A house inhabited by forty guys is exactly what you'd imagine it to be: a pigsty. Questionable choice on my part, pledging for the sole purpose of not having to pay more to live in dorms.

"*Paradise Lost*, more like."

"Milton," she says, looking surprised. "Didn't peg you for a literary guy."

"Not gonna read into what that implies."

"You shouldn't," she counters cheekily.

I can't help the grin that creeps over my face. "Well, sadly, you're right, Donovan. I'm not really into literature. Just made the mistake of signing up for Epic Poetry for my freshman English elective," I explain. "And to answer your question, I do live here."

For some reason, she brightens at this. "My boyfriend lives here too. Maybe you know him?"

I'm surprised at the way my heart sinks. I was still kind of hoping her boyfriend was imaginary... but of course she's dating one of my frat brothers. I mean, look at her.

I nod. "Probably. You in a sorority?"

"Nah, I'm a senior in high school. Steven was in the year above me."

The name hits me like a punch to the gut.

"Steven?" I choke out. I only know one Steven who lives here...

Maybe it's not him.

I pray it's not him.

She blinks up at me. "Yeah," she says, encouraged. "Steven Stanton. You know him?"

As if on cue, the door to my bedroom opens, and the very douchebag in question practically falls out of the room, his mouth attached to the brunette's. Whose shirt is unbuttoned.

Lana's gasp is loud enough to make them both look up.

The girl blushes and fumbles with her buttons as she flashes us a bashful grin. "Oops, 'scuse us."

Steven's eyes widen in horror as they zero in on Lana Mae.

Lana Mae, who's gone the chalkiest shade of white I've ever seen.

She stands there frozen for a few excruciating moments before turning on her heel and bolting, clattering down the stairs.

"Lana Mae!" Steven calls after her, but the jerkwad doesn't attempt to follow her.

For the past hour, all I've wanted to do is go to bed and get as much shut-eye as is possible with the hormonal rager happening downstairs. I don't like drama, or getting involved with it. And with my bedroom now evacuated, now's my chance. I could lock myself in there, go to sleep, and be done with this entire thing.

But I don't.

Instead, for some reason unbeknownst to me, I take off after a girl I've known all of five minutes for the sole purpose of seeing if she's alright. I chase her down the stairs and out the front door, where I find her standing on the street with her head bowed, her breathing heavy.

I approach her slowly. Put a gentle hand on her shoulder. "Hey. You okay?"

Lana Mae looks up, wild-eyed.

She opens her mouth... and throws up all over my shoes.

3

LANA MAE

PRESENT DAY

If there's one thing I took for granted in my old life, it was peeing in peace.

These days, my time spent sitting on the toilet is mostly shared with a nine-year-old who just *has* to get into the bathroom at the exact moment that I need to relieve my bladder, and a ginger tabby who has no concept of personal space. This weekend, I also have the addition of a slobbery puppy houseguest who likes to do his own bladder-relieving on the floor.

I look up, mid-pee, from the shopping list I'm texting myself (*apples, pickles, handsoap, ketchup, tampons*) to where my daughter, Allegra, is standing on her tiptoes by the vanity...

Smearing Maybelline Lash Sensational on every square inch of her face that is *not* her eyelashes.

"Legs! What are you doing?" I squeal, jolting my knee and startling Harry Styles the cat, who has been curled up in my bare lap from the moment I sat down to pee.

Like I said, no concept of personal space.

Harry gives me a dirty look as he hops down and stalks out of the room. Allegra drops the mascara wand onto the countertop (black stain) and reaches for a white hand towel (matching black stain). Sigh.

"I thought I'd look fisticated for school today, but I don't think it worked."

"Fisticated?"

"Yeah. Auntie Annie taught me that word. It means kinda fancy. Like she always is with her red lipstick and stuff." She stops wiping her face for a moment to level me with a critical eye. "You should wear lipstick, Mom."

"Noted," I say dryly. "And I think the word you're looking for is 'sophisticated'."

Legs considers this for a moment. "Nope, don't think so."

I reach for the toilet paper, only to find that Chimichanga—my brother Liam's dog, who is staying with us for the week while Liam whisks his red-lipped, *fisticated* wife off to New York to see *Hamilton* on Broadway—has gotten to it first. There's a trail of Charmin Ultra along the bathroom floor, and at the end of it is a very guilty-looking pup with his mouth full.

"Chimi, no!" I wail, as I try (and fail) to reach for the end of the roll.

The little dog—who is an entirely anxious creature not unlike myself—looks up, sees my displeased expression, and promptly pees all over the floor.

Sigh.

Legs squeals. "Mom, he's PEEING!"

"I can see that." I flap my arms at her like a seagull. "Now, could I get a little help over here?"

She stops screeching long enough to give me a curious look. "Help with what?"

16

Double sigh.

"Could you maybe grab the TP for me?" I ask.

"Out of the dog's mouth? Ew. Gross, Mom. We should probably do something about the pee on the floor, don't you think?"

Nine-year-olds, I tell you.

"Well, yeah. That was kind of the point of you grabbing me the toilet paper. So I could get up and do exactly that."

"Why didn't you say so?" Legs singsongs as she delicately pirouettes over the puddle on the floor and retrieves the roll from Chimichanga's mouth.

By the time I manage to get off the toilet, clean the puddle of pee, and take my makeup remover to my daughter's face, I'm running late. I am also running very hungry, very under-caffeinated, and sans mascara, thanks to Allegra's Lash Sensational trial.

It's not an ideal combination.

Once in the car, I stop en route to pick up Legs's friend Keisha for carpool. I stop for a moment to say hi to Keisha's mom, Imani, who's a friend and coworker of mine, and then finally swing into a ginormous lineup in the elementary school drop-off lane. There's a ton of cars in front of me, and all of them are stuck behind a bus that's evacuating about a million slow-moving children. With what feels like my ten thousandth sigh of the morning, I put my vehicle in park and reach for my phone, my knee in full-blown jiggle mode as I open up my texts.

It's only 8 a.m., and I'm already feeling overwhelmed by the day (and night) to come.

Why? Because I, Lana Mae Donovan, have recently broken out of my safe, comfortable, sweatpant-clad mom routine and am going all carpe diem on the dating scene for the first time in almost ten years.

And so far, it has... sucked. I'm not too sure why. I know

I'm smart, I'm a good mom, and I have a decent career as a travel agent that I maybe don't love, but I appreciate for the flexible hours it gives me as a single parent. I also know I'm relatively attractive (particularly with the help of my Lash Sensational), and I can even be funny when I'm feeling relaxed and at home with the people around me. But not one of those qualities seems to present themselves when I sit down opposite a man at a dinner table. Instead, my anxiety bursts forth in the form of verbal incontinence and sheer awkwardness.

I've been on no less than six dates in the last couple of months, some with nice men, some with not-so-nice men. And I've spent every single one of these dates feeling like a barnacled humpback whale amidst a pod of giggling bottlenose dolphins. I mean, I might only be twenty-seven, but I didn't even realize people went out on Thursday nights. My Thursday evenings are usually spent air-frying cubed sweet potatoes while watching the Food Network.

Wild. But preferable after a long day, if I'm being entirely honest.

Tonight, there shall be no Ina Garten and her choco-latey voice and even chocolatey-er desserts, because it's time for date number seven. I'm feeling cautiously optimistic about this one. My sister-in-law Mindy set me up with him, although I'm not quite sure she actually knows him seeing as she referred to him as a "friend of a friend of a friend."

I add "new mascara" to my shopping list, then open my message thread with Carter, who texted me about an hour ago, as he does every morning.

Carter: I'm giving myself a 9/10 because I clearly get an A for effort, and also because I feel like Gordon appreci-ates both art and happiness.

I snicker as I look at the picture accompanying the text. Today, it's a plate with two overcooked eggs made sunny side up and a smiling, slightly burnt bacon mouth. I truly believe that men are sometimes just overgrown children in big, manly bodies.

Carter's body being particularly big and manly... but I'm trying my best not to notice that anymore. Which is a difficult task, because the whole world agrees that Carter's body is entirely noteworthy—especially after that shirtless *GQ* cover (which I can never look at without my stomach plunging into zero gravity territory).

Besides, *I* was the one who started our little Gordon Ramsay "rate my plate" texting game. It's a tradition of ours that's been going on for years now.

Lana Mae: Oh, please. That's a solid C at best. Where are the toast ears? The blueberry necklace? The strawberry cheeks and shredded hash brown hair? Effort, my ass. 5/10.

Lana Mae: *GIF of Gordon Ramsay exclaiming "you're cooking like a donkey!"

Carter: *GIF of Gordon Ramsay saying "you're getting your knickers in a twist! Calm down!"*

Lana Mae: Don't bring my knickers into this.

Carter: You're the one who started all the ass talk.

Carter: Although in the land across the Atlantic where knickers are actually a thing, I think they prefer the term 'arse'.

I'm chuckling and blushing all at once as I stare down at my screen. So much so that a sudden rap at the window makes me almost jump out of my skin.

"Sorry, sorry," I say automatically as I look up from my phone, but the line in front of me hasn't moved. And then, I see who's knocking.

Oh, great. Mona Freaking McCreary.

AKA Mona the Informer, The National Enquirer, and The Buttinsky.

Which is a real word, believe it or not.

And it couldn't be a more accurate descriptor. Mona's the president of the PTA and one of those people who always acts nice, but not in, like, a nice way. She spreads gossip like farmers spread manure. Every word that comes out of her mouth feels like a thinly veiled insult, and her smile is so forced and wide, she looks like one of those ventriloquist dummies.

Which might be a little harsh. But in case you can't tell, I'm not Mona's biggest fan.

"Cooee, Lana Mae!"

Bang bang bang.

Jeez Louise, is she trying to break the glass?

I reluctantly roll down my window. "Hi, Mona. What's up?"

"Texting and driving, are we?" She laughs and gives a big, exaggerated wink. "Tsk tsk, naughty naughty. My husband's a police officer, you know. He'd have you pulled over for that."

"Would he now," I say halfheartedly, narrowly avoiding rolling my eyes.

"Hi Keisha, dear. Hi Allegra, that's an interesting color you're wearing. Did you pick that out or did your mother... and oh look, how sweet, you got a puppy!" There's finally a pause in Mona's monologue. "Do you have time to raise a puppy, Lana Mae? You know, what with being a *working mom* and all?"

She lowers her voice over the words "working mom" like they're filthy swears. She's leaning forward now, practically tilting her head into the car. On the passenger seat beside me, Chimi lets out a little growl.

"Ooh!" Mona retreats hastily.

"Good boy." I pat the pup's head, and then give Mona a *what can you do?* shrug. "Guess he doesn't like strangers."

Mona smoothes her already perfectly smooth white button-down, and puts her smile back in place. "Anyway, I wanted to drop by to say hi and see if you're interested in running for treasurer of the PTA now that Rebecca is stepping down."

"She is?"

Mona clutches her chest as her eyes widen. "Oh, didn't you hear? *Divorce.* Messy one." She tsks again. "I'm not one to gossip, but from what I hear, there was another woman involved. Terrible. Just terrible." She looks positively gleeful about this poor woman's misfortune. "So, are you interested?"

There's more likelihood of me signing up for naked unicycle lessons than volunteering to be Mona's treasurer-slash-minion, but I simply nod and say, "Maybe."

Mona laughs again, and her next words may be merry, but there's a clear bite to her tone. "Well, with an attitude like that..."

I refuse to feel inferior to Mona because she always seems to have it together. I'd rather be me, stains and lateness and all, than be *mean.* If anything, I just want to find poor Rebecca, whoever she is, and give her a hug.

"Oh, look," I say as cheerfully as I can muster. "The line's moving. Better go—"

"One sec!" Mona's freaking head is back through the window before I can get the hell out of here. "Before you dash off, it has come to my attention that Miss Allegra here *still* hasn't turned in her permission slip for the daddy daughter campout at the end of the month. Will she not be attending? We're raising money for *such* a wonderful cause."

I glower at the steering wheel for a moment and take a

deep, calming breath instead of saying what I actually want to say. Which is *"What's the cause? Making Families Without Fathers Feel Like Crap?"* When I do finally speak, my voice doesn't waver. "We're not sure yet. But I'll let you know ASAP. Bye, Mona."

I drive forward as fast as one can reasonably go between orange cones in an elementary school parking lot, then screech to a halt outside the front doors before turning around to look at Legs. "Honey, you didn't tell me there was going to be a daddy daughter campout."

Allegra shakes her head but doesn't reply.

Keisha smiles and tugs on her braids. "My daddy's bringing stuff for s'mores. And he got me a new unicorn sleeping bag."

Allegra's mouth presses in a thin line, but I don't miss the little wobble in her chin.

I swallow.

As a single mom, I've always struggled with mom guilt—constantly questioning whether I'm enough, and if there are things I'm not giving my daughter that she needs. My brothers have been invaluable in filling that father figure spot in so many ways, but Allegra's old enough now to understand that her biological father is noticeably absent from her life.

"Do you want to ask Uncle Liam or Uncle Luke to come with you?"

"They're not my daddy."

"No, but they both love you very much and love doing these things with you. And I know it's not quite the same as having your actual dad there, but—"

"I don't want *him* there, Mom. I don't even know him."

I'd be lying if I said I didn't feel a touch relieved at this statement. But now, I'm confused as to what she *does* want. "So?" I coax gently.

"I was waiting to see how your date tonight goes."

I blink. "My... date?"

"Yeah." Allegra unclips her seatbelt. "I thought I might have a new daddy by the time the campout comes around."

"You thought you might have a new daddy..." I repeat dumbly.

"That's what dates are for, right? To find someone to marry."

Oh, man.

I lick my lips, then slowly say, "Well, I guess, but—"

"Can I go to school now?" she interrupts.

"Of course. But we should talk about this later, okay?"

Another shrug. "Sure."

I watch as she and Keisha clatter up the pathway to the main doors, Keisha hiking her leggings up, and Legs dragging her backpack along the concrete behind her. I remember the days when I used to carry her backpack for her, holding her hand as I dropped her off for preschool.

How did my baby girl get so big?

Allegra Liana Donovan was born on March 18th, two days after I turned eighteen. Six pounds, three ounces of pink skin and shell-like ears and tiny fingers and toes. Perfect, complete joy and sheer terror. At the time, I had no idea that I'd named her after a non-drowsy antihistamine medication. Turns out, a TV commercial for the drug was playing while I attempted to push through each stomach-splitting contraction, huffing gas and uttering every curse word I'd ever heard in my life.

And Legs—as my brother Liam so charmingly nicknamed her from the get-go—was a fussy, colicky baby with a serious aversion to sleep in all forms. Thank goodness for my mother, who'd been a single mom since my parents divorced when I was little. She died when Legs was just a few months old, but for the short time she was here on earth as both a mother and grandmother, she made the prospect of being a mother myself much less scary. Helped me to realize I could still flourish and grow as both my own person and as a mom.

I didn't graduate high school, but I did end up getting my GED a while later (thank the good Lord above for the world-renowned child hypnotist known as Cocomelon), while my ex, Steven, partied it up at Central Georgia State and didn't visit his daughter once. Or anytime since. Last I heard, he was nursing a nasty case of herpes.

Just kidding.

Well, more like hoping. Past tense.

I've done a lot of therapy since then. Moved past wanting him to hurt for how he hurt me.

I mean, I no longer wish herpes on him... but maybe a bout of explosive diarrhea. Or two.

Either way, Dr. Lemay would tell me it's progress.

Ultimately, I'm glad I got pregnant. My daughter is the crowning achievement of my life. And Steven is an idiot and a fool for not wanting to know her.

But while I'm proud of the job I've done as a single mother, I understand that she's becoming more and more aware that we are a family of two. And I worry sometimes that I'm not always going to be enough for her. Case in point: I may make a mean s'more, but I'm not a great candidate for accompanying my daughter to a daddy daughter campout.

How on earth do I explain to her that she will not be "getting a new daddy" within the month? Or maybe ever?

Because I'm not going on this date tonight to find a husband, per se. Although, long term, that wouldn't be the worst outcome.

I'm going because I'm on a mission to get over my

stupid, unrequited crush on my best friend of almost a decade. Once and for all.

With perfect precision timing, my phone vibrates in my lap.

Carter: What time should I get my *arse* to the mall, then?

4

CARTER

"How about Zac Efron's birthday party? It's two weeks from Friday."

I let out a heavy exhale as I rack the barbell above my head, then look up warily from the workout bench. "Where is it this year?"

Last year, it was on a boat. A big ass boat. In the Mediterranean. Which was actually a lot of fun until a certain former teen pop star took some mushrooms of the magic variety and dove off the boat on the premise of wrestling a shark that he believed was sassing him. I had to dive in after him and fish him out by his neon-pink swim shorts. Idiot.

Anthony checks his notes. "It's going to be at that club you don't like in West Hollywood."

"The one with the aerial dancers?"

"Yeah, that one. Guess he's keeping the party small this year."

I screw up my nose. Anthony's right, I don't like that club. Last time I was there, one of the supposed aerial dancers was much less aerial than she was meant to be and booted me in the head with her stiletto. I still have the scar by my temple. That little puncture bled like a son of a gun, and I don't particularly want a repeat performance. Or more photos of me in the tabloids looking dazed and bloodied in a nightclub.

You'd be surprised how many of those have turned up of late. Or not surprised at all, if you believe the things you read about me.

"Put me down as a maybe," I say as I pick up the bar again. Fourth and final set.

In my peripheral, I see Ant recross his legs and roll his eyes theatrically. He's perched delicately as a bird on the sidebar of a nearby squat cage. "I'd give my left—actually no, my right—testicle to be within twenty feet of Zac. I mean, the man is *every* man's man crush, and you're all *put me down as a maybe because I'm personally offended by aerial dancers.*" He says the last bit slowly, in a grunty, low tone that I assume is meant to be mocking my voice but sounds more along the lines of a disgruntled caveman.

Which is how he probably views me, come to think of it.

I give my assistant squinty eyes. "You have a preferred testicle?"

"You don't?"

I do not. But I *do* want to end this conversation about our anatomy, so instead of responding, I continue extending and retracting my arms, forcing the stacked barbell that's almost impossibly heavy in motion, enjoying the burn of lactic acid through my biceps and chest. I've grown to love working out. It's an important part of my job as I'm expected to keep my body in prime condition. Workouts are necessary, even on my days off like today, but I like the endorphins.

"Okay. So, a 'maybe' for Zac's party," Ant murmurs. "Let's circle back to today's schedule. I need you to be at the airport by noon. We land around three local time in

LAX, and then you have that early dinner with Freya DiMauritz."

"Oh, yeah. Did Elena confirm that's happening then?"

Elena Sanchez is my manager and a force to be reckoned with. To the point where, from the moment I set foot on LA soil after my days off, my schedule is jam-packed to the extreme. Not that I can blame the woman. She's spent the past few weeks having to work overtime herself, thanks to me.

"Yup," Ant says cheerily. "It's an opportunity for you two to get papped together."

"K," I say on an exhale. I hate the word "papped"—it reminds me of pap smears, which I learned about in great detail nine years ago while sitting in the waiting room at the hospital as Lana Mae was having Legs. I accidentally stumbled upon the world's most descriptive pamphlet on the topic, and no matter what I do, I can't seem to delete the information from my brain. But I don't bother to explain this aloud because I really have had enough anatomy talk for one day.

Eight... nine... ten.

I let out a caveman-style grunt—which earns me another spectacular eye-roll from Anthony—and set the barbell back into position with a clatter. I swing my legs to sit up, and Ant extends a towel and a water bottle to me, his nose wrinkled slightly at my sweaty form.

"Thanks," I pant a tad breathlessly as I unscrew the bottle cap. "Appreciate it. But you don't have to fetch me things, you know that."

Anthony's been working with me for five years now. And though I rely on him heavily for many things in my life, I still feel weird having an assistant. I employ him to do my administrative tasks, organizing my calendar and scheduling my travel and appearances, not to wait on me like a servant.

"Please!" Ant flips his hand at me airily. "I do it for my own sake. Nobody wants to see your big sweaty self lumbering around the gym in search of water."

I take a few massive gulps from the bottle before narrowing my eyes at him. "Just for that, I'm going to RSVP 'yes' to Zac's party, and purposely not bring you as my plus-one."

Ant puts a hand to his heart and widens his eyes in mock-horror. "The headlines were right! You are a cruel and brutal man, Carter Callahan."

Which should sting, but it actually makes me laugh. I like Anthony and his sassy attitude. For one, he keeps my ego in check. And for two, it's refreshing to have someone around who challenges the things I say instead of agreeing with me even when I'm blatantly wrong.

This is one of the things I hadn't considered about being in the spotlight: the isolation. I was already pretty accustomed to being alone, but with fame, it's a different type of solitude. Everyone wants to please you, even if you're being a total jerk. And everyone has predetermined expectations of you without knowing you; a picture in their minds that may or may not match a single fiber of the actual person you are.

Right now, the picture most people have of me is a negative one, but I try not to think about it. As long as the people I love know who I really am, I couldn't care less about what a few phony news sources say.

My job is to act. Not make people like me.

But I know that's not always enough.

I swipe my towel across my forehead. "Shoulder press next."

We move across the gorgeous wood-and-white-accented, eucalyptus-scented luxury gym located near the home I bought in South Tuxedo Park a couple years back. I may not be in Atlanta much these days, but I like owning a house here. It makes me feel like I have roots.

As we approach the shoulder press machine, Ant says, "Wouldn't you be taking Sierra Duke as your plus one to Zac's party, anyway?"

"Nah."

Anthony sits on the floor and stretches his purple-chino-clad legs out in front of him. He cocks a brow at me in silent question.

"We broke up," I supply as I load the correct amount of weight, then get to work. First of four sets.

When I'm finished with the first set, I turn to find Ant in the same position, staring at me with his brows alarmingly high.

"Stop that."

"*You* stop that."

"Stop what?" I demand.

"Stop acting like this conversation's over when it's obviously not." He mimes pouring liquid into a cup and taking a sip with his pinky extended. "Hello? I need the tea."

"There's no *tea*. Which is a dumb saying, by the way."

"But who broke up with who?! What happened? *When* did it happen?"

I shrug. "I guess I was the one who called it off. Last week."

"Like I said, cruel and brutal." Ant smirks. "And did that flawless timing have anything to do with you flying back here to Atlanta for a few days?"

"What?"

"Ummm, cute blonde?" Ant says slowly, like he's spelling something out for me. "About yay-high? The one you spend every waking minute with when you're here?"

I scoff at him. "You mean: did my break up with Sierra have anything to do with Lana Mae, my best friend

30

who I'm absolutely, in no way, romantically involved with?"

"That's exactly what I mean." Ant gives me an insufferable smirk-and-raised-brow combo. Which is one of his favorite faces to make in my vicinity. "Because it seems to me that you want to be much more than just friends."

"And how did you come to that conclusion, Ant?" I ask dryly as I begin my second set of shoulder presses. *Anthony and his crazy theories.*

"Because whenever you have time booked off to come back to Atlanta, you call it off with whoever you're seeing in LA right before you go."

"No I don't."

Anthony gives me a smug little smile and wiggles his notebook at me. "I know your schedule better than you do."

I shake my head. Sure, when I'm home in Atlanta, my number one priority is to spend time with Lana Mae and her daughter, Allegra. But that has nothing to do with my romantic relationship status.

My friendship with Lana Mae has been the happiest accident to ever happen to me. She's the most important person in my life, bar none. I've long since shoved down any feelings I may have felt at the beginning in order to preserve our friendship. Because losing her is not an option.

"The breakups are a coincidence," I tell Ant with a shake of my head. "Lana's my friend."

Anthony holds up my phone. "Well, sweetheart, your *friend* just texted you back. She says to meet her at the mall as soon as possible because she needs your opinion on... dresses?"

I practically dive forward to retrieve my phone from his grabby little hands, and the mirthful laugh that inspires is ginormous.

"I didn't realize you were pivoting to personal styling,

Carter?" Anthony hoots, running a gleeful eye over my decidedly unstylish faded Lakers t-shirt and gym shorts. "Rachel Zoe better watch her back."

"I'll have you know that I'm helping my friend for a date she's going on later. With another guy. Because, you know, she and I are *just friends*," I emphasize.

And it's true. Lana Mae is actively dating again after years of not dating at all. She apparently decided out of the blue one day that she wanted to find a boyfriend. Not that we talk about this stuff much. Or ever. We're not really the type of friends who discuss their romantic lives.

"Well, you better run, Carter. I'm sure your cute little bestie can't live without that well-known fashion expert opinion of yours." Anthony chuckles way too indulgently. "In a purely platonic way, of course."

He's still laughing at me as I make my way to the shower.

Like I said, the man is good at keeping my ego in check.

LANA MAE

"I look like a tube of Pillsbury biscuits that someone popped open then tried to reseal."

Carter looks up from his position sprawled in a nearby armchair and chuckles. "Now there's an image that's going to be stuck in my mind forever."

I may be acting like I'm joking around, but I'm serious. This dress is the most unflattering thing that has ever graced my body. The bottom half looks—and feels—like I've been squished into a woman-size finger trap, while the top half has cavernous amounts of room to spare. I could seriously use some assistance in the form of those jiggly chicken-filet thingies you put in your bra, and even then, I don't think my sad little excuses for breasts would begin to fill out the expanse of fabric.

Sigh.

Breastfeeding deflated what little boobage I had to begin with into a sad, floppy situation that I prefer not to think about, ever. Models usually have flatter chests, and people find their figures appealing. So we're going with that train of thought. Because, *positivity*. It's something I learned in therapy: your thoughts contribute to your feelings of anxiety, so learning to change your thoughts can help change how you feel.

I take a tentative step forward, the silky, royal blue fabric straining uncomfortably in a way that suggests that, unlike all my favorite leggings, this material has *zero* stretch to it.

"Nope," I declare solemnly. "This isn't the one."

It's the sales assistant's turn to sigh. "Why not? It looks... good."

She took way too long to think of the word "good" for my liking.

We're in a store in Lenox Square mall because, for some reason, I decided that a new dress might somehow make tonight's date go differently than all the rest. So far, we're not off to a great start. This place stocks merchandise that's a bit of a reach beyond my usual H&M price tags, and I can't afford anything in here. But I don't say that out loud, because then, Carter will do something dumb, like try to buy me something.

"Well, you see... I need, uh, pockets." The lady looks unconvinced, so I keep going. "To store my snacks. I'm a tad hypoglycemic at times."

Melodramatic, more like.

But she doesn't need to know that.

"I'll add it to the pile of rejects," she says through a gritted, pearly-white-teeth grimace, which isn't super becoming of a customer service professional. Maybe it's because she has a perfectly normal-size, perky chest area that looks in the region of a C cup—the Goldilocks of bra sizes. Not too big, not too small, juuuuust right. Clearly, she can't empathize.

"A little help with the zipper?" I ask Perky Chest, but she's already turning away. She quickens her tippy-tappy stiletto step, pretending not to hear me.

34

Charming.

I can't wait until this embarrassing debacle is over and I'm back in my comfy floral jumpsuit that hides all my lumpy bits like magic.

I reach behind me, but the zipper is out of reach. Like, way out of reach.

"I volunteer as tribute," the low, throaty voice comes from close behind me and Carter's minty breath tickles my shoulder. It's cold in the store, and the hit of warmth against my skin makes me shiver. How did he get over here so fast?

"I deeply regret inviting you shopping today." I turn to punch Carter in the arm. "And stop practicing on me for your date tonight."

"Like I need practice." My best friend gives me his best smile. It's the devastating one—the one that makes his blue eyes twinkle like fairy lights, and the dimple in his right cheek pop, and the corners of his eyes crease in a way that gives you no choice but to stare at his face and think "how could anyone not fall in love with this man?"

Anyone except me, that is. I'm officially immune to Carter's Unlucky Charms.

Or so I tell myself. Constantly.

We're just friends. Only ever have been, only ever will be. Couples have meet-cutes. We had a meet-puke. And from that horrific, vomit-soaked night ten years ago, and in all the time that's passed in which our friendship has blossomed and bloomed and grown, he's never once given any indication that he sees me as anything more than just that— his best friend.

Not that I'm complaining. As far as best friends go, Carter is the very best. He's been there for me through everything. The year I met Carter was the hardest year of my life—a year where I unexpectedly became a mother and unexpectedly lost my mother, who was the closest person to me in the world. Day and night, he was right by my side (quite literally) through all of the heartache and bone-breaking exhaustion and tears, squeezing my hand reassuringly. I hadn't known him long by that point, but he became my rock. My light in the darkness at the darkest time of my life. For that, I will always be grateful.

"Besides." Carter smirks at me in the mirror. "Last I checked, *you're* the one who has a date tonight. Mine's a work meeting."

My stomach rolls at the reminder, and to put my growing anxiety on ice for a moment, I roll my eyes at Carter's reflection in the mirror and gesture towards the sales assistant's retreating rear end. "Well, if you're in the market for a date, Miss Perky Chest has been undressing you with her eyes since the moment we set foot in here."

"Nah, she probably thinks she recognizes me and can't place where from..." Carter is halfway through pulling his ball cap down lower when his forehead crinkles. "Wait, Miss Perky Chest?"

Oops.

"The sales lady," I clarify. "She definitely recognizes you, by the way. She's taken about fifty pictures on her phone."

Pictures that I've been trying to block by getting in the way, good friend that I am, despite the death glares she's been shooting me like they're going out of fashion. I know what she's thinking, too. Real-life Carter in his faded ball cap, even more faded jeans, and stubble-clad-jaw-and-flannel-shirt combo looks different from the clean-shaven, dimpled, big-screen sensation who can wear the hell out of a tuxedo. But her question remains the same: What is *the* Carter James Callahan—owner of the sexiest smile in Hollywood—doing with *her*— the Pillsbury Doughgirl incarnate?

Hah. Joke's on you, lady. In an entire decade of friendship, Carter has never so much as touched me in anything close to a romantic way.

Much to my chagrin.

Lana, we're not doing that anymore, remember?

Apparently, I don't remember.

Guess the joke's actually on me, then.

"She's been taking pictures?" Carter's voice is low, and his handsome face tenses for a moment as his eyes flicker from me to the sales lady. He's fiercely protective of his privacy, and even more so of mine.

"Don't worry," I say with a smile. "I made sure my big blue dress got in the way of every frame, so I'm sure she has nothing. Except a great chest, of course."

Carter gives me his small, close-lipped smile, his eyes soft, which I know means he's both thankful and a little embarrassed. He covers it up quickly and his gaze moves to follow the sales assistant, who's now bending over to pick something up, her low-cut shirt working its glorious male-entrancing magic. He turns back at me with a too-innocent look on his face. "I hadn't actually noticed her chest, but now that you've brought it to my attention..."

"Liar." I fold my arms. I love Carter to death, but maybe a girlfriend would've been better suited to accompany me dress shopping. Today is his last day in Atlanta for a while, so we wanted to spend the morning together before I have to go to the office and he has to go to the airport. It might be at the cost of my sanity, though. "And in case you *do* decide to make Miss Perky Chest's dreams come true and ask for her number, let me give you a tip: there is nothing seductive about quoting *The Hunger Games*. Ever."

"Hey, do you want help with your zipper or not?"

"I do." I sigh heavily. "But if you make a single comment about the odds being ever in my favor..."

The corners of Carter's mouth pull upward as he raises his hands in the "surrender" position. "I won't. Promise. I just think I would've played that role so much better than Hemsworth."

"You weren't even considering being an actor yet when they cast those movies," I tell him with a grin. "And I know you saying you'd have played the role better is code for 'I was the one who should have gotten to kiss Jennifer Lawrence'."

"Exactly. You know I can't resist a woman who's handy with a bow and arrow."

"That explains why we had to watch *Brave* three times in a row the last time you were home."

"We did that purely for Allegra's sake."

"I don't believe you."

He shoots me a grin that I can feel crackle through my insides. "You shouldn't."

I laugh, trying my best to appear completely unaffected. "Now that we have your archery fetish out in the open, can you please unzip me?"

"Yes, Ma'am." Carter nods. As he moves behind me, he starts whistling and it only takes me a second to work out that it's the Mockingjay whistle. He genuinely thinks he's hilarious.

Spoiler alert: he absolutely isn't.

"Don't make me hit you again."

"Whistling doesn't count as a comment," he says firmly as he undoes the clasp at the top of the zipper. For someone with such big hands, he's surprisingly deft and gentle while handling the delicate garment. Probably all that practice he mentioned he didn't need.

Ew. That's the last thing I want to think about.

"So, what time is your not-a-date?" I change the subject swiftly, turning around to face him with my hands on my hips before he can pull the zipper down. Because I don't need a physical reminder of Carter's garment-handling along with the mental one.

Carter glances down at his watch. "You mean my *work meeting*?" He shoots me a look and I laugh. He's probably the only man on earth who would label having dinner with Freya freaking DiMauritz a work meeting and not a date. Which, despite Carter's protests, I'm sure it actually is. "5 p.m. Which seems crazy early, but she has a thing later in the evening. I'm hoping I have enough time after my flight to go back to my place to shower and change first."

Carter splits his time between his luxury apartment in Los Angeles and the house he bought here in Atlanta a couple of years back. I'm not sure what possessed him to buy a big family home over another convenient penthouse condo, but I'm not complaining. Legs and I love visiting the immaculate, regency-style build in one of Atlanta's ritziest neighborhoods. Mostly because it has a swimming pool and a movie room.

"How long are you gone this time?" I hope my question doesn't sound as sad out loud as it does in my head. I'm always sad when he leaves. I mean, I'm used to it, but that doesn't change the feelings that accompany it.

"I'm probably going to need to stay in LA for the summer, at least. Have to work with Elena on some PR stuff and trick these *If Only* producers into believing I'm a decent human so they'll still consider casting me for their lead role."

I roll my eyes. "They'd be stupid not to consider you."

"Dunno about that. Apparently, I'm a liability." Carter's smiling in his carefree manner, but I know that the recent tabloid spreads and gossip site clickbaits about him get to him more than he lets on.

Carter got into an altercation in a bar in Vegas a few

weeks back. He hasn't told me exactly what happened—is being uncharacteristically evasive, actually—but from what I can garner from him and what's been reported in the press, it was a bit of a brawl. Which, again, is completely uncharacteristic. When Carter's had a few drinks, he gets animated and goofy, not violent or angry. And when he *is* angry, he tends to clam up and radiate a chilly frostiness, not punch people in the face in the heat of the moment.

So yeah, strange all around. I'm assuming it was about a girl because Carter doesn't take himself so seriously that someone ragging on him would make him snap like that, but I'm afraid I'll never know. For all his stupid jokes, Carter doesn't usually talk about his dating life. And I don't usually ask. Because, well, I don't want to know.

I'm aware that he dates a lot and he has a reputation for being a bit of a playboy, just as he did back in college when I first met him. For as long as I've known him, he's been a serial dater who never engages in serious romantic relationships. It worked in his favor for a long time with the media— the gossip sites ate up and spat out every single nugget about his dating life with glee.

But since the bar brawl, the spin on Carter has taken a turn for the worse. Now, instead of reporting him to be the suave Casanova with a heart of gold, he's the out-of-control wild child with women, substance, and rage issues. Which couldn't be further from the truth.

Carter's a great guy. A stand-up sort of person. And sure, he might be a total ladies' man and heartbreaker, but he's the sort of heartbreaker who breaks your heart then hugs you while you cry about it.

He's considerate like that.

And anyway, all press is good press, right? Carter's definitely got the swagger to be a beloved Hollywood bad boy. And we all know that the media is more forgiving to mishaps made by men than by women. The world in general, really. Hell, a huge part of the romance genre is built around the appeal of the morally gray, bad boy character. The Jess from *Gilmore Girls* versus the earnest Dean (early days Dean, before the whole cheating debacle, of course) or the well-bred Logan.

But I get it. I mean, he's... *Jess.*

"Well, even if you aren't considered for the role, would it be the worst thing in the world?" I ask, "Surely there are a ton of other movies who'd want you to star in them?"

Carter frowns, giving a quick glance around for any onlookers before removing his ball cap and tossing his fingers through his hair. "I mean, yeah, but it would suck because my personal life would be interfering with my ability to do my job. Plus, *If Only* would be the biggest role of my career to date. It already has so much buzz around it; Elena's sure the lead would put me on the Oscar route." His expression is determined, if a little distant. "Which is kind of the pinnacle of the industry, isn't it? You know, proof that I really made it."

"I mean, of course it would be amazing to be nominated for such a prestigious award," I start carefully. "But you know you've already achieved so much to be really proud of."

Carter has always been headstrong in achieving his goals. Working constantly, going above and beyond for every role—and while I will always support him in everything he puts his mind to doing, in my opinion, he's way too hard on himself.

Carter frowns. "It's the next logical step. What else would I work towards?"

"I know... I just think the Boss Lady works you too hard." Elena is Carter's manager and she's a powerhouse of a woman. She's singularly focused on achieving her goals, yet she's consistently multitasking to the point that she never seems to be one hundred percent present in the moment. I do like her, but she can be cutthroat in a way that I could never envision being myself. "It would just be nice if you got to take a break once in a while."

"That's what these past two days were, Llama." He pauses, and the tip of his tongue travels over his bottom lip. I am helpless to only watch, entranced. He has such a kissable mouth. I imagine.

"That wasn't a break." I shake my head. "That was a nosedive into deep exhaustion."

Carter's schedule is crazy. These past couple of days have been the first he's had off in forever, and we made sure to use them well. Almost too well, in that he got no actual rest time. I worked double time in the week leading up to his visit, staying up into the wee hours of the morning so I could take some time off when he arrived. And boy, was it worth it. We stayed up late eating pizza and watching dumb movies like old times, hiked up Stone Mountain, took a drive out to Blue Ridge, and took Allegra to the zoo. Which was fun until a pack of teenage girls chased Carter for his autograph, despite his hat-and-sunglasses combo—AKA the weakest-ass disguise I've ever seen.

And while suggesting he take more breaks may be a *tad* selfish (because of course I'd love him to be around more and travel less—it's almost ironic that I'm the travel agent, yet I'm the one who never travels anywhere), it's more so that I worry about him. I can tell that, underneath it all, these rumors and speculations are bothering him, and I think he's becoming a little worn down as a result of them.

"I'll catch up on sleep on the plane this afternoon, I promise." That beautiful mouth of his suddenly stretches into a smile and I can't tear my eyes away. "But you have to text me later to let me know how it all goes."

"How what goes?" I ask, still fixated on his mouth.

"The date you're going on tonight? Ring any bells?"

Oh, that.

"Will do. I'm sure I'll have much hilarity to report. I'm so freaking nervous, there's no way I'll be normal." I scoop my hair out of the way and offer him my back. "Now, let's actually get me out of this dress."

"Normal is overrated," Carter says as he finally takes the zipper in his hand. "You've got this. And just remember: hope is the only thing stronger than fear."

"Huh?"

"More sage *Hunger Games* advice."

"I hate you."

"No, you don't." The zipper sinks to the base of my spine and his fingertips briefly graze my bare skin, sending a flurry of shivers through me. Carter's voice grows throaty. "Oh, and Lan?"

"Yeah?" I look over my shoulder in time to see him remove his hand and take a big, big step backwards. Message received. Just like I heard it loud and clear when I told him a couple months ago that I was going on my first date in ten years, and he smiled broadly and said, "That's great, Lan". Like he was genuinely excited for me.

He shrugs as my eyes meet his. "For what it's worth, I thought this one looked great on you."

I ignore the tightness in my chest. "I think I'll just wear that wrap dress I wore on my last date. I can't be bothered doing any more shopping."

"Well, you know my feelings on shopping." I'm struck by how sweet it is that he's spending his last day off work in the mall with me instead of doing something he actually likes. "I'm happy to bail at any time. And I'm sure it won't matter what you wear, you'll look amazing."

See? This is why I love him. Always pumping me up,

even when he risks being very, very wrong. As was demonstrated by the great Pillsbury experiment. "Thanks. Now, enough date talk. Let's go get a pretzel or something."

Because there's nothing like a vat of salt and melted butter to drown your feelings.

I start to move away, but Carter puts a gentle hand on my arm, his eyes on mine. "You'll be fine tonight, Lan. He'll love you. How could he not?"

He has this weird look on his face that makes me suck in a breath. Makes me want to state the obvious answer: *Easily. Because you don't. Not the way I want you to, at least, which is why I decided to start dating again.*

I just need to stop comparing every other man on the planet to Carter, and then I'll be fine diving back into the dating pool. Like the adorable little humpback that I am.

Instead of saying any of that, I rip my eyes away from his. "You're right. How could he not?"

Carter's expression changes, blue eyes glinting with mischief. "Just make sure not to tell him the story about when you sat in pineapple juice and everyone thought you'd peed yourself."

I reach for a bust-enhancing, water-filled jiggly thingy from a nearby lingerie display and throw it at him.

He catches it one-handed. Smiles. "A boob? For me? Aw, you shouldn't have."

And just like that, I sweep all my thoughts about Carter not feeling what I feel back under the carpet. Right back where they belong.

6

CARTER

I'm sitting opposite one of the sexiest women on earth.

At least, according to *People* magazine. And I'm very aware that several men in the restaurant would, as Anthony would say, give their left testicle to be in my current position.

They'd be welcome to switch spots with me.

Because despite what *People* magazine says, when I look at Freya DiMauritz, I see a woman who is objectively gorgeous, sure, but her beauty stirs up zero *anything* in me.

We've been making painful small talk since she arrived —mostly about burrata (which we both like) and caesar salad (which we both agree tastes best when the dressing is made fresh with egg yolks). So basically, we've been going over the restaurant menu.

Like I said, *painful*.

She also ordered something named a "Porn Star Martini" in *that* tone of voice. One disbelieving glance at the menu confirmed that this is, apparently, a real drink.

"Don't knock it 'til you try it. These things are delicious... and dangerous," she says in a breathy voice, blinking her long lashes at me in a way that I'm sure is meant to raise my blood pressure. She keeps her eyes on me as she takes a big gulp of yellowy liquid. All I can think is that it reminds me of Lana Mae's hilarious pineapple juice incident that I've never let her live down.

I wonder how her date is going.

While Freya films a video for her social media, I can't help but shoot Lana a quick "How's the date going?" text. You know, casually checking in.

But in reality, it's all I can think about right now. She hasn't dated in so many years and now she's on her, what, seventh date (oh, who am I kidding? I *know* it's her seventh date) in just a couple months. I wish I knew why. What changed for her?

She seemed convinced at the dress shop earlier that I was going on my own date this evening, but she's wrong (and it isn't the only thing she was wrong about—she *did* look great in that dress). This dinner is a work meeting set up by our managers, and it's the first time we've ever met in person. Freya's looking to move away from her squeaky-clean Disney Channel star image, and being seen with me is apparently just the ticket to achieve that. In turn, Elena figured that proximity to Freya would be good for *my* image —a few paparazzi shots of us looking cozy together would give the media something to talk about other than my now-infamous altercation.

Not that I care a dime about my reputation. I'd ruin it again in a heartbeat if I had to.

But my being considered for the role of a lifetime in this *If Only* movie is hanging in the balance of my public image, which is also hanging by a thread.

So here we are. Smoothing appearances to keep everyone happy.

I take a sip of my old-fashioned. Set the glass down. Wipe my hands on my pants. It smells like a bizarre combination of butter and bergamot in here, the scents of freshly prepared gourmet food mingling with notes of designer perfume.

It's kind of giving me a headache. Or maybe it's the fact that everyone in the place is rubbernecking, surreptitiously —and not so surreptitiously—looking at Freya and me like we're goldfish in a bowl.

I know how lucky I am to do what I do for a living, and how lucky I was that one random audition to be an extra in some random movie ultimately set into motion what would eventually become a very successful career. Well, it was a matter of luck plus taking on some pretty odd roles in my early days in LA (which are way too hilariously embarrassing to revisit, trust me). But no matter how many years go by, I'm still not used to being on the receiving end of such stares.

Freya is apparently much more skilled at this; she doesn't seem to notice the gawking one bit. But as she holds out her glass and indicates that I should try a sip of her drink, it occurs to me that she also doesn't seem to have gotten the memo about this evening's not-a-date status.

"No, thanks. I'm good with my drink." I give Freya a pleasant smile.

"Have you seen what I can do with these?" Her green eyes gleam as she reaches over the table for something, and in the process, gives me an eyeful of cleavage.

I avert my eyes in a polite, gentlemanly fashion because, despite what the tabloids might say, I'm not quite the "hit 'em and quit 'em Hollywood bad boy" (their words, not mine) that constantly sleeps with supermodels. Sure, I've done my fair share of casual dates and dinners and dalliances, but the majority of the media stories that romantically link me to other stars are fabrications. Like last summer, when I apparently had a "steamy weekend affair" in Palm Springs with a pop star I've literally never met. I was in Omaha at the time, wrapping up filming on a post-apocalyptic zombie movie, and the only action I got that weekend was an undead actress attempting to eat my brains.

Those stories always seemed harmless to me. Ridiculous made-up crap that people could choose to believe or not. Stories that, according to Elena, were actually *good* for my career progression.

Until they weren't.

Truth is, I find it difficult to date seriously because, while there are lots of wonderful women out there, I don't ever enjoy their company as much as I do Lana Mae's. In fact, spending time at home in Atlanta with Lana and Legs is better than any date I've ever gone on.

This past visit home was particularly good, and I'm sad to be back in LA this evening. Spending time with Lana energizes me. She's like a battery charger for my soul.

"Carter?" Freya prompts.

"Hmm?" I blink, my thoughts on the trip Lana Mae, Allegra, and I took to the zoo yesterday. When Lana read the conservation plaque about deforestation, she pressed her face right up to the glass of the orangutan exhibit, gazed into a primate's eyes, and tearfully swore to never eat palm oil again. At the cafe an hour later, Allegra read all of the labels on her mother's lunch and confiscated her KitKat, much to Lana's chagrin.

Instead, I bought her a double scoop of M&M ice cream (palm oil free, according to Google), and her smile was brighter than the sun. I love that slightly crooked eyetooth of hers, the one she can't stand, but that makes her smile so unique.

"I said, have you seen what I can do with a cherry stem?" Freya flashes her perfectly straight and perfectly unremarkable teeth at me as she dips her long fingers into my drink and plucks out the cocktail cherry.

I try not to wince, but *holy,* that is freaking gross. Sexiest woman on the planet or not, there is nothing attractive about neglecting basic hygiene.

I push my glass away with the back of my hand. "Oh, no, that's okay..." I begin, but she's already placed the cherry stem in her mouth and is making weirdly intense eye contact that feels more like Snape putting a countercurse on Harry at a Quidditch game than a seduction technique.

Needing to look somewhere—anywhere—other than at what is currently being done to that cherry stem, I pick up my phone. Normally, I would refrain from checking my phone too much out of politeness, but honestly, at this point, screw it. The last thing I want is for Freya to think tonight's going to end with me screwing *her.*

I scroll through notifications on my phone until I find the only one that matters: Lana's texted back. Multiple times.

Lana Mae: It went... averagely, maybe?

Lana Mae: There may have been a small choking incident on a particularly hard pea.

Lana Mae: Luckily my date was able to slap me on the back hard enough that it came flying out.

Lana Mae: Which was nice of him. What maybe wasn't as nice is that he has a room in his home dedicated to Kermit the Frog memorabilia.

Lana Mae: He even did the voice a few times. I feel like maybe he is to Kermit as you are to fictional female archers.

Lana Mae: *GIF of Gordon Ramsay saying "Hey, panini head, are you even listening to me?"*

I can't help but crack up as I read the messages, each

one more ridiculous than the last. I obviously have about ten million questions I'm going to need to call her about the second I get out of here.

Carter: *GIF of Gordon Ramsay holding two slices of bread to a woman's ears as she says "I'm an idiot sandwich"*

Carter: First of all, sorry. Didn't mean to ignore you.

Carter: But secondly and way more importantly, if you wanted to escape the date so badly, you could've pulled the old 'oh no, my great aunt has mysteriously fallen ill and I need to drive her to the hospital' trick. You didn't have to almost kill yourself.

Lana Mae: Oh no, I didn't want to get out of there at all. In fact, I'm seeing him again next week.

I love that Lana speaks fluent sarcasm... it's my preferred humor language too, even if people do say it's the lowest form of wit.

Carter: Well then, I take it back. You're the idiot sandwich, not me.

Lana Mae: Like I said, this date was actually average on the scale of dates I've been on lately. So a life of green body paint and amphibian research, it is.

I frown at my phone as I read the last message. Lana has a tendency to foil her own emotions with self-deprecating humor, and it can be difficult sometimes to tell what's a joke and what's actually bothering her.

"Ahem!" I look up to see Freya's mouth stop mid-cherry-stem-wiggle. "I didn't know you had a girlfriend, Carter."

I blink in confusion. "What?"

She spits the cherry stem into a napkin and wipes her mouth. "Geez, I'm so sorry. I wouldn't have been hitting on you if I'd known that."

I start to shake my head at her, wanting to correct her

misunderstanding, but then, I notice the waitress standing at my shoulder. The girl smiles at me. "Calamari for the table."

I nod. "Thanks."

She smiles again and lingers for a moment, her gaze fixed on me, before walking away slowly. She glances over her shoulder twice as she goes.

Freya gives a wry smirk. "Waitress has the hots for you." Her expression turns sheepish and she ducks her head a little. "Like I did, I guess, before I saw who you were texting. I know this is a PR dinner, but I was pretty excited to meet you. Thought we might hit it off, seeing as you appear to have quite the roster of hotties." She places her hands on her hips, shaking her long ponytail. "You should've told me you were unavailable. I'm all for girl code; I'd never muscle in on someone else's man."

I suddenly feel warmer towards my not-a-date than I have all evening. I give her a reassuring smile. "No, you're fine. I..."

I trail off as Lana's reply pops up on my screen.

Lana Mae: Kidding, obviously. I will definitely not be seeing Billy again. And I'm sorry for texting you when you're out with Freya. I'm just... ugh. Dating is hard. How do you do so much of it?

My heart clenches, because there it is: the hurt below the humor. But as far as I'm concerned, all seven of the idiots she's gone out with must be deaf, blind, and also really, really stupid if they couldn't see what a catch Lana is. How lucky they'd be to be with her.

Any guy would.

Lana Mae: Just forget about all that for now and enjoy your date/work meeting. I'll call you tomorrow.

"What's her name?"

Freya is now smiling at me in a totally different way than she has all evening. You know, like a regular human being. She takes a sip of martini, not looking flirty anymore so much as genuinely curious.

"Lana Mae," I answer, then realize that she was asking what my supposed girlfriend's name is, not the name of the person I'm texting.

Who I guess she believes are one and the same.

"Pretty name. Where does she live?"

I don't know why I don't bother to correct her. I'm tired, I guess. My head is somewhere else, wondering about Lana and whatever happened tonight. So I simply say, "Atlanta."

"From the same hometown as you." Freya's eyes widen and she waves her hands excitedly, causing her stack of gold bracelets to clink. "Is it serious?"

She's the person in my life that I'm most serious about, sure. But I know that's not what Freya's asking.

"We've known each other for almost a decade," I say hesitantly. I don't like to lie as a general rule, but is omitting parts of the truth the same as telling a lie? It's a question I've asked myself many times over the years—especially following some recent events—and I'm reminded of a poem I studied in my Epic Poetry elective, freshman year of college. *Oh what a tangled web we weave...*

Lana helped me with the paper for that one. She was always a whiz at that stuff. Before her pregnancy, her plan had been to go to college and get an English Lit degree. But by the time I was writing that paper, she already knew that dream was going to be just that—a dream.

"I thought you just broke up with Sierra Duke." Freya frowns.

"I went on a few dates with her." My hands are itching to pick up my phone so I can call Lana now, not tomorrow. Would it be terribly rude to step out for a minute?

"So you're saying... you and your girlfriend have, like, an open relationship?"

The gleam is back in Freya's eyes and I hastily shake my head. Last thing I need is for the gossip columns tomorrow to be proclaiming I'm a swinger or something.

"No, it's not like that." I lean forward and look Freya in the eye. Because here it is, my chance to come clean and clear up this misunderstanding. "I guess... I dated a lot of people casually for a long time, but none of them ever made me laugh like she does."

Well, frick. That might be true, but it wasn't the truth I meant to tell her.

What I *meant* to confess is that I don't actually have a girlfriend.

"That is the most adorable thing I've ever heard." She's smiling as she reaches into her bag, pulls out her phone, and quickly types something. When she looks up, she tips her head towards the door. "You should go."

"Sorry?"

"You should go. Get out of here and call the girl you love rather than hang out with me."

I want to go. Everything in me wants to go. But Freya's taken time out of her busy schedule to be here. On *my* manager's request. "I don't need to call her right now. In fact, I apologize for being rude and texting her while we're having dinner, she's just had a bad night and I didn't want to ignore her messages. I'll put my phone away now and we can finish up."

Freya assesses me for a long moment, making me feel not unlike that lion stuck pacing in a cage at the zoo yesterday. Then, she smiles that totally normal, totally perfect smile of hers again. "You're not the guy the tabloids say you are, Carter Callahan. Besides, I'm sure that all the noseys in here have taken a million photos of us together by now." She tilts her head to the right, indicating a nearby table where two middle-aged guys are hunched over a plate of nachos. "And I'd bet my grandma that those dudes are paps."

Interesting. She noticed the rubberneckers, too. Maybe she's just a better actor than me.

"I don't want to spoil your evening."

Another laugh. "Please. I'm heading to the opening of that new club on East 11th—you know, the one that rapper owns. And I have about six male models on speed dial who could be my dates for the rest of the evening. I just hit the first one up."

Well, she's definitely organized.

"Um, well thanks. That's really nice of you."

"Not at all." Freya's expression is a genuine one that softens her whole face. "I just wish I had someone who looked like that when they talked about me. Lana Mae's a lucky woman."

I nod in response and then motion to the waitress for the the bill. There isn't anything I could possibly say right now because Lana is not my girlfriend, and never will be.

When it comes to Lana Mae, I'm Icarus, and she's the sun.

Which is why I can never get as close as I want to.

7

CARTER

Lana Mae: Rate my plate: Bonus points for creativity, no?

Through my labored breaths, I can't help but smile at my phone, where a picture of a slightly burnt pizza decorated with a lopsided pepperoni happy-face pops up to accompany the text. Gordon Ramsay would have a field day with this one, but I give it a solid ten out of ten for nostalgia reasons, alone.

Back when we first started hanging out, Friday night was pizza night. I'd come over to her mom's place after classes and work, boxes in hand, and more often than not, we'd eat it while laying on Lana's living room floor. We'd watch reruns of inappropriate 90s' teen movies on AMC, each of us folding dripping cheesy slices into our mouths like we hadn't eaten in weeks. She was going through a hard time at school, feeling ostracized by her friends as she navigated pregnancy while everyone else was worried about prom and college applications.

Meanwhile, I was anchorless, a buoy drifting at sea with no idea what I wanted in life, but just desperate to *be somebody*. I'd grown up believing I'd never amount to anything, and I was desperate for that not to be the case.

I wasn't close with my family, and due to my part-time jobs eating up most of my time outside of classes, I hadn't made a ton of friends at college. Lana Mae's mom welcomed me with open arms, and I grew to absolutely adore her over the one short year that I had the pleasure of knowing her.

These days, Lana Mae is more into those cupcake shows on the Food Network than viewings of *American Pie*, but I'd love to be eating happy-face pizza with my best friend and her daughter in front of the TV right now. Even if they made me watch that ridiculous British baking show while doing so.

Instead, I'm running my usual route in Runyon Canyon Park for the third time in a row this evening. And the only carbs I will be indulging in tonight are the bananas in my protein shake after my run.

Carter: That is a face straight out of my nightmares. The next serial killer movie will have the villain wear that on his face.

I keep my stride as I text, moving my gaze between the trail ahead and my phone screen. All my extra time this week has been spent working out—weights, resistance, and as I'm currently doing, cardio. This role in *If Only* apparently has a very important shirtless scene, and if I can't control perfecting my image, at least I can control perfecting my body. "Train for the role you *want*. Train like you already have it," says my extremely expensive but extremely motivational personal trainer.

It's not like I can complain. Getting to go trail running and take in the LA scenery twice a day is definitely a highlight of my job.

My phone pings again.

Lana Mae: A bit sexist to assume it's a *him*.

Carter: Merely a statistical probability. But I agree, it was an assumption for which I would like to apologize to female serial killers everywhere.

Carter: Either way, 6/10 at best.

Lana Mae: That's totally uncalled for! I'm sending Pizza Face to your apartment tonight to haunt you.

I'm reaching the top of Hero Trail now, and I slow my pace. When I come to a full stop, I put my hands on my knees, catching my breath as I look out towards the city. On a really clear day, you can see all the way to the Pacific, but it's hazy over the canyon today. The late afternoon sun shines through a pale, diluted blue sky—a sure sign that summer is on its way.

I step around a group of tourists taking pictures, have a sip of water, then text Lan back again.

Carter: Carter Callahan stars in *A Marinara Massacre.*

Lana Mae: No way would you get the starring role. You'd be the one who gets killed off first.

Carter: You mean the blonde teenage girl who runs into the woods alone? That's my dream role.

Carter: It's also the role I've never managed to get, no matter how many auditions I go to. No idea why.

Lana Mae: Your boobs are probably too small.

I sputter out a wheezy laugh, which earns me a few strange looks from people in my vicinity. One of them does a double take, says something to their friend and points. Then, after what looks like a hurried whisper-debate, strides over.

"Um, Carter Callahan?" The woman, who looks about my age, blinks up at me.

"Hey." I smile at her warmly, but not invitingly. I know

the drill by now: be friendly, but professional and to the point.

She shifts on her feet, red patches growing on her cheeks. "I, uh, just wanted to say I love you, and I love Freya DiMauritz, and I'm so excited that you're together."

"Well, thank you."

It's been just over a week since I had that initial PR dinner with Freya. The gossip columns went *crazy* for the photos of us, so we've been spending a lot more manager-arranged time together in public, prime photo-op locations. We've neither officially confirmed nor denied relationship rumors, but Elena wants us to lean into the mystery element of it all. She even wants to meet with both of us tomorrow to discuss me taking Freya to the premiere of my latest movie to generate further buzz.

I'm okay with it. I think. The whole faking a relationship for PR purposes thing is a bit weird, but it's definitely not a new concept in Hollywood. Besides, Freya's a nice girl and we're becoming friends, of sorts.

Although Freya's just the first prong of Elena's multi-step approach to "redeem the fallen reputation of Carter Callahan", as she puts it. She also had me take a surfing trip to Malibu so she could curate some clean, wholesome content for my social media and fan sites.

It was actually awesome. I can't believe I've been in LA for the majority of the last nine years but never surfed. I'll definitely go again when I can.

I exchange a few more polite words with the girl, and when she finally wanders off, I turn my attention back to my texts.

Carter: This is LA, there are many, many doctors who can change my boob size.

Then, perhaps against my better judgment, I text again with a subject change.

Carter: No date tonight, then?

Lana Mae: Actually, yes. My new slasher bestie was born out of a dinner date. The guy took me to a make your own pizza place.

What a loser.

Which is a bit uncalled for. Actually, very uncalled for. Make your own pizza actually sounds fun. I guess I'm just hot and a little hangry right now.

Carter: That's a unique first date idea.

There, I can be nice.

Lana Mae: Second date, actually.

Carter: Wait, this is #7 again? You gave Kermit a second chance?

Lana Mae: Nope. This was Andrew. We met for coffee a few days ago, and he invited me out for pizza tonight.

Carter: I can't even keep up! Three dates in one week? You're a certified player, Donovan.

Lana Mae: Speak for yourself, Mr. Just-A-Work-Meeting ;)

I look up from my phone, feeling strangely and inexplicably frustrated, to find a teenage couple looking at me intently. I nod at them, and the girl immediately makes a beeline towards me, tugging her boyfriend behind her.

Dutifully, I say hi, and accept their request for a picture. After a few selfies, they thank me and leave, the girl smiling ear to ear as she taps furiously on her phone.

I watch them go, and a weird little pit forms in my stomach as the boy slings his arm around his girlfriend and pulls her in close. I don't even remember a time when things were that simple, so cut-and-dry.

Because while I'm spending more and more time faking a budding relationship with a veritable stranger, my best friend might be falling for someone for real. I have no idea why I feel so bothered by this.

And even less of an idea if it's in any way my place to feel anything but happy for her.

8

LANA MAE

"I've never been one to objectify men, but that is a seriously nice butt." Mindy points a marinara-dipped breadstick at the TV, sending a spray of saucy droplets in every direction.

Mindy's always been good at making herself completely at home in my home. Or in anyone's home, really.

I arrived home a while ago in a somber mood after my pizza-making date with Andrew the podiatrist (which ended very awkwardly, by the way), to find my sister-in-law camping out on my doorstep with two huge bags of Olive Garden takeout. Apparently, she was bringing me dinner as an apology for setting me up with her Kermit-loving "friend of a friend of a friend", Billy, last week. But she'd forgotten to actually tell me about this apology plan.

And truthfully, *I'd* all but forgotten about Billy and Kermitgate.

But never one to say no to toasted ravioli followed by Chocolate Brownie Lasagna for dessert, I accepted her apology and here we are: Mindy, sprawled on the couch with Harry Styles curled up in her lap while she shamelessly objectifies a butt on TV, and me, seated beside her and shoveling brownie pieces into my mouth while trying my best not to stare at said butt like a lovesick puppy. Because, of all the movies in the world that we could've watched tonight, Mindy had to choose *this* one.

Rubbing salt in the wound, really.

"Oh, please." I take a sip of my wine, then raise a wry brow at her. See, I'm cool. I can watch this movie and be cool. "You objectify men like it's your job."

"Wrong." Mindy rips her breadstick in half like a cave-woman. "I *used* to objectify men like it was my job. Now, I only objectify Luke," she says cheerfully. I give her a *look.* "And that incredible butt on TV."

Mindy then goes on to grab the remote and pause the movie on a close-up of the derriere in question.

Fabulous.

Just to be clear, we're not watching anything weird. It's a regular old movie, and the zoomed-in shot on the TV belongs to an actor who is fully clothed in a regular (but very well-fitting) pair of chinos.

But that's no regular actor.

"Tell me you don't agree," Mindy continues, and when I don't respond, she pokes me in the side with her pink-socked foot. "And before you start on the '*but Mindy, you're married*' train, I'll have you know that there's nothing wrong with married people stating facts. Plus, Luke is a man who's comfortable enough with his sexuality to agree that we're talking about an objectively nice rear end."

I can't help but snort at this. Because while Mindy may have zero filter, she is one hundred percent right on two counts. One, I *was* about to go and get all judgey on her, and that would've been totally without cause because I know that she's just messing around and she adores my oldest brother (to whom she's been happily married for the past year).

And two, she's correct that Luke's the kind of guy who

can objectively appreciate another guy's, *ahem*, assets in an entirely heterosexual fashion. Case in point: at his bachelor party, he took the guys ax throwing, then had way too much to drink (which sounds like a recipe for ending up in the ER, but anyways), and proceeded to smack Mindy's dad on the butt and tell him that he looked like a total stallion for a man in his sixties.

I think Mr. Greene was actually pretty flattered.

"Can you unpause that?" I ask.

"Not until you agree with me," Mindy says. "Or at least tell me why you're being so weird right now. And *don't* even try to blame it on Allegra walking in, I know she's at a sleepover tonight."

I lean forward to snag another piece of toasted ravioli from the mess of takeout cartons and cram it in my mouth. I may not have a man in my life, but at least I have pasta. Which is arguably better.

And yes, I already ate an entire pepperoni pizza earlier this evening. I will not be judged.

"Lan, talk to me," Mindy presses. "Is this about Billy still? Because, girl, that was like a *week* ago. And besides, Billy's small fry. You haven't even been out yet with that doctor from my work. He's a doctor, Lana Mae, a sexy doctor! He said he might be interested, you know—"

"No," I interrupt swiftly, then take a glug of wine for liquid courage. Because the last thing I want right now is another Mindy set-up. I may need to continue my dating quest, but I'm certainly never going to let Mindy set me up again. "No, thank you. That won't be necessary. And it's not about Billy."

"What is it, then? What's up with you?"

I sigh. If I know Mindy at all, she's not going to let this one lie. I take another huge bite of food (emotional eater over here, okay?) as I contemplate whether to tell her the truth. And I don't know if it's the wine talking, or the fact that he's been on my brain relentlessly today, but I can't hold it in any longer.

"ThassCartrshhbutt," I mumble through a mouthful of food.

"Pardon me?"

"On the TV." I swallow and indicate the rear end that is currently infiltrating my living room. "That's Carter's butt."

Mindy's jaw practically hits the floor as she swivels her head back to take in the sight on the screen. She points. "Woah woah woah woah woah.... Carter, like, Carter Callahan?"

I nod.

"You mean to tell me that the butt I was just admiring like a total perv belongs to your famous best friend with all the dumb jokes?"

I swallow thickly. "Yup."

Mindy points at me and narrows her eyes. "Explain."

"He was a body double for the actor who plays the main character for a bit," I say. "Before he hit the big time."

What I don't add is that the famous actor in question—a total Hollywood heartthrob with a huge following of screaming fans—was so insecure about his rear end that he auditioned over two hundred body doubles before Carter was chosen for the role.

"Wait. You're telling me that Carter freaking Callahan started out his megastar career as... a BUTT double?" Mindy blinks incredulously. "I had no idea there was such a thing."

"I didn't know either."

I still remember the moment I got the call from Carter all those years ago. At the time, he'd just moved out to LA, so that he had a bigger pool of auditions and casting calls to attend. He'd gotten a couple of small roles here and there in

Atlanta and found some success with them, so LA was a logical next step.

At that point though, he was nowhere near making the big bucks. Or any bucks at all. Which meant that he was also communal-living in a roach-infested apartment above a bar with a Finnish guy who grew weed in his closet and spent all day astral projecting, and a devout Pastafarian (Yes, pasta with a P) who didn't believe in showering. Or deodorant. Or toothbrushes.

He always sounded so positive, so upbeat on our calls, but I knew that he was struggling—so I was upbeat and positive too, even though I missed him so much it hurt. It was a weird time (for both of us) but a break, of any kind, seemed like a win for him. Even if it was offering up his body in pretense of it being someone else's.

"Hollywood seems nutso," I continue. "They made him stand in the shower with nothing but a cup on his you-know-what so they could see how his butt looked in running water."

At this, Mindy collapses on the couch, staring at the still-paused screen and cackling like a witch from *Macbeth*. "That is literally the best thing I've ever heard. I hope I see him the next time he's in town. I have so many questions."

"I dunno, Min. Maybe I shouldn't have said anything..." I chew my bottom lip, unsure. Carter's very relaxed—he's one of those people who's super secure in his own skin and is happy to make fun of himself. But then again, I've never heard him talk about his butt-doubling days with anyone but me.

"I've never understood why you don't just tap that," Mindy says suddenly.

"Mindy!" I jerk my head in surprise, both because of her ridiculous comment and the change in direction of the conversation.

Mindy takes a slug of her lemonade, unfazed. "Fine, let me rephrase. I have never understood your relationship with Carter."

"We're friends." Friends who definitely do not *tap* anything. Except our phone screens, when we're sending Gordon Ramsay-themed GIFs back and forth. Like normal, platonic, non-*tapping* friends do.

"Yeah, but *why* are you just friends with the guy?" Mindy frowns. "I don't get it. You guys are super close, he's nice, he's funny—except for those dumb jokes, I tell you— and he's also, like, stupid hot."

She's not wrong. His jokes are dumb, and his hotness level is stupid.

"I dunno... Maybe because we don't see each other like that?"

"Nuh uh."

"What?"

"Nuh uh," Mindy repeats.

"Use real words, Min."

"That's not what it is." She shakes her head at me, sandy hair swishing. "I've always been curious about this. Are you into him?"

My cheeks grow warm, and she points at me. "You totally are!"

"Am not!"

Oh good, now I'm six. Maybe I should stick my tongue out, too.

"You are! You can't even look at his bootylicious little booty up there on TV without getting all hot and bothered."

"Not true. He's my best friend, that's all. Friends don't look at friends' butts."

"I beg to differ!" Mindy sounds almost offended. "I'll have you know, I look at my friend Tanya's butt all the time. She does Pilates, and the results are quite spectacular."

"I am not having this conversation with you, Min."

"Yes, you are. You're as in denial as Liam was when he tried to convince me he actually had a life before Annie came along and married him."

She's not wrong—my brother Liam *was* a grumpy workaholic before he met his now-wife. But I fold my arms and glare. "Well, if I like Carter so much, why did I ask you to set me up with Billy?"

"You tell me."

I cannot tell her. Because the exact reason I asked Mindy to set me up with Billy was to stop pining after freaking Carter when I'm freaking eternally stuck in his friendzone. Which is a fact I have never admitted—and will never admit—aloud to another living soul.

Buzz!

As if he can sense that we're talking about him, Carter's picture fills my phone screen. It's a shot I snapped last year when he was briefly in town, fresh from a breakup with an up-and-coming ESPN sports reporter (who had a stunning face and curves for days, of course) and looking to "blow off some steam."

I wasn't sure what he meant by that until we arrived at Six Flags Over Georgia and he revealed his plan to ride the Goliath coaster over and over until we puked our cotton-candy-stuffed guts out. Like I said, men are glorified children. But did I go along with his harebrained plan?

Hell yeah, I did.

The picture that is currently serving as my contact for Carter was taken on our way up the roller coaster for the seventh time. He's got his arm draped around me casually, facing the camera as he laughs, hair tousled, eyes crinkled... meanwhile, I have my head tilted towards him, looking at him like he's the sun and I'm suffering from a crippling Vitamin D deficiency.

"Ooh, is that Sexy McSexerson himself on the phone?" Mindy's beady eyes pivot to my screen and she smiles wickedly.

I grab my phone with lightning speed. "His name is Carter," I hiss, sliding my thumb across the screen to answer. "And he's *not* sexy."

Mindy makes a "pfffft" sound and waves her hand. "Try telling that to his butt."

"Who's not sexy?" Carter's deep voice asks on the other end of the line, playful and teasing as ever.

"Kermit the frog," I reply, and I'm rewarded with a throaty laugh.

"I think we very much established that after your weird frog-themed date last week. Plus, Miss Piggy is the only sexy muppet. Fact."

"I don't know. Fozzie Bear was kinda hot."

"You would think that, you adorable little weirdo." I know he means his comment innocently, just as a joke, but my stomach flips all the same. My body doesn't seem to understand that it shouldn't respond to him like this, including over the phone. I blame that damn sexy voice of his.

"Anyhow, what's up?" My voice, on the other hand, is high and slightly strangled and the polar opposite of sexy. Beside me, Mindy is watching me blush and squirm with ill-concealed delight, like I'm a circus sideshow or something.

"Thought I'd call to see how your date went."

"Didn't we already text about that earlier? Serial killer pizza, the desire to be stabbed in your huge implants on-screen, and so on and so forth?"

Another laugh. "Yeah, but none of that actually told me how it *went*."

For a moment, I'm confused. Does he care about me so much (platonically) that he genuinely hopes it was a great date? Because this feels like a strange reason to be calling on a Friday night when we've already been texting all evening. Shouldn't Carter be out wining and dining Freya DiMauritz right now? Despite his insistence that he's only been meeting her for work reasons, there sure are a *lot* of pictures surfacing of them together online.

And don't even get me started on the shirtless masterpieces that were his Malibu surfing pictures... I didn't even know that Carter likes to surf. Sometimes, his life in LA feels so removed from the Atlanta Carter I know.

"Oh, I guess not." I'm trying to concentrate on the call, but Mindy is now up on the couch, cradling Harry Styles in her arms as she shakes her booty and gets right up in my face while mouthing the words to "Baby Got Back". I wave her off, giving her crazy *shhhhhh* eyes as I say, "It went okay."

"A glowing endorsement."

I reach for my wine and take a gulp. My heart is pounding harder than it did at last year's Six Flags Pukegate, when he held down his twenty-five pounds of turkey leg and funnel cake like a champ, while I projectiled into a trashcan after Goliath ride nine.

Because the truth is, it did *not* go okay.

Andrew is a nice man.

A nice man who holds doors for me and asks me questions about myself and actually listens when I answer, and says please and thank you to service staff.

A nice man who's clean-cut handsome and seems kind.

A nice man who's not Carter.

And this unfortunate little fact hit me like a ton of bricks to the chest when Andrew excused himself to go to the bathroom and the first thing I did was send Carter a picture of my freaking pizza so I could smile at his reaction.

It was immediately clear: Andrew wasn't the guy who

was going to help me get over my feelings for my best friend.

This realization simmered in my gut for the rest of the evening. And because I knew I couldn't give Andrew what he deserved—a fair chance—I did the only thing that *was* fair: I ended things as we were finishing up our pizza, so things wouldn't get awkward if he tried to kiss me goodnight or something.

Andrew, being the stand-up guy that he is, accepted this with grace, noting that he had fun with me. He still paid the bill, despite my vehement protests. Because he's a nice man.

"I ended it. He wasn't right for me," I finally admit.

"Sorry, Lan." His tone is neutral, sincere, but impossible to read.

"Don't be, I'm good." I say this with conviction, but I feel ridiculous. I'm burning through dating prospects like matches while Carter goes on date after date with the actual "sexiest woman alive". I clench my jaw and, most definitely against my best interests, I ask, "How's Freya? You seeing her tonight?"

"Tomorrow," he says. "But there's something I need to be clear about, Freya and I are—"

"Oh, cool. Well, we'll both be on dates tomorrow night, then!"

What?

There's a short pause. "Didn't you just say you ended things with that Andrew guy?"

I look down at my lap and twist my skirt in my hand. "Yup. And now, Mindy's setting me up with a doctor. A sexy doctor. Saving the best date for last and all that."

Liar, liar, pants on fire!

Next to me, Mindy has stopped her ridiculous "Baby Got Back" lip-syncing and taken up open-mouthed staring.

I stare back at her, widening my eyes. She nods in understanding and whips out her phone.

Let's hope the doctor has no plans for Saturday night and loves last-minute surprise blind dates.

Because this is what my life has come to.

"The best for last," Carter repeats, his voice a little far away. And I suddenly feel acutely aware that he *is* far away. Over two thousand miles away, to be exact.

I laugh a tad maniacally. "Well, hopefully last. This guy checks off all the boxes on paper, so fingers crossed he's the one."

I have no idea what I'm doing right now, but here I am. Designating a person I've never so much as laid my eyes on to be my future soulmate. Not crazy at all.

And in exchange for my bucket of crazy, I'm treated to a laugh like a crackling fire in a log cabin—warm, cozy. Something I could bask in forever.

No! Not something to bask in. Something that's too hot to handle. Something that...

Oh, for goodness sakes. I am so freaking screwed.

"I'll cross my fingers for you, then. And if Pizza Face stops by tonight, I'll get him to cross his, too. You know, before he bludgeons me to death."

"I hear he prefers sharp objects. Likes to make a scene." Like someone else I know. That person being me. "Have fun with Freya tomorrow."

"Have fun with McDreamy." Carter sounds highly amused.

As we hang up, I shake my head and gloomily say, "Please tell me the sexy doctor has no plans for tomorrow night."

In response, Mindy simply presses her palms to my burning cheeks and looks me in the eye. "Just friends, *my* butt."

9

CARTER

When I step onto the sunlit patio of the breezy Santa Monica beach restaurant on Saturday afternoon, I'm surprised to find Freya already waiting for me. She's sitting at a corner booth, wearing a brightly patterned short dress and huge wedge heels, and sipping on a glass of sparkling water.

"Hey, you." She looks up as I approach. "Surprised I made it here first?"

"Sure am. You finally master the art of teleporting or what?"

Freya laughs as she lifts her face, and I give her a kiss on the cheek in greeting before sliding into the chair across from her. It's already become a running joke between us that Freya is notoriously late for everything.

I reach for the sparkling water carafe and pour myself a glass. "I don't know if I'm more shocked that you made it here before me or that I made it here before Elena."

Freya crosses one long leg over the other and laughs. "First time for everything. It's just Elena we're waiting for, by the way—Marc's busy dealing with another client who just checked into rehab, so Elena's going to update us both on some circumstances."

Marc is Freya's manager. Nice guy, but a bit schmoozy for my liking. I met him last week after the initial not-a-date, and he complimented my hair—which was a mess—and my socks—which were regular old white socks from Fruit of the Loom. A lot of people in this business in LA seem to communicate this way. I chose to work with Elena because she says things like "you're looking a bit tired" in a tone of voice that conveys, plain as day: "you look like crap."

"Oh yeah, it's probably my fault that your afternoon has been taken up with this."

Freya lifts a delicate brow.

"She wants me to take you to the premiere of my latest movie," I elaborate. "An action thriller that comes out at the start of the summer. Dunno why this had to be an in-person discussion, if I'm honest. I could have just texted you about it."

"Maybe she wants today to be another photo opp now that everyone's shipping us and nobody's talking about your weird barfight anymore."

"Nothing like photos of me stuffing my face with burrata to make me look good," I joke, then glance down at the menu in front of me. "Speaking of burrata, should we order some appetizers?"

"What happened with that, if you don't mind me asking?" Freya runs a critical eye over me, totally ignoring my hunger plea. "The barfight, I mean. You never talk about it, and you don't seem like a coked up, angry drunk kinda guy. And believe me, I know plenty of those."

Poor girl needs new acquaintances.

"I'm not," I reply honestly. "And it was exactly like they reported: a stupid fight."

"Over what?"

My fist involuntarily clenches under the table. "Some guy was heckling me, and I was drunk and reactive," I lie.

Freya pauses thoughtfully, like she's about to ask more questions, and I seize my opportunity to swiftly redirect the conversation.

"Anyhow, enough about me and my misendeavours. How's your new man?"

Freya claps a hand to her cheek and squeaks dramatically. "Oh my gosh, Carter. What a joke that's turned into."

Success.

I relax into my chair as Freya talks about how her new male model "friend"—the guy she's *actually* just started dating—is Derek Zoolander levels of vain. He even has the same habit of checking himself out in the backs of spoons.

I laugh. "Did it make you wonder if there was more to life than being really, really ridiculously good looking?"

Freya grins and quotes *Zoolander* right back at me. "Nope, but it made me realize that a male model's life is a precious, precious commodity."

We're both cracking up when Elena arrives in a click-clack of heels. She elegantly slides into an empty seat, smoothing down her gunmetal gray blazer. Everything about Elena screams *power*—her slicked-back hair, her pants with their razor sharp creases, her fierce expression behind large, black-rimmed glasses as she summons a waitress. The woman's not even our server, but she's by our table in an instant.

"Grey Goose martini, three olives," Elena barks, then places her pointy elbows on the table and scrutinizes my face. "Carter, you look tired. Have you been using the herbal supplements I sent over?"

No.

"Yes."

"Good." She turns her attention away from me. "Freya, stunning as ever."

"Likewise," Freya twinkles, flashing her famous Hollywood smile. "Love the Chanel. New summer collection?"

Elena answers with a half nod, like speaking fashion is beneath her, and dives straight to business. "Sorry I'm late. I had a long talk with Marc on the way here."

"Carter already told me about the premiere," Freya says. "I'll go with him, no problem."

"Good. Marc was sure you'd be up for it. And Marc and I are also in agreement that the premiere is a valuable opportunity to play *this* up as much as possible..." She moves her pointer finger between Freya and me, and then looks at me with a start, like she's shocked to find me sitting in front of her. "Oh! That reminds me, have you had time to go over that script I sent you? The *Endless Possibilities* one?"

"Was planning on giving it a read soon." I shake my head as I hide my smile. Typical Elena, bouncing through a million ideas at once. I decide to get the conversation back on track. "But back to the Freya and me thing, you were saying that we should play it up as much as possible? Isn't that what we've been doing for the past week?"

"Yes. That's right." Elena replies.

I run a hand through my hair and frown, trying to get ahead of the situation. "Well, the dating rumors are everywhere, and we've been photographed together in multiple places. What else would you want us to do? Release statements confirming our relationship or something?"

"Ooh! We could do a hard launch on Instagram!" Freya pipes in helpfully.

"What the hell is a hard launch?" I ask, but Elena cocks her head at Freya, then nods once, like she's actually considering her suggestion and whatever its hardness factor entails.

Then, she says, "Marc and I actually have something else in mind."

She pauses. I wait. Because, if I know Elena at all, I know that there's more coming. And I don't like the look on her face.

It's like she just cleared the area, and now she's about to drop the bomb.

Elena finally steeples her fingers. "Marc and I think you two should get engaged."

Boom. Bomb detonated.

"WHAT?" I practically yell. Multiple heads around the patio swivel, and I offer a small, benign smile of apology. *Nothing to see here, folks!*

"Obviously, it wouldn't be for real. And it would just be until the *If Only* cast is officially announced." She gives me a stern, no-nonsense, very Elena head nod. "If you want any chance at getting this role, Carter, the casting directors need to believe that you can one hundred percent embody this character, play a good man who is truly dedicated to the woman he loves. And what could be better to show this than a real-life romantic commitment?"

"This is hardly fair on Freya—"

"Think about it," Elena cuts me off swiftly. "Hollywood's most notorious bad boy, who's about to star in the most buzzworthy movie of the decade, has cleaned up his act and is now engaged to America's sweetheart, a former Disney star who has reinvented herself as a serious music artist..." Elena looks at Freya like a shark going in for the kill. "Just in time for her new album to drop, of course."

Freya smiles slowly as she twirls a strand of hair around one finger. "Oooh, yes. I can see how that would be a big story. Can I choose my own ring?"

"I have a contact at Harry Winston I can—"

"Wait, you're okay with this?" I interrupt as I gape at Freya. Strategically posed photos for the paparazzi are one thing, but faking an entire engagement? That's lunacy.

Freya shrugs. "Sure. I mean, I did the whole fake relationship thing with that Canadian singer a couple years back when I was looking for breakthrough roles after the Disney Channel and before I switched to singing exclusively. We kept that up for almost a year and it was fine. Don't mind doing it again, especially when I don't have a boyf—" Freya stops abruptly, looking at me with wide eyes. "OhshootwaitIforgotaboutyourgirlfriend!"

I almost repeat my "WHAT?" moment until I remember the lie I put into gear the night we met. "Oh... right. My, uh, girlfriend," I say feebly.

"Your girlfriend," Elena repeats.

"I guess she wouldn't be a fan of this engagement idea," I conclude. Because what else can I do? My lie is already in motion, and it's about to deal me a Get Out Of Engagement Free card.

Which I wouldn't hate.

Plus, Lana will get a freaking laugh out of this. I'll have to confess to her that I used her as a scapegoat when I next see her. She'll tease me mercilessly, I'm sure.

Unless her date with the doctor really *does* go well tonight. Then maybe it's not the best thing that I've been pretending she's my girlfriend while she's seriously pursuing other men for a genuine connection. Because that's highly unlikely to go down well with whoever she's dating.

Which yes, I do still feel weirdly bothered about.

And wish I was a big enough person not to feel that way.

Elena's face is pinched, like she's mentally chastising

77

herself. "Who is this woman then? Are you and Sierra Duke a thing again?"

Before I can give a resounding "no" to that, Freya—who is apparently the biggest cheerleader of mine and Lana's "relationship"—pipes up. "It's a girl from Atlanta. And he's clearly obsessed with her because he's never once looked at my mouth when we've been out together. Or my boobs."

Thanks for that, Freya.

"Hmmm." Elena taps a pointy fingernail to her bottom lip, eyes glazed in thought. "But it's a new relationship, right? She'd understand a publicity-based agreement between yourself and Freya?"

"No, they're, like, ten years serious!"

Thanks again for that, Freya.

Elena arches a sky-high brow at me and I shake my head.

"No, we're not. I mean, we haven't been dating for ten years." I attempt to do some damage control. "We've just known each other that long. We've been friends forever."

"Okay." Elena sighs heavily, like I'm causing her deep, deep pain. "I will need to think about an angle for this. And it's your job to tell me about your relationships, Carter. Way to drop the ball on this one. So before we revisit the engagement idea—which *is* our best plan of attack, by the way— let's turn to the other matter I have to discuss with you both. Which, I believe, will illustrate how correct I am about this plan in the first place."

I look at Elena steadily. "What's the other matter to discuss?"

"It's come to my attention that the bar in Vegas where the, ahem, *altercation* happened has security footage of the incident. And now, someone is threatening to leak it."

"NO!" This time there's no *practically* about it, I yell for real.

"Shh," Elena chides, looking sharply around the restaurant before focusing on me. "I'm dealing with it. But we want you both to get out of town for a bit."

"Ooh, where to?" Freya chirps, but I barely hear her. That tape can't leak. I can't let Lana see it. Maybe I can pay the bar off or something.

Elena looks at me. "Don't you own a family home in Atlanta?"

I nod mechanically. "I bought a place in the Buckhead area a couple years back."

"Good, good. We want you to go there for a couple of months. Together."

"Ew," Freya says with a wrinkled nose. "I don't want to live in Atlanta."

"It's temporary." Elena's steely eyes are now on Freya. "Your little model friend was photographed leaving your apartment the other morning, so in order to make this thing between you two believable, you both need to cooperate."

"I don't understand how us leaving town helps anything," I supply.

"Well, it goes back to my original point in all this: the two of you being seen living together in your family home will divert media attention from your outburst and from Freya's other romantic dalliances. We can even throw in baby rumors—"

"No," Freya gasps, horrified.

"No," I echo solemnly.

"I'm telling you, this is a much better, bigger story than a random hookup with a nobody model or a fight that's old news. Everyone wants a couple they can root for, and together, you two will be America's newest sweethearts. A modern day Timberlake and Spears. Without the patched denim and ramen hair." Elena makes a triumphant hand gesture before delivering the closing line of her argument.

"Hello Carter Callahan starring in *If Only*, and Freya DiMauritz releasing a number one platinum album."

Freya, for some reason, is nodding again. "Kinda makes sense." She looks at me. "And if you're in Atlanta for a few months, you could spend more time with your real girl-friend. In secret, of course."

Just like that, I finally see the potential positives.

Time off of work, staying in my own home, spending time with Lana...

Lana. What's she going to think about all this?

She's always been a passionate supporter of my career, cheering me on and encouraging me to get back up and try again whenever I've failed.

And I think she understands that *If Only* is the next logical step in my career, even if it means going to these crazy lengths. This is what I've always done over the course of my career, used logic. I've never stopped to ask myself if it's what I *want* to do next, or what I *should* want to do next.

Maybe because I'm not sure I can answer that question.

"This could be our angle, Carter." Elena's steely eyes—which exactly match her steely suit—zero in on me. "You want this leaked footage debacle to go away, right?"

I'd do anything for that to happen, so I nod. "Yeah."

Elena smiles, shark-like as ever. "So this is why you need to commit to the engagement. It's the only way to sell it. If this girlfriend of yours can just wait a couple of months, you can marry her then, if you like. Just do this until they cast you in *If Only*. By then, the media circus should have died down, you'll have your dream part, and you and Freya can 'break up' and go your separate ways."

Oh, damn.

I'm all out of moves. Because the only thing that really, really matters right now is not my own wants or needs, but protecting Lana Mae from having any part in this.

The tabloids can be vicious. Fans on social media can be mean, even cruel, with their words, and who knows what they'll make of the footage if it leaks. I can't risk Lana Mae—or, God forbid, Allegra—to be dragged into this part of my world. All because of a stupid fight I got myself into.

"Do you think Lana Mae will mind?" Freya screws up her pert little ski-jump nose. "If I was her, I'd mind."

Once again, I find that I like Freya as a person. I wish she didn't have to get dragged into this either. She's going to make some guy really happy one day, for real. I'm just not that guy.

"I don't know," I reply. *Would* Lana Mae mind if I was fake engaged to someone else? Would she mind if I was *actually* engaged?

Right now, she's probably getting ready for her date with the doctor, thinking only of how her night with him is going to go.

Not-our-waitress appears at Elena's side and places her martini on the table. My manager barely notices. "So marry your friend-girlfriend-whatever when this is all over! Get her a rock the size of Everest to prove your love. Just commit to doing *this* first. If she really loves you, she'll understand."

I glance at the waitress, who's still standing beside Elena, and wait until she's scuttled off before I say, "Okay, I'll do it."

"So in summary, we are good to proceed with the 'Carter Callahan and Freya DiMauritz are getting hitched and moving into his Atlanta mansion' storyline?" Elena asks crisply. "Both of you have commitments in Los Angeles next week, so we can schedule your official 'move' out east together for a couple of weeks from now."

I look at Freya. "This okay with you?"

She nods.

So I nod at Elena. "Let's do it. Just... give me time to talk to Lana Mae before breaking this, okay?"

"We don't have long." Elena's eyes soften a touch as she looks at me. "I can give you the rest of the weekend."

It's already Saturday afternoon.

Guess I'm taking a little preliminary trip to Atlanta tonight.

10

LANA MAE

"Great. Excellent. Fan-freaking-tastic," I mutter as red and blue lights start flashing behind me.

Because of course I'm getting pulled over.

This evening has been a complete dumpster fire from start to finish, so we may as well add some gasoline and roast s'mores on the flames to round out the festivities.

I pull over to the side of the road and wait, fingers tense on the steering wheel. It's only when the cop raps on my window that I realize I've made no move to turn down the stereo, which is blaring "All Too Well" at ear-splitting volume—the ten-minute version, of course.

I quickly turn off the stereo and roll down the window while trying to determine what Carter would do in this situation. Probably charm the absolute pants off the officer in question. Maybe it's time to see whether I've absorbed any of my best friend's natural charisma via osmosis or something.

I peer into the face of a cop looking like he's about to laugh. Is that a good or bad thing?

I take my chances and smile big, hoping it's giving off

more Julia Roberts in *Pretty Woman* than Heath Ledger as the Joker. "Um, good evening, Occifer. Officer."

Admittedly, not a great start.

The amused look slides off the guy's face at my stumbling words and his lips smush together as he studies me. I imagine that I'm quite the sight to behold—streaky makeup, stained dress, singed hair that's still giving off the smell of burnt toast.

"License and registration." He doesn't say please. I don't blame him. I dutifully hand them over and he takes them without breaking eye contact, peering at me like I'm some kind of zoo animal. "Do you know why I pulled you over, ma'am?"

Lovely. I, Lana Mae Donovan, am officially a twenty-seven-year-old "ma'am" who after tonight will be swearing off any and all dating and resigning myself to an entirely hermit-like existence forevermore.

Because enough is officially enough.

"Um... was I speeding?" I bite my lip and pick at the pink polish on my thumbnail.

The guy levels me with a *look*. "You were going 35... in a 60 zone."

"Oh," I reply weakly. Probably best to omit that I'd been too busy shrieking along to Taylor about being crumpled paper—complete with one fist clutching a fake microphone —to focus on the actual task at hand. That being driving.

"Ma'am, have you been drinking this evening?"

"No." I shake my head. Then, I reconsider and nod. "I mean, kind of. I ordered a drink but I spilled it, so I only had one sip."

I don't add that the spilled drink was a foreshadow of how the rest of the evening would pan out.

After my conversation with Carter last night, I knew I had to force myself to get back up and keep trying. Not to be discouraged by my failure with Andrew, but to remind my humpback whale self that there are plenty more fish in the sea, and maybe there *was* a real chance that Mindy's doctor friend would actually end up being my lobster.

That was the mindset I had when I left the house a couple hours ago. I was feeling relatively hopeful. I was wearing the same nice, freshly ironed cornflower-blue wrap dress I'd donned on a couple of my recent first dates. My hair was curled. I was wearing mascara and eyeliner. I'd even contoured my cheekbones, for goodness sakes.

And then, I got to the restaurant. Discovered that it was more of a monochromatic, tight leather pants and backless slinky tops, bandage dresses, and sleek, slicked-back buns sort of establishment. Realized that I looked like a preschool teacher amidst a horde of high-fashion models.

At first, I shrugged it off. Sat down and waited for my date.

He showed up twelve minutes late in a cloud of spicy aftershave looking very, very suavely handsome in a crisp white button-down with the sleeves rolled up. He air-kissed me on both cheeks, signaled the waitress with an *actual click of his fingers*, then flopped down in the chair opposite me and introduced himself as Braxton.

Slightly dazed by both his handsomeness and his audacity, I stared at him for a moment, then asked "Like Braxton Hicks?" before I could help myself.

Apparently, I am beyond help.

He gave me a strange look before saying "Like, Braxton Fletcher, actually."

And that's when I kicked off what would go into the books as the worst date in history by making delightful small talk about contractions for ten minutes.

Braxton—Dr. Braxton Fletcher, the resident doctor at the medical aesthetics clinic Mindy works for—returned the favor by countering my nervous word vomit with a list of treatments he recommended for "improving" a post-baby body. He even gave me a pen so I could take notes on my napkin.

The date went from bad to worse when the waitress appeared and Braxton ordered a Negroni while blatantly looking down her shirt. Apparently, he didn't think she needed any of his "professional help" in that area.

Feeling a little small by this stage, I decided that I would order a cocktail to look classy and like I knew what I was doing, and also because alcohol was very badly needed. But the cocktail menu was written in tiny, swirly script that I could barely decipher, so I panic-ordered a "Cosmopoutan".

Of course, the swirly letters actually said "Cosmopolitan". And while I'd never actually had one before, I've seen enough *Sex and the City* in my lifetime that I should've known that. Guess it serves me right trying to be a Carrie when I'm clearly a Miranda.

When my drink arrived, I managed to spill most of it on myself. Then, while reaching for my freshly inked napkin, one of my hair-sprayed curls fell into the candle in the middle of the table.

Braxton beat out the flames with his Armani blazer, earning him a round of applause from the other patrons and a hug from the waitress with the low-cut shirt.

After a tense hour of picking at our meals, I left with both my leftovers and my pride boxed up to go. Braxton left with the hot waitress.

Cut to the teary T-Swift car concert while I drove like a geriatric. Which is why I'm now stopped on the shoulder of the road, closing my eyes and hoping for a nice coma to give me some sweet relief.

No such luck.

"Ma'am, I'm going to need you to step out of the vehicle."

Of course.

I get out of my car to stand on the shoulder of the highway. Then, on his further request, attempt to walk a straight line in four-inch heels. Which is nigh impossible for anyone —even us stone-cold sober folk.

"Can I maybe try with my shoes off?" I ask with a wobble, shielding my eyes against a set of oncoming headlights.

"That would be fine, Miss Dono... Wait a second!" The police officer squints down at my driver's license. "Lana Mae Donovan? I recognize that name. I think you might know my wife."

"Oh?" I look at his now-twinkling eyes apprehensively. *Please not Mona, please not Mona, please not...*

"Lance." He grins and gestures to himself. "McCreary."

Come on. Really, universe?

"Yes, hi. Of course." I smile the fakest smile known to man, my teeth grinding. "How's Mona?"

It's a dumb question. I saw Mona just yesterday morning when I dropped Legs off at school, and she was the same as ever: a grade-A douchebaguette.

"She's well, thanks. At home with the kids. Wait 'til I tell her I ran into you tonight..." Lance shakes his head, all cheery at the thought of bringing a delicious gossipy snack to his ever-rumor-hungry wife.

I'm no expert but surely this is a tad unprofessional? Isn't there some kind of privacy law in place? If not, then this is pretty much worst-case scenario. Mona The Informer will have a field day with her husband pulling over an unwed former teen mother (who smells like a bonfire and is covered in panda makeup) on suspicion of drunk driving.

By morning, I'm sure every parent at the school will have the memo.

I nod, still at a loss of what to do. "Well, do tell her I say hi."

Hi is absolutely not the message I would like to convey (something of the four-letter variety would be much more satisfying), but so be it.

"Will do. Now, enough chit-chat and back to business, I'm afraid. We need to address those drinks you consumed tonight."

"Sip, singular, of one drink, singular," I correct.

McCreary continues to look doubtful as he mutters, "Well, we'll see about that."

Charming.

It takes Officer Lance McCreary twenty-five minutes, two sobriety tests, three goes of me walking in a straight line, and four rounds of shining his flashlight in my eyes to determine that I'm not crazy drunk, and maybe just crazy.

He lets me go with a warning. Which should feel like a victory, but doesn't.

I drive the exact speed limit the rest of the way home. With the stereo off.

11

LANA MAE

When I finally pull into my driveway after what I hope is my first and final dalliance with law enforcement, I pay the babysitter, shower all my makeup and humiliation away, then change into the comfiest sweats in my closet. You know, the ones with a mustard stain near the crotch that have been washed and worn so many times that the butt is saggier than a soggy diaper and you'd never dare wear them in front of another human being, but you also can't bear to throw them out because they feel more comfortable than anything else you own.

It's a those-sweatpants kind of night.

I flick on the TV in my bedroom, but before I flop on my bed and drown my sorrows in Legs's leftover Halloween candy and back-to-back *Gilmore Girls* episodes, I check to see if Carter's texted me.

He hasn't, which makes sense. Because according to the gossip sites that I may have accidentally-on-purpose googled while Braxton visited the bathroom earlier, Carter and Freya are together today, living it up on a rooftop patio in LA. Looks like they're hitting it off more than ever, and of course they are. Because she's stunning, and he's Carter.

People like that are drawn to each other like magnets. The same way stains are drawn to my disgusting sweats.

What was I thinking anyway, going on a date with a doctor purely to try and make myself feel better about Carter's successful dating life? I should be happy that Carter's forming a connection with someone and seeing her so often, but the little green-eyed monster within me feels no such thing.

I force the image of Carter and Freya out of my mind, send a quick text to my sister-in-law regarding her date choice for me tonight ("Et tu, Mindy?"), and then peek in on my daughter. She stirs when I crack open the door, rolling over in her blue and white plaid sheets.

"Mom?" her reedy little voice calls into the darkness.

I walk in and crouch next to her bed. Stroke her hair. "Hi, sweetie."

Legs studies my face for a long, silent moment. Then she sighs. "On a scale of one to ten, how bad was it?"

For the first time all evening, my smile is genuine. Because my daughter? She has sass in bucketloads. So much so that I know I never have to worry about her future grown-up self sitting through a date like the one I did tonight.

"Ten being the worst it could be?"

She nods.

"Eleven."

Legs sits up in bed and rubs her eyes before looking at me. "Woah. That's pretty bad," she says solemnly, her big brown eyes—she has my eyes—wide and unblinking. "So no new dad for me?"

Her sentence stings my stomach. I want to be everything she needs, but being a sole caregiver comes with a whole lot of nuances and challenges, and I know the best thing I can do for my daughter right now is to validate her feelings, even if those feelings make me insecure. "Honey, do you feel like you're missing out by not having a daddy? Is it something you're thinking about a lot?"

"Kind of. I want you to have a husband. And then I get a daddy, too."

I lean forward to wrap my arms around my daughter. "I don't need a husband, sweetie. I have everything I need right here."

Legs pats my back like she's consoling *me*, then she wriggles out of the hug. "But you watch movies with people kissing all the time and then you cry at the end, but always pretend you don't, and I think it's because you have nobody to kiss."

She's scarily discerning for a nine-year-old, and I could not be more proud of the person she is growing up to be. I've made mistakes as a mother, sure, but Allegra has been my one and only priority these past nine years.

And now, my sweet daughter is apparently tuned into me enough to observe that I'm "sad I have nobody to kiss."

"It doesn't matter if I have anyone to kiss," I tell her.

"Sure, it does. Uncle Luke has Auntie Mindy, and they're always kissing. And Uncle Liam has Auntie Annie now."

She's right. My two older brothers—once known for being a notorious playboy and an incurable grump, respectively—have both found and married women they adore, and who make them better.

"But look at you, Mom. You're all sad and lonely."

"I'm not sure I'd use those exact adjectives."

"You need to keep going on dates until you find the right man to marry."

"I don't know about that, Allegra." I sigh. After tonight, I'm not exactly feeling inspired to date any more. I've given it more than a fair shot, and I'm frankly exhausted with it all. Maybe eternal singledom really is the answer for me.

"Whatever I do, I need you to know that you will *always* come first and I will always love you the most."

Allegra nods. "I love you, too, Mommy. But if the real Harry Styles wanted to marry me, I would love him more than you."

I nod back. "That's fair."

I give her one last kiss goodnight, smooth her hair back from her face, and pad to my room, where Lorelai, Rory and a giant sack of stale candy are waiting for me. Back to normality.

Only not.

Because when I open my bedroom door, my breath catches in a little yelp of surprise.

There's a man sitting on the edge of my bed.

Specifically, the very man I've been having bedroom-themed dreams about for so many years now.

Only this time, I'm awake.

I think. Possibly hallucinating. Maybe my hypo-glycemia has kicked in again?

Carter looks up from the book he's thumbing through, his blue eyes more vivid than ever in the dim bedroom light. "Hey, Lan."

My cheeks turn the color of Snow White's poison apple when I see that he's holding Tessa Bailey's *Hook, Line and Sinker*. The ultimate sexy best friends to lovers rom com book. Those apples only ripen when I notice that he's got the book cracked open to the dog-eared page where Fox and Hannah finally... you know.

Fanfreakingtastic.

I'm definitely awake. Because my dreams would never do me dirty like this.

"Imani lent that to me," I lie swiftly. When in doubt, blame your coworker, as the famous saying goes. Not because I'm ashamed to be reading a spicy book, but because the trope of this particular spicy book hits a bit too close to home.

As in, *I wish.*

Wished.

Past tense, remember? I'm no longer the Lana Mae with a hopeless unrequited crush. Now, I'm the Lana Mae who goes out with rude doctors and gets pulled over by even ruder cops.

"It's funny. And hot." He looks me up and down, then grins cheekily. "Nice pants, Llama. Those new?"

"Har har. Are you gonna tell me what on earth you're doing here?"

In my bed.

And not Freya's.

Carter sets down my book and smiles a tad sheepishly, a flush touching his cheeks. "Oh, yeah. Sorry to show up in your room like a creep. You weren't downstairs and I heard the TV so I figured you weren't asleep. I came over to bring you post-date snacks. Just in case the doctor was a health nut and didn't want to order any dessert."

He holds up a bulging grocery bag as proof, and I can't help but smile. This man knows me so well. I'm *that* person —the one who goes to the grocery store with great intentions, buys a cartful of healthy food... then two nights later ends up raiding her pantry and snacking on old Halloween candy because she didn't have the foresight to buy proper junk food for soothing PMS and bad days at work. Or in this case, bad dates.

It's a vicious cycle, but Carter is one step ahead of me, as per usual. Even with the thousands of miles separating us the majority of the time, he still knows all the little things that make me tick.

"Thanks..." I sit on the edge of the bed beside him— woah, it's been a long time since we sat on my bed together

—and accept the bag. "But I know you didn't take a four-hour flight to bring me chocolate."

"Okay, okay, the snacks were my excuse. I needed to talk to you about something and felt it would be better to do in person than over the phone. Hence the surprise bedroom appearance."

I can't believe that Carter bailed on whatever he was meant to be doing with Freya DiMauritz tonight to fly across the country to talk to me about something. But I'm too exhausted at this moment to read into what could possibly be going on.

"But first and much more importantly, how did the date go?" He flashes me a dimpled smile as he leans back, supporting his weight on the mattress with his hands in a way that makes his corded arms flex tantalizingly.

He's been gorgeous from the moment I met him, but it sometimes dazzles me that this twenty-eight-year-old manly man is the same person as the nineteen-year-old boyish man-in-progress who drove to the store to grab extra diapers for Allegra when I ran out at 11 p.m. one night. He came home with six different boxes of Huggies and Pampers because he didn't know which ones to get, plus Reese's peanut butter cups—my favorite—because he thought I might need the, and I quote, "moral support only chocolate can provide."

Tonight, his shopping bag of goodies has my still-favorite lying on top. It reminds me that although so much has changed over the years, some things remain exactly the same. Carter is still Carter—the best man I've ever met. And I will always make sure I'm a supportive friend to him, too. He's an only child, with parents he's not close to, and he was a bit of a one-man island when I met him. He had casual friends, lots of girls lining up to shoot their shot with him, but he kept everyone at arm's length. Didn't *truly* trust anyone.

He was paying his own way through college when I met him, and he had no concrete idea what he wanted to do with his life. But Carter was so... unique. I knew he was special and destined for big things. He had so much drive and ambition, this unbelievable *hunger* to prove himself, and yet, he was aimless. Had this energy but nowhere to go with it.

Which is why, when he started finding his groove with acting and the opportunity for him to go to LA presented itself, I threw myself behind him. Encouraged him to go and became that person who would always stand in his corner. Because no man is really an island.

It was right then that I realized I loved him. Truly loved him. Because I let him go when everything in me was screaming for him to stay, stay, stay.

"How did it go, you ask?" I look at Carter sheepishly. "Well, there may have been a small fire involved."

"Of course there was." He grins. "Do go on."

"Well, basically, my hair committed arson. And then I got pulled over on suspicion of driving under the influence."

Carter shuffles his position to look at me through narrowed eyes. "I'm going to go ahead and assume that you weren't actually drunk driving."

"I was not. I was pulled over for driving like a blind octogenarian." I rub the back of my neck and make a face. "Yup. I was driving so badly, the guy rudely assumed me to be inebriated."

Carter laughs. "That sounds more like you."

"Hey!" I protest, but he raises his brows and I accept defeat. I am a super competent person, in general—I'm one of the top agents at my office, I mow my own lawn, clean my gutters, and can change a tire with my eyes closed—but I do not have the best driving record, and my car has the scars to prove it.

In my defense, why are there always so many poles in parking lots? It's like they exist to beckon you to back into them.

"And *how* did you set your hair on fire?"

I hold up the singed tips of a chunk of my hair and Carter whistles through his teeth. "The inferno was caused by a horribly placed candle, too much hairspray, and a really hard-to-read drink menu."

"That makes perfect sense."

"'Course it does." At this point, I'm laughing because no matter how bad a night it was, all's well that ends well when I'm spending time with Carter. "I can't believe you're really here."

"I wish it was a surprise visit just to hang out." The smile slips off Carter's face and a ghost of a frown touches his lips in place of it. "But there is something important that I need to talk to you about."

I look at his face and see the pinch between his eyebrows. It's been a long night. I'm exhausted, and I'm happy to have my best friend here with me. When he talks to me about whatever's bothering him, I want to be totally focused, alert, and present.

"Do you think we could relax and watch some TV first? I'm all talked out right now."

"Of course." Carter nods. "We can do whatever you need."

Deja vu moves through me in an instant at his words, digging up memories from almost a decade ago. I look at Carter to see if he's thinking of it too, but he just smiles at me, puts a friendly arm around me, and reaches for the remote. "Let's eat a bunch of chocolate and watch Rory go from boyfriend to boyfriend instead." I raise a brow at him and he laughs. "Oh please, Lan. If I know you at all, I know that there's going to be nothing else on that TV tonight but *Gilmore Girls*."

And this, ladies and gentlemen, is why I love him.

And also why I *cannot* love him. Because tomorrow, he'll talk to me about whatever *this* is—by the sounds of things, something about Freya—and then leave for LA again, and I probably won't see him in person again for months.

Back to normality. Back to the way it has to be.

12

CARTER

Back when I first started acting, I also started partying. A lot.

I was lonely and lacking connection when I moved to LA. I had a lot to be grateful for—the simple act of getting that extra role my freshman year of college led to a couple of small bit parts in shows and movies filming in Atlanta that paid better than my landscaping and warehouse jobs. But I was still purposeless in college, in that I had no idea what I wanted to major in, and acting made me enough money in a few short months that I ultimately dropped out and moved to Los Angeles to pursue something I'd never even considered doing before.

I'd finally found an avenue where it was possible to make something of myself. Something that I seemed to be *good* at.

Other people thought it was impulsive. Risky, even. But it was the only choice that made sense, crazy as it seemed.

Lucky as I knew I was to have an opportunity ahead of me, I missed Lana Mae and baby Allegra desperately. My only friend on the west coast was an actual astral projector named Rasmus who lived in my shared apartment. And I use the term "friend" very loosely. Mostly on account of the fact that he was always astral projecting (which, from what I can gather, is simply a fancy term for having an out of body experience), so therefore he was not very fun (nor mentally present) to hang out with.

I initially only planned to be gone temporarily, but every time I phoned Lana Mae, she was so encouraging that I should stay. Keep trying out for roles. And she sounded like she was doing well, much better than she had the first few months after her mom died. Her nightmares had stopped by then. She was going to therapy. Spending more time with her brothers, who were helping her out. She no longer needed me to fill that gap for her.

So instead, I went to parties. And I drank. Sometimes way too much. Sometimes waking up in weird places with a fuzzy head.

I'm aware of the part I played in earning my playboy reputation—I'm not stupid. But even in the throes of all the Hollywood glamor and glitter and girls, it never once felt good to wake up in a strange bed.

Until now.

Because this bed may be strange to me, but it doesn't belong to a stranger. And somehow, I am lying here, fully clothed and above the covers but not wanting to move a single muscle because Lana is nestled into the crook of my arm, her honeyed hair streaming across the white sheets and gleaming in the morning sunlight. She's still wearing those stained sweats, but now, they're paired with the most serene, peaceful expression on her face as she sleeps. It's beautiful.

She's beautiful.

"CARTER?!"

Lana and I both jolt upright to see Allegra standing in the doorway, wild-haired and wide-eyed. She looks more like her mother every day—big brown eyes, high cheek-bones, and a permanently mischievous look on her face. "What're you doing here? Are we going to the zoo again? Oooh, or swimming? We could go swimming!"

I glance at Lana Mae, unsure what to say or do. We always do activities involving Legs when I come home to visit, but she's certainly never seen me in her mother's bedroom before. I don't want to speak for Lana, so I stay silent as she sits up, rubs a hand over her eyes a little frantically, and says, "Hey, baby. Carter was just—"

"Oh my gosh, wait! Are *you* going to be my new daddy?" She smiles right at me as she twirls into the room, bare feet padding on the soft carpet.

Oh, frick.

"That's what mommies and daddies do," Allegra informs me matter-of-factly. "They sleep in the same bed. I know 'coz I went round to Tara's for a sleepover and that's what her parents did."

"Uh..." I falter, looking at Lana Mae for backup.

I'm surprised when Lan sighs. "Don't sweat, it's a new thing she's on. I'll talk to her later."

Allegra runs to the bed, flops down at the foot of it, and says, "Ooh, *Gilmore Girls*."

Which is still playing on the TV. We must've fallen asleep watching it.

"Oh, shi—I mean, *shoot!*" I correct hastily. I'm due back in LA later today, and Lana Mae and I haven't yet had the conversation I flew all the way here to have.

Lana looks up. "What's up?"

"I'm leaving for the airport soon and we still need to have that talk."

Her brow crinkles. "I told my dad and Constance that Allegra and I would come to church with them this morning, then she has a dance class this afternoon."

"On a Sunday?"

"Yeah, extra practice for the summer recital."

With the Freya story about to break, it's probably not ideal for me to be seen at a public event with another woman and her daughter. Or be seen at that daughter's dance class, even if that woman is just my best friend...

I have to get this done today, as I promised Elena I would. All of my other commitments can wait. I scramble for my phone. "Okay, give me a minute."

Carter: Any chance you can push my flight back?

Anthony: To when?

Anthony: And PS, this is your official written warning that I am now requiring that plus-one invite to Zac's party as payment for making me come to Atlanta with you last minute, then not even showing up at your house, forcing me to hang out alone all Saturday night. And now Sunday too, by the sounds of things.

Carter: Until tomorrow morning, if possible. I'm sorry. For real. There's just something I have to do. You can go ahead home without me, or if you want to stay in Atlanta, you could go shopping today with the incidentals credit card I gave you.

Anthony: Forget everything I said. I always knew I loved you.

Anthony: FYI, have moved the flight for both of us.

Anthony: And AFYI, I totally know where you were all night. I'm assuming you're delaying our flight to canoodle a bit more with your "just a friend"?

Welp. I'll deal with that comment later. For now, I'm just glad I've somewhat got a plan.

"Well, the good news is that I get another day in Atlanta," I tell Lana Mae and Allegra.

"Yay!" Allegra wraps her arms around my leg and looks

up at me. And, strange as this situation is (AKA waking up in Lana's bed and having her daughter pretty much insinuate that I might be her "new dad"), I'm not exactly disappointed to get an extra day with Lana and Legs.

Lana's cheeks are glowing pink as she looks at me. "Want to come around for dinner later and we can talk then?"

"Sounds good. I'll pick up groceries and bring them over. And I can make you both pancakes while you get ready for church," I suggest. Because apparently, I am in full-blown daddy-to-be mode.

The matching sunshine smiles from mother and daughter warm my heart.

Allegra runs out of the room to find Harry Styles the cat, and Lana turns to me with a strange look on her face. "I'm sorry we didn't get to talk last night, CJ. I can tell it's important. We can miss church if we need to?"

"No, it's fine. Later will work."

"Can you at least tell me that you're not sick or dying so I don't worry all day?"

I smile. "It's about Freya actually. Kind of a long, embarrassing story."

"Oh." The single syllable out of Lana's mouth is short and punctuated. And with that, she rolls out of bed and offers me a small smile. "Um, I should shower."

"Of course." I'm on my feet in an instant. "I'll be downstairs starting breakfast."

Conversation is strangely stilted between Lana and me over our pancakes—even our usual "rate my plate" banter is as flat as the pancakes on said plate—and I'm glad for Legs being there, chatting away obliviously.

Maybe Lan's feeling weird about last night. It's been so long since we would sleep next to each other, and I know some of the memories from that time of her life are still painful for her. For me, on the other hand, there were many nights following that period of time where I'd wake up alone and wish she was still there, sleeping next to me—selfish as that thought might have been.

Or maybe I'm overthinking... this might not be about me at all. She could just still be thinking about her bad date.

I can ask her later when I tell her about the harebrained engagement plan that Freya and I are about to be thrown into.

After breakfast, I see Lana and Legs off, clean the kitchen, then let myself out of Lana's house to go by my place and change (whilst avoiding Ant's judgmental raised brows and smirks) before hitting up the grocery store.

As soon as I step out though, I almost run into a guy lingering on the sidewalk aimlessly. When he sees me, he snaps a photo and starts to walk away. I frown at his retreating back, annoyed by the fact that even here, at Lana Mae's house, I'm conspicuous. The last thing I need is for the paparazzi to find out where she lives.

I duck into my Jeep and pull away, filled with fresh resolve to protect Lana and Legs at all costs, along with a lingering mental image of how peaceful Lan looked sleeping next to me this morning... like everything was right in the world.

13

LANA MAE

There are two Lululemon moms waving at me from across the parking lot.

You know the type—skinny in that perpetual-pilates-going, snacks-on-only-almonds kinda way, dressed head-to-toe in form-fitting designer sportswear and sunglasses. Sporting expensive blowouts and diamond engagement rings, which glint in the afternoon sunshine as they jingle the keys to their Range Rovers and sip their oat milk lattes.

Do I sound jealous?

It might be because I am. Just a teensy bit. These women never usually wave at me or speak to me, even though our kids have been in dance together for years. I've always let that niggling little part of me believe that it's because I don't have a husband who's a banker or a lawyer, or because I'm about a decade younger than most of them, or because I'm not one of those perfectly-put-together moms...

I just don't fit in. My mom aesthetic is more "looks like she was dragged through a hedge backwards, someone get that woman a coffee now."

Anyhow, I don't really have time to wave back right this second because I'm dealing with a way more important issue. Namely, the Instagram photo of Freya DiMauritz that I accidentally just liked, and then, in a panic, unliked.

Because, apparently, Carter flew all the way to Atlanta out of the blue to talk to me about... Freya. And then, he slept in my bed all night. Beside me.

My heart beats at a million miles per minute when I so much as begin to think of his soft expression and smiling, crinkly eyes this morning.

And I know that it was just a mistake that means nothing, a friendly accident. But still, the insecure little so-and-so in me couldn't help but look Freya up on social media and lament the ethereal bodily perfection of Carter's latest apparent love interest in comparison to my own, humanly imperfect body, while I asked myself over and over again what he's doing back in Atlanta.

Is he here to tell me that their work meetings blossomed into romance and he's now dating her for real?

Not sure why that would warrant an in-person conversation. Or any embarrassment on his part. He's dated plenty of women over the years, and Freya's freaking hot.

Like, super hot.

In the picture I accidentally liked, she's wearing a Baywatch-red bikini and a million dollar Hollywood smile. Her long hair fans around her dreamily—this pic was taken before she got one of those fashionable butterfly layer cuts that make stunning people like her look like they're doing a modern take on Farrah Fawcett, but would make regular people (i.e. me) look like they'd just stuck their finger in a electrical socket.

The problem is that the picture—the one that my clumsy thumb hearted—was from the dark depths of her feed. I'm talking *three years ago*. And if she *is* Carter's latest girlfriend, she's bound to notice his weird best friend liking her ancient pics like a stalker.

Would I be a terrible mother if I say that Allegra got ahold of my phone and went on a liking spree?

Oblivious to my internal panic, the Lulu Moms get closer, white teeth flashing. "Lana! Lana Mae! Over here."

I blink in confusion at the confirmation that it is, in fact, me that they are waving at, and not the brick wall behind me (which would probably be more plausible). I smile and nod awkwardly in response before hurrying towards the dance studio entrance, clutching Legs's favorite Strawberry-Kiwi Breeze smoothie from Smoothie King in one hand. Because no, I didn't have a moment to make anything from scratch for her healthy post-dance snack, like my ever-present Mom-guilt dictates I must.

Seriously, Mom-guilt is a real thing. And it's a freaking nuisance.

Inside, the studio is cool and air-conditioned, a welcome relief from the summer heat. The music is blaring and the kids are all doing a slightly frantic, leapy dance.

I lean against a post to watch, and my phone buzzes in my hand. Carter's calling.

I silence it. I'll have to call him back.

My phone starts ringing again immediately.

I frown when I see the word "Dad" flashing across the screen. Weird, my father only calls me when he has a bone to pick. And I just saw him this morning at church; can't imagine he would have missed an opportunity to do so in person.

A text comes through.

Carter: Call me ASAP.

Also weird. And demanding. Carter never uses phrases like "ASAP"—he's way too laid back for yell-y capitalized acronyms. And am I not seeing him in a couple of hours?

Lana Mae: Just grabbing Legs from her dance class. Call you when I get home.

I barely have time to press send when my phone rings again. Luke, this time.

Our sibling group chat also has multiple new messages:

Mindy: I knew it I knew it I knew it I knew it!

Annie: Is it for real? Because if it is, my celeb-obsessed former self is DYING.

Luke: Real or not, our dear father is losing his ever-loving mind right now, so if you wouldn't mind calling him back there, Lan...

Luke: And also, if it is real, how does Carter feel about Cabo? Because I'm assuming Vegas is out of the question.

Mindy: You are also assuming you're invited.

Liam: What on earth is everyone blabbering about? I am trying to take an important call, but my damn phone keeps pinging with notifications and interrupting me.

Annie: Welcome to the world of group chats, my love.

Liam: I don't remember consenting to being a part of this.

What in the hecking heck is going on? I try to step around a smiling dance dad to get outside so I can call some of these people back, but I'm accosted by Lulu 1 and Lulu 2 halfway to the door.

"Lana! There you are!" Lulu 1 shrieks as she grabs my arm. "You'll have to tell us everything."

"Yes! How did it happen? I mean, how do you even know him in the first place?" Lulu 2 asks.

I blink at them, wondering if Starbucks accidentally spiked their lattes.

Not willing to take my chances, I smile, shake Lulu 1's

grip off me, and begin to move away. "I'm sorry, I'm not sure what you're referring to, but I'm actually in a rush and..."

But then, Lulu 2 flutters her eyelashes and says, "Carter Callahan, imagine."

Carter Callahan?

The five syllables of his name snag on my eardrums like fabric on a nail, and I stop dead in my tracks.

"You'll have to spill your secrets, because I have to say, I was shocked. *Shocked.*" Lulu 1 gushes, her claws digging back in my arm. "You know, he's my official Hall Pass. My hubby chose Mila Kunis, which is just soooo predictable."

What in the name of all that is holy is this whacked-out woman talking about?

"For me, it was between Carter Callahan and Henry Cavill, but Henry seems more of the settling-down type so I figured I'd have less of a chance if I ever met him. Carter Callahan gives off that sexy, bad boy, eternal bachelor vibe, you know?" She shakes her head, tutting away. "But I was clearly wrong—*obviously!*—seeing as he's getting MARRIED!"

The smoothie cup slips out of my hand and falls to the floor.

What follows can only be described as a Strawberry-Kiwi Breeze explosion of monumental proportions.

Pinkish-red goop splatters everywhere, coating me, the Lulu twins, and all innocent bystanders in a blanket of cold stickiness. It's like the freaking elevator scene from *The Shining*, but with smoothie.

"Agggh!" someone shrieks.

Another person whips off their ruined sweater.

A third comes running with a stack of paper towels.

Me? I stand glued to the spot as my brain short-circuits trying to process this news.

Is this what he wanted to talk to me about? The reason he's back here in Atlanta?

Is he MARRYING Freya DiMauritz?

No. They just started dating. If they are even dating, which has been neither confirmed nor denied. Either way, Carter's not the long-term commitment type, never has been. He goes through girlfriends like I go through Wonderbread.

There's obviously been a mistake.

I need to call him back. Now.

"Sorry, sorry!" I spring to life. Get on my knees on the floor. Start trying to help clean up the mess while throwing out apologies like candy. If I'm not very much mistaken, Lulu 2 snaps a picture of me.

I swear, it must be a full moon or something. But all I'm focused on is getting out of here so I can call my best friend.

"Mom?" Legs's little voice suddenly comes from beside me. "What's going on?"

I look up and give my daughter a beaming smile, hands stacked high with sopping wet, pink-stained paper towels. So basically, I must look like a wayward serial killer.

"Hi, honey! I'm just, um, cleaning up your snack. Is class over? Yes? Okay, we should go."

I load a few armfuls of paper towels into the nearest trash can, not caring that my favorite work dress—ribbed gray material with cap sleeves and a cute side tie—is now tie-dyed bubblegum pink and red beyond repair. Then, I take Allegra by the hand and practically run to the dance studio door. Every pair of eyes in the place follows us, and I'm sure my cheeks are now as red as my stupid dress.

"Mom, I'm hungryyyyyy," Legs whines as she hops onto her booster in the backseat and clips her seatbelt on. "And that is so *embarrassing* that you spilled my smoothie all over everyone's moms."

"I'm so sorry, Leggsy. We'll stop and grab another one on the ride home."

I roll down all the windows to get some much-needed fresh air, and then pull out of the parking lot, needing to get some space between us and the dance mob. I drive for a few minutes before swerving into a Sonic parking lot. Not quite Smoothie King, but Cherry Limeade also contains fruit... of a syrup variety. This is hardly the time to be picky.

But instead of pulling into one of the order bays, I stop in the middle of the parking lot and throw on my hazards, reaching for my phone.

"Mom, what are you doing?" Allegra says in horror. She's just hit that age where she's absolutely mortified by everything I say and do, and it's really making me look forward to those upcoming teenage years. Not.

"One sec, hun. I need to check on something before we order."

Before I call Carter back, I have to be prepared. Have to know what I'm working with. You know, so I don't break down in a fit of hysterical tears or something when he tells me he's engaged.

I ignore all my messages, open Google, and type in "Carter Callahan", like I've done so many times before.

There are a thousand news articles that pop up, and I frantically click on the first one, which reads: "Hollywood's Hottest Bachelor Officially Off the Market!"

And that's when I'm greeted with a full-screen-size picture of my face. It's not a good picture. It's snapped from a distance in what looks to be a park in my neighborhood. I'm wearing sweatpants and my glasses, hair in a knot, and I was probably mid-sneeze, given my expression—face contorted, eyes half-closed, lips puckered above what looks to be an entire collection of chins. The caption reveals me as

"Alana Mae Donovan, Carter's longtime best friend and confidante."

Which is mostly correct, give or take an A, but also how on earth does *E! News* know this, and moreso, why do they care? This seems more like Mona The Informer fodder than national news.

I scroll down furiously. There's a second picture. And while it's another zoomed-in paparazzi shot, I'd recognize that dark, scowling face anywhere. It's my brother Liam, and Carter is next to him. They're in a jewelry store.

Before I can even begin to unpack that one, I scroll to a third picture showing Carter and Freya walking down the street in LA somewhere, Freya looking impossibly cool in that off-duty supermodel kind of way and sporting only a singular chin. Under the photo is the caption: "Freya DiMauritz left heartbroken by revelation."

And then, my eyes land on the last line of the article:

"We have it on good authority from a close source that Lana Mae is very much in love with Carter and always has been. Their friendship was bound to eventually blossom into romance. We wish the happy couple all the best as they plan their upcoming nuptials."

My first thought is "Oh, they got my name right that time."

My second thought is "Aggggghhhhhhhhh!"

Which pours out of me with both the power and speed of a freight train.

"MOM! Why are you shrieking?" Legs demands, covering her ears.

A car pulls up alongside me.

A cop car, to be specific.

The cop rolls his window down. "Ma'am is everything okay here—Oh, it's *you.*"

"Good afternoon, Officer McCreary," I reply tiredly.

Because of course it is.

"I was just about to pull into an ordering bay."

"Okay," Lance McCreary says, skeptical as can be. "Um, you haven't been drinking again, have you?"

"I wasn't drinking last time!"

"But you have been today?"

UGH.

"*No, I...*"

And then, because the universe clearly hates me and my entire life appears to be one big cosmic joke at the moment, a white Lexus pulls into a nearby parking spot and Mona the Ultimate Buttinsky hops out. "Cooee, Lana Mae! Texting and driving again, are we?"

"I'm parked," I reply through gritted teeth.

"In the middle of the parking lot," Mona singsongs. She walks towards the cop car and bends to give her husband a peck. "Hi, muffin. Saw your car so I had to pull in and say hi."

Muffin?!

Gross.

She turns back to me and smiles wide. "Lana, I've been wanting to chat with you. I was looking for you after church this morning. "

I know she was. I saw her. I got Allegra into the car and whizzed off before she could come over.

"Oh, sorry. Mustn't have seen you, was in a rush to get Legs to dance class..."

Mona puts her hands in my open car window and I resist the childish urge to roll it up. "Sure, we'll go with that," she says sweetly. "I was going to call, but I left my cellphone at home this morning, so I'm glad I ran into you. It's vitally important that I speak to you regarding the daddy daughter campout. I *still* don't have a permission slip from Allegra, and then it was brought to my attention

112

that, this morning in Sunday School, she was telling people that Carter Callahan was going to be attending with her." She barely covers a snort. "You know, the famous actor?"

I do know, yes.

And apparently, due to her cellphone-less state, Mona has not seen today's entertainment news. Woman is going to be beyond pissed that she missed the scoop of the century.

"Poor child appears to be suffering under the delusion that he's going to be her new daddy." Mona drops her voice to a stage-whisper that Allegra can still most definitely hear.

"He is!" she pipes up from the backseat. "He slept in my mommy's bed last night and then made me pancakes."

Oh, nooooo. No, no, no.

I go fire-engine red as I look back at Mona, planning to explain the actual innocence of the situation. Instead, I'm startled—though I shouldn't be—to see her covering her mouth with her hand, wheezing with laughter. "Wow, she's got a big imagination!"

Legs crosses her arms and glares. "Nuh-uh. It was real."

I give Allegra a reassuring look before addressing Mona again. "Well, Carter *was* at our house this morning, but it was not—"

"Oh, Lana!" Mona's eyes are full of faux-sympathy as a honk of nasally laughter comes from the police car. I glance over to see that Mona's husband is now joining in, chuckling merrily at the certifiable mother-daughter duo who actually believe that they shared a pancake breakfast with a world-famous actor on a quiet Sunday morning. "Come on. Don't encourage her. I know that you might want to write it off as a big imagination, but she was lying in the *Lord's house*, of all places. And let me tell you, kids who lie like that often turn out to be *sociopaths*."

My jaw sets.

There's only one sociopath here, and it's not my daughter.

Before I can even think about what I'm doing, I'm unbuckling my seatbelt and getting out of my car. I stand right in front of Mona—*yasss, I'm taller than her*—and steel her with a filthy look. "That's extremely rude and uncalled for, Mona. I don't know where you get off calling a child names, for goodness sakes, but in any case, Allegra isn't lying."

Take that, lady. I don't care who messes with me, but call my daughter names and I'm gonna go full mama bear on your ass.

Unfortunately, my impassioned speech is met with a derisive snort. "If you say so, Lana Mae. You know, I expected more from you. Which may have been a mistake on my part, but honestly, involving your daughter in whatever *this*—"

The screech of tires momentarily captures our attention and we look over to see a battered black Jeep swinging into the parking lot. A black Jeep I know very well. In fact, Carter's had this same Jeep since the night I met him and he drove my vomity self home. He won't give it up, no matter how much money he makes. Says that it has sentimental value. I don't know what kind of "sentimental value" he's talking about, but I suspect he may have lost his virginity in it. He has neither confirmed, nor denied, my theory.

The Jeep grinds to a halt and Carter leaps out, looking good enough to eat in a crisp white tee that shows off his toned, tanned biceps, slim cut jeans, and a pair of white Nikes. He obviously went home and showered, got changed and shaved —there's a hint of a five o'clock shadow that accentuates his strong jaw in place of the scruff that was there this morning.

Mona stares at him like she's seen a ghost, but he doesn't

even spare her a glance. His attention is fixed firmly on me. "Llama, thank the Lord! I had to come find you. You said you were picking up Legs from dance class so I drove that way, then I saw your car in this parking lot here, and... I am so sorry, I can explain—"

"Hi!" Before Carter can say another word, I'm launching myself at him, flinging my arms around his neck and pulling him close in a valiant attempt to get him to shut the hell up. Even in the midst of my frenzy, I register how good he smells. Woodsy cologne, clean laundry, a hint of salt. Mmm. "There you are, babe."

He blinks down at me in full confusion. "Babe?"

I wrap both my arms around his middle and smile up at him, hoping to goodness that he gets the memo and plays along. "I've been missing my *fiancé* all day."

"Fiancé..." Carter looks from me, to Mona, then back to me. I widen my eyes at him a little frantically, and I can practically see the penny drop. His stunned expression quickly slides into a confident smile. "Oh... *ohhh*. Yes. Fiancé. Missed you too, gorgeous."

I roll my eyes at him. Isn't this guy paid the big bucks to, yanno, *act*?!

Now onto my little deception, he grins mischievously, his stance visibly relaxing. His vivid blue eyes lock on mine and he reaches up to push a lock of hair off my forehead with his warm, calloused fingertips. "I didn't get a chance to tell you before you left this morning, but you look beautiful today, sweetheart. I love you in that dress."

My entire body blushes and shivers at his compliment and his touch (I know, I'm pathetic and touch-starved). Carter's grin only widens and he puts one arm around me, squeezing my shoulder, and sticks his other hand out towards a gobsmacked Mona. Who doesn't look unlike a big mouth bass at this moment. It's not my least favorite thing I've ever seen.

"Hey, I'm Carter. You a friend of Lan's?"

"I, uh, I...." Mona stutters.

"This is Mona McCreary. She's the president of the PTA at Allegra's school," I offer cheerfully. Never thought I'd see the day that The National Enquirer was stunned into silence. "Oh, and her husband, Lance." I nod towards the cop car, where Lance is looking a little pale and jittery as he sticks his hand through his open car window.

"Very pleased to meet you. I'm a big fan," Lance mumbles, the tips of his ears turning red.

"Thanks, man." Carter shakes his hand briefly before turning back to me. Almost like he can't tear his eyes off me.

Phew, those acting skills are finally coming out.

"What're you doing at Sonic, Lan? I'm making dinner tonight, remember?" The corner of his mouth twitches as he winks at Mona and Lance. "Steak and lobster. Champagne. Anything she wants. Nothing but the best for my *babe.*"

He's clearly enjoying himself way too much right now. And while I have a million questions about how on earth the media got ahold of a story that says *we're engaged,* I can say that, at this moment, I'm actually kind of glad for this misunderstanding.

Because the look on Mona's face?

Priceless.

"I was just getting Legs a drink," I reply with a smile. "You know, before our fancy steak dinner that we totally had planned."

"And how's my other favorite girl doing?" Carter suddenly pivots his attention to Allegra, who's still in the backseat of the car watching everything go down. "Sorry, Leggsy. I didn't see you there."

"I'm doing very good," she informs him with a cat-that-got-the-cream smile. "Can I have steak tonight, too, *Daddy*?"

She asks Carter the question, but she looks right at Mona while saying it, her fierce little expression clearly stating: "See, you idiot?! I was right and you were wrong."

And while I know that we are now locked in a very tricky and elaborate lie, I can't help but feel a swell of pride at my daughter's unwavering sass. And a corresponding swell of complete and utter panic.

Because my daughter just called the man that I am hopelessly in love with "Daddy."

Carter's smile falters for a split second and his eyes widen, but he regains his acting prowess swiftly. Reaches into the car and ruffles my daughter's hair. "'Course you can. I bought enough steak to feed a small army. I know how hungry you get after dance."

"Did you get the filet mignon? Uncle Liam said that's the best steak."

Carter nods. "Your Uncle Liam's a smart man."

"Just like you, Daddy." Allegra smirks, really laying it on thick. I had no idea she was so good at deception—she's as good an actor as her apparent new dad.

Mona and Lance, meanwhile, are still watching us like this is *The Truman Show* or something. Only nothing is true about any of it. Mona's practically catching flies with that open jaw of hers. If she were a golden retriever (ha, yeah right, she's much more rottweiler in her nature), I could fit about seven tennis balls in that mouth right now. And Lance, professional as ever, appears to be snapping photos of Carter on his cellphone.

"Well, we'd better be going." I spring into action and clap my hands like an overeager gym teacher. "Places to be, steaks to eat..."

I laugh a little desperately. Carter gives me side-eyed

look that clearly says "Dude, chill" but I have zero chill right now. We need to get out of here so I can a. figure out what the frickety frick is going on here, and b. die of mortification.

"Okay, bye now, Mona. Lance." I go to open my car door.

"Nice to see you, Lana Mae, and *very* nice to meet you, Carter." Mona's finally found her tongue and is back in full, perfectly presented mode. Instead of her usual saccharine expression, she gives Carter a smile that is closer to a grimace. "And I guess we'll be seeing you next week at the campout then?"

Carter glances at me sideways quizzically.

"Absolutely, you will," I answer for him, flinging open my door while internally cursing every curse word my ears have ever heard.

Mona arches a brow at this exchange, but Carter just gives her an impish grin and a shrug. "I'd say that Lana Mae wears the pants in this relationship, but I personally prefer when she wears no pants, if you know what I mean."

"Hahahhaha!" I laugh like a hyena while smacking Carter in the chest a little too hard. "Always making inappropriate jokes, this one."

At this point, Mona's perfectly groomed brows look like they're about to fly off her forehead, while Lance just looks... impressed. I give my (now former) best friend a look that I hope communicates the full force of what I'm currently telepathically screaming at him in my mind. Which is *shut up, you moron!* Out loud, I say. "Okay. Um, see you at my place in a bit?"

"Absolutely, you will." Carter, clearly not picking up what I'm mentally throwing down, echoes my words and chuckles that deep chuckle of his. You know, the one that's just a little dirty and just a lot sexy. He then gives Mona and

Lance a suggestive little wink that definitely suggests he will be seeing a lot more of me at my place later.

I balk at him, but he's completely undeterred as he leans forward and grazes his lips to my cheek. They skim over my skin for just a second, warm and surprisingly soft, and it's all I can do not to melt into a human puddle in the middle of the parking lot.

"Looking forward to it, *babe*." His whole face is alive with mischief as he pulls back so his eyes meet mine. "Seems we have a lot to talk about."

"That we do."

14

CARTER

I'd say I'm a lover, not a fighter, but that wouldn't be strictly true.

I'm actually highly trained in both areas, professionally speaking. I can simulate the most passionate bedroom scenes for the cameras while my brain is somewhere else entirely—making a mental shopping list or thinking about what I might order for dinner. I also know the basic ins and outs of pretty much every martial art known to man, could breeze through a choreographed fight sequence in my dreams, and fire a (prop) gun while rolling through a (set of a) burning building.

But I've only ever gotten in one real-life physical altercation.

A couple of months ago, at a bar on the Las Vegas Strip, I punched Steven Stanton in the face. And let's just say what happened in Vegas, definitely did not stay in Vegas.

But to be entirely honest, he deserved it.

I'd like to say that it was a slick, one-and-done, alpha move. Like Ryan Gosling's character in *Crazy, Stupid, Love*, when he calmly takes off his ring and decks Kevin Bacon right in the mouth to avenge his friend Steve Carell.

It was not.

My fist connected with Steven's cheekbone, and he staggered backwards. And for a moment, I felt proud of myself. I was defending Lana Mae's honor. Not that she'd asked me to.

But things then took a turn for the worse. Because when Steven hit the floor with a satisfying *thunk!*, his rat friends appeared out of nowhere and grabbed my arms, pinning them behind my back.

I'm strong, but it wasn't like I could take three of them.

Steven picked himself up off the bar's grimy floor and proceeded to let his fists fly at my face until the bouncers separated us. By then, I was spitting blood all over my shirt, but I continued to yell and curse at him like a lunatic through my busted lip and bloody nose.

That was the photograph that made it into every entertainment news article in the nation the next morning—me, snarling and feral and looking every inch the villain. The headlines that accompanied that freaking picture went a little something like, "*Sex, drugs and Rock n Roll throwdowns: Hollywood's bad boy drunk, violent and out of control in Sin City!*" Others questioned if I was on my way to rehab.

It was total B.S. But there was no way to make the situation look any better for me because, not only was everyone reporting me to be the troublemaker, there was also the tiny little detail that I started it. The physical part of the altercation, at least.

But the media only had a sliver of the real story instead of the entire pie.

The thing is, I wasn't drunk or out of control. I knew exactly what I was doing when I hit him. Hearing the filthy words "that stupid slut" come out of Steven's filthy mouth in regards to the best person in the world would've made any good man see red.

I'm not justifying violence, but I couldn't very well stand there and let him talk about Lana Mae—the mother of his freaking child—like that.

Like I said, he deserved it. And I know I could have reacted differently. More calmly. But I'm also saying that if those words ever dared leave his lips again, I'd do the same thing.

If all those stupid gossip writers making me out to be an awful person knew the truth, knew how horribly Steven had treated Lana—how he cheated on his pregnant girlfriend then washed his hands of his daughter—then maybe, they would've been a bit more understanding of what I did. Framed me as the Peter Pan instead of the Captain Hook of the story.

But they didn't know. And I would never tell them.

When Elena asked me what *really* happened that night so that we could release our own statement (after confirming, of course, that my injuries weren't permanent and therefore wouldn't keep me from doing my job), I clammed up. Said I was drunk and stupid and looking for a fight.

No way was I letting Lana Mae get dragged into the tabloids because of my actions.

And I was successful in protecting her from it all...

Until now.

There's no doubt in my mind that this whole fake engagement situation started because of my stupid lie and what happened in Vegas, but I can't understand how the hell we got *here*. I need answers. And if anyone's going to have them, it's Elena. And I intend to arrive at Lana's place in a few minutes with both filet mignon and an explanation.

"Carter, finally." Elena's voice sounds impressively crisp

through the ancient, fuzzy sound set-up in my Jeep. "We really need to talk."

"That we do," I respond, echoing Lana Mae's words earlier as I drum my fingers on the steering wheel.

I used to hate having serious talks with people. To the point where it's actually pretty funny that I ended up in a job that revolves around communication.

But the only reason I learned to act in the first place was *avoidance* of real communication. My parents are decent people, but I don't think they ever really wanted a child. They worked long hours, and from a young age, I got pretty good at being independent and fending for myself. As a result, I never really felt like I had a family who were there for me. It also meant that I spent a lot of time alone with big feelings that I thought nobody wanted to hear... so I figured out how to mask how I felt. I figured out how to put up a wall and guard everything inside it.

It worked. But it also kept the people in my life at arm's length. Friends were surface level, romantic prospects were flings with no strings. Keeping to myself was the safer option.

And then, I met Lana Mae. I don't know if it was the fact that she was going through some serious crap at the time, but she was honest and raw and real and vulnerable with me from the get-go. In turn, I discovered the first person that I could actually talk to without feeling naked and exposed.

But today, maybe for the first time ever, I'm feeling stripped bare at the thought of having a serious talk with Lana. I'm Adam in the garden of Eden, shuffling around bashfully while clutching my modesty. Only I have zero wisdom as a result of my own actions.

"I'll start," I tell Elena. "What's going on? What the hell happened to the story of *Freya* and me being engaged?"

"Yeah." Elena sucks her teeth. "A few things got lost in translation, it appears. Which we actually do need to talk about: translation. Are you still taking those Mandarin classes for that—"

"Elena, what happened?" I repeat steadily. I don't want to sound accusing or aggressive as I don't know what part, if any, Elena played in orchestrating this, but I also have no time for her to get sidetracked right now.

"We think it was the waitress."

"You think it was the waitress," I repeat as I flick on my blinker and pull off the highway. That tells me absolutely nothing. "And so, was it in the living room with the candlestick, or the parlor with the revolver?"

"Ooh, your sarcasm—which is the lowest form of wit, you know—reminds me that they're thinking of doing another *Clue*-type movie, something in the vein of *Knives Out*. I think you'd be perfect for—"

"Elena, for the love of every single deity in the heavenly realms, what the frick happened with the engagement story and what fricking waitress are you talking about?!"

"Fine," Elena huffs. "But don't blame me if you miss out on the most iconic whodunnit role of the century. I'm talking about the waitress from our lunch with Freya yesterday. We think that she eavesdropped on our conversation, misunderstood what she heard, and thought you were proposing to your best friend imminently... then went straight to the gossip-powers-that-be with that information. Who, by the way, happened to already have pictures of you and Lana Mae at a dress store, plus a picture of you with her brother at a jewelry store, no less."

Fricksake.

"You know who visits dress and jewelry stores?" Elena continues triumphantly. "People getting *married*."

Of all the things to be misconstrued, it had to be *this*. I'd rather the media go back to their stupid *Carter Callahan Headed For Rehab* headlines that barely grazed the surface of the truth than drag Lana Mae into any of my messes.

I sigh. "Lana's brother was the one getting married, for goodness sakes. He was picking out a ring to propose to *his* fiancée and I just happened to run into him in the neighborhood. And Lana and I were at a dress store to get a dress for a date that she was going on."

"A date."

"*Yes*," I say, exasperated.

"With who?"

"With—" *Oh, frick.* My tangled web is back to tangle with me. "A date with me... of course."

"Liar! I knew you were lying about having a girlfriend!" Elena practically yells. I can hear the glee in her tone, because if there's anything this woman likes being, it's right. "Nothing gets past me, you fool."

I sigh again. Heavily, this time. Because I am a fool. Clearly. "I—"

"Didn't want to cooperate with my tireless attempts to give you positive PR and get your reputation polished up. I know."

"I wouldn't have phrased it quite like that," I grouch. Around me, the scenery is changing from city concrete to suburban shrubbery. Almost there. And still with no clue what to say.

"I phrased it perfectly," Elena says with a rare laugh. "But you'd better buckle up, buttercup. Believe it or not, your story-spinning has earned you a huge sack of brownie points with just about every official and unofficial media outlet in the country."

I push my hair back off my forehead and grimace. "What do you mean?"

"I mean that thousands of pop culture enthusiasts took

to the internet this afternoon to express their love for you and Lana Mae—that's her name, right?"

"Right."

"And you didn't even tell me she was a single mom! It's all going down *brilliantly*. Such a wholesome angle: Carter Callahan, future stepdad to cute little girl."

"Allegra stays out of this," I growl.

"Sure, sure, we can play that angle down." Elena waves off my fierceness, totally undeterred. "Either way, people are *loving* this. They're tweeting. TikToking. Instagramming. The works. To the point where Nova Khatri, the casting director for *If Only*, called me a few minutes ago..."

I'm not sure where Elena's going with this, so I just say, "Okay."

"She loves Larter!!"

"*Larter*?!"

"I'm experimenting with couple names for you guys."

"Please don't." I pull into Lana Mae's cul-de-sac, and then into her driveway. Kill the engine. "So what does this all mean?"

"It means that you bought yourself a shovel and dug your own hole with it."

"What hole?"

Elena cracks up. Jeez. Now is not the ideal time for my dead-serious manager to develop a sudden dirty sense of humor.

"Elena..." I say with a warning in my voice.

"Sorry, sorry!" She laughs merrily. She really is in a frighteningly good mood right now. "What I mean is that you better figure out a way to get your friend to pretend to be your fiancée, because the entire planet is gobbling up this little love story of yours like pudding."

"And if she doesn't want to pretend to be my fiancée?"

"Convince her. Dust off some of that charm of yours

and make it worth her while. Because it's sure worth *your* while. Larter has taken the internet by storm better than I could've even hoped the Freya engagement story would. For the first time, I think you may be a shoo-in for this role. Like, you could drop a baby on its head and you'd still be in the running after today's press."

"Well, there's a charming thought."

"Forget a modern-day Timberlake and Spears," Elena ignores me. "This is, like, Blake Lively and Ryan Reynolds level of endearing. Do you think you could blast out some funny tweets about your new wife-to-be? A few Larter inside jokes, maybe?"

Every single part of my body is tense. I've always done everything I can to protect Lana Mae from the spotlight, not wanting proximity to me to ever impact her life. And now, I've gone and set fire to the entire house of cards I've built for her. Some friend I am.

And yet... while I certainly wouldn't blame her for being furious that her face is now slapped across every gossip article in existence, I'm also curious as to what on earth she was spinning earlier to that cop and his wife with the big hair and crazy eyes. I definitely was *not* expecting that reaction when I sped into that parking lot like a bat out of hell. I admit that my heart jumped when she flung herself at me, and beat double-time when I teasingly pressed my lips to her cheek.

I know that she's going to have some crazy only-Lana-Mae explanation for the whole charade that has nothing to do with her actually wanting to be my fiancée.

Lana Mae is the person I love most on this entire planet. And while everything in me wants to move on from this stupid bad-reputation rhetoric and step into the type of acting role that could cement my career in cinematic history, the one thing I want more is to make sure that Lan and Legs are both safe and happy.

"I don't think I can do that, Elena. And please stop saying Larter."

"Surely fake marrying your best friend is an easier task than fake marrying a practical stranger?"

Yeah, you'd think that'd be the case, wouldn't you?

"Look, I'll be back in LA tomorrow morning," I say reasonably. "Why don't I stop by your office then, so we can talk about this in person and make a plan?"

"You will do no such thing!"

I find myself, for about the millionth time this week, asking, "What?"

"Stay right where you are in Atlanta."

"What about the commitments you mentioned I have in LA this week?"

"Consider them officially canceled, and your down time in Atlanta officially underway instead. This should be a welcome break for you. Stay put and work on what's important right now: convincing Lana Mae this is a great move for both of you. This does also mean that she will need to attend the premiere of your new movie in Freya's place."

Ha. Freya. I wonder what she's making of all this. She's probably just delighted she doesn't have to move to Atlanta.

"The premiere's in LA."

"Planes exist," Elena counters.

"Assuming she agrees to do this with me," I remind Elena.

"And *when* she agrees, you should also see if you can negotiate for her and her daughter to come live with you at your house. We'll move forward with the original plan I had for you and Freya, just with Lana Mae instead. Ooh, do you think she'd be open to pregnancy rumors?"

"Absolutely not!"

"Okay, fine. No pregnancy. But the rest isn't up for negotiation, Carter. You need this. Once the movie cast has been announced and your role is safe, you can stage a breakup right around the time some starlet has another meltdown. I'm sure Kim Kardashian is due another marriage soon. We could sneak something in around that."

"That's kind of ruthless."

"It's my job, Carter. I'm doing mine. Now I need you to do yours."

After Elena hangs up, I get out of my Jeep warily, pulling my ball cap low in case any paparazzi noticed my Jeep sitting here in the driveway for the last ten minutes. I rap my knuckles on Lana Mae's cherry red front door, which, despite the whole heap of crazy that has happened today, draws a smile from me.

Lana's always painting her front door. In the time that she's lived here, it's been baby blue, citrus green, buttercup yellow, and, for one strange season, glittery gold.

"OH HEY!"

Allegra flings the door open, revealing that she's changed out of her dance clothes and into what looks to be a ball gown made of silky fabric and covered in bows. On her head sits a bonnet. A literal bonnet.

Before I can ask any questions, she gives me a sweet grin, grabs my hand, and yanks me inside. All while yelling, "MOM, CAR-DURRRRRR'S HERE!"

"Dude, I'm digging the olde worlde get-up," I tell her. "Do you have a theme day at school tomorrow or something?"

Legs beams. "No, silly. I'm playing *Bridgerton*."

"You're playing *what*?" I balk. I've never seen the show, but a good friend of mine is in it, and I know enough to know that it's not exactly standard viewing material for nine-year-olds.

"Carter, hey!" Lana's voice comes from the top of the stairs and I look up instantly, everything in me drawn to her like a moth to a flame.

For so long, I've forced myself to look at Lana platonically. But waking up next to her this morning, followed by her (quite literally) launching herself into my arms this afternoon, has me gazing at her in that hazy, romantic light that I barely ever dare to do. Has she thought about our sleepover as much as I have? Or shaken it off without so much as another thought?

A zero-gravity feeling fills my chest as I take her in slowly, eyes moving over her like I'm trying to memorize every detail and store it away for later, even though I have already long memorized everything about her: slender limbs, messy dark-blond streaked ponytail, sparkly brown eyes, lips the perfect shade of dark pink.

She's changed clothes, too—she's now wearing lilac running shorts and is in the middle of pulling an oversize sweatshirt over a black tank top that clings to her every curve. Her feet are bare and there's not a stitch of makeup on her face. She's smiling at me tentatively, almost shyly, her dark eyes full of anticipation. She finishes shrugging the sweatshirt on, covering that incredible body of hers, and I have a sudden urge to burn the baggy garment.

"She's not actually playing *Bridgerton*, by the way. She just thinks 'Bridgerton' is a catch-all word for anything set in regency times," Lana explains as she comes to a stop in front of me in the hallway.

I can only laugh. "Checks out."

We stare at each other for a long moment, a million

things unsaid stacked between us. I hurriedly hold up the paper grocery bags in my hands. "Three filet mignons on Lady Allegra's request. Plus asparagus, sweet potato wedges, and of course, dessert."

Legs wrinkles her nose suspiciously. "What kind of dessert?"

"Crumbl cookies." They're her favorites, and I'm rewarded with a beaming smile.

"Yay!" Legs cheers. "Thanks, Carter!"

I grin at her. "That's 'Daddy' to you."

This makes her laugh a cute little belly laugh. "That *was* funny earlier. Do you think I could be an actress?"

"You'd blow all the other child actors straight out of the water," I tell her. "But didn't you want to be an astronaut when you grow up? That's way cooler than boring old acting."

"It is, isn't it?" she says thoughtfully. "Maybe I can be both." Then, she sweeps into a deep curtsy before dashing upstairs to "call the Duke."

Lana shrugs at her daughter's retreating, ball-gowned figure. "Weird phase she's in. Shall we grill those out back?"

"Sure." I follow Lan to the kitchen. She reaches into the fridge and produces two bottles of Corona, holding one up to me.

"Yeah, please."

She smiles, still tentative, as she turns to the counter and begins chopping a lime. She shoves a slice in the neck of one bottle, licks her fingers clean, then hands it to me. "I figured beer might be necessary."

"For this completely insane conversation we're about to have, you mean?"

A laugh. "Yeah. That."

She fixes her beer up with lime too, and we head

outside. It's still sunny and warm, the evening breeze full of the scent of fresh-cut grass and honeysuckle.

Lana curls into an outdoor chair, and I fire up the grill. I lay out the seasoned pieces of meat one by one. Take a long pull of beer. Adjust the heat settings.

Am I stalling?

Absofreakinglutely.

Because how does anyone go about a conversation like this one?

I finally sit down in the chair opposite Lana Mae, bending to pet Harry Styles as I do so. Lan's picking at her beer label, piling a ton of tiny little paper pieces onto the armrest of her chair. I watch her long, slim fingers pick and peel and tear for a few moments before finally saying, "This wasn't meant to happen."

She looks at me, curious. "What *was* meant to happen?"

"It was meant to be Freya."

A strange flicker dances across her face before her expression becomes carefully neutral again. "Go on."

"The media was meant to think that I was marrying Freya. Elena and Marc—Freya's manager—thought it would be good for my image and for buzz around her upcoming album. I found out yesterday that that was the plan, and that's why I flew home to talk to you last night. I wanted to tell you that I'd agreed to be Freya's fake fiancé."

Her face pinches. "Okay... But how on earth did I end up involved?"

"Well, the original plan was for me to appear to be dating Freya, which is why we were always out in LA together and had all those photos taken. But, on our first fake date, I sensed she was hitting on me, and so I kind of let her think you were my girlfriend."

Lana's mouth drops open. "I beg your finest pardon?"

I rub the heel of my hand in my eye and take another

swallow of beer. "I told you that this was embarrassing. I... may have purposefully misled Freya to believe that you were my girlfriend the first night we met so she wouldn't get the wrong idea about how I felt about her."

Lana looks at me incredulously and I make a sheepish gesture.

"She assumed that you were my girlfriend and I simply never corrected her," I explain. "So when Elena suggested that Freya and I fake a marriage, Freya mentioned you, my alleged girlfriend, and how you'd feel about it. Someone must've overheard our conversation—Elena thinks it was the waitress—and leaked the wrong story so you, instead of Freya, were named as my fiancée to the entire world. And now, Elena's dreaming up stupid couple names for us and wanting me to convince you to attend premieres with me and play along with the whole thing." I give my head a quick shake. "I'm so sorry, Lan. I'll fix this, I promise. Get you out of this mess."

Lana stares at me.

And stares at me.

And stares at me.

Until, finally, she starts to howl with laughter.

"You freaking idiot!" she cackles, and my entire being relaxes at her laughter, relief flooding me as I realize that she's not angry. "Only *you* could end up married to the wrong person."

"Engaged, not married," I correct lightly, but I don't miss the strange little sting in my gut at her use of "the wrong person."

"What does Freya think about all this?" Lana asks.

"I dunno. I haven't talked to her today." I shrug. "Like I said, I don't know her that well. She was happy to go along with fake marrying me, but I don't think she was super invested in the idea. Either way, we can't very well spin a story about me being engaged to *her* now, but you don't need to worry about it. I'll handle this and do what I need to do to make sure you're no longer a part of this ridiculous narrative."

"You sound like Taylor Swift after the whole Kanye and Kim showdown."

"Well, Taylor Swift is clearly onto something because she's right—it sucks to get dragged into someone else's drama. Like I said, I'll fix this. Tell everyone there's been a misunderstanding."

Lana Mae screws up her lips, making her nose wrinkle. "I don't want to you to lose a role because of me."

"I won't," I assure her with a dry smile. "If I lose out on the role, it's entirely because of me."

"You're too hard on yourself." Lana lifts a shoulder, eyes back on her beer bottle. "And you seem to be forgetting that I used the story to my own advantage this afternoon..."

In my haste to make things right and explain myself, I'd forgotten about what went down earlier in the Sonic parking lot. "Oh yeah, what was that about... *babe*?"

A smile creeps over my face as her tan skin flushes, a red blush dusting her high cheekbones. "I can't stand that Mona woman. She basically accused Allegra of being a liar and a sociopath because she told her friends at Sunday school today about us being in bed together and mentioned that you were going to be coming to the daddy daughter campout school fundraiser. Which is what you said yes to at the end, by the way."

"Oh." I blink. "Damn."

"'Oh damn' is right." Lana shakes her head. "I tried to set Mona straight, but she was going on and on, being such a jerk about everything. And then you turned up and I just... went with the story I'd seen online."

It's my turn to laugh. "Well, Mona was clearly very shocked, so the story worked."

"It did. And now, I'm going to have to figure out what to tell her..."

"Or I could just go. With Legs. To the campout."

Lana frowns. "Oh, no. I couldn't ask you to do that."

"I'd be happy to. I'd do anything for her, you know that."

And for you. I wish you knew that, too.

"Plus, I'm under strict instructions from Elena to stay here in Atlanta for awhile," I continue. "So for the first time in forever, I actually have a clear schedule."

"That's exciting that you're going to be here for a bit." She smiles a cute little smile, eyes sparkly, then tilts her head. "But I don't know about this whole campout thing. I'm scared that she might actually start believing that you're going to be her new daddy and then be disappointed. She's been really fixated on this 'new dad' thing lately, as you discovered this morning..." As she talks, her smile fades, and her thumbnail scratches more insistently at her beer label. I can tell she's stressed, and I don't want to make that stress worse for her.

I try to keep my expression neutral. Nonplussed. But before I can find an appropriate way to address the accidental sleepover we have not talked about yet, Allegra appears, bonnet askew. "I won't be disappointed. I know we were lying to Mona the Moaner."

I can't help but crack a smile at that, and when I look at Lana Mae, I see that she can't, either. Until her mothering instincts kick in and she purses her lips. "It's not nice to call someone names, sweetie," she tells her daughter, her face reddening slightly, and I know she's mentally chastising herself for being a hypocrite right now.

"Sorry, Mom."

"And—" Lana starts, but before she can deliver any kind of lecture on lying, Allegra waves an airy hand in her mom's direction, cutting her off.

"Yeah yeah yeah, I know lying is wrong and we shouldn't ever do it. But please, Mom, can Carter come with me to the campout? Even if *I* know he's not really going to be my new daddy, nobody else will know. I don't want to be the only one there without a daddy…"

Lana's expression crumples and her fingers tense on her beer bottle. "Legs, can you get me a plate from the kitchen, please? I think the steaks are about done."

"Okay, but think about it. Please."

"I will." As Allegra runs off, Lana turns to me and looks me dead in the eye, suddenly all business. "Okay, CJ. What if you help me and I help you?"

"How so?"

"If I pretend to be your fiancée, Elena's reputation-fixing plan is still on the table and you still have a shot at the *If Only* role." She looks at me for confirmation and I give her a nod. "In return, Allegra can bring you to the daddy daughter campout and have her daddy moment."

I sit still, absorbing this. "Lan, I can go to the campout with Legs without you having to pretend for me."

But Lana's face is resolute. Staunch. "No. We can help each other here, and I want to do this for you. Friendship is a two-way street, so if we're doing this, I'm playing the part of the fiancée."

A million strange feelings are flooding through me, each as jumbled and indecipherable as the next. "So you're saying… let's get fake engaged for real?"

Lana leans over and clinks her beer bottle against mine. "That's exactly what I'm saying, Callahan."

15

LANA MAE

What on God's green earth am I saying right now?

Seriously. My voice is steady. Confident. Casual, even.

But the words that just came out of my mouth are enough to freaking unravel me. Because I just told Carter James Callahan I'd be his fiancée.

Fake fiancée, to be exact. But details have never been my strong suit.

While Carter was speaking a few moments ago, kindly reassuring me that this was all his fault and he'd fix it... all I could think about was the fact that he flew all the way to Atlanta to tell me that he was fake-marrying Freya.

Why?

Why not text or call? A simple *Oh hey bestie, just a heads up, if you see any headlines about me being engaged to a world-famous,* People*-magazine-certified sexy pop star, don't sweat. They're fake. Just a little publicity stunt, not actual upcoming nuptials I forgot to invite you to. Hope the date with the doctor went well.*

And something occurred to me: he must've flown all this way to make sure that my feelings were spared. He knows how badly dating has been going for me, and maybe he didn't want me, even for a second, thinking that he, in turn, was so blissfully happy with his new girlfriend, he'd proposed to her.

That's the kind of friend Carter is—one who can have a million important things going on in his life, but he still spends his time and energy on the insignificant little problems of the people closest to him.

And that's when I realized that getting over Carter—finding a man as good as him, one who I could remotely see myself falling for—is an entirely fruitless idea.

Stupid, in fact.

I didn't have to go on on a bunch of disastrous dates with other men to know that Carter is the best man there is. And my most disastrous date ended with me sleeping next to Carter, anyway. Shifting even closer to him.

So maybe, just maybe, I need to change tactics here. Switch it up.

Instead of trying to get over Carter by dating other people, maybe I need to get over him by pretend dating *him* and getting him out of my system that way. I know it's fake, but it could be exactly what I need to do to get rid of these feelings. See what it would be like to date Carter without actually dating him.

And if my playing the part of his fiancée helps Carter get the role he so desperately wants, it's just all the better, isn't it? No matter how I feel about him working too much lately, I know how important this is to him. Winning this role would be the crowning achievement of his Hollywood career, and I could never forgive myself if I stood in the way of him getting there.

Or maybe it's the Corona doing the talking.

Who knows? Not me.

"Okay, Donovan. I'll bite." Carter tilts his head and studies me, his blue eyes questioning. "We stay fake engaged, you make some public appearances with me and come to my premiere, I go to the daddy daughter campout with Legs... And then what?"

"We call it off when you want a real girlfriend?"

Carter narrows his eyes. "No, I mean what about you? Like, what are you getting out of this?"

"Well, Legs—"

"Not Allegra, Lana Mae. What are *you* getting out of this?"

I can hardly tell him the half-baked plan I've just semi-tipsily concocted, so I throw out, "I get to help my friend?"

"Try again."

"I get..." *Think, Lana, think. Something he'll actually buy.* "I get clout," I finally say.

Carter's eyes narrow further. "Clout?"

"Yeah," I go on, suddenly inspired. I take a sip of liquid courage, then continue, "Instead of being the weird single mom who sets herself on fire, I'll be Carter Callahan's ex-fiancée. Surely, that's a way more desirable angle when I hit the dating world after this is over. You'll be the Jess to my Rory. My bad boy boyfriend who gives me the edge I so desperately need to finally find my Logan."

Which is probably the stupidest thing I've ever said because I've always been Team Jess.

But Rory doesn't end up with Jess, does she? He just helps her get over her cheating ex, becomes one of her best friends, and though they fall in love, he eventually leaves.

And she moves on.

"I never liked Logan." Carter frowns. "And Lana, for what it's worth, I think you're set in the clout department. You were the one who broke it off with that Drew guy. You're obviously desirable."

"Sometimes I don't feel it." I chew on my bottom lip. This is weird conversation territory for us, but I do want to

139

be honest with him about this. "I've been anxious on a lot of these dates. I don't feel particularly sexy or confident... but maybe pretending to be your fiancée will give me a boost. Brush me up on my dating skills and all that."

His frown deepens. "Well... pretending to be my fiancée would mean that you can't date anyone else, at least not publicly, for awhile. And that's not what you want, is it? You've been dating like crazy lately, and wasn't the goal of that to find something like what your brothers have?"

I pick at my fingernails as I consider this. Before my first date a couple of months ago, I gave everyone around me a half-truth. I mean, I couldn't exactly tell people that I was finally ready to move on and get over my romantic feelings for my best friend. So instead, I leaned on the fact that both of my brothers are now married and happy, and I'm ready to find my own happiness.

A lie of omission, really. Same as I'm about to do now.

I swallow. Smile. "Up until two months ago, I hadn't dated in almost a decade. What's a few more months? If anything, it'll give me practice for when I find the real thing."

Carter's blue eyes narrow a touch. "So I'd be, like, a trial run for when you find the person you actually want to marry?"

"Sure," I say with a shrug. Casual casual casual. That's me right now. "I need practice. You're the expert. Teach me your ways, O wise oracle."

Carter takes a swig of beer and wipes his mouth with the back of one big, tan hand. Maybe I'm wrong, but he looks kind of bothered. Is the idea of fake dating me for a few weeks or months so repulsive to him? *How lovely*.

"It can be as long or short as you want it to be," I add. "I'm ready to be dumped whenever you're ready to dump me."

Carter's dimple pops as he smiles at me, but the smile doesn't quite reach his eyes. "Who's to say that I'd be the one doing the dumping? You'd be breaking my heart if you run off with your real true love, which would make you the dumper and me the dumpee."

"Oh come on, CJ. We gotta make this story believable."

"Exactly." He gets up, moves towards the barbecue, and begins flipping the steaks. What on earth was *that* supposed to mean?

He's quiet for a few moments as he works, and I watch him. His broad shoulders are tense and I wonder if maybe the part in this *If Only* movie—and his reputation—mean more to him than he lets on. When he eventually closes the lid of the grill and turns to me, his face is composed. Neutral. The Switzerland of facial expressions. "K, how 'bout this? We can *mutually* part ways when this is no longer *mutually* beneficial for us."

I nod. "That works."

"When's the campout?"

"Two weekends from now. How long does Elena want to keep this going?"

"Just until the *If Only* cast is officially announced. Elena thinks that, after that, we'll be safe to split up quietly. In the meantime, she basically wants me to hang around Atlanta and do what I can to look tame and domestic and in love. And she thinks it would be good for you to come to the premiere of my latest movie in LA—it releases the week after the campout." He glances at me quickly. "Assuming you can get a couple days off work and we can find someone to watch Legs."

"I can ask Imani to cover some shifts for me, and I'm sure one of my brothers can take Legs." I somehow manage to say this like it's a totally normal thing to be discussing the logistics of attending a freaking Hollywood movie premiere with the hottest actor on the planet.

"Oh yeah," he tacks on. "She also wanted you and Allegra to move in with me, but I can obviously tell her that's not happening."

This conversation is now taking a right turn at bizarre and barreling straight into the realm of the completely insane, but I nod. I love Carter's house, but this is... a lot to take in. "K. And what do we tell our families?"

But Carter doesn't reply. His eyes are focused somewhere behind my head...

Where there's a sudden burst of chaotic noise.

I whirl around to see Allegra, who was taking an eternity to fetch that plate she's still not holding, leading my brothers, their wives, Chimichanga the dog, and—oh, for the love of Moses—my father and his wife, Constance, into the backyard. My entire family, whom I have failed to text and call back regarding the sudden national news of my upcoming nuptials.

Frick.

Allegra is grinning from ear to ear, Luke is smirking his face off, Liam is sporting a small, close-lipped smile, Annie looks like she's about to capsize with glee, and Mindy is... holding a cake.

A cake that's clearly in the shape of a big, round butt.

Fabulous.

"Surprise!" my daughter yells, then blasts on a kazoo like a madwoman.

"Indeed, it was," my father mutters behind her.

Unfazed, Allegra turns to Luke and Liam, who both smile at me mischievously before unfurling a banner that reads: "Congratulations, Lovebirds!"

Chimichanga promptly lifts his leg on it.

Carter lets out a long, low whistle, and when I look at

him, his eyes are already on me. "I have a feeling that maybe, just maybe, Allegra might've already told your family it's real."

"Oh no. Oh no no no no no no." I cover my eyes then peek between two of my fingers, as if I can ostrich this entire situation away by sticking my head in the sand.

My leg is jiggling a million miles a minute and I can physically feel my face pale in anticipation.

And then, a warm, strong hand is on my thigh, gently but firmly stilling my anxious movements.

"Hey Lan, look at me." His voice is the same as his touch—gentle, but commanding. Reassuring.

I do as he says, and he holds eye contact in a way that further melts away my nerves. His hand is still on my thigh.

"What's the plan?" he asks, eyes capturing mine. "Keep up the pretense for your dad and Constance and find a quiet moment to tell the others what's really going on?"

Once again, Carter proves that he knows me better than I know myself. Knows how my father wouldn't approve, and is likely to give endless lectures and derisive comments that are sure to break down my confidence more than they should after all these years...

I nod. "That's a perfect plan. We'll placate my dad first, then divide and conquer to tell everyone else the truth. You take my brothers, and I'll tackle Annie and Mindy."

"Will do."

"I can do this." I give myself a little pep talk as my family gets closer. "I've got this."

"No." Carter gives my leg a tiny squeeze, but the miniscule motion feels more reassuring than a huge gesture would from anyone else. *"We've* got this."

16

CARTER

Our fake engagement party is turning into quite the rager.

And by "rager", I mean that, since arriving not five minutes ago, Luke has carted in an entire crate of champagne, cranked up the music, and is doing a strange, thrusty dance around the yard, a bottle in each hand.

Lana snags his sleeve as he dances by. "You look like you're auditioning for a two-bit traveling stage production of *Tragic Mike*."

Luke momentarily stops hip-thrusting and wrinkles his forehead. "You mean *Magic Mike*?"

"Nope, said it right the first time."

"Relax, little sis," Luke drawls with an eye roll. "This is a party."

"A party with dad in attendance," Lan hisses back. Luke, Liam and Lana's dad is known to be a bit of, well, a dick. To put it nicely.

"I don't care what dad thinks." Luke shrugs, takes a huge swig of champagne, then resumes his hip gyrations. "I'm a grown-ass man."

"Could have fooled me," Liam mutters darkly as he

144

drinks his beer, looking vaguely horrified by his brother's dance moves.

Before Luke can respond to that, his wife, Mindy, starts prancing across the yard, all smiles. She's still holding the cake she brought, but now it's covered in sparklers that flash and twinkle. "Okay now, everybody, on the count of three: *Happy engagement to youuuuuuu, happy engagement tooo youuuuuu....*"

"Where was the count of three?" Liam demands as everyone else obediently breaks into song.

I peer at the cake, which seems to be in the shape of a bare butt for some unbeknownst reason. On the right cheek, there's a heart with an arrow through it and the letters "CJC + LMD". It looks like a cross between a tattoo and something that's been hack-carved into a tree by a madman.

Mindy sees me eyeing the cake and holds it out towards me. "Do you like it? I bought it at the adult cake store and added the little love heart myself."

That explains the madman hack job. But not the existence of an adult cake store.

I glance at Lana, my brows raised, but she's just shaking her head and smirking. I'd love her even if she'd been raised by a pack of wolves, but her awesome, completely crazy family are just an awesome, completely crazy bonus to hanging out with her.

Well, they're all a bonus except her dad and his wife, who are currently standing nearby, tight-lipped and not joining in on the raucous round of singing.

When the song ends and the sparklers fizzle out, Allegra claps with glee and Annie tops up the champagne glasses. Meanwhile, Constance peers at the cake in Mindy's hands with puckered sour-lemon lips. "Melinda, that cake is vile. And entirely inappropriate!"

Mindy—whose full name is Mindy and not Melinda, to

Constance's perpetual disbelief—looks right at me and smirks. "Oh, no. Trust me, it's *very* appropriate."

What?

"There is a *child* present," Mr. Donovan Senior hisses at Lana, as if this is somehow her fault. I wrestle the urge to stand in front of her like a shield.

Allegra looks up at her grandfather with big, innocent eyes and a wide smile. "Don't worry, Grandad. I know what butts are."

Liam snorts. Luke full-on laughs. Their dad's face turns red as a tomato.

"Who wants a slice?" Annie interrupts hurriedly, grabbing the platter from Mindy's hands. I don't know Lana's sisters-in-law super well—especially Annie, who's the most recent addition to the family—but she is clearly the resident peacemaker. The one to try to calm situations before they escalate. "I can take this to the kitchen and cut it up."

"I will very much pass." Constance sniffs. She should probably have some; might sweeten her up a little.

"Now, tell us more about how this happened." Mr. Donovan glares at me. *Up* at me, to be exact. He's a big guy, but I have a couple inches on him. Which I'm pretty happy for at this moment.

"I realized I'd been in love with Lana Mae for a long time. Maybe for as long as I've known her," I say, grabbing Lana's hand and interlacing our fingers. "She's incredible."

"Aw." Lana's cheeks pinken and she smiles bashfully.

But her dad scowls. "I didn't get a phone call asking for my blessing."

I want to echo Luke's earlier sentiments and tell the man that I don't care what he thinks. But he is Lana's only living parent, and as much as my own parents and I no longer have any kind of close relationship, I know that Lana tries to foster a civil relationship with her dad. Mainly for Allegra's sake.

I open my mouth to say something along the lines of "I guess I just couldn't wait another moment to propose" when Luke inserts himself into the conversation. "Oh, he couldn't get ahold of you, so he called me. I gave him my blessing to marry my one and only sister."

Gave his blessing to marry his sister? Aside from sounding like we've stumbled into an episode of the Sopranos (like, I wouldn't be overly surprised if Luke whipped out a huge cigar right around now), I'm more than a little shocked by Luke's quick and casual lie. I look at him with wide eyes, but he just winks at me. I pivot my eyes to Lana Mae, but her expression of surprise looks exactly like the one I imagine I'm currently wearing.

Needless to say, Donovan Senior also looks rattled at this revelation. "You had no place to do that."

"Sure I did." Luke nods confidently. "No man was ever going to be worthy of my little sister, obviously. But this guy here..." Luke reaches out to sling an arm over my shoulder and shoots me a little wink. "Well, he's the closest we're ever going to get."

I'm not sure why he says this. Or why he's not a professional actor himself seeing as he's clearly mastered the craft. I also have no idea why he's covering for me when I clearly didn't call him and ask for his blessing to wed his sister. But no matter what Luke's playing at right now, his words create a small, very uncalled-for lump in my throat.

"I don't know about that," I reply. Mr. Donovan looks at me darkly, and I swallow the pesky lump and keep my voice steady. Because for someone who's always been good at pretending, I don't have to act in the slightest with what I say next. "I do know this, though: I will try my damnedest to make this woman feel safe, loved, and happy for the rest of my life."

The flicker in Lana Mae's eyes is everything.

I finally get a moment alone with Luke and Liam on the premise of steak.

Namely, when I see a billowing plume of black smoke coming from the barbecue and remember the existence of said steak.

I sprint over, throw open the lid and frantically wave the smoke away, but I can already tell it's too late. RIP filet mignon.

With a sigh, I poke the blackened, shriveled lumps with a pair of tongs. Behind me, Luke clicks his tongue sarcastically. "It makes me suspicious when a man doesn't know his way around a grill. I may have to rescind my blessing."

"Your *blessing* was what distracted me in the first place," I shoot back with a grin. "What was that about anyway? I definitely didn't call you, dude."

"Um, I was saving your ass from my father's weird wrath. You're welcome, by the way."

I poke the coal-steaks again. "But why?"

I've hung out with Luke and Liam a bunch when I've been home over the years, but I've never spent too much extended time with them. I like the guys, and I know they like me, but Luke jumping to my defense with his dad so fiercely was a surprise to me. Especially now, when so many... less than ideal stories about me are floating around.

Luke pops the top off a beer and takes a swig, about to answer, but Liam beats him to it. "Because all we want is for

Lana to be happy, and you make her happy. We all saw this coming a mile off."

Oh, jeez.

Liam's not a talker at the best of times, and it's very unlike him to start a sentimental conversation. I'm also sure he won't take kindly to being lied to. But there's no time like the present to bite the bullet. Lana's brothers need to know the truth before this web gets any bigger.

I turn my head to check that Donovan Senior and Constance aren't in earshot, and I spot them on the porch with Lana Mae and Allegra. Lan has a hand on Allegra's head, affectionately stroking her daughter's hair. The way her eyes are shining with pride and her mouth is pulled up at the corners, I'm sure she's talking about one of Allegra's recent achievements. She always lights up when she talks about her.

It's beautiful to watch. And for just a moment, I let myself imagine how different this night would be if this was real. If I stopped all the casual dating crap because Lana really wanted to be with me, and we were really engaged to be married, and she was really mine. How, when everyone else went home, I could tuck that stray lock of hair behind her ear and tell her I loved her. Listen to her say those same three little words back to me, then tug her towards me and kiss the living daylights out of her. Tasting each of them on her tongue...

Where the hell did *that* come from?

I take a deep breath and yank myself out of my runaway daydream before it runs so far that I won't be able to catch it again. Then, I face her brothers and hold up my hands. "It's not real."

"Yeah it is," Luke scoffs.

"I'm serious, it's not. It's a long story, but my manager

set up this stunt where I was pretending to date Freya DiMauritz—"

"Hot," Luke interjects helpfully. Liam rolls his eyes.

"—but when I tried to get out of it, I kinda botched it, and the press got hold of the wrong story."

"Well, yeah, we figured something like that had happened. Our sister wouldn't just *forget* to mention that she had a serious boyfriend that she was considering marrying," Luke says reasonably. Like *I'm* the one missing the point here. "But what I mean is… it *is* real in that, even if the story was fabricated, it was obviously meant to happen."

"I dunno if a deception that was meant to help out my public image but ended up mistakenly involving Lana Mae and Allegra was 'meant to happen'," I reply a little glumly. "I didn't want to drag Lan into this, but for some reason, she's insistent that we go along with it."

Luke smiles, all coy. "'Course she is."

"Why were you trying to get out of dating Freya in the first place?" Liam asks.

"Because I don't feel that way about her."

"Precisely." Liam retrieves the tongs from my hands without asking, then starts removing the ruined meat from the grill. "And yet, you're saying that it's not real with you and Lana Mae, but I don't see you trying to get out of it."

Luke nods along like this all makes perfect sense. "You guys are clearly more than friends, and now, you have an actual reason to take things to the next level. Like with Mindy and me—we were friends first and Mindy actually liked another friend of ours. It wasn't until she saw that guy with another woman that she started to look at me differently. See me as more than a friend."

I step back from the grill, the acrid scent of smoke clinging to my shirt. I'm not sure Luke has a point. Lana Mae said herself that this would be a sort of trial run for when she finds the real thing. No matter how many of my old feelings for her have been coming to the surface lately.

"Nah," I say with a shake of my head. "Sorry to break it to you guys, but Lana doesn't see me like that. Never has, never will."

"Bull," Luke singsongs.

Liam shuts the lid of the grill and sinks into a nearby chair. "I'm no expert on this stuff, but the girl hasn't so much as *looked* at another guy since she met you. She spends any time she can with you. Talks about you all the time. And if that's anything to go by, I'd say you're very, very wrong, my friend."

I sit down in the chair opposite Liam's. "What about her dating? She's been out with a ton of guys lately."

"No offense," Liam says with a shake of his head. "But I think that might be because she's sick of watching *you* date all the time."

I frown. My years of casual dating never seemed to even be on Lana Mae's radar; she's never so much as asked me about anyone I was dating. My heart might want to do a funny little leaping motion in my chest at Liam's words—at even the *thought* that they might be true—but I keep it together.

I buried my feelings for a reason all those years ago. Lana Mae was dealing with a lot at the time. And her first love was a guy who shattered her heart and left her pregnant and alone. I might've had feelings for her back then, but I would never have acted on them. At the time, she was vulnerable and scared and needed me as a friend. Needed someone who would, and could, never hurt her like Steven did.

And what I wanted came second to what Lana Mae needed.

Today, that sentiment still stands.

"Even if Lan *did* have feelings for me, I could never make a pass at her," I say resolutely. "I vowed to be there for her as a friend a long, long time ago, and I could never go back on that."

Luke gives me a hard look. "While we appreciate how good a friend you've been to Lan over the years, especially after our mom died... well, with all due respect, you are being a complete and total dumbass right now."

That sentence didn't end the way I was expecting it to.

I blink at Luke. "I'm being a dumbass how, exactly?"

"You promised an eighteen-year-old girl who had just lost her mom and just become a mom herself that you'd be there for her as a friend. And you kept that promise. But aren't you missing the tiny little detail that an entire freaking decade has passed since then? Lana's now a twenty-seven-year-old woman who's actively dating again."

"Yeah. Other people. She's dating other people."

"Yet here we are, celebrating her engagement to *you*." Luke sighs, then adds "dumbass" under his breath.

"Need I remind you that the engagement is *fake*."

"But are your feelings for her fake?" Liam raises a brow.

"I love her as a friend, and she loves me as a friend. End of story."

But is it?

"Hmm," Liam responds skeptically, then levels me with a dead-serious, dark-eyed look. His eyes are so like his little sister's except... scarier. Way scarier. Where Lana's eyes are melted dark chocolate, Liam's are nuclear bomb casings. "Well, as her older brother, I feel the need to say this, and I'll only say it once. My sister is an adult and I will never tell her how to live her life. But hurt her, and I will break every bone in your body."

Luke claps his brother on the shoulder. "That was deep,

bro. And a bit dark, even for you. But I like the sentiment. We just want what's best for Lana."

I look at them both and nod. "Me too. And believe me when I say that I would never, ever do anything to hurt her. She's the most important person in my life and the best friend I've ever had."

Which is the truth.

Yet the Donovan brothers' declarations that she might see the potential for something more snags on my brain and won't let go... Could she really have started dating again because of me? Is it possible that she, too, feels something she's tried to squish down and suppress for the sake of our friendship?

Liam nods back at me, then breaks into a rare wide smile as he holds up his beer bottle in a salute. "Glad to hear it. Conversation over, then."

"Conversation *almost* over," Luke corrects. "Because there's something I do need to confirm: Mindy was telling me that the butt cake has to do with you doubling as a famous Chris's butt in movies?" He grins at my gaping expression. "At least, that's what Lana told her."

It may be true that I will never hurt her. But I am going to kill her.

17

LANA MAE

Later, after Allegra has gone to bed, Mindy, Annie and I are cleaning up in the kitchen while my brothers and Carter straighten out the yard. It's coming up on midnight, but the air breezing through the open windows and doors is still sticky hot and sweet as we stack the dishwasher, put leftovers in Tupperwares, and rinse glasses. All while stepping around a sleeping Chimichanga on the floor.

After the cremation of the steaks, my father and Constance decided that their visit was over. Thank goodness. Carter then ordered in a ton of Vietnamese food, and the rest of us spent the evening sitting outside eating spring rolls and vermicelli and sipping on champagne, our conversation and laughter carrying through the night as the world darkened around us.

I can't remember the last time I felt so happy. I was surrounded by all my favorite people, and Carter's arm was casually lying along the back of my chair, thereby giving me a delicious proximity to his warmth.

He was so sweet earlier, when we were speaking with my dad. I had to remind myself countless times during the evening that everything he said was for our ruse, and not because he meant it. But even still, his words gave me a thrill...

"I will try my damndest to make this woman feel safe, loved, and happy for the rest of my life."

What a guy.

One day, Carter is going to get tired of casual dating and flings, and he's going to settle down for real. Whoever gets to be Mrs. Carter James Callahan is one very lucky lady.

"That was a wild night," Mindy says from where she's sitting on the counter, stabbing a fork into the remnants of the butt cake. She scrapes up peach frosting and shovels it into her mouth. "And believe me, I know a wild night when I see one."

I put the last plate in the dishwasher, then lean against the counter next to her and stick my finger into the cake, scooping up a big dollop of frosting for myself. "I still can't believe that Allegra called you to organize this party."

I already filled Annie and Mindy in on the little engagement arrangement, but I still haven't gotten the full story about how and why on earth they all ended up here tonight with cake and champagne.

Annie looks at us from the sink and tuts at Mindy. "Don't blame the child, you cruel creature!"

"Okay, fine." Mindy rolls her eyes. "When I saw the story earlier today, I figured that it wasn't real and you would've told us yourself if you were actually engaged. But then, you weren't responding to any of us on the group chat, so I thought it would be hilarious to throw you an engagement party."

"And you invited my dad?!"

"Uh, no." Mindy scratches her ear. "That actually *was* Allegra. I get the feeling she knows what's going on but desperately wants it to be real."

155

I blow out of the side of my mouth. "Yeah, I think you got that right."

Annie gives me a sympathetic look. "That's a tough one."

I nod. "The last thing I want is for her to be confused."

"So just marry him for real then," Mindy says easily, licking the back of her fork and peering out the window to where the men are hard at work.

"Ha. If only it was that simple." I follow Mindy's gaze and find Carter's athletic form all the way at the end of the yard. He's stepped away from my brothers and is now pacing back and forth while speaking on the phone. He's still in a t-shirt, and despite the sweaty temperature and late hour, he looks fresh as a daisy.

Who's he talking to at this hour? Elena? Anthony? Some other bigshot celebrity?

Mindy clocks what I'm staring at and smirks. "I'd say 'just look at him' but there's no point, is there?"

"He *is* easy on the eyes." Annie shakes her head in wonder. "The whole thing is a bit surreal."

As the newest member of our family, Annie has spent by far the least time with Carter. She's still getting used to being around someone whose picture she once admitted to cutting out of magazines.

"I'll say—I'm the one who's fake engaged to one of the biggest stars on this planet."

"But like I said," Mindy insists with a twinkle. "Does it have to be a *fake* engagement?"

"He's not looking for commitment. The reason we ended up in this mess in the first place is because he didn't even want to be in a *fake* serious relationship with an actual romantic prospect. He's my best friend, but he's also a total ladies' man. I'd bet it'll be years before he settles down."

And when he *does* find the woman he wants to spend

the rest of his life with, he'll need someone who can keep up with his jetsetting lifestyle. Not a single mom whose roots run deep in suburban Atlanta.

"I dunno about that." Mindy winks theatrically at me. "Maybe he was just waiting for the right person to have a romance with."

"Well, if that's the case, he's going to be waiting awhile longer."

"Waiting for what?" Luke asks, suddenly appearing in the kitchen with his arms piled high with white paper plates. He immediately dumps them into the recycling.

"Waiting for me to call you guys an Uber so you can get your drunken asses home and leave me alone to go to bed," I say.

"I already ordered an Uber." Liam comes in next. "I need to be at work early tomorrow for a call with London."

"What call with London?" Luke—who is also Liam's business partner—frowns in confusion.

"The one I didn't tell you about because I knew you'd be sleeping off a hangover."

Luke looks like he's about to be pissed off at this revelation. Then, he apparently thinks better of it and smiles. "How responsible of you. Thanks. I will enjoy my sleep in, then."

Ten minutes later, after I've managed to shoo my brothers and their wives out the front door, Carter walks in through the back, his face a little tense.

"Sorry about that," he says quietly, glancing around the kitchen. "Has everyone left?"

"Yup. Here's hoping that Liam doesn't care about his Uber rating. Last I heard, Luke and Mindy were getting a little handsy in the backseat."

Carter chuckles and his eyes return to me. Move slowly over me, in fact. I'm wearing the same thing I've been wearing all night—an old, oversized Braves sweatshirt over Nike running shorts (i.e. the least sexy outfit ever)—but something feels different now. Somehow, the very feel of his eyes on my bare legs draws a huge, hot shiver out of me that I disguise by pretending I'm having a sudden leg spasm.

He cocks an eyebrow at me. "You okay there?"

"Restless leg syndrome." I hop up and down a bit to punctuate my lie. "Comes out of nowhere at times."

"Oh yeah?" He grins, and I know I'm not fooling anybody. "At the same time as your hypoglycemia, or at other times?"

I glower at him. "That depends."

"Sure it does."

"Who was on the phone?" I ask, and then immediately pause. It's a question I'd never usually think twice about asking, but now that we're "engaged", do we need to give each other privacy in certain areas? What if he was on the phone with another woman? I have no idea how fake-engaged-to-your-best-friend-you're-secretly-in-love-with etiquette works.

Before my thoughts can spiral too far, Carter saves me by answering, "Anthony. Well, Elena and then Anthony."

"At midnight?" I frown.

Carter crosses the kitchen and stands right in front of me. There's six inches of space between our chests, but every millimeter is electric. "They want to throw us an engagement party."

My breath catches in my throat. "Is that a... normal thing for your manager and assistant to do?"

Carter's blue eyes darken as he worries his lower lip with his teeth. "Not really," he admits, his expression pinched. "But nothing Anthony and Elena ever do is normal."

"Oh," is all I can manage to get out. I was anticipating

having to meet people at some point, make a few public appearances where I can be a total wallflower whilst indulging my inner fan-girl, like at the premiere. But I never expected to be the center of attention at a star-studded party. Anxiety does not even begin to cover what the introvert in me is feeling right now.

Carter's steady eyes study me and I offer him a wan smile. "Wasn't tonight our engagement party?" I joke hopefully.

He smiles back at me. "I'm not sure too much paparazzi action was happening, unless you count Mindy's half-drunken selfies."

"I do not," I reply.

"The idea for this one is to do an official bash. Get some famous bodies in one place and get them talking and posting. Elena offered to organize it all and even have it at my house here in Atlanta so it's not too much of a disturbance for your schedule. But I can tell them you're busy next weekend, find an excuse—"

"What on earth am I going to wear?" I interrupt him hurriedly. Because of course we're doing this. We have an agreement and I intend to hold up my end of the bargain. Mildly crippling anxiety or not.

Carter's concerned expression fades as he laughs and shakes his head. "Anthony's on it. He'll bring over a few wardrobe options on the day. You'll just have to pick the one you like best."

I gape at him. "You set that up for me?"

He taps me on the shoulder and smirks, blue eyes dancing. "For me, really. I didn't want to spend any more time sitting in dress stores."

"Fair." I smile up at him, my heart beating a million miles a minute. This sweet, thoughtful man, I tell you. "And thank you."

"Don't mention it. Like I said, it was mostly selfish. Now, are we watching *Gilmore Girls* or what?"

"You don't want to get home?"

"I'm still pretty wired from this evening, so I'm up for hanging out for a bit, but I can order an Uber if you're tired. I had a few drinks so I shouldn't drive." His dimple pops as he grins at me. "Don't want your good friend McCreary to pull me over."

"You can stay over, if you like." The words pour out of my mouth before I can think them, and the second they do, I wish I could scoop them all up and shove them right back where they belong. "Um... because it would look good for our story if the paparazzi catch you leaving my house tomorrow, wouldn't it?"

He raises his brows. "It would. But I'll probably have to kiss you goodbye on the front porch to get the full effect for the media."

He's messing with me, I know he is. But I feel my entire head go red at the thought of his mouth on mine.

"We didn't discuss the physical stuff, did we?" I yelp. "How are we going to make people believe we're together if we don't even kiss?"

Carter takes a small step towards me. Those six inches between us become three. Two. One. He's right in front of me now. So close, his scent—woodsy and clean laundry, tonight layered with a hint of barbecue smoke—surrounds me in such an intoxicating way I can't help but breathe in.

He trains his eyes on mine. "We don't have to kiss. We can do lots of other things to make it look believable between us."

"L-like?" I stutter.

"Like this." He reaches out and smoothes a warm palm down my arm. Even through the sweatshirt, I feel his heat. I gulp.

"And this." His hand moves, traveling up to my shoulder and around to tangle in my hair, anchoring at the base of my neck. It's all I can do not to squeak aloud.

"And, of course, this." His hand is on the move again, and I'm dizzy and short of breath and sure I am way, way, way too red and flustered for him not to know what's currently going on in my body. He gently runs the back of his index finger along my jawline, and this time, it's impossible to hide my shiver.

When I dare look at him, his eyes are boring down at me, a little hazy and dark. "Lan..." he starts, his voice gravely, his fingertips still possessively on my jaw. Man, this guy can act. It is an act, right?

Just an act.

"Cold!" I squeak, jumping backwards so fast that I bang the small of my back on the countertop. "Is it cold in here?"

I spring into action, moving around the kitchen and closing windows. Carter remains still, watching me as I flap around like a disorientated bat. By the time I'm done and dare look at him again, he's rubbing his eyes with the heels of his hands.

"Tired?" I ask.

"Yeah, I am actually. Maybe I should get an Uber and let you get to bed. We could probably both do with a good sleep after today."

The thought of him leaving fills me with a strange sadness. I have no idea what's going on with me, too much champagne or something. I mean, I'm used to him leaving. He leaves all the time. Why would now be any different?

So I shrug and say, "Your Jeep will still be parked out front, which is probably enough proof. Plus, there were people lurking out there when I came home earlier. They've likely already gotten a ton of pictures."

He studies me for a long moment, eyes guarded. "I hate

the thought of you being hounded like that," he says quietly. "And honestly, forget adding credit to our story. I'd feel better if I stayed tonight in case one of them is dumb enough to ring your doorbell or harass you or something. I want to make sure you and Legs are safe."

He looks so serious, so earnest, I can't help but hug him. He responds right away, pulling me almost roughly towards him and holding me tight in a bear-like cuddle.

I've never felt safer.

When we eventually pull apart, he smiles down at me. "If you're good with that, we could still watch one quick episode before we go to bed? I can sleep on the couch so we don't confuse Allegra."

"I'm definitely good with both the you staying over plan and the one episode of *Gilmore Girls* plan." I find myself nodding in agreement way too fast. I'm like an overeager beaver at the thought of him staying.

I'm also sure that he can see right through me because he smiles widely. Then, he starts walking towards the living room, calling over his shoulder, "Come on then, Wifey. We don't have all night."

But we do.

And even if it is all pretend, I'm going to savor every damn second of it.

18

LANA MAE

True to his word, Carter slept on the couch that night.

And the night after that. And the night after that, too.

"May as well make this as believable as possible, right Lan?" he said last night before once again retrieving the pillow and blankets from the linen closet and making up the couch. "And, of course, I should be here in case anything happens."

And even though I was sure his back must be in agony, I agreed all too eagerly. Because having this much time with Carter is incredible. When he's gone, I don't let myself miss him because it hurts too much. It's only when he's here with me that I can feel the hole his absence leaves in my life.

It's going to be so hard to see him go when this is all over and he's back in LA or New York or wherever *If Only* is going to be filmed—because I'm sure he'll get the part—and I'm still here. But I've done it before and I'll do it again, supporting him without ever wavering. Cheering him on in his success.

But still, I'm trying not to think about it too much just yet. Because carpe diem and positivity and all my mantras that I actually have to start living by.

This morning, I wake to the unmistakable smell of pancakes wafting from the kitchen. Voices and laughter carry up the stairs, mingling with the cooking scents, and I roll over in bed to look at my alarm clock. It's almost eight. Allegra has field day at school today, so she doesn't need to be in until later, and my shift at work today doesn't start until noon, so I decided (wild and crazy person that I am) that I wasn't going to set an alarm this morning. This has gotta be the latest I've slept in years.

I stretch luxuriously before stepping out of bed, and pad to the bathroom to brush my teeth. The woman staring back at me in the mirror might have crazy bedhead hair and no makeup and is wearing a mismatched pajama set consisting of a faded Snoopy tee and shorts with burgers all over them. But she looks rested. Content.

Happy.

After I rinse my mouth, I consider going to my room and getting dressed, but I change my mind and head downstairs instead, gathering my hair into a loose knot on top of my head.

The morning sunshine is streaming through the windows in the living room, casting the house in a golden glow. That sweet, mapley smell is filling the air to the point that my mouth is practically watering.

Carter's standing at the stove in my tiny kitchen, looking altogether too large, but at the same time, perfect for the space. He's wearing a pink plaid "Kiss the Cook" apron (I wish) over a ridiculously sexy white-t-shirt-and-gray-sweatpants combo while he spoons ladles of pancake batter onto a griddle pan. He doesn't look so much a DILF as a DILTSMELWAHAHB (Dad I'd Like To Spend My Entire Life With And Have All His Babies, for those of you who are not fluent in acronyms).

I don't know what his secret is. Carter never cooks and

seems to order all his meals from nice restaurants and those nutritionally balanced, fresh-prepped dinner companies— you know, the ones that arrive premade in pretty packaging and cost a pretty penny, too. But somehow, the man makes the best pancakes this side of the Mississippi.

Allegra is sitting at the counter next to a huge pancake stack, inhaling them like they're going out of style. She likes hers with Nutella and strawberries, and she's got chocolate all over the corners of her mouth.

Carter smiles at my daughter softly as he flips the latest round of pancakes. I love that pure look of adoration on his face when he looks at her almost more than if it were directed at me.

There was no love lost between Carter and my ex, Steven, who were both roommates *and* enemies during their freshman year of college. So I'm really glad that Carter's able to look at my daughter, and see and love her for who she is rather than seeing her as the daughter of someone he can't stand.

Genetically, Allegra may be half Steven, half me, but she's one hundred percent herself and one hundred percent perfect in my eyes.

Plus, it's not all bad. She inherited Steven's natural athleticism over my hopeless lack of coordination. The kiddo can throw a fastball with impressive speed and accuracy. And she's a beautiful dancer.

I watch from the kitchen doorway as my daughter smiles up at my best friend with a similar look of adoration in her expression. "My friend Keisha got a new unicorn sleeping bag for the campout."

Carter tilts his head. "Did she now?"

"Uh-huh. She says it's purple and sparkly, so I'm sure she will have the coolest sleeping bag there. But that's okay.

My sleeping bag is green with leaves on it. What color is your sleeping bag?"

"Um, I don't think I have one." Carter scratches the back of his neck. "But I'll go buy one this week."

"Okay, good. You're definitely gonna need one. And a tent, too. But I guess we could use ours. Mom put some duct tape over the leak so Tara and Ella and me could camp out in our backyard last month."

"'Course she did." There's a smile in Carter's voice. "And you don't need to worry about a tent. I have a tent that I think you'll like."

He's such a liar. But a good one, because Allegra nods. "Good. I'll write on my campout list that the tent will be your job. My jobs so far are marshmallows and flashlights."

"Those are great jobs." Carter transfers another few pancakes to the stack, then returns his attention to the stove. "Both are super important. What other jobs can I do?"

"So first, you have to act like you love me and like you're going to be my new daddy for real."

"I do love you," he says immediately. "New daddy or not, that never changes. I'm always here for you, Legs. You're my number one girl."

She gives him a little wrinkle-nose smile. "Duh. *I* know all that. I just mean that you have to act like it for our audience."

"That shouldn't be too hard." He swallows a laugh as he turns to look at her, and in the process, catches me lurking in the doorway like a weirdo. His eyes roam over my face and messy hair, then up and down my body, taking in my pajama-clad form. A slow grin creeps over his face. "It lives."

I poke my tongue out at him and walk towards the food. "I can't believe how long I slept, but oh my gosh, did I need it. I feel like a new woman."

"I love to hear that," Carter says thoughtfully as he scrapes the last of the batter into the pan.

Sitting down at the counter next to my daughter, I drop a kiss on her head. "Morning, princess."

"Morning, Mommy. Can Carter use your sleeping bag for the campout? You know, because you're not invited and he is?"

"Nice reminder, thanks for that. And sure." I reach for a pancake and fork it onto my plate. Slather it in syrup and add a pat of butter on top, which slowly slides off.

"Good. I'm gonna get dressed for field day!" Legs scrambles down from her chair and heads for the stairs.

"Don't forget to wash your face!" I call after her.

"You working today?" he asks as he sits down on the stool next to me.

"Not 'til later," I say through a mouthful of syrup.

He raises a dark brow. "Fancy a morning trip to Target?"

"Who are you and what have you done with Carter Callahan?"

Carter gives me a lopsided smile, and with his one dimple popping, he looks positively boyish. Even though there is not one boyish thing about this man's incredible physique. "I'm a *fiancé* now, didn't you hear? Don't domesticated couples love Target?"

I punch him in the arm for that one, because he knows I love Target with all my heart.

"I'm taking my new family-man role *very* seriously," Carter continues. "And that means that my mission for the week—aside from taking you, my beautiful fake bride-to-be, to our official engagement party on Saturday night, of course—is to find a certain little girl a sparkly unicorn tent."

A blush crawls over my body at this endearment, and my mind flashes back to the way he touched me in the kitchen the other night. I catch myself thinking about this way too much, to the point where I'm actually looking forward to the engagement party. Even the thought of him touching me like that again is enough to make me giddy with anticipation.

But I force my mind away from Carter's sexiness, and back to my daughter's upcoming campout.

"Didn't she want a unicorn sleeping bag?"

"Yes. That too." He cuts himself a piece of pancake and fixes those vivid blue eyes on me. "All the unicorn camping stuff we can find. Don't tell her though, k? I want it to be a surprise."

Just when I thought I couldn't possibly fall for him more.

19

CARTER

I've never understood the appeal of Target to the majority of the female population.

But as Lana Mae and I walk the aisles, pushing a huge red cart and sipping coffees, Target (which, up until five minutes ago, was just another generic big box store I rarely frequented) becomes my new happy place.

Because it's just Lana and me. No crammed, scheduled visit. Just time to relax and enjoy ourselves and each other. She's bouncing along next to me, chatting my ear off as we chuck a wild assortment of items into our cart. Most of which are not even camping-related.

After that moment between us in her kitchen the other night, I wasn't sure what to think. Something was *definitely* there, in her eyes, almost daring me to lean in...

And then, just as quickly, the moment was over. Evaporated like smoke. And I'm still not sure what to make of it.

"This is so much better than dress shopping," I tell her as I add a case of Olipop to the cart, then point us in the direction of the snacks.

"I don't think we've ever been grocery shopping

together. I thought you were going to be one of those Erewhon snobs."

I laugh. "I've never even set foot in an Erewhon. Anthony arranges it so that all my stuff gets delivered to my apartment when I'm in LA."

"So spoiled." She rolls her eyes.

"I know," I reply seriously. It's always bugged me that, since I came into money, Lana has refused to take a penny from me. I know she's stubborn and proud and determined to do things herself (which I admire), but I still wish she'd let me help. It's not personal, though—her brothers have a super successful tech company, and the most she'll let them pay for is Allegra's dance classes.

When I found this out, I also found my loophole: Lana Mae may not want my help, but she'd never deny her daughter anything.

So I've been doing what I can in *that* way. Mostly unbeknownst to my best friend.

Lana takes a sip of her Starbucks cinnamon dolce latte. "I always imagined that your LA apartment has a really fancy coffee machine that you learned how to use for the sole purpose of impressing all your guests."

"Well, you do know how much I love to impress guests. The King of England was positively blown away by my coffee game when he swung by for a latte and a chat," I reply flippantly, and when she rolls her eyes and whacks my arm, I add, "But you're half right. I *do* have a really nice coffee machine that I don't know how to use. Anthony does, though."

"What, you don't offer all your lady friends coffee in the morning? Or is it part of Anthony's job to come round and barista for them?"

There's a little flash of something in my stomach at her

question. Like I said, we don't usually talk about my dating life, but here she is, suddenly asking questions.

I reach over and tug gently on her hair. "What're you talking about, lady friends? I'm engaged to be married, you know."

She looks at me with a silly smile. "I did know that, actually. Think I saw a story about it on *E!*"

"You should meet her, she's incredible," I say with a matching silly smile.

Lan looks down at her feet bashfully as I toss some honey roasted cashews and Milano cookies on top of our haul. I realize with a start that I've barely given a second's thought to the shirt-less scene in *If Only*. All that stuff is starting to pale and fade around the woman upon whose couch I've been camping out.

"She's also going to be late for work if we don't find this tent soon," she jokes lightly.

"Okay, okay."

Then, as she turns to walk towards the Outdoors section, I grab her from behind. My arms wrap around her petite body, holding her close as I pick her up... and dump her onto the cart.

I start jogging. "Hold on!" I call as I race towards the camping equipment.

Lana squeals. "Stop, you big oaf!"

But she's laughing her head off. We both are as we blast through the aisles like over-sugared kids, me swerving and weaving the cart around displays while she holds on for dear life. A tinny version of Taylor Swift's "Paper Rings" starts playing over the store's speakers, and I could not think of a more perfect soundtrack for this moment as Lana Mae throws her head back and sings along, like she doesn't have a care in the world.

Our fake engagement feels like a paper ring right now—

171

it might not be the real thing, but it doesn't make this moment with her any less perfect.

We're both practically crying with laughter by the time we get to the camping aisle, where we find two serious, outdoor-enthusiast types in North Face fleeces and zip-off cargo pants. The two men are examining a propane camping stove like they're trying to mine it for the secrets of the universe. One of them looks up and gives us an annoyed glance, and Lana snorts her snorty little laugh again, which sets me off.

The fleeces move away and I grin at Lan while offering a hand to help her down from her sprawled position atop the cart. She places her hand in mine, soft and small, and a little zing travels up my arm as I pull her to a seated position. She looks at our intertwined hands for a long moment, hops off the cart neatly, and I let myself hold onto her for just a bit longer than could be considered accidental. Just a touch longer than I *should* hold on for.

Then, I let go and begin to throw every pink, sparkly, remotely camp-ish looking thing into the cart.

Lana stands behind me with her arms crossed, shaking her head. "You don't do a lot of camping, huh?"

"Nope," I answer cheerfully, adding a pink multi-tool pocket knife, a matching pink first aid kit, and a purple hammock to the cart.

"You know that it's going to be in the school field, right? With access to a medical tent and washrooms?"

"I like to be prepared." I hold her gaze for a moment, and my stomach drops as a spark of something glimmers between us.

Neither of us notice the designer fleece twins come back into the aisle until one of them says, "Lana Mae?"

We whirl around to face them. The one who spoke is the guy who didn't look up earlier, but is now staring at us

172

like we're two pieces of bacteria in a petri dish. Lana, meanwhile, has paled.

"Can we help you?" I ask shortly.

"Thought it was you." Even though I asked him the question, he's talking directly to Lana, and he's now got a smug expression on his face that I don't like. "We're shopping for a guys' camping trip, and I noticed Lana Mae over here and wanted to say hi." He does this vile little smirk that automatically makes me clench my fists by my side. "I didn't know you liked the outdoors, Lana. Sleeping under the stars, telling stories around campfires... And speaking of open flames, how's your hair doing?" Before Lana can say anything, the guy elbows his buddy in the ribs. "*This* is the girl I was telling you about."

His buddy hoots. "You're the chick who set herself on fire? Dude! That was the most hilarious story I've ever heard. Priceless."

"I just *had* to tell people. It was too good not to share." The guy is looking at Lana with an insincere smile. She's smiling back, but it's strained. And I start to put the puzzle pieces together.

A date where Lana set fire to her hair... Which is, admittedly, hilarious in its own right, and we did laugh about it together.

But the way this guy is smirking at her. Like she's *beneath* him or something. It's enough to make my blood boil.

And then, the guy takes one long look down Lana's body and says, "I've been keeping an eye out for you, but it doesn't look like you made an appointment at my clinic yet."

What?

I step close to Lana Mae and put a possessive arm around her shoulder. The dude looks at me like he's really seeing me for the first time. He does a double take when he recognizes me, but manages to cover his surprise pretty swiftly.

"I'm Braxton." He sticks out a hand, which I ignore, and instead pull Lana Mae into my side.

"And what clinic is this?" I say so coldly, there's a noticeable chill in the air around us.

"I'm the resident doctor at a medical aesthetics clinic." Braxton actually looks *proud* of this. "Lana Mae was interested in having a consultation for some 'mom-bod' skin tightening treatments—"

"My wife is perfect just the way she is, thank you very much," I snap, cutting him off. "She isn't interested in anything of the sort."

Beside me, Lana audibly sucks in a breath. But I just tighten my arm around her shoulder and glare at Dr. Moron. Did Lana really go on a date with this jerk?

"You should write a book about dating disasters," his buddy continues, oblivious to the growing tension in Aisle 19. But he blinks when he registers my last words. "Wait... your wife?"

Braxton, too, is frowning, obviously confused. "I'm sorry, I don't think I'm following." He points between us. "You two are married?"

"Engaged to be married, but I can't help but refer to her as 'my wife' already, because I'm counting the days until she's officially mine forever." I laugh, then give him a pitying look, like I'm registering his surprise for the first time. "Oh... you didn't think that was a *real* date, did you?"

Braxton's expression slackens further and I look down at Lana Mae, who's still nestled under the crook of my arm. I lift my free hand and run my fingers over her jaw adoringly. "Isn't that wild, honey? He thought it was a real date."

"Wild," Lana echoes, also sounding vaguely stunned by this turn of events.

Braxton's face is darkening further and further by the second, storm clouds rolling in. But I continue to ignore him, and instead, look at his buddy. "You're right about one thing—she *is* writing a book. Her editor wanted her manuscript to include a horrible date, which was something I obviously couldn't help her with research-wise, so I told Lana that she should get set up with the worst per—uh, I mean *first* person, she could find to fit the bill. Guess her sister-in-law's doctor work friend came to mind."

I finally turn back to Braxton and give him a sympathetic smile. "Sorry you got caught in the crosshairs, bro."

"Very unfortunate," Lana pipes up. She's now sporting a barely concealed grin.

"Maybe you should send him a signed copy when it's done, Lan."

"Absolutely. Without you, Braxton, there would be no book. So, thank you for that."

And with that parting blow from my girl, I steer us out of Aisle 19 and away from the fleece-clad creeps. My arm doesn't move from its secure place around her shoulders.

The second we're out of earshot, she comes alive, sputtering with laughter. "Carter, that was... Brilliant! His face! How on earth did you come up with that so quick?"

I shrug. "Didn't want him to have the satisfaction of thinking that he got to go on an actual date with you when you're clearly a million miles out of his pitiful D-league."

"I think we might've ruined his weekend hiking excursion," she says cheerily. But then, her expression clouds. "Let's just hope that Mindy doesn't get fired."

I shake my head and squeeze her tighter. "Oh, please. Mindy would never let herself get fired."

After we (barely) manage to cram our Target haul into the back of my Jeep, I drive Lan to work. She works part-time from the office, part-time from home, and I know she ends up putting in a lot of extra hours late at night to keep on top of everything. It's impressive, how she juggles parenting and working like she does, and I was excited she had a proper morning off today. Until that freaking Braxton idiot almost ruined it.

Though I played things off as cooly and jokily as possible with Lan afterward, my blood pounds in my temples at the memory of his snooty, sneering face. How *dare* he think he was too good for her.

I glance over to the passenger seat, where Lana Mae is sitting quietly, picking at her nails, and I know she's thinking about what just happened, too. I don't try to fill the silence, because I know my best friend. Know that, sometimes, she needs space to gather her thoughts and process what she's feeling.

When I finally pull up to the curb outside her office building, I wait for a moment. She does too, making no move to get out. We sit like that for a minute before she quietly says, "Carter?"

"Yeah?"

"Thank you."

"Thank *you* for being a willing cart race participant."

I'm gratified to see her smile. "I'm not sure I'd say 'willing'."

"Fine. Thank you for letting me throw you in the cart and push you around the store like a maniac."

"That's more like it. But I don't just mean thanks for the shopping trip, I mean it for everything. For being so sweet with Allegra this morning. For pretending in front of Braxton."

"That guy's a total moron. I can't believe they gave him a license to operate on people."

"I think he mostly does Botox."

"He's probably poisoned his brain with the amount he's self-injected."

"That would explain a lot, actually." Lan fiddles with her door handle, then gives a chuckle. "I guess, with all the dates lately, I've been feeling like a fish out of water. Or, more like a humpback out of water."

My forehead creases. "Humpback... Like the whale?"

"Long story, not important." She waves a hand. "What I mean is, every time I go on a date, I feel out of place. Like I'm living someone else's life and not mine. The bad dates sucked, sure, that's a given. But the good ones did, too. Even when I liked a guy, I just wanted to go home and be alone the entire time we were together. You know, like a real idiot sandwich type of person."

She laughs, but I see the pinch in her eyes. The hurt behind the humor.

I wait for her to take a breath before she continues, "That date with Braxton wasn't just awkward or sucky or made me feel like I was out of place. That night, I felt less than. The funny thing is that, even though I disliked the guy on sight, he still somehow made me feel like *I* wasn't worthy of *him*." She's fiddling with her fingers now. "So, thank you. I know this engagement stuff is fake and you're a world-class actor, but you really made me feel... special back there. Desirable. As you know, my romantic history hasn't really left me feeling all too confident in that area, but I've been trying to get over that."

Her face is a little withdrawn, the uncharacteristic vulnerability peeking through her usual humor.

Anger rises in me, simmering like steam. I'm angry that she doesn't see how incredible she is. Angry that she went through such a brutal relationship when she was so young, and it's tainted how she sees herself.

Frick. I'm glad I punched that jackass in the face. He deserved it.

"You are no less than entirely worthy. Entirely beautiful, all the time. Any guy would be lucky to have you, Lana Mae. Trust me."

Lan's eyes meet mine, and she gives a little nod, eyes flickering. Then, she smirks at me, her shield of humor back in place. "What's this talk about, any guy? I'm engaged to be married, you know."

"Oh yeah, I think I heard about that. To the really, really good looking actor with the incredible bod?"

She giggles, and I'm happy to hear the sound. "Six out of ten at best. On par with my pepperoni pizza."

"Excuse me?!" I widen my eyes at her and she laughs harder.

"Oh please, CJ. You know you're a perfect ten."

And with that little comment, she gets out of the car, waves at me, and walks away.

I don't make any move to drive off. Instead, I watch as she hurries towards the revolving door of her office building, gorgeous in her floral sundress and sandals. And completely oblivious to the guy leaving the building, who stops midstep to check her out.

She really has no idea how other people see her.

How *I* see her.

Because despite all my best efforts, I can't ignore my feelings anymore. Feelings that I may have pushed down for years, but never actually left.

And while I'm still not sure what it is she might feel or not feel for me (if anything) all I want is for her to *feel* as beautiful as she really is, inside and out. So, I resolve to use every avenue I have as her fake fiancé to make that happen.

Starting with our engagement party in a couple of days.

The second Lana disappears inside her building, I pick up my phone.

Anthony answers on the second ring. "Hello, stranger. How's betrothed bliss?"

"Pretty blissful," I say with a smile. "So listen, I have a favor to ask you..."

20

LANA MAE,

The day of our "official" engagement party starts with a bang—literally—when a crash from the living room had me racing downstairs to discover Carter spreadeagled on the floor in a tangle of blankets...

Wearing nothing but navy-blue boxer shorts.

Tight ones. Like the ones that hug... everything.

I immediately covered my eyes (oh, who am I kidding? I peeked through my fingers and ogled the absolute hell out of his sculpted body) and squeaked a "sorry" for walking in on him. Carter sat up, which made his abs flex distractingly, and then rubbed the back of his head, which made his biceps pop even more distractingly. I was so entirely distracted by that point, I barely heard his explanation that he'd been having a particularly active dream and rolled clean off the couch.

Poor dude is way too big to be sleeping on that little thing.

He stood up (cue me dying behind my strategically placed fingertips) and stood there for a full second before seeming to fully wake up and cover himself with a blanket (boo).

Meanwhile, I lingered not six feet away and tried with everything in me not to throw myself on top of him like a hungry lioness.

He looked at me with his head tilted, almost like he was daring me to do... something. "Hey, Llama?"

When I finally managed to croak out a shaky "Yes?", he just smirked.

"You don't have to peek through your fingers, you know," he said before striding past me and into the bathroom. I simply stood in his wake, dropped my hands, and stared at his (literal) million dollar butt retreating to the shower.

Six hours later, that image is still engraved on my frontal lobe as I start to get ready for the big event. Alone. Allegra's at Liam and Annie's place for the afternoon, and they'll take her to the party later. As for Carter, he left for his house awhile ago to help Elena, who just flew in from LA, and the party planners. He'll be back to pick me up at seven.

I've never been to such a fancy event before. But unlike the lead-up to my multiple dates with other men, any impending anxiety about tonight is overshadowed by excitement at the thought of spending the evening with Carter. The thought of him being by my side, guiding me through our first public appearance as a couple, is enough for me to feel safe.

I still can't believe the way he came through for me at Target, when we ran into Number One Worst Date Braxton and his little buddy. The way he vouched for me, built me up when Braxton tried to tear me down. Put his arm around me almost possessively, like I was his to protect.

And let's not get started on the way he *looked* at me.

I know he was playing his part, but even still, the memory of those searing hot eyes is enough to send chills through my body.

So today, I'm like a teenage girl on her first date, blasting a 2000's pop playlist that is all One Direction and T-Swift classics while I run myself a bubble bath. With Legs gone, Chimichanga back at his own house, and Harry Styles curled up in the sunny kitchen windowsill, this may be the first time in years that I've had the washroom to myself.

My peace doesn't last long, though. My phone pings, then pings again, and again as I sink into the soothing hot water. With a sigh, I reach for it. About a hundred messages have poured in on my family group chat.

Annie: We're all SO excited for tonight. Send pics of the dress options.

Mindy: And make sure you shave your legs ;)

Luke: And your chest. Saw a bit of a neck beard forming the other night, Lan. You might be taking after me in the stubble department. Lucky you.

Liam: Can we please not discuss body hair in the chat? Some of us are trying to work.

Luke: This is way more important than our stupid company.

Liam: Our sister going to a party and shaving her legs is more important than the multimillion dollar tech business we built from the ground up?

Annie: *GIF of David Rose rolling his eyes and saying "Obviously"*

Liam: Don't you start.

Mindy: I tried to give myself a bikini wax once.

Liam: Or you.

Annie: Noooooo that sounds horrific.

Mindy: It was a hot wax nightmare. Not unlike that Paris Hilton slasher movie.

Luke: Believe me, she has the scars to prove it ;)

Liam: Seriously people, this chat is for emergencies

and event reminders. This is not what I want to think about while I'm eating my lunch.

As much as I agree with Liam that I'd rather not dwell on the thought (or mental image) of Mindy's bikini wax blunders, I can't help but laugh as my fingers move over my screen to respond.

Lana Mae: Just jumping in to say that I will be shaving my legs thoroughly. Thank you all for your concern and input on the matter. And Mindy, I recommend going to see a doctor.

Luke: Wait, back up a second. Why is it such a big deal that you shave your legs?

Annie: Duh. In case Carter touches them.

Mindy: Not "in case"... he will definitely be touching them. I saw that hand on your thigh the other night looking very comfortable.

Annie: Yassssss get in there, Lan.

Mindy: Want to watch one of Carter's butt movies while we get ready for tonight, Annie?

Lana Mae: The ones you weren't meant to tell anyone about, Min?

Mindy: Yup, one of those :) Luke is still trying to guess which famous Chris he was butt doubling for and I'm planning on leaving him guessing.

Annie: Absofreakinglutely I do. That way, we can be there in spirit.

Luke: I don't know what the big deal is. I could've been a killer butt double if someone had asked me.

Annie: You sound jealous.

Mindy: Some may say... *butt-hurt.*

Luke: I am not butt-hurt!

Lana Mae: And I am not honoring any of this with a response. Goodbye and talk to you all later.

Liam: Everyone except me, because I am blocking all of you.

Liam has left the group chat

Luke: Wow, what's he so butt-hurt about?

I'm still laughing to myself as I wash my hair, and yes, shave my legs. Because while I'm a little mortified that Mindy noticed Carter's hand on my leg the other night, she's not wrong—it felt *very* comfortable there. Felt like that was where it belonged, had always belonged, and should always stay.

I run a quick hand over my knees and ankles to check that I got all the stubble (you know, just in case). Then, I throw my wet hair up in a claw clip, put on my robe, and walk to my bedroom. I'm in the middle of studying my underwear collection, trying to decide what pair one might wear under fancy cocktail attire, when the doorbell rings.

I run downstairs, barefoot and damp, to find Anthony on my doorstep. Well, the top of Anthony's head. The rest of his upper body is hidden behind the ton of garment bags piled high in his arms.

Whoa.

"Hey!" I throw open the door for him. "Can I grab some of those for you? There's so many!"

"No, no, I've got it." He steps inside. "Where shall we set up?"

"Living room," I suggest. "And *we?*"

Anthony sets the dresses on the couch with a loud exhale and stretches his back. "Whew. Who knew dresses with so little coverage could be so heavy?"

"Little coverage?" I balk.

Ant laughs indulgently. "Let's just say that we have a selection of options and not much time to choose. And by *we*, I mean that hair and makeup will be here in an hour so chop chop"—he claps his hands—"grab the first bag and get to trying."

"Wait." I blink, feeling more than a little perplexed. "I thought I was doing my own hair and makeup."

A satisfied little smile. "Not today, girlie. Your fiancé called me a few days ago and specifically told me to pull out all the stops. Bring all the dresses you—*and I*—could dream of, hire a whole team of people. Make you look, and more importantly, *feel* like a million bucks tonight."

My heart stutters as Carter's words from the morning of our Target trip dance through my brain. *You are no less than entirely beautiful, all the time.*

"Anthony," I venture. "Did he happen to call you Wednesday around lunchtime?"

"He did," Anthony confirms, and my smile is immediately a mile wide.

Carter James Callahan. What did I ever do to deserve him as a fake fiancé?

I grab the first garment bag, dash to my bedroom, and soon feel like I'm in a movie montage as I slip into a pink dress that's cute, but too bright. This is followed by a black dress that looks sexy, sure, but whose neckline is *way* too revealing for my own personal comfort level.

"Oh, come on," Ant tuts when I come downstairs to show him the slinky black one. "Your boobs look great in that. Carter will love it."

"Next!" I choke out hurriedly, my cheeks flushing at the thought of Carter seeing me in this dress. Let alone drawing his attention to my chest.

Anthony looks at me slyly, knowingly, and passes me a third garment bag. "Okay, fine. We can try the next one. I guess we *do* want you to be comfortable as well as super hot."

I run back to my bedroom, shimmy out of the plunging-neckline nightmare, and unzip the next bag.

The second I see the dress, I am in love. As I pull it over my hips, I pray it fits, and I'm filled with hope as the garment slips on perfectly.

I turn to the mirror, and I'm almost rendered speechless. It's perfect. Not quite beige, not quite gold, the dress is long and slinky with a slit up one leg that's just daring enough. The bodice is covered in delicate beading that shimmers when it catches the light. I turn around to examine the back, and even unzipped, the dress clings to my curves without being too constricting. The teeny spaghetti criss-cross straps on the back are the perfect finishing touch.

The wide-eyed look I get from Anthony when I walk back into the living room confirms my gut feeling—this is the one.

The perfect dress.

Anthony makes a circle with his index finger, and I obediently rotate so he can zip me up. Then, he pats my hips triumphantly, steps back, and admires the dress. "Amazing. It's like it was made for you."

I awkwardly pat my damp, still claw-clipped hair as I try to receive the compliment graciously. "I think it'll all come together when my hair and makeup are done."

"It absolutely will."

And you know what?

He's right.

Two hours later, my makeup artist, Cherry, is flicking the last drop of lip gloss over my mouth while Marvin, the hair stylist, mists a coat of hairspray around my head. Anthony directs me to the mirror, and even *I* am impressed by the smokey-eyed woman with the sleek updo and chiseled cheekbones looking back at me.

I look... beautiful.

Even better, I *feel* beautiful.

"Thank you, everyone," I say, all of a sudden a bit choked up.

Cherry tuts. "Don't cry, you'll ruin your mascara."

I snort out a laugh and give her, then Marvin, a big hug.

I turn to Anthony. "Thank you."

He grabs both my hands and squeezes. "Hush now. You already said that."

"Well, I'm saying it again."

"Fine. I'll accept full responsibility for this masterpiece standing before me," Anthony declares. "Now, pics or it didn't happen."

I reflexively flinch as the three of them point their phones towards my face and start snapping. Anthony gives me a small smile. "Better get used to it, honey. Everyone's gonna be wanting to take your picture tonight."

And just like that, some of my happiness is replaced by a tightening in my stomach as a knot starts to form. Will people really believe that Carter chose me over, by definition, the sexiest woman in the world? Will I live up to everyone's expectations as the fiancée of Carter Callahan?

I shove my anxiety away and focus again on my reflection. Recall the hope I felt before my date with Braxton, and how it failed so spectacularly because of...

Him.

Yes. Because of him, not me, dammit.

He was the problem.

Our run-in at Target the other morning only confirmed that.

Tonight, I'll have the most unproblematic man by my side. A man that my heart aches for. And while the romance between us might not be real, he's the only man (besides my brothers) who has never made me feel anything other than safe and accepted as I am. A man who has never judged me for my mistakes.

The rest of the world might see him as a player, a bad boy and heartbreaker, but I see the best person I've ever met. And that's all I need not to feel anxious anymore.

When the doorbell rings, I turn to Anthony with a squeak of excitement. "It's him! He's here!"

He winks at me. "Girl, he is going to lose his ever-loving mind over you."

21

CARTER

I can pinpoint the exact moment that I realized I was falling for Lana Mae. Remember it like it was yesterday.

Because it was the same day that I realized that having feelings for her was not an option.

It was a cold November day during my freshman year of college. I overheard Steven on the phone to Lana Mae, promising that he'd be at her high school homecoming dance later that evening.

It was the third or fourth time that I'd heard them on the phone discussing the dance—it was obviously important to Lana Mae, and she was obviously feeling a little unsure about whether her boyfriend would turn up. They'd gotten back together the day after she caught him cheating on her. I was surprised, to say the least. Bothered, actually. What was a girl like that doing with a guy like him?

But their relationship wasn't my business.

Or at least, that was what I told myself until later that same evening, when I spotted Steven on his way to a party on sorority row instead of heading to Lana's high school like he'd promised. The guy had clearly risen to new heights of douchebaggery, because he was standing Lana up at her senior homecoming dance. After he cheated on her.

I hardly knew the girl, but my heart went out to her. And so, I did the only thing I could think to do: I threw on a suit and drove to Lana Mae's high school.

I strode in through the front door of the dance and picked her out in the crowd in an instant. Honey hair. Caramel skin. Chocolate eyes. Sweet all over and wearing a baby-pink sparkly dress, which I thought, at the time, was the prettiest thing I'd ever seen a girl wear.

And that's when it hit me. I wasn't selfless, or good, or kind. I was selfish. I *liked* her. Had liked her from the moment I laid eyes on her. And I wanted *her* to realize it, too. See me being there instead of him as a sign—a signal to lose the fool boyfriend and get to know me better instead.

My palms were sweaty as I approached her. I put a hand on her shoulder, and when she turned around and saw that it was me and not him standing there in front of her, my hope quickly dwindled.

"He's not coming."

She said it as a statement, not a question. But I nodded anyway to confirm what she already knew. "He's not," I said. "But Lana, he's a cheater and a liar. You can do so much better than him."

And then, she looked up at me with the biggest, saddest eyes I've ever seen, and choked out the words, "Carter, I'm pregnant."

She found out the day after we caught him upstairs with that other girl. It was why she took him back all those weeks ago. She hadn't told anyone else, and didn't know what she was going to do. How she was going to make it work.

Seeing as I was completely unqualified and in no position to give her any advice whatsoever on her situation, all I could do was comfort her. Give her someone to lean on. I pulled her towards me and she buried her head in my chest and cried mascara tears all over my slightly crumpled suit as I stroked her hair.

When she eventually pulled away, she wiped her nose and sniffled. "Well, that's embarrassing. I've only met you twice and already managed to both puke and cry on you."

Desperate to make her smile again, I joked, "As long as you don't pee on me next, I'm okay with it."

It worked. Through her tears, she laughed and laughed, doing that weird snort thing she does. And I knew, in that moment, that I'd found my new favorite person. Somebody who could laugh at a terrible joke in the face of the worst, most painful moment imaginable.

That's Lana.

Tonight, as I stand on her doorstep with nervous anticipation pricking at my skin like needles, I feel like I've been transported back to the night of her homecoming dance. Only this time, we're grown, mature adults who might know each other better than we know ourselves.

And I'm wearing a tailor-made Armani tux in place of a too-small, thrift store suit. Which I'm sure is an improvement.

I shift the bouquet of wildflowers to my other hand. It's an eclectic collection of lilacs, garden roses, succulents, sweet peas and ranunculus, according to the florist. He did a great job putting together something that looked "beautiful but unique, tasteful but untamed" for me.

The door finally opens a few moments after I ring the bell, and I'm stunned into silence. Because standing here, staring at Lana Mae in that dress, I suddenly realize that I was a fool to think those feelings had ever gone away. I've been in love with her all this time. How could I have ever been anything but?

I mean, *look at her*.

I *definitely* don't want her like a best friend.

"What?" she asks as I drink her in, laughing awkwardly as her petite hands smooth over the front of her silky, slinky dress, which makes that pink dress from all those years ago pale in comparison. "Is it okay?"

I realize I'm staring, but I can't seem to tear my eyes away. Or pull my thoughts out of the gutter. Her dress clings to her body like a glove, accentuating her soft curves that are all *woman*. Her hair is pulled back to show off her delicate collarbones and long, graceful neck. But best of all, her beautiful face is... happy. Those plump lips of hers are parted and smiling, and her eyes, when they sweep over me, light up in a way that sparks something within me.

"It's way more than okay," I finally reply, my voice low and thick. "You look incredible."

"Thanks. You don't look so bad yourself." Her cheeks are pink, and she extends a hand to touch my clean-shaven jaw gently. "I don't think I've ever seen movie-star-Carter in the flesh before. I'm used to my Carter being scruffy and flannel-clad."

My Carter. That tiny two-letter word almost undoes me.

If only she knew that any and all versions of me share one thing in common: they're *all* hers.

And this version of *her* Carter has turned into a prepubescent schoolboy who has zero game and can't get a single word out. Case in point: in reply to her intimate, face-touching gesture, I thrust the oversized bouquet of wildflowers into her arms. "These are for you."

Her eyes go soft and wide as she looks at the flowers that I've practically just thrown at her, smooth operator that I am. "Thank you, CJ. I love them so much," she tells me with a huge smile. "I'm going to put them in water and we can go."

As she retreats into the house, Anthony appears at the door, smirking in satisfaction. "Isn't she a vision?"

"She is."

Anthony looks past my head and into the driveway, and his expression immediately sours. "For the love of all that is holy, Carter, you drove that old thing tonight? How do you expect to sweep a woman off her feet in that rustbucket? I'm all for vintage, but only the good kind."

I shake my head, laughing. "Ant, I—"

"Am a lost cause, I know," he finishes for me with a roll of his eyes.

"I was going to say that I like it. And I don't think Lana cares what I drive."

"But if she's not after your money, what could she *possibly* see in you?" he teases.

"I think she's into my massive ego that's constantly inflated by my compliment-ladling assistant."

Anthony snorts. "Happy to be of service."

Lana has a theory (which I've never debunked) that I have an automotive kink, but the truth is that I keep my Jeep as my primary vehicle in Atlanta because it was the first place she ever told me she loved me—platonically, of course. Those words coming out of her mouth as I drove her and baby Legs home from a postpartum checkup did something to my insides. Wallpapered them in sunshine and wholesome goodness. Every time I climb into my battered old SUV, even now, the distant echo of her words makes me smile.

But I don't tell Anthony this because the memory is so special to me. I selfishly want to keep it all to myself. Even if that makes him believe that I'm a cheapskate who won't shell out for a new ride despite my healthy bank balance.

"Ready to go?" Lana reappears, holding a gold-beaded clutch.

I offer her my arm and she takes it, her small hand slipping through my elbow and circling around my bicep. I like how her hands feel on me. And this close, I can breathe her in. She smells different tonight—the cherry blossom and vanilla shampoo she's been using for years mingles with an unfamiliar perfume that makes my head spin.

I can't remember the last time I so badly wanted to taste someone's skin.

Don't think there was a last time.

Anthony catches the pained looked on my face and grins wickedly. "You two have a good time tonight, you hear me?"

Lana smiles wide at him. "We'll see you there, right?"

"Of course." Anthony kisses her cheek. "But I had to say it now because I'm sure you'll both be so busy mingling at the party, you'll hardly have a second to spare for me." My assistant then looks at me and holds up his hand. Waggles his fingers. "Aren't you forgetting something? I brought a few options."

I shake my head. "Nah, man. I have it covered."

My smile stretches at the look of abject shock on Ant's usually smug face. For once, I've surprised *him*.

"What was that about?" Lan asks as I steer her down the driveway and towards my Jeep. The evening air is thick and muggy, perfumed with damp heat and the smell of impending rain.

"I'll show you when we get there."

I open the passenger door for her, and she scrambles in, hiking her dress up as she does so. "Damn thing might look good but I forgot to check if I could sit in it," she mutters with a laugh.

But I can't reply because my mouth is full of sawdust looking at the smooth, tan thigh that's currently on show through the dress's deep leg slit.

Lan follows my eyes and hastily rearranges her dress. "Oops, sorry."

I quickly (reluctantly) avert my eyes from those long, slim legs of hers. "I'm the one who's sorry. I forgot you were my *fake* wife there for a moment."

She grins. "Well you're very good at getting into character."

Like I need to get into character right now.

"Let's just hope that I never have to play a serial killer." I grin back. "*Pizza Face Returns.*"

Her laugh fills the air as I duck around to the driver's side of the Jeep. Inside, the smell of her perfume is headier, and the air is thick with an unspoken tension that my Pizza Face joke didn't seem to lessen.

"Need any help getting into character yourself?" I turn the keys in the ignition and the Jeep sputters reluctantly to life. *Pretend everything's normal and everything will be.*

"Definitely. I'm pretty concerned about how I could ever pretend to be in love with a handsome, rich, funny movie star."

"Quite the difficult assignment," I reply. "Would it help if I give you my character's backstory?"

A smile. "Maybe. And if this is going to be a romance worth its salt, it's going to need a meet-cute and a grand gesture."

I turn out of Lana's cul-de-sac and lean back in my seat. Inside, my heart is pounding, but on the outside, I'm fully calm and composed. No cracks in the façade.

"Well, what if Carter—my character in this fake engagement romance, by the way—met his best friend Lana Mae at a frat party a decade ago and he thought that she was the prettiest girl he'd ever met. And then, she called him insufferable and he couldn't believe his luck: she was funny too! Carter wasn't deterred by her insults though, and was confident that he could win her over because, at nineteen years old, he already had serious game."

"Did he now?"

"Totally. He had a shared room in a frat house with this awesome tiny twin bed that was too small for him and sheets that definitely weren't changed enough. Wore excellent quantities of Axe body spray. Had an affinity for cheap keg beer."

"Wow, how could Lana—she's my character—not have loved him? He sounds like such a catch."

"I know." I flick my eyes sideways at her and she's laughing, like this really is a made-up story and not an account of the whole truth. "He even had this gross old Jeep with duct-taped door handles. Can you imagine?"

Lana runs her hand over the duct tape on the passenger door handle. "Ah! There's the dealbreaker. Never trust a man with duct tape on his car."

"Or anywhere about his person, one would think." I look over as I say this, and our eyes catch long enough for us to share a goofy smile.

"So what happened after Carter showed Lana his A-game and attempted to woo her with his duct-taped Jeep?" she asks.

I breathe out slowly. "Life got in the way. Lana wasn't in a place to date, so Carter respected this boundary. They became friends instead. Best friends. Until years later, when Lana finally started dating again and Carter begged her to give him a chance. Plot twist: she turned out to be head over heels for Carter too, and she said yes. He seized his opportunity and put a ring on it ASAP."

I pull up to a red light in time to hear her sharp intake of breath. My palms become clammy.

"Ha," Lana says, fiddling with the clasp on her bag.

When she finally turns to look at me, her neck and chest are flushed and her breathing is labored.

Just like it was when she shivered at my touch in the kitchen after our first engagement party.

Just like it was when she peeked at me in my underwear this morning, face beetroot red behind her shaky hands.

The spark of hope that's been flickering in me ignites.

Because all these things I'm finally letting myself feel for the first time in years? I'm starting to wonder if she might feel them, too.

22

LANA MAE

I think he knows.

Frick. Frick. Double freaking frickety frick.

Because what was *that*? We were just sitting here in the car, joking about getting into character to pull off our fake engagement charade for the evening, and the next moment, Carter's spouting some story about how I was the prettiest girl he'd ever met, but respecting my "boundary" by just being my friend—and then he finished by saying that, in a huge plot twist, I turned out to be in love with him, too.

I know we were technically joking around about our "characters" for the evening, but what he said felt... pointed. And the only conclusion I can come to is that he's onto me. He knows that I've been harboring very real feelings for him this entire time and is letting me know, in his way, that he'll be sensitive to this in case I get the wrong idea about our little arrangement and start reading into it.

Which, again, proves how well he knows me, because we've only been doing this fake engagement thing for a few days, and already, my mind is blurring the lines between what's real and what's not. What's true and what's for show.

So much for fake dating Carter as a way to get him out of my system. I currently feel more wrapped up in him than one of those gag Christmas gifts with a million layers of paper and tape that you have to pry open using your teeth like a feral wildcat.

I mean, the man's so good at playing his part that he was looking at me earlier like he wanted to devour me. He even confessed that he'd gotten so into the role that he forgot it was fake for a moment. What's a girl to do but physically respond to that?

I swallow, hard, and look away from the scenery passing by outside to see him smiling at me, the corners of his eyes crinkled. I haven't been able to say anything since uttering that lame "ha!" a few minutes ago. I mean, what am I *supposed* to say in this situation.

And why on earth is Carter now looking at me like he's a child who's high on too much cotton candy?

"Open the glove box."

"What?"

"That thing I said I'd show you when we got to the party. We're almost there." He turns off the 19 and onto East Andrews. "It's in the glove box."

The wooly mammoth-sized elephant in the car momentarily forgotten, I flip open the small door and pull out a velvet ring box.

Oh my giddy goodness.

"Is this...?"

Those blue eyes move all over my face, and he nods. "Open it."

I crack open the ring box and suck in a breath. Nestled on the little blue velvet cushion is the most stunning ring I've ever seen in my life. A flawless emerald-cut diamond sits atop two tiny, delicate, diamond-studded gold bands that come to meet at the back. I've literally never seen anything so beautiful.

"Holy sh—"

"It looked like you." Carter smiles at the look on my face. "Of all the rings I've ever seen, this one looks like it belongs on *your* finger."

My heart is practically hammering out of my chest. "It's gorgeous. But you know I can't accept this, Carter. It's way too much."

"You need to have a ring, Lan. Can't have everyone thinking I'm a terrible fiancé," he teases, eyes glinting as we turn into his property and drive down the long, densely treed driveway. "A violent brute *and* a cheapskate? Not a good look."

"Nobody thinks you're a brute," I say automatically, then look at the ring again, my head spinning. "But you can't spend this kind of money on me. This ring must cost more than my house."

"Nah," Carter says as he comes to a stop at the top of the driveway and kills the engine. The courtyard in front of his house is all lit up, and there are staff in full black tie attire darting here, there and everywhere, adding last minute touches to the party preparations. Elena is in the middle of it all, clutching a clipboard and barking orders.

Carter doesn't even seem to notice the hive of activity surrounding us though. Instead, his focus is wholly on me as he gently takes the box from my hands and extracts the ring. He reaches for my left hand, his skin warm and his fingers calloused. The graze of them over my knuckles turns my bones to jelly.

"I knew you'd freak out if I bought you a real ring, so this one's just an imitation. A prop. Keiko from the wardrobe department of my last movie hooked me up."

"Oh." I let out a huge sigh of relief. "In that case, thank

you. It's perfect. More beautiful than any real diamond ring I've ever seen. And I don't have to worry about accidentally flushing it down the toilet, or having Harry Styles eat it then barf it back up or something."

I'm rewarded with my favorite smile: his dimple-popping one. "And with that beautifully romantic mental image... Lana Mae Donovan, will you do me the very real honor of being my fake wife?"

"Absofreakinglutely."

Carter slides the diamond ring onto my finger. It fits (gosh, this thing is heavy, what are fake diamonds made of?) and I look at my hand in awe. "Woah."

"Perfect," he says softly. "Ready to do this thing, Mrs. Callahan-to-be?"

Honestly? I have no idea.

But the show must go on.

So I brush a stray lock of hair out of my eyes, pushing away any lingering anxious thoughts about tonight along with it. I smile. "Born ready."

"Thank you so much for being here tonight, I appreciate it." I pull my work friend, Imani, into a big hug, and when I step back, she's laughing. It's a couple of hours later, and I'm standing in Carter's backyard—if you can even call this vast expanse of space a "yard"—still in absolute awe of the party unfolding before me.

A scene that's happening in *my honor*.

"Oh please, I wouldn't have missed it for the world," she twinkles, fluttering her fingers at the scene surrounding us. "It's like something out of a billionaire romance in this yard right now."

"Or *The Great Gatsby*," I agree.

"Totally. This is all going to feel like a dream come Monday morning when we're back at work."

"I'll say."

We chat for a few more minutes, before Imani jerks her head in the direction of a waiter carrying canapes. "Welp, I'm sure you have a ton of people to chat to, and I should probably go find Jared. I think he's eaten his bodyweight in caviar blinis already."

"Sounds good," I laugh, and as she floats off, instead of making more polite small talk with guests, I'm still for a minute, allowing myself a silent moment to take it all in.

The gardens of Carter's huge property are decked out with soft, twinkling fairy lights that sparkle overhead and along the treed perimeter. Incredible floral arrangements—white roses and deep green ivy, stunning but unable to hold a candle to the wildflower bouquet Carter brought me earlier—are strategically placed around the property.

There's even an archway swathed in hundreds of roses with a swing beneath it. It's been a hotspot with the Insta crowd this evening.

A massive marquee is erected over the swimming pool, which is covered by a lit-up perspex dance floor. Within the tent, a six-piece band plays instrumental contemporary classics, and waiters mill around carrying trays loaded with champagne flutes and caviar blinis. At the center of the lawn sits a grand table with a behemoth, six-tier red velvet cake frosted with a million sugar flowers and handcrafted lovebirds.

I'm still standing here, gaping like a guppy, when Mindy sidles up beside me, gorgeous in her teal, backless dress. "It's nice, but I don't think it beats the butt cake."

"Agreed." I gesture my champagne flute towards the

thing. "Dare you to give it a hack job heart tattoo when nobody's looking."

"Challenge accepted." Mindy holds up her own flute of what looks like sparkling water. "But only if you can figure out how to get that stupid dance floor off the pool so I can start the skinny dipping and this party can *really* get going."

I'm so freaking glad that she's here. That *all* my favorite people are here for me tonight. Carter and I made our entrance earlier to thunderous applause and a champagne toast. Then, we mingled, kissing cheeks and shaking hands and thanking people for coming. I was so grateful that, among so many strange faces (and familiar faces that belong to famous strangers), I could hug and welcome Mindy, Luke, Annie, Liam, and Imani and her husband. And Allegra, of course, who's currently busy buttering up a deeply wrinkled ex-Hollywood starlet wearing a fox stole and sucking on an empty cigarette holder.

"I already tried jumping up and down on it. That dance floor ain't going anywhere."

"Boo." Mindy pouts, then her mouth drops open and she grabs my hand. "Wait wait wait... what in the crown jewels is this freaking rock on your finger?!"

I look down at my hand, which is still in her death clutches. "I know, isn't it amazing? Fake, thank goodness. But looks the part, don't you think?"

"It looks like a literal princess ring from a fairytale," Mindy declares. "Show that thing off, lady. There's going to be about a million girls across America wanting to claw your eyes out with jealousy this time tomorrow. So you may as well *enjoy* this moment. Flash that rock, and let the world know that he's yours and they don't stand a chance."

Mindy's words make my stomach twinge, and I recall the conversation Carter and I had in the Jeep. If he really *does* know that I have more-than-friendly feelings for him, and he really *was* trying to let me down gently, then this moment in time and this fake engagement really is the closest I'll ever get. And if this whole arrangement isn't helping me overcome my feelings for Carter, well... maybe Mindy's right—the least I can do is make the most of this time I have living this crazy fairytale.

I'm reminded of that old saying, *Don't cry because it's over, smile because it happened.*

For so long, I worked with Dr. Lemay in our sessions to heal from the past. To let go of resentment and hurt when it came to my sad memories. To be able to look back at them without feeling pain. And I did it. I worked through it all, and I freaking did it. And now, maybe what I need to do is create memories that will always make me smile when I look back on them. Real romance or not. And right now, standing in this beautiful party, wearing this beautiful dress —feeling beautiful—I realize that I have the power to do just that. Tonight is an opportunity for me to carpe diem the crap out of this party.

I give Mindy a sudden spontaneous hug. "I love you. I'm so glad you married my brother."

She gives me the side-eye. "Love you too, weirdo. And me too, mostly."

I'm still laughing as I excuse myself to find Carter so we can continue our mingling efforts. I spot him over by the bar, sipping out of a crystal tumbler as he talks to two former James Bonds, both of whom I was introduced to earlier and discreetly fan-girled over.

But, let me tell you. Carter Callahan in a tuxedo? Yeah, he puts any James Bond in the corner.

He sees me coming, because of course he does. No matter what I've been doing this evening—who I've been talking to or whatever he's doing—I find those gorgeous azure eyes trained on me every time I look his way. Like he's tracking my every movement, action and emotion, determined to make sure that I'm doing okay.

"Hi, love," he says when I get close enough, slipping an arm around me and pulling me into him like he did at Target. And just like at Target, his sexy, woodsy, clean scent envelops me. I relax into his side like I've been doing it all my life, and he trails a casual hand softly down my bare arm, his fingertips leaving fire in their wake.

"Excuse us," he says to the Bonds, then unwinds his arm, takes me by the hand, and leads me across the garden

"You didn't have to leave your conversation for me." I smile up at him, trying to ignore the fact that my entire body is tingling from his touch.

"It was painfully boring," Carter replies with a twinkle in his eye. "You saved me. How's your night going?"

"Good. I can't believe Elena did all this; this party is out of this world. But I do admit, my feet hurt."

Carter laughs. "Well, no fear. Let me teach you a little about the ways of Hollywood parties. There's this little thing called the afterparty, when the cameras shut off and everyone gets barefoot and reckless."

"Sounds like my kind of party. But Allegra's here, I'm going to have to take her home..."

"I arranged for Mindy and Luke to take her back to their place before any craziness goes down. Mindy's happy to bow out early seeing as she's not drinking tonight."

"Thanks. That was really thoughtful of you," I say steadily. Secretly, my whole body is coiled tight at the thought of a late night out with Carter, no cares or worries.

"There you two are!" Elena's crisp voice punctuates the air as she marches up, tip-tapping in her stilettos. They're much higher than my heels, but I have the feeling Elena is the sort of person whose feet never hurt.

"Hey, Elena." I smile warmly. "I was just saying to Carter that you put on an incredible party."

She looks momentarily touched and surprised, but she swiftly thanks me and moves onto the next order of business. "I have a photo op for you two set up on the dance floor. The band is going to play a love song, or Ed Sheeran is going to come out and sing for you or something. I don't remember that exact detail. But way more importantly, there are photographers milling around the tent, ready to capture the perfect "candid" of the couple in love. And I'm not talking tabloid rags, I'm talking all the reputable news sources and entertainment outlets."

Wide-eyed, I nod as she talks, brain snagging on the fact that Ed Sheeran's presence isn't considered an important detail to someone like Elena. Or Carter, who looks like he's barely even listening.

"Got it?" Elena concludes.

"Got it," I reply.

"Great. Be on the dance floor in ten minutes."

She departs in a cloud of perfume. I turn to Carter, who, like he has been all night, is already looking at me. "You okay with all this?" he asks.

"All in a night's work for me." I nod, then take a deep breath. "And anyway, I've been thinking—"

"Oh, that's always dangerous."

I smack him in the arm and he wraps my hand in his, pulling me towards him.

"Tell me what's going on in that beautiful head of yours."

"Well," I start nervously, biting my bottom lip. "I've been thinking that our engagement is not going to look very realistic if we don't kiss."

Carter looks momentarily surprised before a slow smiles creeps over his face. "Oh yeah?"

His blue eyes are glinting with... something... but I don't want to be distracted by that right now, so I spit out the rest of what I have to say before I lose my nerve. Carpe diem, right? "And we need tonight to look realistic because Elena went to so much trouble setting this all up. Plus, this is meant to be practice for me anyway, and at some point, I'm going to have to kiss someone for real, so I should probably practice that, too. Let's face it, I haven't been so much as touched by a man in, like, ten years, so I'd appreciate a trial run. And um, yeah. Forget it, it was a dumb idea..."

I finally manage to stop my utterly humiliating ramble long enough to try and pull my hand out of Carter's so I can go jump in a hole somewhere. Instead, Carter catches me gently but firmly by both of my wrists. Holds on steadily as his eyes bore down on me and he smiles. "Lana Mae Donovan, are you trying to tell me that you want to kiss me?"

The scalding embarrassment is back, tenfold. Of course I want to kiss him... but I cannot believe I approached the subject like this. What is wrong with me? Kissing isn't even a subject you approach anyway, is it? It's just something people do.

Well, normal people do. All the time.

"Yes? Maybe? I don't know, I just thought..." I stutter, entirely flustered at this point.

"Okay."

"What?" I'm shocked by his calm demeanor.

"I think you're right." His smile grows wider. "A kiss would make everything look *way* more believable, and a trial-run kiss should be part of your trial-run engagement, no?"

My stomach nearly boils over at the fact that we are *actually* having this conversation. For a plan that we might *actually* put in motion in mere minutes. A plan that involves me kissing Carter Callahan.

His eyes level on mine. I muster up a confident smile. "Exactly. Plus, what's a kiss between friends?"

"That's a great question," Carter replies. "I guess we'll find out in just a few minutes."

"I guess so!" I squeak, simultaneously elated and terrified.

I am not ready.

But, at the same time, so ready. Because positivity and carpe diem and all that.

As we move towards the dance floor for the photo op, Carter seems completely cool and collected, his hand placed tantalizingly on the small of my back when a legendary director stops us to congratulate us on our upcoming nuptials.

But for all of his bravado, as soon as we step onto that dance floor, Carter's behavior changes. He moves towards me slowly, at first. Tentatively.

A hummingbird might as well have flown into my chest cavity. My palms are prickling with sweat as Carter comes to a stop right in front of me.

He looks at me from under his eyelashes. Gives me that lopsided little half-smile that most women would think is entirely confident and self-assured, but I know better. I know it's the one he gives when he's unsure. Bashful. Not in control.

And somehow, this makes me relax. This is Carter's life, not mine—with a million flashing lights and clanging sounds and cameras pointing right at us—but he's as nervous as I am.

"Hey," he says. His blue gaze is so piercing, I can feel it moving over my body, but his hands are still at his sides. "You ready?"

I puff out my bottom lip and blow a big breath upwards,

attempting to blow some stray hairs out of my eyes as I hold his stare. "Yes?"

He extends a hand to tuck the pesky hairs behind my ear. Lets it linger there for a moment. "Don't worry, Donovan. We got this."

And then, his arms are around me. With one swift tug, our bodies are flush together, his broad, hard chest pressed up against me.

A stifled whimper slips out of my mouth as I try not to inhale too much of his dizzyingly warm, clean scent.

Acting, Lana. We're acting.

Well... he's acting. I'm trying my best to breathe over here.

I coil my arms around his neck, and my diamond ring glints with the flashes of the cameras. Carter presses his forehead to mine. Skin on skin. His fingertips follow a path along my spine. Fire on fire.

My whole body stills under his touch and he shakes his head against mine.

"Don't stop," he murmurs as his fingers tighten on my back, gently guiding me from side to side until our bodies are moving together. In sync. We're on a dance floor, being watched from every angle, but the world beyond Carter is blurring. Slipping further and further away with each movement, each touch, each caress. My pulse is jumping all over my skin, and his breath is as jagged as mine.

"You sure you're ready?" he whispers, his voice throaty, his hands moving to cup my face.

Hell yes. Hell no.

How could I ever be ready for this?

His eyes lock on mine and I see heat crackling there. Someone give this guy his Oscar, already!

"Because you don't have to do this," he continues. "We don't have to do this. Just say the word and I'll make it stop."

The thought of stopping this right now fills my body with boiling outrage. Because all I can think is that I need to know what those lips feel like on mine, or I might actually, literally die. (Melodramatic, remember?)

"Ready as I'll ever be," I manage to croak. "Let's do this."

And then, his mouth is moving towards mine.

Closer, closer. Painfully, tantalizingly, beautifully closer...

"Great, thank you very much!"

Elena's barking voice shatters the moment. It's quickly followed by the abrupt sound of her clapping her clipboard against her other hand. She's addressing the photographers, who I'd all but forgotten were there in my Carter haze.

"I appreciate you all being here tonight on such short notice," she goes on.

Meanwhile, I'm struggling to catch my breath. My head is reeling from what almost just happened as Carter and I pull apart. Carter looks equally pained, his pupils dilated, his breath catching as he stares at Elena in what looks like total incomprehension.

She throws him a smirk and says quietly enough for only us to hear, "Figured since you're not *really* together, I'd save you the trouble of a *real* kiss."

23

CARTER

I'm a tsunami stopped in its tracks mere inches from reaching the shore.

She was finally *right there*, in my arms, breathing jaggedly and trembling as she looked up at me with big, dark eyes that were screaming for me to touch her, kiss her, taste her. Steal that breath away altogether and claim her lips as *mine*.

And then, Elena just had to jump in and "save us" at the exact wrong moment. Although, judging by the smirk on her face, she knew what she was doing—playing with us, having a little fun of her own. It was the opposite of fun for me; getting cut off like that was almost physically painful. My heart is still beating too fast, my skin too warm.

So, I do what I've been doing for years now and stuff down my emotions. Paste on a pleasant expression, even as my hands stiffen by my sides.

"I need a drink," I say lightly, like we're standing around chatting about the weather. "You too, Lan?"

She looks up at me with those liquid dark eyes and shakes her head. "I think I'll run to the bathroom first."

And with that, she's off, legging it out of the tent and

across the lawn. She looked like she was going to do the same exact thing right after she proposed that we kiss.

But I couldn't let her take off after suggesting *that*.

I'm still on a high from hearing those words come out of her mouth. Even if it is just for practice on her end, the thought of kissing Lana Mae in that moment was almost too tempting to bear ... but what's she thinking now? Everything in me wants to run after her. But everything in me also knows that I need to give her space—give us *both* space—to process the insane fireworks of whatever *that* was.

Or, *almost* was, I should say.

I turn to Elena and arch a brow. "Really with the 'save you the trouble' B.S.?"

My manager smirks. "Please. You don't want your first kiss to be for the cameras. You want it to be special, private. All yours, without the world bearing witness."

I'm first taken aback by her surprisingly sincere response, and then by how *right* she is.

If Lana wants me to kiss her, I'll do it properly. Take my time and wait for the perfect opportunity where it's just me and her, in our world. Together. No matter what it means or what it doesn't, the least I can give her is that.

"Thanks, Elena. That's actually kind of... sweet of you."

"Don't be ridiculous, Carter. I'm not being sweet, I'm being practical." She snorts at me before whisking a very full flute of champagne off of a nearby waiter's tray without spilling a single drop. "And have I mentioned that you're looking flushed tonight? You sure you're taking those herbal supplements?"

"Nope," I respond cheerfully.

Elena sighs a very, very deep sigh. "For the *last time*, you really must start thinking about ——Oh Harriet, darling!" She suddenly beams as she spots a familiar face over my shoulder. "What was I saying? Ah, it doesn't matter. Duty calls."

And with that, Elena rushes off with barely a parting glance. I roll my eyes at my easily distracted, undeniably practical agent's back before making my way back to the bar, where I order a whiskey. Neat.

Because hell yeah, I'm flushed.

Luke comes sauntering up, the top button of his dress shirt undone and his eyes a little glazed. "Hey." He hiccups. "Great party. 'Speshly"—*hic!*—"the shrimp"—*hic!*— "cocktail."

The guy definitely looks like he's enjoyed more cocktail than shrimp tonight.

"Thanks," I reply. "I had precisely nothing to do with any of it."

Luke laughs and points at me with his beer bottle. "Hey, now that we're family, can you tell me"—*hic!*—"washhhh it Pine?"

I smirk. "I have no idea what you're talking about."

"Hemsworth, then? Or Pratt?"

Fueled by my silence, Luke gasps. "Not Captain America?! He's a *national treasure*."

"I'm under NDA, dude," I say with a laugh, shaking my head. "My lips are sealed."

"But you told my sister?"

"Yes," I acquiesce. "I told your sister."

Luke smiles and looks across the party. Points his beer so aggressively that a spurt of dark liquid sloshes out. "You wan' know something else?"—*hic!*—"I haven't seen Lan this happy in *aaaages*."

I follow the bottle to see that Lana has come out of the bathroom and is now standing on the patio, chatting with a best selling author. I smile at the sight. Her face is animated, sparkling. She *does* look happy, and I can't help but wonder how much of that has to do with me. Whether it has anything to do with what almost just happened between us.

"I'm glad to hear that," I tell Luke. "She makes me pretty damn happy, too."

"Dunno why you're talking to"—*hic!*—"me then, dude. You should go talk to her."

"True. I like you plenty, but your sister is way prettier than you are." I clap Luke on the back. "Maybe we should get you some water before I leave."

It takes me ten minutes to get Luke a bottle of water and a couple of Advil from the medicine cabinet in one of my many bathrooms. Mindy's already gone home with Allegra, so I order Luke a cab and wait for it to show up. I make sure he's safely in the car and the cabbie has the right address so he doesn't end up in, like, Augusta or something. Which may or may not be based on not one but several true stories involving Luke and beer.

I'm feeling like a pretty good fake brother-in-law-to-be by the time I amble back to the party, where the "barefoot and reckless" portion of the evening seems to be well underway.

The press have packed up and gone home, the band has been replaced by a semi-famous DJ, and the dance floor in the marquee is crowded with a throng of sweaty bodies and flashing strobe lights. I spot Elena chugging a Jager Bomb with an NFL player, Anthony cozying up to the drummer from the band, and Annie and Liam dancing in a surprisingly provocative fashion, attached at the mouth without a care in the world.

And then, there's Lana Mae in the middle of it all, shoes kicked off, hair falling out of its updo. The sequins on her dress catch the light, and her eyes are closed, head thrown back in bliss and celebration.

Pure perfection.

A Hollywood playboy who actually deserves his "hit 'em and quit 'em" reputation is eyeing her like she's a tasty snack, his eyes roaming over her face and body hungrily. A swift shot of jealousy courses through me, unleashing my inner caveman mentality: *Mine. My wife.*

The guy spots me and winks. I reply with an absolute death glare, cold and unwavering, until he backs away slowly, step by step, like she's a bomb that's about to go off.

Yup, that's it. Back off, bozo. Call me Borat if you must, but this woman is definitely MY wife.

When he's at a suitable distance (i.e. all the way across the party and out of my eyeshot), I stride across the marquee. I'm a man on a mission with one goal in mind: to slide my arms around my fake bride-to-be, pull her close until she's pressed against me, and dance the night away with her.

And that's exactly what we do.

24

LANA MAE

We Donovan siblings aren't big on traditions, but we do have a couple that we always honor.

The first is Chinese food on Christmas, which has been a constant since our mom passed away almost ten years ago.

The second is... softball. We gather in a local park once a month on a Sunday afternoon for a family softball game. Though it usually involves much more heckling and laughing and talking than any actual softball playing.

The tradition was born a few months ago, when Annie and Liam showed up after a vacation to Mexico and announced that they'd eloped. Which was rude. As penance, Luke, Mindy and I teamed up and insisted that *we* organize the wedding party they were planning to throw for the friends and family who hadn't gotten to be there for the big day. After a lot of wheedling, Liam and Annie acquiesced. And because the happy couple had pretty much fallen in love at a company softball tournament, we thought it would be hilarious to throw them a softball party for their wedding bash.

And hilarious, it was.

An entire crew of formally dressed wedding goers

engaged in one riotous game together. And of course, we put the newlyweds on opposing teams. Annie sliding for home base in a white, floor-length dress in a passionate effort to win against her new husband was the funniest thing I've seen in forever.

Our little family of siblings and spouses always gather at that very same park for a smaller, much less chaotic version of the wedding softball bash, and today, everyone arrives a little worse for wear. Luke's wearing dark sunglasses and clutching a bottle of blue Gatorade with a shaky hand. Liam and Annie, meanwhile, are not only looking exhausted, but sporting matching guilty smirks which makes me think that they did it in the bushes or something last night.

Which does not bear thinking about, especially in my current delicate state.

I only had a couple glasses of champagne, so I'm not hungover, but I *am* exhausted. My feet ache from dancing, and I'm pretty sure there's still about a hundred bobby pins in my bird's nest hair that I didn't bother to wash, nor brush, this morning. Even Allegra is drooping, tired and a little cranky from what was a super late night for her.

Mindy is the only one who looks perky and fresh. "Come on, chop chop!" she calls, clapping her hands as the rest of us grumble and settle ourselves on camping chairs. "Let's make hay while the sun shines."

Liam looks at her like he would happily kill her. He points towards some food trucks gathered in the parking lot across the park. "First, coffee."

"I second that." Annie agrees.

"I want churros!" Legs chimes in, eyeing the Mexican food truck.

"Mmphf," is Luke's contribution.

I blink up at my oldest brother angelically. "You sure you want coffee, Lukey? Maybe you'd prefer some sushi?

Or really runny eggs with hollandaise sauce? Or wait, how about a platter of raw oysters... you know, the ones that have that slimy texture like snot?"

In response to my hilarity, my brother grabs the back of my camping chair and tips it over.

"Eeeek!" I tumble to the ground.

With a satisfied nod, Luke turns on his heel and makes his way to the coffee truck with Liam, Annie, and Legs in tow.

Nothing like sibling love, right?

Mindy hauls me up, cackling with laughter, and we sink down in our chairs.

"I can't believe you married him," I grouch.

"Oh, relax," Mindy says with a laugh. "You know he'll feel bad and come back with a latte for you."

"He better." I close my eyes, arching my face towards the sunshine. "And hey, thanks again for taking Legs last night."

"No problem. You have as much fun as Luke did?"

"I don't know if anyone had as much fun as Luke did," I say lightly. But even as I speak, my mind fills with memories of the intense look on Carter's face as he lowered his lips towards mine last night. Quickly followed by his tortured expression when our kiss didn't happen...

And I may be entirely imagining it, but I could have sworn his hand flexed—Mr. Darcy style—when Elena interrupted our moment.

Which, if it did happen, is quite literally too sexy to even comprehend.

"Girl, don't downplay your night," Mindy admonishes. "I might've been boring and went home early, but Annie told me all about you ripping up the dance floor with that hunk of man meat fiancé of yours."

My stomach clenches tightly. After our interrupted

moment, Carter didn't try to kiss me again, but for the rest of the night, his hands were on me. Pulling me towards him, trailing over my arms, across my shoulders, and down my spine as we moved with each other, dancing close, our bodies in perfect rhythm. The man is a phenomenal dancer, and I was a more than willing dance partner.

"Fake fiancé," I correct.

Mindy waves a hand. "Details!"

"There's not much to say."

"I'm calling B.S. I think you had more fun than you've ever had in your life."

She's not wrong. And the thing is, nothing about last night *felt* fake.

Carter really is an incredible actor. A man of many talents, it seems.

I swallow down my recollections of last night, then lean over and pat Mindy's arm. "I feel like we've done nothing but talk about me lately. How're you doing? You don't have to tell me anything, but I noticed that you weren't drinking last night, and you haven't had any wine at my place the last couple of times you've been over..."

Mindy and Luke have been trying for a baby for awhile now, but it hasn't been going smoothly for them. It always baffles me that some people (me) can get pregnant after having sex precisely once, where other people can try and try and nothing happens.

I'm hopeful that her not drinking means that there's some good news, but Mindy shakes her head against the back of her chair. "We weren't going to say anything yet because of everything going on with you and Carter, but we've decided to try IVF. You don't have to give up alcohol right away, but I'm doing everything I can to help our chances. I've started giving myself the shots." She laughs abruptly. "Well, Luke's giving me the shots. But he hates hurting me, so he always closes his eyes, which freaks me out to no end."

My heart goes out to my sister-in-law. I take her hand and squeeze it. "You're going to make a great mom one day, Min. I know you are."

"Just like you." She squeezes back.

"That means a lot," I tell her. And it does.

Because becoming a mother at seventeen? Not exactly what I had envisioned for my life. Especially after the loss of my own mom and the guidance she provided.

Thanks to her, the first few months with baby Legs weren't that bad. She kept me sane and stable through all the sleepless nights, and latching difficulties, and constant fear of peeing myself as my pelvic floor (very) slowly recovered. She reassured me that she was proud of me, always. Proud that I'd made her a grandmother, even if it was accidental. She made me believe that I could still achieve the things that would make my daughter proud of me, too.

And then, one day, she was gone. A freak illness took her life way too soon. Allegra was barely six months old.

At first, my grief took the form of numbness. A dulling of my senses as I went through the motions of working with Luke and Liam to organize a funeral, trying to keep up with what the lawyers were saying about our mom's financial situation (selling our family home was the only way we were able to pay everything off), and thanking countless people I didn't care about for coming to pay their respects.

And then, it was over. The urn of her ashes was placed in a cemetery, and the well-wishers stopped calling. Luke went back to work and Liam started job and apartment hunting in the area.

That's when it all became real.

That's when the nightmares started.

Anxiety and depression hit me like a ton of bricks, to

the point where, some days, going outside was hard. Other days, it was impossible. I was at Walmart once, Legs strapped to my body in a carrier, and suddenly the edges of the store became blurry and I started feeling like the walls were closing in.

I set down a basket full of unpaid merchandise, ran to my car, and sat there for forty-five minutes, trying to breathe while Legs shrieked and screamed.

That evening, Carter found me lying in bed, crying my heart out. We'd become close since the night he showed up at my homecoming dance. He'd been there for me as I went through my pregnancy, and I found myself relying on his non-judgmental, smiling presence as my bump grew. We hung out when we could (between his college classes and auditions), and when my mother died, he was the first person I called.

As the crowd of well-wishers subsided, he kept turning up to keep me company.

Sometimes we'd talk. Sometimes cook. We'd often watch movies—comedies, action flicks, sci-fi, horror, but never anything sad or romantic. I'd curl up on the couch under a blanket and Carter would sprawl on the rug next to a cooing, gurgling Legs and her activity gym.

Over those months, he became the closest person to me in the world. And though I still missed my mom terribly, he calmed my anxiety and filled so much of the painful void from her loss. He supported me, believed in me, and helped me be the best person and mom I could be.

He does the same for me today. Calms my anxiety. To the point where being fake engaged to him feels less stressful than the simple act of having dinner with any other man.

Which is a little mind-blowing.

"Do you think you want more kids someday?" Mindy

asks, startling me from my thoughts. Then, she says, "With Carter?"

"What?!"

A smirk. "You heard me."

"We were talking about you and Luke. Not me and Carter."

"Nah, I wanna be nosy and ask you invasive personal questions."

"Min, I have no idea if he even wants kids to begin with."

"'Course he does. He looks at you like he's dying to put a baby in you at all times."

"Mindy!"

"Just sayin'."

I look at my left hand and twist the diamond ring on my finger around and around. "Carter is one of the most important people in the world to me, but this fake engagement thing is all an act for him. If anything, I'm worried that I'll blur the lines of this whole thing and start thinking it's real when it's fake. And then, it'll be over and he'll leave again."

"Lana Mae, that man absolutely adores you, fake engaged or not. He's not *that* good of an actor—nobody could possibly fake the way he looks at you."

"Even if that was true, it wouldn't matter," I reply, still twisting my ring. "His job, his life... they're thousands of miles away."

"But I bet he'd move back for you in a heartbeat."

"I'd never want him to give up who he is for me. That's ridiculous."

"Your job doesn't make you who you are, dummy." She rolls her eyes in a very *duh* manner that I'm not sure I appreciate. "I'm sure he'd stay for you, if you asked him to."

And there it is. The sting of the next memory—him moving to LA—makes my chest constrict.

The thing is, he already left. And I'll keep on encouraging him to pursue his dreams, because that's what friends do. I'd never hold him back.

"I felt bad and got you a latte."

I look over my shoulder to see Luke walking our way. Allegra is trotting alongside him while stuffing a huge churro in her mouth, and Annie and Liam are hanging back a bit, holding hands, whispering, and giggling—yes my big, tattooed, macho brother is *giggling*—about something.

"Told ya," says Mindy.

"Thanks, Lukey." I accept the delicious beverage and inhale the coffee scent. "Mmmm."

"Also got you this." He throws a newspaper down on my lap.

"Um, thanks, but I'm not really a big *USA Today* reader."

He smirks at me. "Turn to the entertainment section."

With a slight frown, I do as he says.

And *ho-ly,* there we are.

An almost full-page photograph of Carter and me, dancing for the photographers last night. Our faces are mere inches apart, and the look on Carter's face is, well, *devastating.*

He's staring at me like he's looking at the most beautiful thing in the world. Like I'm priceless. Cherished. It's an expression of such abject love and tenderness, a literal chill runs through my body.

"Holy hell," I say.

"I KNOW!" Luke yells. "Literally cost more than my brand new car."

"Wait, what?"

My brother rolls his eyes. "Third line down, slowpoke."

And that's when I see the words "custom-made, ethically sourced, three carat diamond ring from Tiffany."

I look down at my hand. Could this beautiful rock on my finger be the real freaking thing?

Whoa.

"Whoa," Annie says the word out loud, her straw lolling out of her mouth, and for a moment, I think she's reading my mind.

But then, I notice that she's staring across the park, slightly starry-eyed.

"Take a picture, it'll last longer," Liam grumbles.

"I'm *sorry*," Annie laments. "I had his poster on my wall in college. This is still weird for me."

I follow her gaze, and there he is. Carter in motion, jogging across the park and laughingly calling to Legs as he tosses a frisbee her way. He looks like sheer perfection—long and lean and muscular, hair tousled and full lips curved in a smile. Wayfarer sunglasses hide his eyes, but I'm sure they're gleaming.

"You made it!" Luke calls, all jolly all of a sudden.

"You invited Carter?" I squeak, frantically patting my bird's nest hair.

"Um, if you mean 'did I invite the newest member of our family to our family softball game', then yes. Yes I did." Luke looks at me as if to say *duh*.

"But..." I protest, still staring at Carter. He's getting closer by the second, lifting his sunglasses onto his head and smiling warmly at me. I can almost *feel* the look in his eyes physically, like his hands are skimming my hips again.

"Mom, look, my new daddy's here!" Legs yells. She sees my expression and rolls her eyes. "What? I'm just *practicing* for the campout."

Carter laughs and ruffles her hair. "Morning, everyone."

"Morning," Liam says gruffly, then points to the cardboard tray of coffees next to him. "Got you one."

"Thanks, man." Carter scoops up a coffee and takes a

casual sip. Like he's simply drinking coffee to enjoy it, and not chugging it like it's a lifeline to fix a hangover and/or exhaustion like the rest of us.

"Great party last night, by the way."

Despite Liam being the one who spoke, Carter looks straight at me. His blue gaze sears with heat as he says, "I know I had fun."

His words are like a caress dancing down my spine.

"You, um, don't happen to have CCTV on your property, do you?" Liam goes on. "In case of... party crashers or whatnot?"

Beside him, Annie goes scarlet.

They *totally* got up to no good last night!

Carter's eyes dance knowingly as he replies, "I do, yes. But all tapes from last night will be erased for privacy reasons."

"Oh. Good, good." Liam clears his throat. Carter catches my eye and makes an O shape with his mouth, eyes popping. We are clearly on the exact same train of thought about my brother and his wife's extracurricular activities from last night. I hide a snort of laughter behind my hand.

It's almost enough to forget that I'm mad at him.

Almost.

Because the man bought me a freaking real diamond engagement ring. What on earth was he thinking?

I rearrange my snort-laughing expression to a bit of a glare, enough to communicate: *I'm onto you, I know what you did and I'm not best pleased about it.*

He scans my face, and then smiles. Like this is no big deal. When this is a ginormous deal of astronomical, Jupiter-sized proportions.

"Well, Luke might've invited you to a softball game," Mindy says. "But I don't know how much game playing will actually happen today."

"No problem," Carter says easily. He's still smiling, and I'm still fixin' to give him a piece of my mind. He could have bought himself a brand new Jeep for that pricetag, for goodness sakes. And Lord knows, he could do with replacing that rust bucket he drives.

"I, um, actually think we should play softball!" I say, rising from my chair. "Immediately. In fact, Carter, can you accompany me to the car? I think I left my glove in there."

"You don't own a glove," Luke says, scratching his head. "You say you only come to these things to make daisy chains in the grass and eat Spitz."

"Sure she has a glove!" Mindy shoots her husband *a shut the hell up* look. "Go, you two. Now."

"Okay..." Carter says, shrugging as he falls into step beside me. "Wouldn't want Lana to have to carry one whole imaginary glove all by herself."

The second we round the corner and are out of sight of the others, I grab him by the sleeve of his t-shirt and yank him to the first private place I can find, which happens to be behind an ancient gear shed that has a rusting metal roof. It maybe isn't my finest idea because there's a fence behind the shed too, meaning that we have approximately six inches of room between us.

As we stand so close together, practically chest to chest, the air suddenly feels thick and warm.

"You park back here?" Carter's eyes dance as they move over me.

"You bought me a Tiffany ring?!" I shoot back.

He smirks. "Is that a rhetorical question?"

"Yes." I glower at him. "Wait, no."

He takes a sure, purposeful step forward, backing me into the fence as he places a palm flat on the chain link behind my head. He's effectively caging me in.

"Hey, is this our first fight?" he asks, amused.

I'm gulping for air as I say, "What do you mean?"

"Well, if we're going through the motions of a relationship, there's got to be a fight at some stage."

"Carter, be serious right now."

A smile. "I am serious."

"Why did you lie about the ring?" I poke a finger into his chest, and he reaches for it with his free hand, wrapping his fist around it. Now, I'm really trapped.

And oh my gosh, does he smell good today. He's so close, I can feel the heat from his body, sense the thrum of energy radiating off of him.

"Because you didn't want the truth," he says calmly.

"I—what?" I try to shake my finger loose but he doesn't budge, holding me hostage as he levels those scorching blue eyes on me.

"You. Didn't. Want. The. Truth."

"Of course I want the truth," I scoff, trying to ignore the heat gathering in my belly. Our bodies are mere inches apart right now.

"Yeah?" Carter smirks.

"Yes!"

"Okay." He drops my finger and steps back. Crosses his arms. "Here it is: I bought you a real diamond ring, but where it's from and what it costs doesn't matter. I bought it because I *wanted* to buy it for you. End of story. I'm a grown-ass adult who made my own decision on how to spend my own money."

"Well, that was a crazy decision."

"No." He moves forward a touch, his face dangerously close as he lowers his voice. "It was a perfectly rational thought process. I saw this ring and thought it was made for you. I wanted you to have something as beautiful as you are."

My cheeks fill with blood and my heart begins to

227

thump. There are no paparazzi here, no onlookers. Nobody's watching us. He has no reason to act right now. It's only me and him. "Carter..." I start, unsure.

"Fine," he says lightly, narrowing his eyes at me in challenge. "Let's go with last night's story instead: I didn't want the media to think I was a cheapskate, and a real ring was the safest bet. No personal or sentimental meaning whatsoever."

I shake my head. "I... I don't believe you."

He suddenly pushes back from the fence, righting himself. The gesture frees me from my Carter cage and puts some physical space between us, but the smile he gives me is so electric, it lights up my entire body from the inside out. "You shouldn't."

25

CARTER

I've played a father before. In a thriller movie, where it turned out that the baby was not actually mine, and his mother was trying to kill me. It was a really heartwarming story.

I've also had a father. A man who, last I heard, had moved to Texas with his new girlfriend.

But I've never actually *been* a father.

Which means that I have no idea what to expect on a camping trip with twenty-five nine-year-old girls and their fathers (or their stand-ins, like myself). I'm actually nervous to make sure I live up to what Allegra's hoping for. Who comes up with these fundraising events, anyhow? Especially ones like this, that are so non-inclusive to so many families.

My money's on that Mona character.

But while I might be wary of the night that's about to unfold, Allegra is positively gleeful as we unload my Jeep and make our way to the fields behind the school where this shindig is taking place. She walks right beside me, chattering nonstop as she clutches her bumper-size bag of marshmallows and bounces up and down in her high-top

Converse shoes, ponytail askew and smile turned up to a million watts.

"There's gonna be games and s'mores and hot dogs and campfire songs! Ashlynn is gonna be sooooo jealous when I tell her my daddy is better than hers."

"S'mores and hot dogs sound awesome... wait, what?"

"Campfire songs, Cart—I mean, Daddy."

"No, I mean, what was that other thing you said about being better than someone's dad... Ashlynn, was it?"

"Oh, yeah. She's gonna be *so* jealous that my daddy is in movies and her daddy is just a police officer."

My heart constricts a little. Why our society looks up to celebrities so much, I'll never know. In my entire career, I've never made any significant positive difference, injected any sort of good into the world. Sure, I donate money and support good causes, but that seems almost lazy to me sometimes. Like I could be doing something much more meaningful with my time and with the money I've been lucky enough to come into.

I'm just glad that I had the foresight to set up a college fund for Allegra after I got my first big role. Not that Lana Mae knows about this. While she may refuse to accept money from me, history dictates that she can't be mad if I did it for her daughter.

And she did accept the ring I got her, in the end. Although it took some convincing. I smile as I think back to her pulling me behind the equipment shed last Sunday, eyes fiery, then softening as I told her the truth behind the ring. Because it was true, I wanted her to have something as beautiful and special as she deserves.

"Is Ashlynn, by any chance, Ashlynn McCreary?" I ask Allegra, redirecting my train of thought onto our conversation.

"Yuppers. Her mom is Mona the Moaner."

I can't help but chuckle at her earnest expression. "Okay, yeah. Between you and me, kid, I agree that Ashlynn's mom does seem to be a bit on the moany side of things from time to time. But being a police officer is a pretty cool job—you catch real-life criminals. Acting is just... pretending."

"I like pretending. That's what we're doing tonight, right?"

"Right," I agree hesitantly. Because the truth is that the longer this goes on, the more real it feels...

The more I *want* it to be real.

And not only the whole "engaged to Lana Mae" thing, but being here, with Legs. I might be unsure about what to expect tonight, but being her support and the one she's excited to invite on her daddy daughter campouts feels good. Really good.

"I'm going to tell everyone that you're the best dad ever, even though my friend Ella's mom told her that you're not a nice man and you get into a lot of fights." Legs blinks up at me. "Is that true?"

I pause. I don't want to lie to the kid, but at the same time, how do I explain this one? I've been parenting for all of ten minutes and it's already a roller coaster of emotions. "Kinda. I got in one fight a little while back."

"Whoa. Fighting is bad."

"I know," I tell her. "And it's definitely something I'm not proud of."

"Why did you do it?"

Well, that's a loaded question.

I think very carefully for a moment before finally asking, "Have you ever seen anyone do something really wrong or unfair, and it made you mad?"

Legs nods vehemently. "Yeah. Zeke Williams stole

Kayden Oberstein's lunch and threw it on the floor of the cafeteria so he had nothing to eat."

"That's a great example. What happened next?"

"I went up to him and told him that he was being a bully."

I try my hardest not to smile at her fierce little expression. She's like a mini Lana Mae when she's passionate about something. And, same as with Lana, I'm sure this isn't the full story. "And then what?"

"I threw his lunch on the floor, too."

Man, I love this kid.

I try my best to keep a grave, fatherly expression. "Did you get in trouble for that?"

"Yes!" Legs squawks. "Both Zeke and I got clean-up duty from the lunch monitor. She's a big meanie. It was no fair, I was just helping Kayden. He's nice."

I sling an arm around Allegra. "I bet she told you that the right thing to do was tell a grown-up and ask for help instead of throwing Zeke's lunch on the floor."

"Yeah." Allegra pouts.

"And, you know, Legs, getting a grown-up probably would have been the right thing to do." I pause. "But were you secretly kinda glad that you threw his lunch on the floor because you were defending someone who needed help?"

Legs's big dark eyes widen. "Yes! Exactly!"

I smile. "Well, that's what happened when I got in a fight. Sometimes, we do the wrong thing for complicated reasons. That doesn't make it right, by any stretch, but when we care about people, sometimes we can be a bit blinded when it comes to protecting or defending them."

"So... you got in a fight because you were defending someone? Were they hurt?"

I bite the inside of my cheek. "Well, the person who needed defending wasn't actually there. Basically, I heard someone being really mean and unkind about someone I really, really care about. They were being a bully. I wanted to stand up and defend the person, but I got so mad in the end, I wasn't kind either. And I got in trouble for it."

Legs smiles back at me. "But you were still secretly kinda glad you did the wrong thing because the bully kinda deserved it?"

"Hel—*heck* yeah, I was."

"Well, I guess that's okay that you got in one fight, then. Ella's mom is wrong." The little girl leans against me, snuggling up to my side. "I like you, Carter. I'm having fun with you pretending to marry my mom."

Me too, kid.

"You know I love you and your mom so much, no matter what, right?"

Legs's little brow puckers. "And Harry Styles?"

I laugh. "That cat is my ride or die. I love him more than I do the person."

We reach the field and our conversation is seemingly over as Legs shrieks, "Ahhhh, there's Keisha! HEY KEISHA!" This is quickly followed by, "Oh my gosh, this is even better in real life than it was in my head!"

It's a sentiment I've been relating to often, lately. I smile at her quickly retreating back fondly as she sprints ahead to catch who I presume to be Keisha.

The kid isn't exaggerating about the set-up this evening: the back field of the school has been transformed into the ultimate sleepover. Fairy lights hang in the trees, a row of tents ring one side of the field, and a batch of extra chipper-looking dads man a line of grills at the other end. Lawn games are spread out in the middle, and there's even a huge outdoor movie screen, along with cotton candy, slushie and popcorn machines.

I catch up to Legs in a few long strides and find her

chatting to a cute kid with box braids and chubby cheeks. She's standing next to a man who already looks very, very tired. He raises a wry brow at me. "You think there's going to be a bar at this thing?"

I decide on the spot that this dad is going to be my buddy for the night. "Carter." I stick out a hand. "And sadly not."

He shakes my hand firmly. "Jared." Then, a grin. "I'm a big fan of the *Switchblade* franchise, so I'm pumped to be meeting Agent Jackson Palmer in the flesh."

"Ah, I wouldn't be too excited. I'm nowhere near as handy in hostage situations in real life."

He gives a big laugh and shakes his head. "Well, I'm very sad to hear that because this sleepover kind of feels like one." I laugh along with him, and he continues, "Anyhow, I'm sure you hate that kinda movie fan talk, but I really am pleased to meet you. My wife, Imani, works with Lana Mae, and Keisha and Allegra are great buds. I hear congratulations are in order?"

"Thanks, man. First time being a husband and a dad, so I'm on a steep learning curve. Starting with this campout."

At that moment, Allegra and Keisha utter matching ear-splitting shrieks as they dart off towards another friend of theirs who is rapidly approaching from the far end of the field. Jared and I don't follow, and it's probably best for our ears and our sanity that we kept our distance because, when the girls reunite, there's an actual racket of excited screams.

I tilt my head towards the tent village. "Shall we grab some Dr. Peppers we can pretend are Coors Lights and set up our unicorn tents?" I wrinkle my nose. "Wow, there's a sentence I never thought I'd say."

Jared shakes his head and smiles. "Welcome to being a girl dad, dude."

234

Forty-five minutes later, I've assembled one pink unicorn tent for Legs, and one regular black tent for myself. Our sleeping bags are rolled out in each (also one unicorn, one regular—they didn't have a unicorn bag in my size at Target, for some reason), and the airbeds are blown up.

Next door, Jared is putting the finishing touches on his own camping set-up.

"Looking good." I hold up my can of soda and cheers him. "Shall we find the girls?"

"Sure," my new friend replies, standing and stretching. I appreciate that he's treating me like a regular person. Though I'm wearing a navy hoodie, shorts and a ball cap (seemed like good campout attire), I far from blend in with the other dads, who've mostly been shooting me surreptitious glances.

In the end, the campout is an absolute blast. Hot dogs and hamburgers, three-legged races and cornhole tournaments, roasting s'mores on the fire, and finally, everyone gathering around the big screen for a viewing of *The Parent Trap*, which Legs thoroughly enjoys. She sits criss-cross-applesauce on the grass, resting her head on my shoulder. Every so often, she cackles with laughter or looks up at me with a *did you see that?!* expression. Especially when the twins hatch the plot to fool their parents.

After the movie, she's so sleepy that I have to practically carry her back to the tents. But when she sees the unicorn tent, she wakes right up. "Oh my gosh, is that for me?!"

"Sure is. There's a matching sleeping bag inside."

Legs squeals and unzips the tent. When she gets inside and sees the bag, she squeals again. "Keisha, I have a unicorn tent and sleeping bag, too!" she calls to her friend.

"Woah," Keisha says excitedly. "Now we both have the best tents. Ella's going to be sooooo jealous. Let's get ready for bed and see if we can find her. I think she went to the bathrooms."

With a huge smile on her face, Allegra grabs a comically large bag of night things that Lana Mae packed for her (some of which has to be unnecessary... I mean, fleece sleep socks? In this weather?) and then ducks off with Keisha. Jared comes over and claps me on the back. "Seems you're doing absolutely fine with the father stuff so far, dude."

"If buying things with unicorns printed on them is all I've gotta do to ace this, I'll be fine," I joke.

"I wish." Jared's eyes twinkle in the dark.

I duck into my own tent and flop down on my air mattress, which sputters a bit, making me offer up a quick prayer that I don't end up on the ground by morning. Multiple nights sleeping on Lana's couch has got my back in agony. I'm going to have to move in with my chiropractor when I get back to LA... Which I really don't want to think about right now.

I pull out my phone.

Carter: Legs loves the tent.

Lana Mae: Knew she would. You two having fun?

Carter: So much fun. But don't be surprised if Legs suddenly starts pretending she's her own long-lost twin.

Lana Mae: So, basically, if she starts using the word arse?

Carter: Don't forget knickers.

Lana Mae: I never forget knickers.

Carter: Glad to hear that ;)

Lana Mae: You know what I meant!!

I laugh as I click my phone screen off and put it down on my chest. Since our engagement party last week, all I can freaking think about is Lana Mae. How she feels, how she smells, how close I was to kissing those lips and finding out what she tastes like...

Jeez, how badly I wanted to kiss her as we danced, our bodies close and our lungs breathless.

But I held off, remembering Elena's words. If—*when*—I kiss her, I want it to be perfect. Just for us.

The morning after the party, Luke invited me to the Donovan family softball game. I went, unable to stay away from Lana for even a morning. Something changed in the way my best friend looked at me, the way she blushed when my eyes lingered on her face, the way her breathing sped up when I told her why I bought the ring. Like she, too, was remembering how our lips almost touched mere hours before...

It's new territory for us. And I've been continuing to hold off all week, unsure what my next move should be. Unsure what all of this means.

Legs pokes her head into my tent, cute as a button in the thick flannel pajamas and infamous fleece socks. You know, for this positively balmy late May evening. "Hii!" she squeals, still high on sugar and unicorn consumerism.

I grin. "C'mon, kiddo, let's get you set up in your tent."

I get to my feet, and follow her into the pink tent next to mine.

"Wee!" She dives onto her air mattress (which doesn't groan like mine did) and scrambles into her unicorn bag. "I still can't believe I have my very own unicorn sleeping bag and tent!"

"I wanted you to have the best stuff for the campout."

She flashes me her gap-teeth in the glow of the little wind-up camping light. "I have the best everything. I'm so happy you came tonight."

"Wouldn't have missed it for the world."

She snuggles her head into her pillow and sighs. "Do you think it could happen like in the movie?"

"What's that?" I ask as I crunch myself into a seated position on the neon pink floor next to her mattress. I link my arms around my knees, feeling not unlike a giant oaf from a fairytale. But it's worth it—I'm sure all the best actual dads chat to their daughters while tucking them in.

"Like... do you think if I planned to set my mom up with someone, my plan could work? Like in the movie?"

I go very still as I try to read her face. Try to figure out what cogs are turning in her head right now. "You want to set your mom up?" I prod gently.

"Yeah." She waits a beat. "With you." Her voice rises with hope.

And I'm touched. Like, actually touched. In a way that makes my chest warm and my stomach buoyant. She would really want that?

"Well." I lean back and prop myself up on my hands. "That would depend on what your mother wants. You'd only want to set her up with someone she *truly* wants to be with in order for her to be happy."

"She wants to be with *you*. For real."

"Is that something you think, or something you hope, Allegra?" I ask, my voice soft.

"Both?" She shrugs. "I dunno much about love except that my uncle Liam used to be sad and grumpy, and then he married Auntie Annie, and now, he's way less sad and grumpy. And my mom's not grumpy, but sometimes, I think she's sad. Unless you're around. Then she's happy."

There's a lump growing in my throat. "She makes me happy, too. You and your mom both do."

"So why not be my new daddy for real? You could actually marry my mom."

I let out a long, low breath, my mind full of Lana Mae's smile and that one crooked tooth of hers I love so much. "It's complicated, Allegra... Your mom is very important to me. She's my best friend. If I told her I wanted something more and she didn't feel the same, or if things didn't work out with us, well..."

I can't lose the most important person in the world to me. She's everything to me, and I'd rather have only her friendship than risk loving her and losing her altogether.

"Then you'd go back to being only friends. Right?" Allegra finishes, nose screwed up in confusion. "I don't think it's complicated at all. My friend Daria used to like Jack. I mean, everyone at school *loves* Jack, but then, she and Jack started to hate each other when Jack and his friends were hogging the soccer fields at recess. But now they're friends again. So," she concludes. "No matter what, you can always go back to being friends, right?"

Those innocent little words, spoken by a nine-year-old girl wise beyond her years, hit me square in the chest. We say our goodnights and I give her a hug before returning to my tent, but those words run through my mind over and over on repeat.

Because she's not wrong. Lana Mae and I have a decade of friendship behind us. I was there for her first heartbreak, present in the waiting room while she had her daughter, sitting right behind her at her mom's funeral. And she's been there for me through everything, too. Supporting my career, cheering me on, believing the best in me when the rest of the world saw the worst.

It's like her friendship is the puzzle piece that slotted in next to me. Fit with me so I was no longer alone. But maybe I've been so focused on hanging on to that one puzzle piece, keeping it next to me, that I haven't considered the possibility that I could be missing out on building the entire puzzle with her—having friendship, family, *and* love around me. Around *us*.

My friendship with Lana Mae is a permanent fixture in my life. No matter what.

And I love her, no matter what.

So, really, no matter the outcome, what's the worst that could happen if I just... go for it?

26

LANA MAE

"Thank you so much for coming at the last minute." Mona's voice, for once, completely matches her facial expression. And for once, both look entirely sincere. "I really appreciate it."

I pull on my brand new *I'm a Mom Volunteer!* tee over my long-sleeve shirt and smile at her. "No problem. I wasn't busy."

And by not busy, I mean that I was lying on my couch, watching a movie with the best famous Chris in it. And for once in my life, I was letting myself ogle the butt-that-definitely-doesn't-belong-to-Chris.

"Well, I figured that would be the case."

Ah, there it is.

"What would you like me to do, Mona?" I ask, my smile a little more forced than it was before.

Mona called me fifteen minutes ago to say that one of the moms volunteering at the campout had come down with a sudden bout of food poisoning and asked if I could come and help in her place. At first, I was a bit torn. For one thing, I was already wearing my strictly indoors sweatpants. For another, being in close proximity to Carter this week has had me continuously concerned for my health.

On the surface, everything's been normal. I worked and dropped Legs off at school and dance practice. Carter worked out and had meetings and cooked every one of our meals in my tiny little kitchen (well, he cooked one meal and then ordered in for all the rest). But every time his eyes met mine, or he touched me casually, or he said something dangerously flirtatious, it was like a device was detonating in my stomach.

I mean, the man gave me a diamond ring. A *real* diamond ring. From Tiffany's. That likely does—as Luke so eloquently put it—cost more than *both* my house and vehicle. And not only that, but since the almost kiss at the engagement party and the spine-tingling way he trapped me against the chain-link fence at softball, he hasn't made any move to kiss me again. Not even once...

The moment he told me he got me the ring because he wanted me to have it—because it looked like it should be mine—was almost enough to make me scream, "Just kiss me already!"

But I didn't.

And he hasn't.

Meaning that my mind and body are shaky messes, tense with want and anticipation.

I feel like we've been orbiting one another like satellites. Keeping our distance because we had to, even while the space between us crackled with tension and electricity.

The problem is that if and when we collide, I worry that the fallout is going to be spectacular...

But I can't think about him leaving again right now. Going there involves too many layers of pain, and I resolved to celebrate this thing between us. So here I am, last-minute volunteering and hoping to steal another precious few minutes with him tonight if he's not already asleep.

"Well, before she got sick, Padma was on campsite duty," Mona says as she neatly fastens the lid on a large rubbermaid bin full of lawn games.

"What does that entail?" I crouch down to tie the lace on my tennis shoe. All around me, moms are milling around helping the clean-up effort. I didn't sign up to volunteer because, until Carter showed up in the Sonic parking lot that day, I had no idea that Legs would actually be attending this thing.

"Checking that there aren't any girls out of bed, making sure that all the trash in the area is picked up..." Mona holds out a black garbage bag.

"Sounds good." I finish tying my shoe, then grab the bag. Armed with that and a flashlight, I set off for the camp area across the field, where I'm greeted by a cacophony of snores coming from several tents.

How are the girls sleeping through this?

I do a quick lap, pausing by the new unicorn tent and boring black tent that sit side by side and contain the two most important people in the world to me. I smile, wondering what they talked about this evening. What they did together. I hope Allegra got what she needed out of tonight. I wish I could creep inside the first tent and kiss her goodnight, then slip into the other one for a few minutes to watch Carter sleep. Like a creep.

As I move through the rest of the campsite, all seems quiet (save for the snoring) on the western front. So, I get to work gathering a bag full of trash.

By the time I'm done, there's only one small group of moms left, all huddled around the remnants of a campfire and blowing on hot chocolates while chatting. A few mom volunteers will keep watch tonight to make sure no little girls go rogue in the forest. But Mona didn't say she needed me for a shift, so I hesitate, bouncing on my toes.

Maybe I can sneak into Allegra's tent for a second?

Before I can give it too much thought, I'm unzipping the unicorn tent and climbing in. Through the darkness, I can vaguely make out the lines of my daughter's peacefully sleeping face. She's cuddled up and looks perfectly comfortable. I kneel to stroke back her hair and give her a little forehead kiss before slipping out and quietly rezipping the tent.

I pause for a moment, dithering, before I unzip the black tent too.

I poke my head in, and then, upon hearing the steady breathing coming from the Carter-shaped lump in the dark, I creep closer.

"Hey." A hissed whisper comes from the air mattress as Carter bolts upright, and I find myself looking straight into midnight blue eyes that are wide and wild. "You just about gave me a heart attack!"

"I'm sorry, I thought you were asleep," I whisper back, feeling a strange mix of happy that he's awake, and sad that I missed out on watching him sleep. Like the weirdo I am.

"Light sleeper," he murmurs, a sleepy grin creeping over his face. "What're you doing here?"

I crouch next to him. "I'm helping clean up. One of the volunteer moms got sick."

"Not surprised. If anything, I'm shocked that there weren't any more puking casualties with all the games of chubby bunnies."

I laugh at the thought of Carter and Allegra, smiling and happy, with their mouths full of marshmallows. "I'm going to miss Legs so much when we go to LA next week."

"I told you, she's welcome to come. Although I'd want to get some extra security if she does. Can't be too careful."

His concern warms my heart. "Better she doesn't miss

school. Plus, she's super excited to stay at Annie and Liam's."

I don't add that, as much as I'll miss my daughter, I'm also excited to have some time alone with Carter. The premiere is only one evening, so we'll have a couple days to explore LA. I've never been to California. Carter's offered a bunch of times to pay for Allegra and me to fly out, but I've never been able to accept that offer. I always figured that he'd actually be paying for us to get in his way—I know how busy he is when he's working.

But this time, I can't wait to experience a taste of his life out there with him. See what *my* Carter looks like in *his* city.

"It's only a few days," Carter says in this low, husky whisper that probably isn't meant to be sexy but totally is. "We'll be home before she knows it."

Home.

His use of the word is so casual, it could've been acci-dental. But it makes my heart soar with hope. Could he really see Atlanta being home again for him? One day in the future, maybe?

"That's true. And she made me promise to bring back some In-N-Out Burger. She saw a documentary about it and is quite convinced that it'll top Chick-fil-A."

"It's a grave possibility. That shiz is delicious." Carter laughs softly, and then, quick as a cat, reaches out and grabs my hand, pulling me out of my awkward crouch and onto the air mattress next to him.

"What're you doing?" I whisper-squeal.

"Saying hi." He says, his face close to mine. "Hi, by the way."

"Hi, you weirdo. We've been talking for, like, the last five minutes." I speak as casually as I can, but my heart is thumping a million miles a minute. His warm body is so close, his heady scent surrounding me.

"Yup. But what're you doing now?" Carter, meanwhile, is cool and calm, like we're standing in line at the bank and not sitting together on a too-small air mattress, inches from each other in the dark.

"Going home, I guess." I shift my butt on the mattress gingerly. "I'm all done with my chores for the evening."

"Why don't you stay a while?" he murmurs softly, running his hand down my arm and wrapping it around my wrist. "I mean, I'm awake now, and holding you accountable."

"Don't you mean holding me hostage?"

"Semantics."

"Hardly," I reply with a snort. He's still holding my wrist, and he gives it a tug so that I tumble down beside him. The air mattress is, indeed, very small. Much too small for both of us. But Carter slings an arm around me and pulls me into his chest, and I'm immediately comfortable. "That's better," he says with a smile in his voice.

"I guess I could lie down for just a minute."

"Good girl."

"Do you say that to all your hostages?" I blink up at him innocently, and his chest rumbles with laughter.

"Only the cute ones," he replies, and I jolt, remembering his same words to me the night we met, ten years ago. A coincidence, or does he recall that night as well as I do? The way his eyes danced as he flirted with me, our fiery, funny back-and-forth before my night descended into total chaos...

In all the time I've known him, he hasn't flirted with me again. Until this week.

"Gee, glad I made the cut." I repeat my own line from

that night, and his arm tightens around me, a silent communication that he *does* remember. I shiver in his grip.

"Hey, Llama?" he says sleepily, burying his face in my hair.

"Yeah?" I look at the shadows dancing on the roof of the tent.

"You should stay tonight."

"I..."

"Don't overthink it," he says quietly. "Just do what *you* want to do. Don't worry about anyone else."

In this moment, in Carter's arms, I'm right where I want to be.

I don't want to leave, don't want to go anywhere else.

So I don't.

Ow.

No, seriously, ouch.

What the frick am I lying on?

An exploratory pat confirms that I've been sleeping on a rock. I shift lightly on what is now a very flat air mattress and rub my back, opening my eyes. I'm surprised to find that the tent is empty, save for me, my aching back, and what is sure to be a very unattractive bedhead of hair.

This is the second time in two weeks that I've had the luxury of "sleeping in" (AKA not being woken up by an alarm set to an ungodly hour or by Legs jumping on my bed in the morning wanting pancakes). Being fake engaged is working wonders for my sleep schedule, apparently. I have no idea how Carter managed to sneak out of here, but I must say that waking up alone in a tent with a jagged little rock digging into my back is definitely not how I imagined this morning going.

Poor Carter, sleeping on a totally deflated air mattress after so many nights on my uncomfortable couch. I should probably offer him a massage. Mmm, I should *definitely* offer him a massage.

I close my eyes and rest my head on the pillow for a moment more, remembering the warmth of Carter's strong, muscled body next to mine as we drifted off to sleep last night. Unlike our last sleepover a couple of weeks ago, there was cuddling this time. And despite the faulty mattress and the rock in my spine, I slept like a baby snuggled up next to the literal man of my dreams.

Outside the tent, I hear a shout and a smattering of excited, high-pitched voices. Breakfast is clearly underway by the picnic tables currently doubling as the campout's dining area.

Is Carter flipping pancakes again, I wonder?

And can I stealthily sneak to the bathrooms to freshen up before I make my appearance?

And oh my gosh, speaking of appearances, how am I going to explain my being here?! I wasn't meant to be an actual participant of the daddy daughter campout. Which means that my stepping out of Carter's tent is going to look like... a walk of shame.

A walk of freaking shame.

At a children's campout.

Holy freaking moly, Mona is going to have an aneurysm.

With a strange, crab-like scramble, I get myself off the air mattress and over to the door of the tent. All I have to do is get out of here, leg it to the bathrooms unnoticed, and then come strolling over to breakfast all casual, like I turned up only a moment ago. In the same clothes that I was wearing last night. Without brushing my hair. Or teeth.

Oh, frick.

I unzip the tent and stumble out into the blazing sunshine. Unfortunately, I attempt my getaway before getting my bearings, and so I promptly run into the tent next door. Which caves in at the side, resulting in me effectively squishing the sleeping person inside.

"Ouch!" comes a startled yelp from within.

"Sorry, sorry!" I cry, leaping to my feet and taking off in the other direction. The person inside the tent was clearly male, and I am not sticking around to find out if I just assaulted Officer Lance McCreary.

By the time I make it out of the bathrooms (looking even more like I was dragged through a hedge backwards than usual, but unable to do anything about that unfortunate little fact), breakfast is over, the food wrapped up and cleared away. Volunteer moms and bleary-eyed dads sip on coffee while sitting around a firepit, and the girls are over at the baseball diamond...

Where Carter is pitching for them.

Be still, my heart.

I draw in a breath as I watch. He throws a softball for each kiddo, laughing and cheering the girls on when they swing and make contact with the ball, or encouraging them gently when they don't. And ho-ly is he a sight to behold in the cool, clear light of morning. Dressed in all black: a tee that's *just* snug enough, shorts, baseball cap, and sunglasses. The dark outfit enhances his golden tanned skin.

He looks like a literal tall drink of water that I'm thirsting for so freaking bad.

Pedro Pascal better hope there are no cameras around, because if pictures of this scene end up online, the internet will officially have a new favorite daddy.

"He's good with kids." Mona suddenly appears beside me.

I hastily pick my jaw up off the ground, cheeks turning red at being caught practically drooling. "He is."

"You know, Lana, I was skeptical at first. Almost called an emergency PTA meeting to discuss the likes of Carter attending an event like this."

"The likes of Carter?!" My voice goes up an entire octave so that I sound like I've inhaled a tank of helium.

I must look like I'm about to lose my ever-loving mind at her, because Mona holds up her hands. "Lance talked me out of it. And, I'll admit, I was wrong."

What? Who is this person wearing a Mona skin suit right now?!

I turn to gape at the woman I've known for years, but wouldn't call a friend. She continues quietly, "I was concerned about what the tabloids have been saying about him, but Lance reminded me that none of the dads at school are perfect. For goodness sakes, Alistair Wright practically gambled away the family home last year, and Tommy Ellison has been having an affair with Amand—oh, I probably shouldn't say that. It's not public knowledge yet."

I shake my head with a wry smile. *There's* the Mona we know all too well.

"Anyhow." She clears her throat. "I realized that we know more about Carter's life because it's splashed all over the internet, but it doesn't necessarily mean that he's a bad guy. Doesn't even mean that the rumors are true. When I saw him last night and this morning with Allegra—with all the kids—I could clearly see that he's one of the good ones. And it's clear that he truly loves you and Allegra."

I blink at her, vaguely stunned by the appearance of this woman's softer side (despite the inevitable gossip), and very glad to see it. In the same way that Carter isn't as he appears to the world, Mona is more than what I see on a daily basis, too. I suppose we all are, and it's such an important thing to remember when you form opinions of others—to be slow to judge, and kind, especially when you don't know the whole story.

"Thank you," I say sincerely. "I appreciate you saying that, Mona. He very much is one of the good ones."

She shakes her head as she watches him with the kids. "Do you think he could share his workout routine with Lance? Because those forearms are…"

"Yup," I say in full agreement as we both look at him (and his sexy firm forearms) in wonder.

After a few moments, he looks in our direction and waves. Says something to the girls before jogging over with a smile. "Hey, Mona. And good morning, beautiful." He comes to a stop in front of me. "How's my sleepyhead?"

"I'm good, *babe*," I reply with a teasing smile.

He seems to see my sass as a challenge, because he shoots me the cheekiest dimpled grin before moving into my personal space, stopping an inch from my body and holding eye contact steadily. My heartbeat is in my stomach as he moves tantalizingly close. And then, for the briefest, most blissful, painful second, he barely—just barely—skims his lips over the edge of mine. He steps back with a gleam in his eyes.

Meanwhile, I am barely—just barely—avoiding melting into a human puddle.

Because good lord.

"Saved you breakfast," he says, eyes still dancing. "Pancakes and coffee?"

"Mmpf," I manage in response, which makes his smile stretch further.

He takes my hand, and the three of us walk to where the other volunteers are sitting, Carter making casual conversation with Mona as I try to keep my legs from buckling beneath me.

There are only two empty chairs and Carter indicates that Mona should take one before he grabs a plate of pancakes and sinks into the other. He wraps an arm around my waist to pull me effortlessly into his lap.

Holy moly, he is *really* playing this up for our audience right now. And I am here for it. Because oh my gosh, his legs are firm and solid and he smells like clean laundry and fresh-cut grass and goodness. We talk while I eat my pancakes, but I'm wholly focused on where my thighs are touching his. How his hand moves casually over my arms.

And this? It feels so right. Me, on his lap, like I belong here.

When there's a quiet moment, Carter rests his forehead against my back. "I was thinking you guys could come to my place after we're done here today. Legs is dying to go swimming."

His warm breath on my t-shirt sends heat up to my cheeks. "That sounds good."

"And then, I was thinking that we could do Thai for dinner? I can head to the Asian grocery store in Decatur to pick up ingredients. Want to try my hand at making that stir fried basil dish you loved the last time we got Thai takeout."

"You're turning into quite the house husband," I say with a laugh.

Carter wraps a big arm around my waist and squeezes. "I prefer the term 'domestic god'."

"'Course you do." I smirk. "Always punching above your weight class."

He moves his head slightly and grazes his lips to my neck, brushing across a sweet, sensitive spot that sends a literal flurry of chills down my spine. "'Aim high' is what I like to say. I got you to agree to marry me, didn't I?"

I have no idea if this is for the benefit of the other parents present, or if he's just teasing me, but the sensation of his lips against my skin short-circuits my brain, and my body explodes into an electrical fire.

"True," I say shakily, trying my best not to melt on the spot. And then, maybe because of the aforementioned short circuit and complete system malfunction, or because I can't bear the thought of him having to spend another night squished on my couch when he has a perfectly good bed twenty minutes away, I add, "Actually, what if we *didn't* go back to my place tonight?"

He chuckles, those blue eyes crinkling adorably at the corners. "Where are you planning on going?"

"Well, maybe... we can stay at yours?" I turn so I can look him in the eye, and lower my voice so nobody else can hear. "Your place is so much bigger and more comfortable. I was thinking it'd be nice to escape there for awhile, and give you somewhere more comfortable to sleep."

"My back would be very thankful."

"I'll have to run home first and pack some things for Legs and myself. You don't mind if Harry Styles comes with us, do you?"

"I don't mind at all. Harry's stayed at my place before."

"No, he hasn't." I frown in confusion at Carter's playful expression. Then, the penny drops and my eyes grow to be saucers. "Holy moly... You don't mean the cat, do you?"

"I do not."

27

CARTER

This morning, I woke up in a tent with my arms wrapped around Lana Mae.

And yes, we were on the floor, and my back was aching like I was very, very elderly instead of a mere twenty-eight years old. But it was perfect.

Because last night, in the darkness of our late night conversation, I told Lana Mae to do what she wanted to do, and she chose to stay.

It's making me feel like everything I'm feeling, she's feeling too. That this push and pull between us goes beyond sheer tension and attraction for both of us. That it's not fake at all, but real and deep and meaningful. That if I kiss her now, it would be real for both of us.

I've never had a serious relationship in my life. Since I moved to LA, I've had nothing but short-lived flings. I never knew why this was the case, never gave it too much thought. But now, I'm starting to think that there's a simple reason: if it wasn't with Lana Mae, I didn't want it.

How could anyone else come close to stealing my heart when it was always hers?

I walk around the guest wing of my house, making sure

that everything is perfect before Lana Mae and Allegra arrive. They're at their place, packing, and it's given me time to appreciate the newly renovated and decorated section of the house.

After the engagement party last week, I flew Anthony back to LA so he could have some well-deserved time off while I lay low here in Atlanta. But before he went, he managed to source a great husband-and-wife team who run a local renovation and interior design business to decorate the guest wing of the house. Just in case Lana and Legs ended up staying here during our arrangement.

I've seen enough of Lana Mae's Pinterest boards over the years to know what she likes, and I wanted her and Legs to feel comfortable and at home. Somehow, the designer was able to pull off some amazing work from the stilted, vague and entirely questionable descriptions I gave her. Which included "she likes those hangy plant things" and "maybe add some natural-looking stuff."

I've been coming to the house every day to check in on how the project was going while Lana Mae was at work. The designers wrapped it up in perfect time—yesterday.

Allegra's room now features soft pink walls, a custom-built four-poster bed, and an array of sparkly, unicorn-themed touches. Lana's room is what the lady called "boho chic"—all muted tones and soft furnishings, and finished with a few of the designer's own art pieces that she commissions for interior design clients.

Best of all, they were able to fully renovate my unused office space upstairs to create the perfect surprise for Lana. I was inspired by the *Gilmore Girls* ten years later show (or whatever it's called) that I've been watching with her at her place since I started sleeping on her couch.

I didn't like a number of things about the show, but I *did* like the way Jess helped Rory realize a dream of hers.

No matter what happens between us, no matter what we are to each other, I will always try to do the same for Lana Mae.

Downstairs, the doorbell rings.

They're here.

28

LANA MAE

"Mom, can we stay here forever?"

I look down at my daughter, who's ensconced within a puff of bright white, billion-thread-count sheets on a behemoth king bed in a pink room that looks, feels, and somehow smells like you'd imagine a unicorn would. Like bubblegum and vanilla and freshly baked cookies. How Carter managed to capture this particular essence is completely beyond me.

But then again, how Carter has managed to do *any* of the things he's done lately is beyond me...

"Wouldn't you miss your bedroom? All your stuff and your backyard?" I stroke her hair back from her face, keeping my voice as light as possible in an effort to avoid answering her question head-on.

But Allegra Liana Donovan wasn't born yesterday.

"Nope," she replies with a smirk. "The backyard is *way* better here. I could have Keisha over for pool parties! Plus," she adds with all the gravitas a nine-year-old can possibly have. "This room is much bigger than mine at home. I could bring all my things with me. And Carter might even buy me some new stuff if I asked nicely."

"You sound spoiled, my dear," I tell her with a smile, chucking her chin.

"I'd say lucky," she murmurs as she snuggles further into her nest.

I kiss her on the forehead, smooth her hair back one more time, and let myself out of the bedroom, closing the door almost all the way behind me.

Tonight, Allegra and I are sleeping at Carter's house. Specifically, in two gorgeous spare bedrooms with an adjoining bathroom that's bigger than the kitchen in my little duplex.

We've been over to his house a lot over the past couple years—we were here just last week for the engagement party. But I haven't spent much time in this part of the house, save for when he gave us a tour after he bought the place. I was amazed earlier today to find that the guest rooms are now as beautifully decorated as downstairs. The rooms—except for Allegra's, which is clearly meant for a unicorn-obsessed child—carry the same palate of warm whites, oat hues and sage greens. Each is filled to the brim with home-like touches.

It's like someone let my favorite Pinterest boards loose in here. When I asked Carter about his decorative choices earlier, he shrugged, looking almost embarrassed, and said he'd been lucky enough to find a really great interior designer.

But the best part by far was the library room.

The spare bedroom across the hallway has now been converted into a little wonderland. It's incredible—built-in bookshelves that go from floor to ceiling, comfy padded reading chairs, houseplants, and gorgeous glowy lights...

When I pressed Carter on that room specifically, he shrugged again and said, "Well, I needed somewhere to store all my books."

Which was a mildly surprising answer coming from a man who has read maybe five books in the last decade. All on my recommendation.

But hey, I'm certainly not about to judge what Carter does with his money.

I pad down the hallway and duck into my room to shower and change. We spent the afternoon and evening running through the sprinklers in the yard, eating popsicles, and grilling burgers after Carter's first foray into Thai cuisine was a spectacular fail (Allegra almost cried when she tried a mouthful of his "green curry", and I say this in quotations because I've never seen a green curry that gray in my life. Don't even get me started on his basil stir fry).

Harry Styles is curled up on my bed and I give him a scratch under the chin. He's obviously at home here, stalking around like he's lord of the manor. I hope that Carter's housekeeper isn't too annoyed with all the orange fluff. I make a mental note to find out when they're coming next, and will do a thorough vacuum beforehand.

In the bathroom, I peel off my sticky t-shirt and shorts, then stop to look at myself in the mirror. My skin is sunkissed and pink, my hair is wild and frizzy, and a smattering of freckles are blooming across the bridge of my nose. But the woman in the mirror?

Still happy.

I'm about to step into the steaming shower when my phone pings.

Carter: We never got to swim today.

Lana Mae: I know :(Legs is in bed and I'm gonna hop in the shower. Will be down soon.

It's such a domestic bliss kind of text, it gives me the warm and fuzzies.

Carter: Hey, before you shower... You fancy a night swim?

Lana Mae: *Fancy?*

Carter: I've decided to be British when we're texting.

Lana Mae: Course you have. And yes, I do fancy a swim. Good sir.

Carter: See you at the pool in 10, m'lady.

I click off my phone screen and look at myself in the mirror again, suck in a breath. Has Carter ever seen me in a bathing suit?

Doubt it. For one, swimsuits are not my favorite.

It's not that I'm embarrassed of my body. If anything, I'm proud of it. Proud of every mark and scar that indicates that I brought Allegra into this world. But even still, it's hard not to feel exposed with so much flesh on show.

It's Carter, I remind myself. Carter, who never judges me. Carter, who's done nothing but make me feel beautiful and desirable and... *sexy*... since the moment I admitted to him that I didn't always feel this way with men.

I take a deep breath, change into my swimsuit—a nondescript black one-piece—and wrap a robe around my body.

And then, I go downstairs. Red face, frizzy hair, and all.

He's already in the water, swimming laps, when I get out to the garden. In the dark, the pool glows, and I stand on the patio for a moment. His broad upper back tenses, the corded muscles in his arms rippling as he glides through the water with long, clean strokes. Effortless.

When he turns to start a new lap, he sees me and swims

for the edge of the pool instead. He pulls himself out in one graceful motion (so basically, the opposite of how I look when I get out of a pool, which is more on the beached seal end of the spectrum). He walks towards me, eyes focused on me.

Ho-ly. That torso in all its tanned, muscled, water-slicked glory is a beautiful, beautiful thing. It's almost surreal.

This is *surreal*, I remind myself. Not my regular, real life. Or his, for that matter.

But it's still happening.

"Hi," he says, coming to a stop in front of me. In the moonlight, his eyes are like deep blue velvet.

"Hi," I squeak back, looking everywhere but at the perfectly fitted hunter green swim shorts he's wearing.

He takes another step forward—he's close, oh so close. I suck in a breath as he leans towards me...

And reaches for the bottle of wine and two glasses on the table behind me.

"Refreshments." He smirks as he takes in my wide-eyed gaze.

"Of course!"

"Come on." Carter reaches for my hand with his free one, like it's the most natural thing in the world. His fingers twine through mine and he squeezes them gently—his wordless signal that everything's okay. We're okay.

We sit at the edge of the pool and I dip my legs in, swirling them around in the cool, refreshing water, relishing the way it slides over my skin. Carter pops the cork on what I now realize is champagne like a pro. He pours the fizz into two glasses and extends one to me.

I accept mine with a smile. "What's the occasion?"

"We're celebrating."

"Your decision to be British over text?"

"Almost as good as that." He grins. "We're celebrating a big relationship milestone."

"Oh, yeah?"

"Didn't you hear? My fiancée moved in with me today."

"That *is* big news. Think I heard something about her wanting to hire a chef as soon as possible. Isn't Gordon Ramsay himself in the running?"

"No way. Not my fault that my Thai food was too hot for her to handle."

"Honestly, I think the thing that was too hot for her to handle was the library room upstairs." I drum my fingers on my glass. "That's, like, every reader's wildest fantasy."

I get treated to his lopsided smirk—my favorite of his smiles. "So you're saying that I made your wildest fantasy come true?"

My cheeks turn red at his words. "I'm *saying* the place is so beautifully decorated. And I know you said that the library room was just for storing your books, but I'm going to spend all my time reading in there from now on. In fact, you might never see me again."

"Actually, the room's designed for both reading and writing." He looks at me with a secret smile. "There's a desk in there with a special chair and a screen to plug in your laptop."

"Are you writing something?" I ask, puzzled.

"No, silly. But *you* could be."

I pause for a moment. "What?"

"I've been thinking a lot about what happened at Target last week, and I think you *should* write a book now that Allegra's a bit older and you have more time. Obviously, it doesn't have to be a bad dates book—I would never expect you to relive a date with that douchecanoe if you didn't want to. But you're a great writer, Lan, and you could totally do this. Your mom would have been thrilled."

A chill runs through me despite the heat of the night.

I love that he thinks this. Love that he understands my love of literature, and that when I was younger, I wanted nothing more than to spend four years in college soaking up every drop of prose and poetry I could like a sponge. Back then, I wanted to become a literary critic. Or a professional book reviewer. Or work at a library. Become an editor.

Better yet, I would have loved to write my own book.

Over the span of my childhood, I escaped into books and I wanted my adult life to be as bookishly wonderful as possible. My father laughed at these notions. My mother celebrated them. She devoured every short story I wrote. Buddy read everything from Dickens and Rowling to Steel and King with me.

When I found out that I was pregnant with Allegra and college wasn't going to be an option—at least, not like I'd originally planned it—she offered to look after Legs while I studied for my GED. Picked up a million brochures so that we could pore over potential evening classes at the community college.

And then, Mom was gone, and the dream slipped through my fingers.

I thought it was gone forever and I made my peace with it, eventually. Literature and writing was something I could never pursue. I fell into being a travel agent, and let myself forget all about it.

But Carter James Callahan didn't forget.

He knows me better than I know myself. He's the total Jess to my Rory right now, and I wish there was a way to communicate to him that I don't give a crap about finding my Logan. Because I was team freaking Jess all along.

"Carter, that is... incredible. The most thoughtful thing anyone has ever done for me."

"Figured it was worth doing on the off chance that you

and Allegra *did* stay here while we did this whole engagement thing. I wanted you to have time and space to explore that part of yourself again. If you wanted to."

"I don't know what to say."

"Then don't say anything. Just write."

There's a lump in my throat as I say, "I will."

"And if it's anywhere near as sexy as that book I found on your nightstand, sign me up to be the first reader." He winks at me and our eyes catch, and though he's laughing, I see heat flare in his gaze.

"Ha," I say, a little breathless. "Enjoyed that one, did you?"

"I like that they started out as friends."

"Me, too." I bite down on my bottom lip, and his gaze moves to my mouth. The same heat in his eyes simmers in my core.

"I think I need to cool off." Without warning, Carter pushes himself off the edge of the pool and into the water. Swims to the middle, then ducks beneath the surface and disappears for a few long moments as I sit here, heart pounding in my throat, skin prickling with anticipation.

When he finally surfaces near the edge, close to me again, he shakes out his hair. "You getting in?"

My stomach is clenched tight. I know what he's doing, ducking into the pool like that. He's giving me time and space to process, to make my own decision about what's going to happen next. And there's only one possible answer.

"Yes."

I stand, peel off my robe, awkwardly adjust the butt of my suit...

And look down to realize that I had no reason to feel insecure about my body for even a moment.

Because Carter's eyes are stoked with molten heat as they move slowly, deliberately, over every one of my curves.

The look in them is ravenous, like he's never seen anything he wants so much.

And suddenly, I know with every fiber of my being—as sure as I know my own name—that his expression is real. That his want is genuine. This is a face I've never seen on a movie screen. No. This look is all for me.

I don't stop to question it. I don't stop to doubt it. Doubt him. Doubt myself. For once, I let my instincts guide me and do what I want to do.

I slide into the cool water, every inch of my body tensed with want. It's a balmy night, and the shock sends goosebumps all over my body.

He's by my side immediately, wrapping his arms around me and pulling me to him.

"Cold?" he asks in a low voice, running his hands down my arms in such a way that produces more goosebumps than the water did.

I shake my head. "Not anymore."

He tilts his chin down and his eyes fix on mine. I see the clench in his jaw, feel the tension in his body as we look at each other for one moment. Two moments. Three.

We're a rubber band. A rubber band that's been wound so tight, for so long, that when all resistance finally—*finally*—gives way, the snap is sure to feel like an explosion of supernova proportions.

"Hi," he says again. His voice is gravelly, and his eyes—still trained on mine—darken, his pupils dilating inkily into the blue of his irises in a way that makes me suck in a sharp breath.

"Hi," I practically wheeze out in response.

And then, he's kissing me. And I'm kissing him, and my hands are tangled in his hair, and in this moment, he is everything and nothing else exists.

Carter's kisses start slow, deliberate, controlled. His

skillful mouth moves over mine, drawing a moan out of me within seconds. It's a sound he clearly likes, because the kiss goes from sweet to fiery instantly. His hands slide up my body, fingertips skating across my collarbones and along my throat before cupping my face almost desperately. His hot, searing kisses light a match inside my belly, and I'm burning.

There's a poem I love by a poet named Angie Sijun Lu, and in it, there's a line where the narrator asks her friend what drowning feels like. Her friend replies that "not everything feels like something else."

And this, *this*, is exactly how it feels to kiss Carter—like nothing else I've ever experienced. For so many years, I dreamed of what Carter James Callahan's mouth would feel like on mine, how he would taste, what he would sound like, what his hands would feel like on me...

Now, I know that every single wild fantasy I've ever had couldn't begin to capture the pure, unadulterated bliss of this moment. Couldn't possibly encapsulate how it feels to experience his pulse quickening beneath my fingers, hear his breath catch in his throat as his control begins to unravel...

Those big hands move to my thighs and he picks me up so I wrap my legs around his waist. His body is flush against mine and everywhere we're touching feels like an electrical storm crackling.

If this *is* what drowning feels like, I'd be happy to drown forever.

Because here, cradled in Carter's arms, I understand desire in a whole new way.

Ten years ago, I gave my virginity to a man—no, a *boy*—who didn't want it. I gave him something as a way, I wrongly thought, to make him love me more. A move fueled by desperation, not desire.

But one kiss from Carter is enough to, not erase, but ease those past hurts. There's something healing in his kiss, an experience of true desire for the first time. Something that makes me understand at a deep, core level that my experiences with sex and sexuality are nothing at all compared to what they can be. What they're meant to be.

In Carter's arms, I finally understand how a simple kiss can bring two grown people to their knees. I understand wanting to experience everything with him, the two of us together. Because I love him and want to show him love, rather than do something to make him see me.

This kiss tells me that I am already seen.

29

CARTER

Peaches.

She tastes like peaches.

Cool and sweet and perfect. Something I'm now craving in every form...

"Hellooo? Anyone there?"

I blink, startled out of the memory by the voice coming through the speaker. Thank goodness there are no other vehicles in the drive-thru right now, my head was a million miles away. "Sorry! Sorry. Yes, I'm here."

"What can I get for you?"

My eyes return to the menu board, where the famed summer special is featured front and center. "I'll have the peach milkshake, please."

"Alrighty. Anything else?"

"Um... actually, make that two. Thanks."

"My pleasure."

I pull my Jeep around to the pick-up window, and at the same time, try to pull my head out of the clouds.

Last night, I kissed Lana Mae, and it was... unforgettable. In a way that makes me wonder how on earth I've been living all these years without once doing it. Kissing someone you love, someone you have such deep feelings for that they're rooted in an inextricable part of you, is a whole new world. An experience unlike anything I've ever felt.

I can't get enough. All I can think is that I want to do it again. When we leave for LA in two days, I plan to do nothing but kiss her every second that we get to be alone on our trip.

With the milkshakes securely in cupholders, I swing onto the highway. Lana's got work today and Legs is at school, and I've decided to ditch my usual schedule of work-outs and meetings to see my new buddy Jared.

Yup, this past week has held a lot of new things for an old(ish) man, because in chatting to Jared for hours at the campout, we hit it off. For the first time in years, I have a new friend (who is not also employed by me) and he doesn't care that I'm Carter Callahan, the actor. He simply enjoys spending time with Carter Callahan, the human who is in no way as cool, glamorous, wild, or promiscuous as his public persona might suggest.

When I arrive at Stone Mountain Park, Jared's already in the parking lot, tying his shoes.

"Hey, man," I holler as I jump out of my Jeep.

Jared straightens. Looks from me, to my vehicle, to me again. Then, he smiles and nods at my Jeep. "Nice ride." He says this with obvious jokey sarcasm—the man speaks my language.

"Top of the line model from about two decades ago." I match his smile, then awkwardly hold out a drink topped with a huge dollop of whipped cream, suddenly aware that it might be a bit weird to buy another man a milkshake. "Uh... stopped to get a shake and thought you might like one, too."

"Didn't realize this was a first date," Jared says, then gives that booming belly laugh of his.

"If it was a first date, I would've at least brought flowers," I shoot back.

"I'd take a milkshake any day."

"Me too, actually." I take another sip of mine. Peach is my new favorite flavor.

"Gonna be a bit hard to trail run with these, though."

I shrug. "Let's walk, then."

Jared looks a touch relieved. "I'm down."

And so, the two of us big, grown-ass men, set off on one of the area's most popular hiking trails, the sun beating down on us as we drink matching pink-hued milkshakes and stroll up the mountain at a leisurely place, chatting the whole time.

My trainer would have a literal heart attack. But he's three thousand miles away.

And I'm here. In Atlanta. Climbing a mountain and feeling on top of the world. Also feeling a little stitch forming in my side already, thanks to the thousand calories of dairy I'm currently consuming.

"I hear you and Lana Mae moved in together?" Jared asks, and a smile splits my face.

"We did."

"You guys set a date yet?"

I look at him, uncomprehending. "For?"

He gives me a funny look. "The wedding...?"

"Oh!" I clear my throat and look at the path. Adjust my sunglasses. "Um. No, not yet."

"Guess you have to plan around your filming schedule?"

"Something like that," I reply as nonchalantly as I can. Because the last thing I want to think about right now is going away to film. Not when I'm enjoying the here and now so much. "How long have you and Imani been married?"

"Ten years." Jared wipes the sweat from his brow. "We were both fresh out of college when we became pregnant with Keisha. We tied the knot right away and made our little family official on paper."

"Congrats, man." Keisha and Legs are the same age, so if Jared was fresh out of college when Imani got pregnant, that makes him three or four years older than I am. "That's a big achievement. Ten years ago, I was a college freshman with an attitude problem and no clue what I wanted to do with my life." I smile. "And then, I met Lan."

"Imani mentioned you guys have been friends for years?"

"Yeah, we met when she was pregnant with Allegra. We became friends, and we stayed friends, even when we were on opposite sides of the country for huge lengths of time."

"Did you always want to be an actor then?"

I rub the back of my head. "Nah, man. Not at all. I started out as an extra, picking up little roles here and there just for the money. But then, I sort of fell into it. Got really lucky, I guess."

"I'd hate to be famous," Jared says bluntly. Then, he holds up a hand. "No offense, man. But I can't imagine strangers knowing who I am, being everywhere I go."

As if on cue, a hiker passing on the other side of the trail looks at us, does a little double take, and loses her footing. She slips, then before I can offer a hand to help her, she scrambles to her feet, her cheeks pink.

"You okay?" I ask.

"Yulp," she says. Goes redder. "I mean yep. Yep."

She disappears down the trail in a flash.

Jared watches her go. "Case in point, right there."

"You never really get used to it," I tell him. "But it's part of the job. I'm honestly way more interested in what you do."

By the way Jared lights up, it's clear that he, too, is excited by his work with at-risk youth around the city. It's a non-profit organization he started himself that helps teenagers in need access supports for mental health and wellness, life skills, education and even safe housing. When he talks about the kids he works with, he speaks with passion. With love.

I ask him tons of questions, and he launches into fascinating stories about his plans, his dreams, and his visions.

We talk so much that the eleven-mile hike flies by, despite the ever-growing stitch in my side. By the time we get back to our vehicles, the sun is on its descent.

"Thanks for a great walk, man."

I look at my new friend seriously, happy to have spent such a good time with him. Even happier to be going home to Lana and Legs. "It was a solid first date."

"Shall we make the second one a double date? Bring the wives and kids?" Jared jokes back lightly. But I feel almost giddy at the thought of us all spending time together.

"Absolutely. You guys should come round to our place for dinner when Lan and I get back from LA."

"When are you off?"

"Day after tomorrow. It's just for three days. Taking Lan to a movie premiere."

We say our goodbyes, and when I climb into my Jeep, I check my phone to find a few texts waiting for me.

Luke: Welcome to the sibling group chat, Carter.

Liam: Did you get non-consensually roped into this too?

Mindy: Too late to run, Butt Boy.

Annie: Surely we can come up with a better nickname than that?

Luke: I dunno, I like Butt Boy.

Liam: You would.

Lana Mae: I swear I don't know these people.

I laugh as I read the messages, touched that they've included me in the infamous family group chat that Mindy set up a couple of months back, much to Liam's chagrin. I love the Donovan clan, and with every day that goes by, they all feel even more like family.

Then, I click to my other message.

Elena: Great news, C! Nova Khatri has personally requested a meeting with you when you're in LA. I think *If Only* is in the bag. Great job on laying low in ATL, the whole "engaged to your hometown girl" bit has def paid off.

Just like that, my warm feeling turns cold. For one, reducing what I feel for Lana to a "hometown girl bit" is plain wrong. And for two, there's not a flicker of excitement within me at the thought that I might have landed the biggest role of my career.

Sure, wanting to win this role was the catalyst for this entire fake engagement fiasco, but honestly, it's barely crossed my mind lately. How Jared feels about his work with the at-risk youth? *That's* how I should feel about winning this role in *If Only*. Inspired. Passionate. Committed.

I don't feel any of these things. I'm not sure I even want the role, if I'm being honest with myself.

What I love is here in Atlanta. If I land the role in *If Only*, it means that soon, I'll have to leave again.

I never even wanted to leave in the first place.

30

LANA MAE

Stepping into LAX to the flash of a million cameras was something I never thought I'd experience in this lifetime. Or in any of the next thousand.

But here I am, bathed in morning sunlight as I walk hand in hand with Carter through the Arrivals area. We're flanked by two huge security guards and I'm trying my best not to panic as we get closer and closer to the mildly blinding lights.

I look up at Carter and his expression is blank. Dark sunglasses, baseball cap pulled low over his face, features carefully neutral as he walks slightly ahead of me, almost possessively shielding me from the cameras.

I try to emulate what he's doing, keeping my eyes firmly fixed on the exit up ahead. And tilting my chin up so we don't have a repeat of the paparazzi photo of a thousand chins.

As we approach the mob of lights and shouting camerapeople, Carter squeezes my hand, and when I squeeze back, he runs his thumb over my skin in a smooth, steady, reassuring motion.

Everything's okay. You're okay. I've got you.

My eyes flicker to his face, and he's still calm, composed. Nobody would ever guess that we're communicating in secret right now.

We stop for a moment right before the exit, and Carter gives a smile, a wave, a nod—saying hello to his fans. How he can tell the difference in the blur of bodies is beyond me. The whole thing seems entirely exhausting.

Outside, the security detail helps us into a vehicle with tinted windows. As soon as the door shuts behind us, Carter lets out a huge exhale before pushing his sunglasses up on his head and turning to face me. He reaches out and cups my face in his hand, his beautiful eyes trained on mine. Always checking on me. Always making sure. "You okay?"

I nod. "Yup. Glad that's over, though."

"I'll say. I bet Elena arranged that circus."

"She's good at her job."

"She is," Carter agrees, closing his eyes before pulling his hands from my face. As he swallows, I watch the strong, tanned column of his throat in awe. Today, his jawline is dotted in designer stubble. I can only imagine how that would feel against my cheeks as he kisses me. "Since the engagement party, the media have been hungry for more pictures of us together, and I guess that's what Elena delivered. We'll go in the back way to my place to avoid any more of that."

My place.

It's almost crazy to me that Carter's got this entire life out here. He drops into *my* life as and when he can, but I've never seen California Carter in his habitat.

I always blamed my lack of visiting him on not wanting him to pay for my flights. But maybe, possibly, there was a tiny part of me, deep down, that was scared to see this side of him. His fame, his high-profile relationships, his work and networking... I worried that all it would do was remind me

275

how established he is here. He moved to LA in the first place to pursue exactly *this*, and despite his beautiful house in Atlanta, there's a very real chance that he might never come back for good.

But I'm not going to go there right now. There's another very pressing issue weighing on my mind.

"I'm intrigued to finally see this famous coffee machine of yours."

Carter gives me a hot look that sears my insides. "I might have to learn how to use it, just for my latest guest."

"Oh goodness, no. Please no. Call Anthony to come make me a latte in the morning. I like my coffee drinkable."

"And I like my women sassy and insulting of my barista skills." Carter laughs as he puts an arm around me and slides me across the backseat until I'm curled up against him. His touch sends a hot shiver through me and I bite down on my bottom lip like I'm forcibly trying to contain my feelings from spilling out of my mouth.

We haven't kissed since that magical makeout in his pool two days ago, and I feel permanent pins and needles of anticipation for it to happen again. We've done lots of fun activities with Legs, cooked dinner together, and swam in his pool. But there's been no more kissing.

I'm hoping that he's simply waiting until he gets me alone. Mostly because I don't think *I* can wait any longer.

"Oh, heads up, Anthony's coming over when we get to my place to review our schedule for the visit and our wardrobe for the premiere."

So much for being alone.

"Sweet, I'd love to see him," I chirp. It's not a lie, exactly... I'd just prefer not to see *anyone* but Carter when we get to his place. For a while.

"Anything in particular you want to do while you're

276

here?" Carter asks, absentmindedly running his fingers through my hair and smoothing it as he talks.

I love that he's aware that this is a big deal for me to be here, that I'm the ironic travel agent who's barely traveled. But, as excited as I am to be in California, I've hardly glanced out the window of the vehicle. Being with Carter tops whatever setting we're in.

I move my eyes slowly over his chiseled features. So familiar, yet still so breathtaking after all these years. "What's *your* favorite thing to do when you're out here?"

He pauses for a moment, his expression almost unsure. Then, he turns to me with his trademark, dimpled grin. "I went to Malibu and surfed for the first time when I was here last. It was awesome."

"Let's do that, then."

"You don't want to go to Rodeo Drive or Santa Monica Pier or Disneyland?"

"I do. But I like the surfing idea more. I want us to do the things that make you happy, the things that you enjoy doing whenever you're out here. Get a sneak peek of your LA life." I pause. "If that's what you want, too?"

Carter gives me a curious look, like something's running through his mind. But then, he nods and opens his phone. "Surfing, it is. I'll set it up now. We might even be able to get over there this afternoon."

While Carter types away, I let my gaze drift out the window. I register the scenery around me for the first time, reflecting again on how weird it is to be here with him. Not a bad weird though. Never a bad weird when it comes to Carter.

But is it weird for *him* that I'm finally here, in this part of his world? Right after we kissed?

A kiss that he hasn't brought up. But then again, I haven't brought it up either...

How does one approach this kind of a conversation? Is it entirely unusual to say *"Oh hey, that was an insanely amazing, world spinning, groundbreaking kiss and I'd love to do it again but I can't tell if you want to as well, so just let me know."*

As though he can hear my thoughts, Carter's hand moves from my hair and slides around my waist, giving me a little squeeze. I feel his heartbeat through his shirt, warm and steady and reassuring.

Everything's okay.

I need to get out of my head and enjoy this trip to LA. Make memories. After all, attending the premiere completes the last step of our fake engagement agreement. Maybe Carter's waiting until we're over that hurdle to talk about what's going on with us. If he doesn't bring it up then, I will.

It'll be much less confusing when the pretenses are stripped away and it's only me and him.

Him and me.

No matter how many miles separate us.

31

CARTER

Have you ever wanted someone so badly that everything inside you aches to touch them, to hold them, to kiss them? Wanted them so much that the mere *idea* of proximity to this person flares desire inside you that's almost untameable in its urgency, its intensity?

That's Lana Mae for me. Now that I've actually allowed myself to lean into all the love and desire I've carried within me for so many years, I've discovered that the desire runs *deep*. I don't know if I could ever separate myself from it. It's part of me, carved and inked into all my grooves and edges.

And not kissing her for the past couple days has been an exercise in self control that I would gladly never repeat.

But I had to hold on. Take it slow. Lana's been hurt so badly in the past, the last thing I wanted to do was move too fast or risk making her uncomfortable in any way. After all, she and her daughter *just* moved into my house. I don't want her for a second to think that I expect anything from her. Especially when we haven't talked about what's going to happen when this trip is over—when this *If Only* role is in the bag and our fake engagement can officially be called off, according to Elena.

This is why I want to enjoy every moment together while we're in LA. And, hopefully, find another perfect opportunity to kiss her again. Show her how much she means to me.

I was so happy when she said that she wanted to go surfing earlier, when she said that she wanted to do what I love instead of all the tourist trap stuff. I would've gladly done those things with her, also. But it fills me with a special kind of warmth to know that she wants me to show her more of myself. The parts of me that she doesn't see when we're apart.

It made me wonder why I'm even preparing for us to be apart again. What would happen if I just...

Stayed.

And speaking of staying, I cannot seem to get rid of freaking Anthony. He's been here for, like, two hours. So basically an hour and forty-five minutes past his welcome.

"So, um, we should probably head out." I shift from foot to foot, check my watch, then realize I'm not wearing a watch, and hastily shove my hand in my pocket.

Anthony tracks the gesture with glinting dark eyes from the huge, U-shaped couch where he's lounging beside Lana, chatting away like they're BFFs. Mostly making jokes about my terrible cooking and coffee-making skills while I hover beside them, shooting him what I hope are sneaky death glares.

He arches a brow at me and stretches like a cat. "Trying to get rid of me, Carter?"

Yes.

Lana Mae looks at me with interest, and I shake my head, not wanting to appear rude. "No, no. Nothing like that. It's just that the truck is loaded up and ready to go downstairs, and it's probably going to take an hour and a half to get to Zuma at this time of day, and..."

"I get it, I get it." Anthony climbs to his feet. He does a wink-wink-nudge-nudge gesture to Lana, then stage whispers, "I think *someone* is trying to get you alone."

Lan's cheeks turn pink, and she hops up, too. Gives Anthony a quick hug. "Good to see you." She glances at me. "I'm going to change before we go."

"You can use my bedroom," I tell her.

"You don't say," Anthony purrs.

As Lana walks away, I punch him in the arm. "Would you quit it?"

"Would you get over yourself and tell her you're in love with her?"

Touché, Ant.

"I will."

And I mean it. I just need to figure out the perfect way to do so.

"You better, you idiot."

I roll my eyes at him. "Love you, too."

"Tell her." He points at me as he backs towards the door. "And remember, 9am sharp tomorrow. I can keep Lana Mae company while you're gone, if you like."

I smile at him gratefully. "Thanks, I'll let her know to text you." Then, I frown. "Just don't make her coffee from my machine, okay?"

"You celebrities and your weird requests."

And with a flick of his scarf, he's gone. Though why he's wearing a scarf today, I'll never know. It's like seventy-five outside. Fashion is clearly not my forté.

"Don't tell me you're gatekeeping the caffeine." A laugh makes me whirl around, and Lana's standing by the door to the living room with her arms crossed, an adorable smirk on her face. She's sporting a high ponytail and a lemon yellow sundress over a white bathing suit that makes me take a very sudden U-turn in my opinion of fashion.

"Beautiful," I breathe, my eyes moving over her face, her lips, her neck, her body. "You look beautiful."

"Thought I could at least look cute, pre-wetsuit. What's happening at nine tomorrow?"

"Meeting with the casting director for *If Only*."

My stomach tenses at the thought. I realize that I'm nervous in case I *get offered* the part.

For the love of all that is holy... All of this effort from Elena, Anthony, and Lana—from the people who care about me and support me—and I'm hoping I don't get it.

Lana smiles brightly. "How exciting that this whole fake relationship thing actually worked. I haven't read a negative story about you in ages."

The words *it's not fake to me* are on the tip of my tongue.

I swallow them down. Smile back.

"Come on, let's get you on a surfboard."

We spend the afternoon at Zuma Beach—a gorgeous, very beginner-friendly spot along the coast in Malibu. And today, the waves are perfect. Foamy white crests break along the shore, and the pale sandy beach is quiet. Serene. Romantic, even.

Not that this matters whatsoever.

Lana Mae is an entirely hopeless case on a surfboard. As in, she bobs around like a cork out there on the waves, laughing hysterically and asking endless questions about what it was like when *Baywatch* was filmed here. Like I was around back then.

After a few wipeouts, she gives up and sits on her board to watch me surf and cheer me on. I'm getting better, and enjoying myself immensely—the cold water, the rush of catching a wave, the way wiping out feels like you're being tumbled around in a washing machine...

I got news the other day that *If Only* is currently slated to film in New Zealand. I wonder if there's any good surfing out there. I look over at Lana, bathed in afternoon sunshine, her dark eyes shining as she maps my movements, and then wonder if I'd have half as much fun without her by my side.

When our lips are turning blue and the skin on our hands and feet is shriveling, we towel off and pull our clothes on over our damp bathing suits. I carry both our boards back to the truck and fasten them on while Lana sits shivering in the cab, the heat cranked all the way up.

We drive along the coast as the sun melts along the horizon. I have one hand on the wheel and the other arm propped on the center console. Lana reaches over and takes my hand, twining my fingers in hers, and when she squeezes, my heart does the same.

I don't want to go back to the apartment yet. Out here, everything feels so perfect, so removed from my actual life in LA.

On impulse, I take a left after Topanga Beach, turning us inland.

She looks at me through half-closed eyes, tired and peaceful and beautiful. "Where we going?"

"Fancy a detour?"

"Always."

Twenty minutes later, I pull over at a trailhead in the state park. We're surrounded by desert scenery blending with woodlands—scrub and rock and brush mingling with large oak trees. It's close to dusk now, and there are no other vehicles here.

We're all alone.

Lana and I get out of the truck and she scrambles into the truck bed, shielding her eyes with her hand as she spins around to look at the view.

"Oh, I love this song!" she says.

I'm still standing by the door, so I reach back into the truck and crank the radio up. It's some pop country song, and she knows all the words. She tilts her head towards the setting sunlight as she sings, looking like a sunflower. Tall and golden.

She shakes out her hair and closes her eyes as she begins to sway to the music, her lemon yellow sundress fluttering in the wind. She's still singing, looking both so sweet and so sexy that I can barely stand it.

Lana opens her eyes and catches me staring. Smiles and beckons to me.

I don't hesitate.

I hop into the bed of the truck with her and take her hand. Spin her round, then pull her close, one hand on her hip and the other intertwined with hers as we begin to slow dance. The arid evening air is warm and smells of salt and citrus. In the glow of the setting sun, Lana now looks like she's on fire. Bronzed skin, honeyed hair, eyes so dark that they spark like coal set alight as they catch the last glimmer of daylight.

Her head comes to rest on my chest as my arms circle around her, holding her against me as we sway gently. The entire world feels sweet and good right here, right now.

As her heartbeat moves through me and I feel the heat of her skin against mine, I'm turned upside down and inside out by a realization that hits me square in the chest: I'm not just in love with her. No, a simple 'love' isn't enough. I'm hopelessly, entirely, absolutely, unequivocally, go-to-the-ends-of-the-earth-for-her, head-over-heels in love with Lana Mae Donovan.

She's all I've ever wanted. All I'll ever want. And I'll do whatever I need to do to prove that I'm the man who can make her happy. Which means that I no longer need to be nervous about my meeting tomorrow morning. Because the answer's been there the whole time: If they don't offer me the part, great. If they do, *I can say no.*

I don't need this role to prove myself or my achievements. Those aren't what's important.

She is.

Lana Mae looks up and our eyes meet. "Hi," she whispers.

"Hi, yourself." I hold her gaze, and then, I take the plunge. "I have a confession to make."

"Oh?" Her lips part, and I slide a hand along her jaw, running rough fingertips over her smooth, silky skin. If only she knew how many times I've thought about running the pad of my thumb over her full bottom lip, coaxing a breathy sigh out of her before my lips find hers...

"I can't stop thinking about kissing you."

Lana's pupils dilate, her pulse hopping erratically as she says, "Me, too."

"In fact, it's taken all of my self control over the last couple of days to stop myself from leaning in and doing this..." I brush my lips against hers. She tightens her grip on me, almost reflexively pulling me closer as I kiss her. Her reaction drives the need in me for more—more of this, more of her, more of everything—and our kiss goes from sweet to scalding in mere moments.

My hands move into her golden hair, and she moans into my mouth. I run the tip of my tongue over her bottom lip, eliciting a shiver from her as her lips part. I tilt her head backwards to deepen the kiss. Taste the peaches on her tongue. Pulling her closer still.

I pour everything I have into her with this kiss, communicating everything I possibly can with my touch. Because how can I leave again when everything I've ever wanted is right here in front of me?

I love you, my lips say as they move against hers.

I believe you, her breathy gasp replies.

You should, my hands insist as they slide down her arms and find hers. Squeeze.

Everything is more than okay right now.

32

LANA MAE

It's perfect.

Everything is perfect.

Carter's hands are on my body and his mouth is on mine and I'm on fire.

But yet, even in the feverish rush of our kiss, he's watching out for me, checking on me. His hands suddenly find mine, and he squeezes.

It's a gesture he's made a million times. The one thing I can always rely on from him to calm me. Center me. Every time.

Yet this time, it almost undoes me.

A sob catches in my throat and he pulls back, his blue eyes flooded with concern.

"Hey, hey, hey." His voices is low and soothing as he cradles my face and tilts my chin up so I meet his eyes. "What's wrong? Is it something I did? Did I go too fast or—"

I shake my head in his hands, hot tears pricking at the corners of my eyes that I try—and fail—to blink away in mortification.

"No, you were perfect," I choke out on a sob, my stupid,

stupid tears now blurring my vision. "It's just..." I trail off as my voice wobbles.

"Hey, it's okay," he says softly, his thumbs moving to wipe the tears from under my eyes. His forehead comes to meet mine. "I'm here. Take your time."

I nod in response, leaning into his touch, and we stand there, my face in his hands, foreheads pressed together, until I finally catch my breath.

"Thank you," I whisper.

He pulls back enough to look into my eyes, then kisses my forehead. His lips burn against my skin, and despite my tears, I shudder at the sensation.

"You want to talk about it?"

I swallow. Nod.

"I'm sorry," I start as I sink to a seated position in the bed of the truck. Cross my legs and wrap my hands around my knees, holding on tight as if to hold myself in place.

"You don't ever have to be sorry for the way you feel." He pulls off his hoodie and drapes it over my shoulders, pulling it snug around me. He sits opposite me.

I sniffle as I rub my cheek to the sweatshirt, breathing in his scent as I try to form a cohesive sentence. "I guess I'm feeling a bit overwhelmed," I finally say.

"Why's that?"

"Because that was, like... *wow*."

"It was."

"And the last time we kissed, it was no different."

"I agree."

"And you're always so nice to me."

His mouth quirks. "You think I was kissing you like *that* to be... nice?"

That draws a smile out of me. "Well, no." He leans over and wipes my nose with the sleeve of his hoodie, and I laugh through my tears. "I don't know much, but I'm pretty sure nice boys don't kiss like *that*. What I mean is that I just appreciate you looking out for me, making sure I'm okay, no matter what."

"Lan, you mean the world to me. I'll *always* look out for you."

"I just... I wasn't lying the night of our engagement party when I said that I hadn't been touched in, like, a decade. I haven't even come close to kissing anyone else since, well... since Steven."

His face falls for a moment. Then, his expression changes. Becomes carefully stoic. "Was it that you weren't—*aren't*—over him, even though you want to be?"

"No!" I exclaim sharply. Take a deep breath. We might've never talked about dating in the past, but this is something I should tell him. Something he should know before things go any further between us.

I inhale through my nose and look up to the sky as I breathe out. The stars are arriving for the night, flickering overhead like candles in the darkness.

"I... only slept with Steven once."

Carter's face is a question mark, but he remains silent, his eyes calmly telling me that I can keep talking if I want to. And I do.

"Don't get me wrong, it was my decision to do it. I'm not saying he pressured me or anything, I just want to make that clear." I hold up my hands, and Carter nods. "But at the same time, he used to become distant whenever I said I wasn't ready. Was kind of hot and cold with me; one minute telling me nice things about myself, the next minute talking about so and so girl he thought was hot. It made me insecure. And I thought that, if I slept with him, it would make him like me more. Which was dumb, I know."

"Not dumb," Carter corrects immediately. "You were seventeen, Lan. And that sounds like gaslighting to me."

I shrug, my shoulders slumping. "That's exactly what Dr. Lemay said. But he didn't pressure me. I made the decision. And the second it was over, I felt the shift in him. It was like the very thing I thought would make him love me more pushed him away. I felt so inadequate, like I'd done something wrong."

His hands come to rest gently on my shoulders, his big hands anchoring me. "Still gaslighting. You did nothing wrong."

My bottom lip trembles. "And I know this is stupid, but a part of me thought that maybe *I* was the problem. Like I'd done something wrong, and that was why he slept with other girls while we were still together."

Carter's hands tense, then slide off my shoulders as he makes a sound in his throat that's akin to a growl. "He slept with other girls 'coz he was a complete jackass. Not because of anything you did."

"Deep down, I know that. But at the same time, I carried that insecurity with me. And when I started dating again, it all bubbled back up to the surface, amplified by the fact that I am now a single mom with stretchmarks and ten years of being out of practice." I fist his sweatshirt in my hands, exhale before I continue. "Even though I knew, logically, that it wasn't true, I couldn't fight the nagging feeling that I was a disappointment, or bad at sex or something."

Carter shakes his head at me. "I can assure you that it definitely wasn't that."

"Again with the being nice to me." I smile feebly. Since my mom died, he's been there for me, every step of the way. Even before she died, before we even knew each other that well, he would show up for me.

We needed each other then, and I still need him now.

And right now, he's showing up again, making me feel safe and wanted.

"Since we've been doing this thing, you've calmed so much of my anxiety surrounding relationships and sex." I take a deep breath. "I never thought I'd get to experience this stuff in such a positive way and with someone I trusted so much. For the first time in a long time, I actually feel like I can love someone, and be somewhat worthy of being loved."

"Entirely worthy," Carter corrects, and my eyes well up again as he adds, "And I'm still not being *nice*, silly. I'm being honest when I say that getting to kiss you, hold you, touch you, is surreal for me. You don't realize how incredible you are."

"Is this... normal? How good it is between us?"

"The earth-shattering kisses and insane, off-the-charts chemistry?" Carter grins. "No. No it is not."

"But you've dated, literally, some of the most beautiful women alive."

"That means nothing."

"'Course it does. I just mean, like, I'm not really your usual type."

"Wrong. You are my entire type." He looks at his hands for a moment before training his eyes back on my face. There's something in his expression that makes me feel weak. "None of those other women ever made me laugh like you do. Made me feel like you do."

"Carter, what're you saying right now?" My voice is barely above a whisper.

"I'm saying that you're my favorite person on this planet, and I don't know anyone more worthy of love than you are."

I do the only thing I can think of doing in response to words like those: I lean forward and kiss him.

He immediately wraps his arms around me and kisses me back, and this time, it's different. Not heated or feverish or desperate, but soft and sweet. Tender. Entirely unhurried.

By the time we pull apart, the sky is midnight black and dotted with hordes of twinkling stars. My lips are swollen and tender, my hair is a mess, and the saltwater from the ocean earlier has dried in cracked white patterns on my skin. Yet, I've never felt more beautiful. More desirable.

More *loved*.

33

CARTER

They say the third time's the charm.

And I've woken up next to Lana Mae three times over the last few weeks—the first time, a little frantic after a mistaken sleepover; the second, content at the sight of her curled up next to me but with an aching back from a very flat air mattress; and this morning, sheer perfection at the sight of her in my arms in my bed in LA, infiltrating my life here on the west coast in the most welcome of ways.

Her suitcase is unzipped on my floor, her sweater is draped over the back of my armchair, her toothbrush is in my bathroom, and this place has never felt more like home in all the years I've lived here.

I wrap my arms around Lan's golden shoulders and pull her towards me, happy that I got to be here with her all night, cuddling her close. My fingertips move her hair out of the way so I can inhale the scent of her skin, place a kiss on her neck above the edge of her t-shirt. In response, she murmurs something in her sleep and snuggles into my side, pressing her body against mine in a way that makes me smile—like she'll do whatever she can to get closer.

I know the feeling all too well. I can't get close enough to the woman right now.

And just as Lana is here with me now, filling the hole that's been at the center of my years spent out here on the west coast, last night, she let me into the part of *her* life she'd never unlocked before by candidly discussing her dating history and hurts.

I only had two thoughts running through my head as she spoke.

The first was that I'm glad I punched that gaslighting asshole in the face.

The second was that, over all these years of watching her closely, reading her body language and facial expressions, watching her eyes for telltale flickers so I could be there for her, soothe her anxiety and help ease her stress... well, I never would have guessed that she thought I didn't pursue more than friendship with her because she wasn't my *type*.

It's insane to me that she could've ever thought that. Even if she had purple skin and six legs and a horn in the center of her forehead, she'd still be my freaking type. She's *Lana*. She's perfect to me, exactly the way she is, and I love her more than words could say.

This fake engagement is technically over after the premiere later today, but this whole thing has felt real for me since day one. The realest thing to ever happen to me. And after we get through tonight, I want to make it real every day for the rest of forever.

All the focus will be on me at the premiere, and I want this to be about *her*. So, tomorrow, I will find the perfect way to tell Lana Mae everything I'm feeling. Let her know that I'll move as slow and respectfully as she needs me to, physically, mentally, and emotionally. As long as I'm with her.

I hold her close for another few moments before I drag myself out of bed, letting her sleep. I shower, dress, then place an order on DoorDash for coffee to be delivered straight to our door—venti cinnamon dolce latte, extra hot. Just how she likes it. And also because I still literally have no idea how the coffee machine works.

Then, I text Anthony.

Carter: Hey, slight change of plan. Wanna grab a coffee with me before the meeting this morning?

Anthony: Sure thing. Name a place and time. Lana going to be okay on her own?

Carter: Yup. Made sure she has coffee and everything.

Anthony: Please tell me you didn't make it.

Carter: Don't worry, Starbucks made it.

Anthony: Phew, I like her alive.

I couldn't agree more. And as I sneak out of my apartment quietly so as not to wake her, I'm filled with a brand new sense of purpose. I'm no longer nervous and uncertain, but sure that the path that lies ahead has both been chosen by me, and chosen correctly.

It's almost poetic that Lana's here in LA to close this chapter with me. To stand next to me at a movie premiere tonight and taste a piece of the life I had here before it's gone. That way, when we look back, we can smile at the fact that we shared a part of it together.

Because moving forward, if it's away from her, I don't want it. I want Lana Mae everywhere I go, and in everything I do.

And I'll do whatever it takes to make that happen. No matter where I am on this planet, *she* is home to me. *She* is my happy.

Her, and Allegra.

My found family.

And I'm a man who plans—no, *vows*—to always be there for his family.

34

LANA MAE

It's wild to think that, a few weeks ago, I couldn't believe that people went out on Thursday nights.

And now, here I am in a limousine on my way to the world premiere of a blockbuster movie. With the most handsome man in the world at my side.

Thursdays have certainly come a long way since air-fryer potatoes and Ina Garten cooking shows.

"You okay?" Carter has an arm around me, and his fingertips are moving up and down my bare skin, creating a patchwork of goosebumps. I've got a slinky cream silk dress on (picked out by the ever-reliable Anthony), and Carter's wearing the absolute crap out of a custom-tailored suit—black pants and a jacket over a black dress shirt, unbuttoned at the collar and showing the most delicious sliver of tanned chest that makes me want to scream "stop the car!" to our limo driver so I can climb on top of him (Carter, not the driver) and lick it. Which is honestly pretty indicative of my current state of mind.

i.e. a tad unhinged.

"Um, I'm not sure." I look into Carter's blue, blue eyes

as I say this, and the buzz that floods through me feels like shooting a triple espresso.

Make that a *lot* unhinged.

"How can I make it better?" He slides his hand onto my thigh. Squeezes. And then, he smiles. Really smiles.

In fact, he's been in a remarkably good mood all day. He got back from his meeting with the *If Only* people this morning surprisingly quickly, and when I asked him how it went, he twinkled as he said, "Really great". My stomach rolled a little as he said the words, but I pushed those feelings away. After last night, I know everything's going to be okay between us, no matter what happens.

We then hopped in his truck and drove down to Huntington Beach. Spent the rest of the morning eating açai bowls while watching beach volleyball games and strolling the boardwalk. And got absolutely soaked when Carter unceremoniously picked me up and ran into the water, plunging us both into the shallows fully clothed (which made me splutter), before he kissed the absolute hell out of me (which totally made up for it, and then some).

We got back to his place after lunch, and I spent the afternoon getting my hair and makeup done. Carter, meanwhile, took a quick shower then laid on the couch next to me so we could watch *Gilmore Girls* together.

It's been a pretty damn perfect day so far. A fairytale. And now, I get to stand next to the man I love at the premiere of his newest movie.

I don't even think about later, when we get to be alone together. The desire coursing through my veins for Carter— for the way he looks, and smells, and touches me, and kisses me—is a brand new feeling to which I am in grave danger of becoming addicted. It's like a whole new part of myself is bursting through the surface, a side of me that is no longer a confused teenage girl, but a sensual, desirable *woman*.

"You can make it better by kissing me," I tell him boldly as I look at him from under my lashes.

He gives me an impish look. "Aren't you worried about ruining your makeup?"

"Are *you*?" I counter.

"Screw the makeup!" he proclaims. And then, he kisses me wildly, in a way that confirms that he, too, is feeling a bit unhinged right now.

When we finally come up for air, the limo is coming to a stop. He brushes his lips against the sensitive skin of my collarbone before giving me a rueful look. "Should we just get Ted to turn the car around?"

I laugh and shake my head. "Tempting, but no. This is your night. Let's go celebrate."

"As long as it's with you, I'm there." He brings the pad of his thumb to my mouth and drags it along the line of my bottom lip. Smiles. "Good as new. You ready to do this thing?"

"Born ready," I reply. And this time, I mean it. Because we have tonight, and the lights, cameras, and the buzz of people are all background noise for me. It's me and him.

Him and me.

At this moment, nobody and nothing else matters.

We step out of the limo to a roar of screams and cheers. There are throngs of people pressing up against the barriers for a better look at Carter Callahan in the flesh. Security are physically restraining people. Flashbulbs are going off, and cameras are rolling, and I even catch a glimpse of a girl with a "Marry me, Carter" sign in the middle of the crowd.

Sorry girlie, he's taken.

Carter, slightly ahead of me (protective as usual), reaches for my hand. Squeezes.

But despite the cheering, and the people, and the lights, and the cameras, I feel... totally fine. Nervous, sure. Who isn't nervous walking down a red carpet in front of the entire world in four-inch heels? Kendall Jenner, probably.

Yet, underneath those nerves, I don't feel much anxiety. *Any* anxiety, in fact. That voice in the back of my head telling me that I'm not good enough, that I'm unworthy, is silent.

And sure, Carter and I haven't talked about what's going to happen next, haven't addressed the role in *If Only* that I'm assuming he accepted this morning, and how everything will unfold for us after this trip is complete and he leaves again for work. But I'm trying to just stay in the present tonight, focus on the fact that right now, I have my hand in his. That's all I need.

I squeeze, then tug on his hand, signaling for him to slow down. He doesn't have to worry about me. So, he takes his time. Stops to talk and pose for pictures with fans. Sign an autograph for a pre-teen boy. Smile and wave at the cameras. And while he gives his fans the love and attention they deserve for showing up for him tonight, I watch the whole thing with a grin on my face. Because *he's* the one who's always shown up for *me*.

When we get to the top of the carpet, there's a bunch of press waiting. He grabs my hand again, pulling me in close to his side.

He smiles down at me affectionately as the cameras click away, and leans down as if to kiss my cheek, but instead, brings his lips to my ear and whispers, "You look so hot right now, I am having a very hard time keeping my hands off of you."

I bite my lip, hard, as my stomach turns to jelly.

Click. Click. Click.

Carter smirks at me, clearly pleased with himself and the reaction he's invoked, and I resist the urge to poke my tongue out at him. Revel in the fact that, though he touches me and kisses me and says sexy little things like that to me now, he's still my best friend in the world.

We finish posing for pictures, then move down the line towards the video cameras and interviewers standing by to ask questions. I attempt to step out of the way, let Carter take the spotlight, but he holds onto my hand tightly. So I stay next to him, running my thumb along the edge of his hand.

"Hi, Carter!" A peppy woman in a double-breasted lipstick-pink suit jacket beams at him. Then, she looks at me, still beaming. "Lana Mae."

"Hey, Angie," Carter says easily.

"Hi," I squeak. How bizarre that she knows my name. And that she actually got it right and didn't call me Alana.

Angie then asks a few questions about the movie and Carter's role in it, and what he hopes people will love about it. He answers with a dazzling smile, natural self-confidence, and that touch of boyish charm mixed with self-deprecating humor that made every red-blooded woman in America swoon in the first place.

Angie is holding the microphone towards him, looking like she'd happily rip all her clothes off and beg him to have her babies. In the background, people are still screaming Carter's name. Cheering and clapping for him. The cameras are still flashing.

Our plan worked. The world is once again on Carter's side.

As if she can hear my thoughts, Angie then asks, "Before I let you go, Carter, do tell us, are the rumors true?

Can we expect tomorrow's press conference for *If Only* to officially announce your casting as the lead?"

Frick, I'd like to know too, Angie.

"I'm afraid you'll have to tune in tomorrow to find out, Ang." Carter lifts a shoulder. "Tonight, I'm here to talk about this movie and the incredible cast and crew who came together to make such a phenomenal action flick." He shoots the camera a cheeky smile as he slings his arm around me. "Oh, and I'm taking my beautiful fiancée on a great night out too, of course."

"Oooh. So much secrecy." Angie's smile becomes a little predatory as she looks away from Carter and over to me. "Lana Mae, I have to know, do you think that Carter's hush-hush stance on the *If Only* situation has anything to do with the recent revelation that he assaulted your ex-partner in Las Vegas, and that said partner is officially pressing charges?"

I frown in total confusion as she sticks the microphone in my face, eyes widened dramatically, like she's playing this all up for the cameras. But I barely notice her. Her words are bending and twisting around me, a pattern of syllables that make no sense, no matter how hard I try to make them.

Steven... is pressing charges because... Carter assaulted him? In Vegas?!

No. There's no way.

Anxiety begins to brew in my stomach, then claw up my chest like a wild animal. I turn all of my attention on Carter, and immediately, the rest of the world blurs and fades away behind him.

His hand is still around my shoulder, and I confidently wait for him to squeeze. Let me know that the media are spinning another story and this is all a total lie. Because it *is* a lie, right?

I wait.

And wait.

He looks... *off* right now. His face is strained, his eyes dark, his mouth pressed in a harsh line. Carter, who's usually so unshakeable, currently looks entirely shaken.

No words have been spoken, but I have my answer.

He swallows and leans towards the mic, looking like he's about to say something, but I swiftly cut him off.

"It wasn't Carter's fault!" I'm amazed that my voice is even working right now, let alone that it sounds confident and steady. I keep on talking. "He can press charges all he wants, but nothing will come of it because Carter wasn't the one in the wrong."

Angie's eyes are practically bugging out of her head with glee, and I can only imagine what on earth my defensive response looked like on camera. "Do you really think—"

Carter holds up a firm hand, though his voice has a strained quality that I don't think is noticeable to anyone else but me. "No further questions, thank you."

With that, he steers me away from Angie and her intrusive questions and down the carpet. Behind us, the other interviewers are yelling our names, calling after us with questions and comments like this isn't a movie premiere, but some kind of courthouse press conference. Carter keeps walking us forward, eyes fixed ahead and expression entirely void of emotion.

And as I'm at a total loss of what else I could possibly do right now, I follow suit.

35

CARTER

I don't know what I'm expecting her to do, but I'm definitely not expecting her to laugh.

"Wow, Angie sure is a real Buttinsky. Mona McCreary is clearly in the wrong line of work." She smiles flimsily. "Shall we find our seats?"

We're standing in the foyer of the movie theater, and as she moves to go inside, I grab her arm. Spin her back around to look at me.

She doesn't. Instead, she looks at the floor.

"Lana Mae," I say firmly. "We need to talk about this. "

We've been through a lot together over the course of our friendship. I was the one who sat in the waiting room while baby Allegra was born, the one who cuddled her in bed to help her sleep after her mom died, the one who watches *Gilmore Girls* reruns with her like it's my damn job.

I'm now also the person who punched her ex-boyfriend, the father of her child, in the face. Then let her find out about it while she was being interviewed on live TV.

The crazy thing is that, while that revelation literally confirmed everything the press was saying about me and all those terrible rumors, she *still* publicly defended me.

So basically, this conversation can no longer wait until tomorrow.

She finally raises her eyes to meet mine and says, "People are watching and I'm assuming that the headline 'Carter Callahan seen fighting with his fiancée at movie premiere' isn't exactly what Elena has in mind for tonight. We should take our seats. This is *your* night and I don't want to spoil your moment."

"Lan, I don't give a damn about all that right now."

She gives a casual wave of her hand that I know isn't casual. "Carter, we're here for the show."

I can tell that she's going to fight me on this. So, with my hand still on her arm, I do the only thing I can think to do: I grab the handle of the nearest door... and drag her into a supply closet.

"Hey!" she squeaks as the door swings shut behind us. I flick on the light. It's tiny in here, cluttered with shelving and cleaning supplies. I'm not unaware of the ridiculousness of this situation: me in a custom-made Ralph Lauren suit, her in a stunning evening gown, and my foot planted firmly in a mop bucket.

But desperate times call for desperate measures.

"What do you think you're doing?" she whispers. We're standing so close, I can see her pulse moving in her throat.

"Talking to you. I know you're mad that I didn't tell you it was Steven I got in a fight with, so I'll start by saying that I'm sorry you found out like that. But I'm not apologizing for doing it."

Her eyes are huge as she stares at me incredulously. "You think I'm mad that you punched Steven?"

I nod.

She throws up her hands. "I'm not mad about that! I mean, I'm a little shocked, sure. And it would've been nice to find this out without a camera in my face. But whatever. I'm sure he deserved it. He's not exactly Mother Teresa."

I monitor her expression carefully. Note the way she still won't meet my eyes, the way her lips are curved down at the corners, the way her body is angled.

This isn't the full story. Something else is bothering her.

"What's going on, Lan?" I ask on an exhale.

A couple of long, drawn out seconds go by. Seconds which, in this tiny broom closet, feel like years.

Then, Lana puts a hand in the middle of my chest, spreading her fingers across my heart and spreading warmth all over my skin. She looks up at me, and her eyes are no longer flat, but liquid. Dark and stormy. "Carter. I know you, and you would never do something like that unprovoked. But I need you to tell me, did you do it because of me? Did he say something to you?"

I swallow, my skin prickling. What he said to me is the exact reason I never brought it up to her. But it's one thing to keep something from her to protect her, and it's another to lie to her face about something that indeed *does* directly involve her.

She's looking at me, challenging, and I do what I need to do. "I'm not going to repeat what he said. But yes."

Her expression pinches. "So I'm the cause of all this crap that's been happening to you lately. You've been dragged through the mud by the press, made out to be a total dick by the media... all because of me and my baggage."

"No." I shake my head quickly. "It was *my* decision to hit him, and I'd do it again. Plus, Lan, it's not about them. I only care what *you* think."

She swallows slowly, her eyes darkening even further. "I almost cost you the role of a lifetime in *If Only*, and now, you're standing in a freaking janitor's closet at your own freaking movie premiere because of me. What I *think* is that this isn't what you deserve. The last thing I want to do, ever, is hold you back. And it seems like that's all I've done lately."

I open my mouth to respond to this, then register her words. "What do you mean, 'almost' cost me the role in *If Only*? They haven't announced the cast yet."

"You came home from the meeting this morning walking on air. And you didn't tell me how it went, so I assumed you were holding off on breaking the news that you were leaving again for filming soon. Tonight was our last event as an officially engaged couple, so I thought you were giving me tonight before telling me." She sniffles, her voice wavering a touch as she smiles, setting her jaw. "New Zealand, right? I looked it up this morning, they have great surfing there. You can keep practicing."

She has it all so, so wrong.

"I turned down the role."

"What?"

"I was happy today because I turned it down. Said thanks but no thanks when they offered it to me. Explained that I was taking a break from acting to spend time with my new family."

"So... you turned it down because of me?!" She looks almost indignant, her lower lip trembling.

"Because of *us*." I take her hands in mine. "Because of *this* between us. Because I want more than anything for this fake engagement to be over, and it will be tonight. So, starting tomorrow we can have something entirely real together."

"No," Lana says, so softly, so quietly, I almost don't hear it. But as the tiny syllable touches my eardrums, the roar of sound is deafening.

I scrub my hand over my face. Suck in a breath. "We can do this, Lan. We've got this."

"I don't belong in this part of your world."

I catch her wrist with my hand. "Llama, I don't want any part of my world not to have you in it."

But she's still shaking her head.

"I need to go." She gently places her other hand—the one I'm not holding—on top of mine, and I obligingly release my grip. It's not like I'm going to hold her in here against her will like a broom closet psycho. "And right now, *you* need to get back inside and attend your premiere. Just like you needed to go all those years ago."

With that, she's gone. And all I can do is stand there for a long, long moment, suddenly confused.

What the hell does she mean—I *needed* to go?

Needed to go to LA? Needed to leave Atlanta? Needed to leave *her?*

That's not how I remember it. At all.

Nine years ago, I went to an audition on Peachtree Street in downtown Atlanta, where an agent gave me her card. She thought I had promise. Potential.

Her name was Elena.

I must've twirled the card in my hands a thousand times before Lana Mae encouraged me to pick up the phone and call her. So I did. Elena invited me to come here to LA to start auditioning for bigger roles, said that she would help me along the way.

I was so torn about going. I couldn't imagine leaving Lana and Legs, but this was my opportunity, and Lana was so encouraging and supportive. Since her mom had died, I'd been there every night when she needed me—was more than happy to have done so—but everything about her demeanor suggested that she didn't need me in that way anymore.

So, even though I didn't want to leave her, I did what I thought was best. I dropped out of college, and took off for the west coast. It was hard at first, and I was surprised. Before I met Lana, I'd been so good at being alone. She'd changed me, and I was comforted by the fact that it was only meant to be a temporary move. A chance to give acting the best shot I could.

I always planned to come home... but every time I talked to Lana on the phone, she sounded like sunshine. Happy. She had her brothers, got her GED, and baby Allegra was growing into a strong, confident, sweet little kid.

As time went by, things slowly but surely got easier for me, too. I started getting callbacks. Booking roles. I got my feet under me, and, somewhere along the way, my move became not-so-temporary.

What I wanted was purpose. To feel proud of myself and like I'd achieved something. I found this in LA with my acting career.

But what I *needed* was her.

And, like I didn't need to go back then, I don't think she needs to go now. Things are different today. We're no longer just friends, that much is clear. There's no longer any good reason we should be apart. When we met, Lana was a teenage girl who was about to go through more heartache than a lot of people experience in a lifetime. And I was just a kid who kept to myself, only looked out for myself, and was desperate to prove something.

She changed me in a way I could never have imagined. And I know my presence in her life changed her, too. But, on top of that, we grew separately. Today, Lana is a grown woman who's both resilient and remarkable. And though I will always try to protect her, she is my equal partner in whatever relationship we have. Which means no more keeping things from her...

So I'm going to give her space to process everything she's feeling, and then, I'm going to go out there and find her and tell her everything I feel. Fight for her.

Because sometimes, fighting *is* the answer. And I'll be damned if I let anything separate us again without putting up my best fight.

And with that resolution, I step out of the closet, tripping over the damn mop as I go, so I end up stumbling out into the foyer. I must look crazed and out of control all over again, falling out of a random closet at my own movie premiere, my suit slightly crumpled. I'm sure the paparazzi are going to have a field day with this one, but I don't care.

They can call me what they want because they're gonna forget my name soon, anyway.

Tomorrow, I'm going home. For good.

I have a different—much better and brighter—future ahead of me with the woman I love.

36

LANA MAE

I've never been the one to leave.

And to be honest, it's not all it's cracked up to be. To start with, I'm standing on a dark street with absolutely no idea where I am or where I'm going. My feet are aching from my heels and I didn't have a bag with me for the premiere, so I don't have a phone, or a credit card, or even a Kleenex that I can use to blow my nose.

What the hell am I even doing right now?

Was leaving the right thing to do?

I'm not good when put on the spot... but I should have tried to explain what I was feeling instead of just legging it out of there. Or at least told Carter that I needed some time to think, to process, instead of just saying "no" to him when all I've ever wanted to say is "yes."

He's always been there for me when I've wanted to talk, or not wanted to talk. The man can read me like a book, see what I need before I do.

After my mom died, the night of my Walmart panic attack, we didn't talk. Not a word. Carter just looked at me, read the situation, then slipped out of his sneakers and crawled into bed with me, drew me close to his chest and wrapped his arms around me.

We fell asleep like that.

And the night after that, and the one after that, and the one after that.

Bit by bit, the nightmares stopped. The anxiety eased enough so that I felt like I could breathe.

It was like stepping out of a fog. But once my vision cleared, I realized that if I didn't do something, Carter would sacrifice too much. Sacrifice what he couldn't afford to lose.

Back then, when the opportunity came up for him to go to LA, I was the first to smile and congratulate him. I supported him from the beginning because it was the right thing to do. He had a bright future to chase, and I had a baby to care for. As much as I wanted him to keep holding me each night, I knew that, to grow, we had to be apart. So every time he called, I was strong. I never let him know how much I missed him. I would never hold him back by making him think that he needed to be in Atlanta with me. I couldn't bear for the person I loved to sacrifice their future for me.

But somehow, he's still gone and done that. Put me first when he should have been thinking about himself. We could have made a long distance relationship work while he went to New Zealand.

Surely he knows that I would wait forever for him, if I had to?

"Need a ride?" The voice makes me just about jump out of my skin. I didn't see the sleek, black limo pull up next to me. It's the same limo that drove Carter and me to the premiere, but now, Anthony's staring at me through the open back window with a vaguely amused expression on his sweet face.

"I absolutely do." I stumble towards the car, tripping on my heels as I go.

Anthony is next to me in a flash, putting a steady arm around me as he helps me into the limo, where I inelegantly flop backwards onto a bench seat. Which happens to be leather, so I almost slide right off it in my silk dress.

I manage to claw myself back into some semblance of a seated position, and a box of Kleenex is proffered my way. I smile at Anthony gratefully as I take a wad of them

"You okay there, girlie?" He gives me a sympathetic pat on the knee.

I don't know if it's his kindness, or the fact that his well-meaning pat makes me think about Carter and how he'd give my knee a squeeze to make me feel better, but I suddenly feel the weight of what just happened and burst into tears.

Go Anthony and his preempted Kleenexes.

"Does Carter have a good lawyer?" I ask through a dramatic sniffle, then blow my nose. Loudly.

I'm sure I'm the pinnacle of attractiveness and poise right now, but Anthony, bless his heart, does not comment on this. Instead, he gives me a wry, crooked smile. "Yeah, 'course he does."

"Do you know what happened?"

He pauses for a moment, then nods. He knows exactly what I'm referring to. "A tape of the footage was leaked earlier today—probably timed with the premiere to make a bigger splash. From there, your ex boyfriend was identified. I guess, when the media reached out to him, he said he was going to press charges."

I'm seething all of a sudden. How *dare* Steven.

But before I can boil over, Anthony gives my knee another pat. "You've got nothing to worry about, honey. He doesn't have a leg to stand on. Several witnesses have come forward saying that Carter was provoked, and by the end of the fight, it was three on one. Your boy won't face any charges in the end, don't you worry."

"Wait, it was three on one?" I gasp, horrified.

"Probably shouldn't have mentioned that bit." Anthony looks bashful.

"He never told me what happened that night," I admit in frustration. "I guess he was trying to protect me from whatever Steven said... but I can't believe he'd do that at the expense of his entire reputation. I nearly cost him the biggest role of his freaking career."

"Girl, come on." Anthony sits forward, crosses his arms and levels me with a *look*. "Enough with that nonsense."

"What nonsense?"

"You know as well as I do that that boy only wants one thing in his life. And it sure ain't no movie role."

"But *If Only* is—"

"*If Only* is what he *was* going for before he knew that he had the option to be with you. Carter doesn't care about the Oscars. Or being in any more movies. Or even going to Zac Efron's parties, which is beyond my comprehension. Carter's not himself when he's not with you, and between you and me, I think he spends most of his time here in LA counting down the days until he's home in Atlanta again."

I blink, caught off guard by Anthony's words that I so desperately want to believe, but don't know if I can let myself. "He does?"

Anthony shakes his head and casts his eyes heavenward. "Child, why do you think he went and bought a family home and decorated it in all your favorite colors? That boy is *nesting*, I tell you."

Nesting. My mind flits back to the library room. A custom-made room that looked like it was produced straight

314

from my wildest dreams. A room that I, specifically, know I belong in.

He, quite literally, made room for me in his house.

"I...I was just trying to protect his future," I say feebly, embarrassed to feel a sob catching in my throat.

A smile. "And what if *you're* his future, but you're too busy trying to give him something you *think* he wants when what he really wants is you?"

Anthony's words run over me like water, and I finally—finally—let myself drink them in. I spent so much time in therapy over the years, working through my hurt and grief, and trying to change my thought patterns about myself. Yet, when push came to shove and I was confronted with Carter saying that he was choosing me over his career, I straight-away panicked and fell back into old thoughts about myself: that he was a Hollywood star with the world at his feet, and I was a single mom tied to Atlanta who would only ever hold him back.

I know that he's what I want; the person who's best for me. But I never stopped to consider that, maybe, I'm what's best for him, too. That we're better together, and our careers, and the places we live, and the things we want to achieve will always come second to having each other. Our safe place. Together.

And yeah, he didn't tell me what really happened. But it wasn't for his own gain—he was trying to protect me from blaming myself. He was clearly right to do so, because as soon as the truth came out, that was what I immediately did. Guess old habits really do die hard.

But I am so much more than what those negative, anxious thoughts tell me I am.

Plus, didn't I hold back from him, too? All this crap about clout, about wanting to use our fake engagement to ultimately find my Logan. Which is ridiculously idiotic because everyone knows Rory should've ended up with Jess.

That lie was the only thing about mine and Carter's engagement that was fake for me.

As long as we're together, everything will be okay. But for that to truly happen, I need to start treating myself as someone I love. Someone who's worthy. Someone who's worth staying for.

My actions tonight were out of fear, not love. And I feel like a total jerk, leaving him like that. Leaving him when he needed me, when he asked me to stay. He would never leave me if *I* asked *him* to stay.

Because he's Carter. The best man I've ever met.

I need him. And maybe he needs me. Which means that I need to change my thinking for good, and fix this.

Leaving was definitely not what I should have done.

"Anthony, I think I need to go. Now!" I wave my hands frantically at the divider separating us from the driver. "Ted, stop the car!"

Anthony puts his hands on my arms. "Girl, we are parked. The car never even started moving. Now, get your butt out there and go get your man."

37

LANA MAE

I fling open the door and stumble out of the limo as inelegantly as I first stumbled into it. I race back down the street, half-blinded by old tears and mascara, and I push the doors to the theater.

Locked.

A security guard is standing nearby, but without Carter by my side, I must look like a rabid, crazed fan trying to enter the place to throw my panties at him. Or whatever it is that stalkers do.

I take a step back, trying to think of my next move. Carter's got to be watching the movie now, so I guess I can sit here for the next hour and a half and hope I don't get the urge to pee. And also hope that he exits through this particular door afterward.

Yeah, solid plan, Lana Mae.

I sniffle and scrub my hands over my face. I've only got myself to blame for this, but all I can do right now is hope that he's okay.

After a thorough inspection of the curb for rogue discarded gum, I sink down to a seat. Clearly, I've reached new lows, quite literally. In the corner of my eye, the security guard frowns and reaches for his walkie-talkie as he comes towards me. I get ready for him to tell me to move on.

But when the voice comes, it's not the one I expect. It's that sweet, sexy, low voice that's simultaneously the most familiar sound in the world, and the most exciting one.

"Is this seat taken?"

I look up to see him standing next to me, dashing as ever in his formal suit. His hair is tousled, and his expression is determined. Passionate. He looks so heartbreakingly perfect that it's all I can do to hold back a fresh flood of tears.

"Didn't mean to leave you sitting out here on your own," he goes on with a confident smile. "But I realized I should have given you time to process rather than demanding you talk to me in a supply closet. So I waited a few minutes before following you to allow you to gather your thoughts."

I don't deserve this man...

No, wait. Scratch that.

I *do* deserve this man. And he deserves me.

Because together? We're like two puzzle pieces. A perfect fit.

"I... I... Rory should have ended up with Jess, dammit!" I blurt.

Carter looks momentarily taken aback by the fact that my first words to him are a passionate statement about two fictional characters, but he recovers surprisingly quickly. "Duh. 'Course she should have, everyone knows that." He smiles almost sadly. "But Jess never should have left. He should have fought for his place in her world."

I wipe the back of my arm across my still-watering eyes and blink up at my best friend.

Instead of pulling me to my feet, he sits down next to me on the curb. Puts a gentle hand on my thigh. Squeezes. And the actual, non *Gilmore Girls* speech I had prepared dies on my tongue as we communicate silently, in our own little language.

I'm sorry.

I'm sorry, too.

It's okay.

We're okay.

"I tried to get back inside but I couldn't," I eventually say softly. "I realized I made a mistake the second I walked away. I came back for you."

His eyes sparkle. "It's always nice to come back."

"It is." I dip my head in a nod. "Turns out, I didn't really need to leave after all."

"Lan, I need you to know something." Carter's voice is soft and crackly, like a bonfire kindling. "The last thing on planet earth I ever wanted—or needed—to do was leave you. Not then, not now, not ever. And despite anything you say, I'm never leaving you again."

"Good," I choke out. "Because all I want is to be with you. I was so focused on not holding you back, I didn't stop to think that what we actually do is hold each other together. We've always been there for each other and I never want that to change. Because I love you, Carter. Always have. Always will. No matter what."

He swallows shakily. "I love you too, Lana Mae."

The scalding, piercing, incredible feeling of saying I love him, hearing him say it back, and accepting it, rather than running from it, washes over me like a tide. I feel cleansed. Right. Like everything is exactly how it should be.

Carter continues, "I've been looking for the perfect way to say that for a long time now, to give you a perfect love story. But sometimes there isn't perfect. Life is messy and confusing and throws us curveballs, and those can hurt. So, maybe, I can't promise perfect. But what I can do is promise to protect your heart at all costs. To love you well. You're it for me. My person. And I know I can't change the past, can never be your first love... but I can be your last. I want to be your last. If you'll have me."

I've said it before, and I'll say it again: There is no better man than this one.

"Yes," I whisper as my hands come to his face. "Yes. A thousand times yes."

He leans over and kisses me, and despite being on a dirty curb in a busy street and all his words about not being able to give me perfect... well, it's pretty damn perfect.

When we pull apart, I shake my head at him in wonder. "But I still think you should have gone to watch your premiere before coming to find me. There were so many people here to see you."

Those blue eyes pierce right through me. "Don't you know yet, Lana Mae? I'd rather be in the gutter with you than anywhere else on earth with anyone else."

"I... believe you."

"You should."

38

LANA MAE

ONE YEAR LATER...

"Knock, knock."

I'm sitting at my desk in a pool of late afternoon sunshine, typing so furiously on my keyboard and feeling so in the zone that I barely hear the words coming from the doorway behind me.

But I do. Because how could I ever *not* hear, nor respond to, that voice.

I swivel around with a smile on my face and look in wonder at the sight of his big, muscular body leaning against the door frame. "Hey, babe," I say softly. "What's up?"

"Dinner's ready... and everyone's almost here."

I rub the heels of my hands into my eyes and loll my head back against my chair. "Already? I must've lost track of time."

"Hours." My husband grins at me, his eyes sparking with heat as he moves out of the door frame and takes a step towards me. "But I'll forgive you because you look so sexy when you're writing."

A little shiver runs through me. Almost a year of marriage and he still makes me feel weak at the knees with a single look.

After we got back from LA, we were quick to put wedding plans into motion. Carter and I decided that there was no point in waiting to tie the knot—be it fake or not, we were already officially engaged, and Allegra and I were already living in his house.

We were married in a small, intimate ceremony in his backyard at sunset, surrounded by close friends and family and Allegra as the world's most enthusiastic flowergirl. The opposite of a big, flashy Hollywood wedding. And not a single camera or reporter present. It was exactly what I wanted.

What we wanted.

It was a casual wedding, but I wore white. And not just any white dress, but a gorgeous empire-waist bohemian gown that was straight out of my childhood wedding fantasies. The ones I thought would never be a reality for me... until Carter changed everything.

And do I mean *everything*.

He crosses the room in a few quick strides, stopping right in front of my desk chair.

"Hi," he says, and then, in one swift motion, he scoops me up, sits in the chair in my place, and pulls me down onto his lap so I'm straddling him. He nuzzles into my neck, the tip of his nose gliding over the delicate skin there, pulling a shiver out of me. "Get much writing done?"

As of three months ago, I am officially a full-time writer working on my debut novel. Quitting the travel agency was harder than expected—for so long, that little job had served me so well and helped me stand on my own two feet as a provider for my daughter. But Carter helped me realize that

I no longer have to do that. He's here for me and Allegra, always, and I can lean on him, if I want to. When I want to. Use that support to pursue yet another dream I never thought I'd make a reality. And while I am still an independent woman in so many ways, it's wonderful to know that my husband is here, by my side, and never going anywhere.

"Tons," I tell him a little breathlessly, as I thread my hands into his hair and tug, trying to urge his head upwards so I can press my lips to his.

But he resists, a man on his own mission right now. His nose is replaced with his lips, and he kisses, then gently runs his teeth over the same, delicate spot. "Any sexy bits?"

I laugh even more breathlessly as my pulse begins to pound in my throat. I was actually working on writing a very non-sexy scene about a crime investigation, but he doesn't need to know that.

"That's for me to know and you to find out... when the book comes out," I tease.

He huffs out a laugh of his own as his hands move down the length of my body and find my hips. He wraps his hands around them firmly, pulling my body even tighter to his as he levels me with a searing look that makes my insides melt into a puddle. Not unlike in the crime scene I was just writing.

"Need some inspiration?" Carter's voice is low, throaty. The voice I have now come to realize is the voice he uses when he's thinking about doing all kinds of incredible, unspeakable things to me.

Yes. Yes I do need some inspiration.

"Isn't everyone arriving for dinner soon?" I ask, running my palms across his chest longingly.

Carter gives me a teasing smirk as his thumbs move on my hips, making dizzying little circles that make me want to lock the door and cancel all other plans for the evening. "Yup. But we have a few minutes. Last I heard, Annie and Liam were swinging by the grocery store for dessert, and Luke and Mindy were on their way to pick up Legs from dance."

"Well, what are we waiting for?" I eagerly reach for the hem of his t-shirt, but he wraps his hands around mine, stopping me.

My face is a question mark as I turn incredulous eyes on him, and his smirk grows. "I changed my mind..." He leans forward and gently nips my skin with his teeth a second time. His breath is labored as he brings his lips to my ear and hoarsely says, "I think I want to make you wait until later, when we can savor every single second."

As if on cue, downstairs, the doorbell rings.

I do not get up.

I am officially a puddle.

CARTER

I spend all of dinner giving my wife furtive glances and playing footsie with her under the table.

Over the past year, I've realized I love teasing her.

Love when those cheeks redden and I know she's thinking about *me*.

"Carter, this is actually really good?" Mindy says as she loads up her fork with more papaya salad, momentarily pulling me out of my what's-definitely-happening-later fantasy. Beside her, Luke grumbles in agreement, his mouth full of penang curry, and his forehead covered in a light sheen of sweat from the spice.

I give Lana Mae a final glance before turning to Mindy. "Thanks. But why did you say that like it was a question?"

"Because, Daddy, your Thai food used to royally suck," Allegra helpfully pipes up. She's sitting at the head of the table—the spot she claimed when she and her mom moved in for good—and is holding court over the rest of the family. She's even wearing a freaking tiara for the occasion.

Mindy shrugs and grins. "What she said."

I laugh, then look over at my daughter and smile softly. "I guess I'll take that as a compliment."

Since quitting acting, I've upped my cooking game spectacularly. And when I say spectacularly, I mean, I've spent many hours in the kitchen each evening, wearing Lan's "Kiss the Cook" apron and experimenting wildly. For a while, everyone had to endure some very questionable culinary creations. Making edible Thai food was my first achievement...

No, second achievement, actually.

The first was learning how to use my coffee machine, so that every morning, I can bring my wife coffee in bed.

"It wasn't really a proper compliment, but that's okay because Auntie Mindy's right, it is really good." Allegra smiles back sweetly, and I swear, that little girl looks more and more like her beautiful mama every day. I'm so freaking proud of the person she is becoming. So honored to get to step into this role in her life.

Liam wipes his mouth with a napkin and props his elbows on the table as he addresses me. "So I was thinking I'd stop by around ten in the morning. Get everything wrapped up on the internships before Annie and I head out."

"Works for me," I reply easily.

Annie bounces in her chair. "I'm so freaking excited!"

"I'm already jealous. The surfing out there is meant to be unreal."

Annie and Liam leave for a three-month backpacking trip to Central America tomorrow—Nicaragua, Costa Rica, and Panama. And while I cannot, for the life of me, picture Liam Donovan—the eternal suit—tenting it up, and riding overnight buses with no air conditioning, and trekking through the jungle, and dancing on the beach at night, I think it's all the more awesome that they're going for this very reason.

The guy's life used to revolve around work, and being married to Annie has clearly broadened his horizons. Made him see life differently. Right now, they're just enjoying spending time together as a couple in love.

Lana smiles at me warmly. "You should talk to Jared about doing a surf trip with some of your boys. Take them down to Cocoa Beach or something."

Oh yeah, did I mention that I finally found a job that I feel passionate and excited about?

Work, these days, involves no cameras or agents or Hollywood glamor, but working side by side with my new friend Jared at his foundation. After our first hike together last year, my mind wouldn't stop turning over the information he'd given me about the work he does. I kept thinking about all the teenage kids out there who were experiencing the same things Lana Mae and I went through at that age—absent parents, an accidental pregnancy, struggling with what to do with their lives and who they want to be...

And so, I gave Jared a call. A few calls, actually. Because while my first intention was simply to donate to the program and fund Jared's charity with the means that I had, as I talked to him, I realized that I could do more than simply give money. I could make myself useful by getting involved and meeting these kids face to face, helping them with their needs.

Now, it's my full time job, and I couldn't love it more. And Jared and I have become close friends and confidants, as well as colleagues. We have joint family hangouts all the time—Lana and Imani, and Legs and Keisha, are close as ever. And the two of us still go hiking together frequently. Often with matching milkshakes in hand, like the manly men we are.

"That's a great idea," Luke chips in. "I'd come too, if you needed an extra hand."

Yup, even Luke and Liam are involved now too—their company is partnering with the charity by setting up a paid internship program for kids who are interested in careers in tech.

I nod. "And I'm sure Anthony would love to come. If only to lie on a lounger on the beach."

Before my cross-country move and permanent departure from acting, I sat down with my assistant and offered him a severance package. But he surprised me by telling me he was coming to Atlanta, too—he'd enjoyed his time here and wanted a change from LA. He also wanted to keep getting to know the drummer from the band, who he'd been chatting with ever since the night of the engagement party. They're now officially a couple, and Anthony works at Jared's foundation as his executive assistant.

Elena, of course, stayed in LA, and Freya dumped Marc to enlist my former manager as her new one. Which was apparently the right move as her album went double platinum.

Mindy smiles wide at Lana. "Perfect, if the boys clear

off for a while, that'll give us time to have girlie movie nights."

Luke whirls around to point at his wife. "You are officially banned from watching *any* movie with *any* Chris in it until one of you spills the beans on which one it is."

"Never," Mindy cackles, then pats her blooming belly. After three rounds of IVF, they are pregnant with twins, and I've never seen them happier. "I'm actually thinking of naming our firstborn Chris, just to keep you guessing."

"What if it's a girl?"

"Christabel."

Luke throws his hands up and rolls his eyes, then turns to Lan for support. Which he does not get. My wife is too busy laughing and mimes locking her lips.

And me? I smile. Because as we sit around the table, laughing and joking and teasing, I'm filled with a fierce love for my nutty family. I'm blessed to be a part of a family where love is freely given and received, no strings. I don't need to achieve anything to be recognized, or to feel like somebody. I just need to exist as the person I am, love the people around me, and let myself be loved by them, in turn. And that's enough.

I'm still smiling hours later when we hug our family goodbye, and bid Annie and Liam safe travels.

Allegra requests that I be the one to tuck her in tonight, and when I return downstairs, I find Lana Mae stacking the dishwasher.

I walk up behind her and slip my arms around her waist. She instantly straightens, leaning back into me as I embrace her.

"Hi," I say softly, leaning down to kiss her collarbone. She shudders, pressing herself even closer to me.

"Hi, yourself," she whispers back, her voice throaty as her hands move along my forearms. Seeing this side of Lana, now so confident and assured and aware of how much I want her, and of how beautiful and desirable she is to me, is, well... It's sexy as all hell.

"Why don't we leave the dishes for now?" I slide my lips along the length of her collarbone, then press a line of soft kisses up her neck. "I feel like I've waited long enough."

I can feel Lana's smile. "Oh, I don't know, I'm suddenly in the mood to scrub some pots."

"Is that so?"

She turns around to smirk at me, her dark eyes hot and sparking with desire. "Two can play at your teasing game, as it turns out."

"Yeah, but only one of us can do this." In one swift motion, she's whisked up into my arms and thrown over my shoulder.

"Hey, put me down, you big oaf!" she squeals with laughter, hitting my back.

"Never," I declare as I stride towards the stairs. "I am never letting you go. And right now, we are both going upstairs because you and I have unfinished business that I'd like to take care of immediately."

The shiver that runs through the length of her body is both gratifying and insanely hot.

I carry her all the way to the bedroom, and by the time I lay her down on the bed, she's not squealing and laughing anymore. Instead, her face is soft, eyes crinkled at the corners and shining. She reaches for my hand. Squeezes. "I love you so much, Carter. I've never been this happy in my entire life."

"You *are* my entire life," I respond simply. Squeeze back. "Deep down, I think I always knew that it was you. That the love of my life could never have been anyone else but you."

And when I'm done telling Lana Mae how much I love her, I show her how much I love her.

Always. For real.

Want to keep in touch? Follow me at @authorkatiebailey on Instagram or @authorkatiebailey on TikTok.

A NOTE FROM KATIE

Oh my goodness gracious me, book FOUR!

This one was very close to my heart, and journeying with Lana Mae through losing her mom, becoming a mom, and overcoming her past and her anxiety to fully love herself and let herself be loved, was a journey I poured so much of myself into.

And I know so many others feel this way, too. So I wanted to take a moment to say to all of the moms out there: whatever your situation looks like, just know you are doing great. You're amazing. You're worthy. And you've got this.

Now, onto the thank yous, which are vast, because this one would not have been possible without a number of very important people.

First and foremost, a MASSIVE BOTTOM OF MY HEART THANK YOU to my ride or die girl SJ. Your patience, thoughtfulness, careful considerations, and ability to actually create a real, cohesive story out of a pile of my half-witted, hare-brained thoughts is nothing short of remarkable. Without you, there would be no Katie Bailey books in existence. But many half-written pages of random scenes. So for that, I thank you eternally.

Also huge thanks to Madi, for providing such an awesome pair of fresh eyes that saw things in such a different way than I did - your input was invaluable. I appreciate your time and effort so much and I hope you never have to go camping again. Loveyoubye.

Thanks to Leah, who listens to all my complaining and

also keeps me (somewhat) on the straight and narrow. Haha, jk, we lead each other astray constantly and I am so here for it. Glad we're on this journey together.

A huge, heartfelt thank you to my ARC readers. Thank you for taking the time to read this love story and sharing all of your thoughts, tips and (of course) typos with me. What would I do without you all?! You're the best.

To the entire wonderful community that is Bookstagram. I am so overwhelmingly grateful for you all, and for this beautiful, safe, supportive, uplifting corner of the internet we share together.

And last but certainly not least, thank you to my family, who have all contributed to this book in their own way:

To my MIL, the accidental inventor of the Cosmopoutan, thank you so much for all the time you spent babysitting so this book could even be written.

To my husband, who actually had to beat a small inferno out of my hair at a restaurant once. You are my favorite non-reader ever, and also my real-life DILTSMELWAHAHB.

And finally, to my kids and my dog, who never, ever, let me pee in peace. It's a privilege to love and raise you, and to experience mom guilt in all its ever-present, anxiety-inducing glory. I wouldn't change it for the world.

Thank you one and all, and also TEAM JESS FOREVER!

ALSO BY KATIE BAILEY

Donovan Family

So That Happened

I Think He Knows

Only in Atlanta

The Roommate Situation

The Neighbor War

Made in the USA
Columbia, SC
15 July 2023